COVER UP:
HOLLYWOOD STYLE

"The last item that we have to worry about is Stevie Tree," Sy said. "Now I think that Stevie will be on the phone to me in a little bit. I won't be too easy to find. I'll be in town . . . and then I'll be resting . . . and finally I'll talk to her. I'll listen to everything she has to say. That's what I should do as head of the agency. Now what you gentlemen should do is make sure of your other people . . and it would be a good idea if the funeral for the poor child were tomorrow . . . Sunday is a good day for a funeral. It shouldn't be too large . . . a simple, small thing appropriate for the loss of one so young." The two of them nodded at the correctness of Sy's judgment.

Laurel Canyon

Steve Krantz

PUBLISHED BY POCKET BOOKS NEW YORK

Another *Original* publication of POCKET BOOKS

POCKET BOOKS, a Simon & Schuster division of
GULF & WESTERN CORPORATION
1230 Avenue of the Americas, New York, N.Y. 10020

ISBN. 0-671-82801-0

First Pocket Books printing October, 1979

10 9 8 7 6 5 4 3 2 1

Trademarks registered in the United States and other countries.

Printed in the U S.A

FOR JUDY

Friday Night—10 P.M.

The Nicholas Long place on Bellagio Road, in Bel Air, was typical of the neighborhood—a million-dollar mansion, resting luxuriantly on three acres of choice California. The gatehouse at the East Entrance housed private patrolmen, who guarded the serpentine roads intertwining the canyons and hillocks of this ultra-rich neighbor to Beverly Hills.

The Long residence, carefully hidden behind a ten-foot brick wall, covered with years of ivy growth, lay on an incline, at the end of a driveway protected by electronic gates.

On Friday nights, the Longs show a film in their private screening room in their poolhouse, down a slope of lawn, just across from the tennis court and swimming pool. Spray from a fountain, lit from below, steaming from the condensation of the warm water in the cool night, was the only noise one could hear outside, except for the muffled sound of the movie.

Valerie Long, wife of motion picture producer Nick Long, was just leaving the screening room, tortured by the pain of a persistent headache and torn by the demands of etiquette—no one ever leaves a private screening until the very end. This film, *Young Dillinger*, had been produced by her husband, and that made matters worse.

The headache had started at dinner, but three vodka Gibsons had made it nearly bearable. When she could stand to watch the movie no more, she unceremoniously walked out and headed for her medicine cabinet and

1

the codeine it contained. Nick would be furious, but it was *her* headache . . . and it was *her* money that made it possible for them to live the way they did.

Valerie maneuvered out the door, scarcely making a sound. The flickering light of the projector gave shape to the wisps of smoke rising from the overstuffed chairs. When she was outside, she breathed deeply. It was chilly, and the cool air helped clear the fog of the Gibsons, but that only seemed to intensify the riveting pain in her head. She gulped the cool air and set out briskly across the tennis court, up the bricked pathway to the back patio, and up the stairs to the second-floor living quarters.

Valerie Long stood for a moment on the wide upper landing, hearing the muffled sound of water splashing violently from a tap. The sound came from her daughter Melinda's room. She saw the door ajar. As she walked to the door, the sound of cascading water grew louder.

Lying on the bed, she saw the form of Morgan Oliver, the star of her husband's film, the one she had just left. Morgan Oliver on screen was dark-haired, with incredible blue eyes, boyishly handsome still, though the years had not dealt kindly with him. Now he lay nude, spread-eagled and unconscious across the pink satin sheets on her daughter's bed. The sight was unbelievably grotesque. His dark body hair contrasted to his flaccid white skin. Once beautiful, young and princelike, he suffered from years of drink and drugs.

The door to the bathroom was partly open, and Valerie pushed against it. She pushed harder and finally was able to slip inside. What blocked the entrance was the body of her naked sixteen-year-old daughter, dead. A hypodermic lay shattered on the shining tiles of the floor. Valerie's breath stopped for a moment. Then she screamed.

Averting her eyes from the figure on the bed, she ran down the thickly carpeted stairs. Nearly falling, she stumbled onto the patio, and raced across its expanse to the screening room. The lights had just gone up, as she crashed the door open. The screening of *Young Dillinger* was over.

Nick Long stood in the center of the room, as the audience circled him like a victory huddle. He was grinning broadly.

"Nick . . . fantastic. You can count your money."

"Thanks, Fred."

"I loved it, Nick. The audience will go crazy."

"Thanks, Jerry."

"Nick . . . you'll get Best Picture in a shoe-in. You deserve it, baby."

And thanks to Zelma, Walker, Randy and the other guests, who were sincere in their enthusiasm.

Valerie raced to his side and grabbed his arm. Nick Long saw the tortured face of his wife and hissed at her, "Don't you ever leave a screening. I don't give a goddam what you have to do. Pee in your pants."

Valerie was in tears.

"Shut up, damn you. Melinda is dead," she sobbed. "Heroin. That son of a bitch Morgan Oliver." With a wail, she screamed, "She's dead, Nick, in the bathroom. Morgan's unconscious. He's lying on her bed naked."

Nick Long raced out of the screening room. A tall, beautiful blonde followed. Stevie Tree, agent for Morgan Oliver, wasn't going to be left out. In seconds they were in Melinda's bedroom. Morgan had not stirred. Stevie pulled up a blanket from the foot of the bed and covered him. She and Nick Long pushed their way into the bathroom to see the twisted figure of the once beautiful young girl.

Stevie put her hand on Nick Long's shoulder. "I'll phone the ambulance, Nick . . . and the police. I don't know what to say." Nick Long was sobbing as he knelt on the floor.

In the screening room, the guests were quiet, waiting for the news. They wanted to leave, but were fearful of the consequences. Each of them saw himself in the newspapers splattered with the scandal.

As Stevie Tree reached the foot of the stairs, a

serious-looking young man stood in her path. Jerry Fentris, heir apparent to International Artists, a picture of youthful success from the tips of his gleaming shoes to a perfectly tailored suit, custom-made shirt and an extravagant tan. At thirty-five, Jerry Fentris was trim and handsome, a smiler and a cutthroat. He took Stevie's arm and motioned for her to follow him into the small library.

"Jerry, I've got to call an ambulance . . . and the police . . ."

"Come on in here. That'll wait. Nothing's gonna help the kid. Come on."

The two of them walked into the library. In bookcases on the wall, in chaste splendor, were row upon row of first editions, photographs of Nick Long with prominent industry figures, and next to these a Corot, two Degas's, a Van Gogh and a Renoir. It was part of an instant art collection provided for Nicholas Long when he married money.

Fred Wine, administrative head of IA was nervously sitting on a couch, clenching and unclenching his fists. Fentris looked at him contemptuously.

Stevie, flushed with the adrenalin on the moment, had almost lost her poise. She had seen a terrible tragedy just moments ago. The sight of the young girl, dead on the floor, still sent shock waves to her brain.

"Stevie, sit down."

"Not now, Jerry."

"Now, dammit."

Stevie sat down. Her anger served to quiet the shock. Fentris stared at her. At twenty-seven, Stevie Tree was the most important female in the entertainment business, the most successful agent, the most imaginative purveyor of actors, writers and properties that the industry had ever known. Her appearance made one think not of an agent but a movie star. Tall, ash blonde, Stevie's deeply riveting blue eyes stared back at him. Dressed in an expensive Oscar de la Renta gown, she stood impressively before him.

Jerry Fentris smiled. "We've got a little problem, Stevie." The men exchanged dark glances.

Stevie looked at them both incredulously. "My God, Jerry, what are you talking about? A girl is dead."

Fred Wine looked at her for a moment. "Stevie . . . just listen to Jerry . . ."

"Fred and I were talking while you were upstairs," Jerry Fentris continued. "Morgan Oliver probably gave the kid the heroin. Obviously he was fucking the ass off her . . . He's our client and we've got a lot of money tied up in that guy. If the story gets out . . . he's dead. Some of our other clients who are here right now are going to be smeared too . . . and if I guess right, they'll get antsy about the agency—and split."

Stevie was stunned. Her eyes darkened. She wanted to shout out, "The girl is *dead!*" And now she heard the quiet drone of Jerry Fentris outlining a game plan as one might read the directions for assembling a model airplane.

Fred Wine chimed in. "I know a doctor that we can get . . . and I think that we can get him to say the girl died of a heart attack, or some other legit-sounding thing."

Stevie looked at Fred. It was as if he were discussing an employee pension plan or use of the executive washroom. Fred Wine, in his forties, undistinguished and gray, was excellent on mechanics. He was detached, sincere and serious. But what he was suggesting was criminal. They could all go to *jail*.

Fentris continued. "The big problem isn't the doctor or the cops. We can handle that. I think that we can finesse the whole goddam autopsy and newspaper publicity if we can get the cooperation of two people. One is Nick Long . . . our host . . . and not very much of a producer, who just happened to luck out with *Young Dillinger*. Jesus, when I think about the luck of that guy. The film could do a hundred million easy, and he isn't even a client. OK, with him we have two cards to play. He won't want to see his name all over the papers and his little girl's reputation ruined. Of course she was balling every star all over town, but Nick won't have that problem anymore." Jerry seemed to chuckle at the thought.

Fentris lit a cigarette, sat down in an easy chair and stretched out. It was just like any other negotiation. There was always a buyer for the right package. "OK, so we appeal to the reputation bullshit, and if that doesn't work, then we've got Morgan Oliver."

Stevie thought, 'Yeah . . . our hero.'

Fentris continued. "*Young Dillinger* is gonna be a smash and the whole industry will be after us for Morgan."

Stevie added, "Would have been . . ."

Fentris corrected, "*Will* be, and we can give Morgan to Nick for another picture—or two—on some kind of terms . . . We can up this last deal substantially and get a piece of the gross on the next two pictures. Now that leaves the director, Walker Perkins. He's probably drowning in his own sweat this minute. He's a goddam faggot and we should have thrown him out of the agency years ago, but he's gonna be hot after this monster gets out. Walker has a boyfriend who can't get arrested . . . some tightpants little twat who works as a reader at one of the studios. He writes shitty scripts in his spare time, and it would be a kind of transaction he might dig if we got a studio to commit to a script for his current boyfriend. We'll handle the deal. It'll take a little lovemaking to do it, but our house faggot's the one we put on just for this kind of stuff . . . and we'll point him in the right direction and tell him to go sic 'em. We can make *that* work."

Stevie sucked in her breath. She unconsciously tugged at an earring. She looked at Fred Wine. He was staring at his shoes.

Fentris continued, "OK, Stevie . . . now you've got a lot of stuff you've got to pull together . . . Zelma Hurwitz, your discovery. Yeah, you can claim credit for making a star out of Miss Bronx Bitch. You've got to keep Zelma and her black stud quiet. The world ain't gonna be happy to find out super-star Zelma is heavy into coke, and her black boy has a prison record for dealing hard drugs. The two of them will forget they're alive if you scare the shit out of them."

There was a knock on the door and Jerry Fentris opened it. It was Zelma. She looked frightened to death. Fentris told her, "Zelma, don't worry. We're working the whole thing out." He shut the door in her face and resumed his planning.

"Now there's Randy Davis. Randy has more money than God, and should have retired years ago, but he keeps looking for reassurance that chicks will think he can still get his pecker up. Randy could use a new picture. If he plays along, we can get the studio we lay the Morgan Oliver picture on to commit to some piece of shit with Randy. We can work *that* out."

Fred Wine stirred. "What about Morgan? He's got a mouth a mile wide!"

Jerry Fentris interrupted. "He's out of the house even as we are sitting and talking."

Stevie looked at him. "What do you mean, out of the house? He's upstairs naked on Melinda's bed."

Fentris smiled. "He was. The projectionist is now on our payroll. I got him to dress Morgan and get him out of the house. It'll cost the agency five or ten grand, but that's peanuts."

Stevie was pale with rage. She was used to a lot of cute dealing in the business, but this was unbelievable. Morgan Oliver was responsible for the death of a sixteen-year-old girl. Stevie felt the anger in her burn to such an extent she could hardly speak.

"OK, Jerry . . . what about Sy Rosen? As the head of International Artists, he might have other thoughts."

"Stevie, don't worry. Sy is down in Palm Springs recuperating from an operation. I'm gonna fly down to see him tomorrow morning, first thing . . . but I know my uncle. He'd approve of everything I'm doing."

Fred Wine interjected. "What about Valerie? Nick can be handled with the promise of a couple of pictures, but his wife is a different number. She's unpredictable, and she has money of her own. She's the missing link."

Jerry Fentris tapped on the side of the chair. "No need to get into it now, but I can deliver her for sure. Now the way I look at it, Stevie . . . Fred . . . this whole shitpot could do us some good, too. We can keep some of our *pissant* clients under control when their contracts come up for renewal . . . and with the new business we can generate on this transaction, it could mean a couple of million dollars' worth of new commissions to the agency . . ."

Stevie faced them angrily.

"Jerry . . . Fred . . . you've got the whole thing figured. Something for everybody, OK? *Not* OK! You forgot me. My client, Morgan Oliver, has gotten away with destroying people, ruining reputations and running roughshod in this community. He's a prick in a town where you've really got to work for that distinction. I took him on because you forced me to. You know that Morgan and I go back a long way . . . and I'm telling both of you that I'm going to destroy that man. You can fix every man, woman and child from Bel Air to Pasadena with deals and payoffs, but I'm going to see that Morgan is dead in this industry. I give you my word."

With that, Stevie Tree left the library, banging the door shut behind her, and walked down the marble corridor to the entrance of the house. She passed no one on the way to her Porsche. They had sixty hours to put the fix in, to make all the deals. Stevie vowed that in sixty hours, Morgan Oliver would be no more, and she had the best of reasons.

Jerry Fentris sat for a moment in the library.

"What do you think?" Fred Wine asked.

"I think that the minute this weekend is put to bed, I'm going to burn that young lady. She just isn't going to find a place to sit her ass in this business. We've got problems to deal with, and the toughest may be Miss Stevie Tree."

"How soon will the doctor be here?"

"He said right away . . . that could mean any damn thing."

Fred Wine moaned, "Why the hell do these things happen to me?"

Jerry stared at him hard. "You asshole, these things aren't happening to you. If I let you go on your own, this could blow the whole agency to bits. Now you wait for the doctor and you give him the message. Heart attack. I'll be upstairs if you need me, massaging our grieving producer. Come on, Fred. You're making enough money to do a little work now and then."

Fentris walked out the door of the library and upstairs. From the sound of crying, he located Nick in his bedroom suite. Nick was talking quietly to Valerie. Jerry Fentris thought to himself, The key to this is the first half hour or so. Stabilize the damn thing and keep it from exploding. If it can go through the first twenty-four hours buttoned up, then it will develop its own momentum. That's the way you make a deal. Sell a customer a bill of goods and stick around for a little while to calm his buyer's remorse. When that's over, the deal begins to live on its own. Then, pour concrete over it, and make it immortal.

Stevie left Bel Air in her red Porsche, narrowly missing disaster as she scorched through the winding roads of the palatial community on her way to Sunset Boulevard. She turned east and drove at a more leisurely seventy miles per hour toward home—past the enormous luxury of Beverly Hills, into Hollywood with its fleshpots ablaze, strip places, punk-rock havens, hamburger and pizza joints and then farther east to the silent world of Laurel Canyon.

Further along, she slammed on the brakes for a moment and looked at the dark form of Schwab's Pharmacy, closed for the night, which stood at the south end of Laurel Canyon. Laurel Canyon ended at this watering place that had been her first stop when she arrived in Hollywood ten years ago.

Stevie remembered the specific day as a landmark of sorts, and the many times after that she had been there for meals, for supplies and for human contact.

She gunned the motor and made a left up the high, twisting road of Laurel Canyon, where Stevie had spent virtually all her Hollywood years. Laurel Canyon was a country in itself.

It was a steep climb that took you across the Santa Monica Mountains, an age-old canyon, twisting and turning through a labyrinth of dark scrub pines, overhanging rocks and secret, silent roads nearly invisible to the casual eye. There were still hippie establishments in the woods, tiny houses where out-of-work actors and actresses would hole up in communal life, a small Country Store midway up the canyon where Hell's Angels bikers would stop on their route to Northern California, and where you could always find groups of locals gathered in the parking lot, meeting as you would in a small town. Near the top, where Stevie lived, the canyon changed its complexion, and there were some of the most luxurious, most secluded homes in Hollywood, lying in private and mysterious splendor.

The high climb brought memories of places and people. Stevie had spent her adult life here. She had also been near death here. Hollywood's highs and lows walked hand in hand in these mountains alongside Laurel Canyon.

1

Stevie Tree had joined International Artists four years earlier, following an interview with its president, Sy Rosen. The interview had hardly started when there was a string of interruptions of "urgent" phone calls. Each time, Sy Rosen excused himself to accept the call. While he talked, Stevie glanced around the room and looked at the symbols of power of one of the most powerful men in Hollywood.

The IA office was on Santa Monica Boulevard in Beverly Hills. IA had been there for fifteen years, and its offices were adequate but not grand. The building they occupied had formerly belonged to a real estate conglomerate that went bust in the late 1960's. It was a large, white colonial monster that had been built by the now defunct outfit to give an impression of solidity. When IA bought the building, it acquired all of the furniture belonging to the former owners. Consequently, in the last half of the twentieth century, International Artists employees and executives were dealing from chairs, desks and furniture reproducing the eighteenth-century world of colonial America. It was very quaint and decidedly uncomfortable. After a while, its particular style gave it a curious cachet that was both incongruous, effective and reassuring to IA clients. Any organization that was so cheap as to buy a used building with used furniture—and the rumor was that for five or six years IA used the conglomerate's old stationery as second sheets and scratch pads—had to be goddam smart.

Sy Rosen wasn't concerned about that part of public

relations. He knew where it really counted—the concept of power that made customers call IA first, because even though they knew the dealings would be tough, they were dealing with professionals who would see things through to the end, even when their clients failed to.

At forty-six, Sy Rosen wore the dark blue suit and black tie that were his trademark and the trademark of all his top people. In fact, he had twenty such suits, and virtually no other clothes. He was short—five foot four—trim, athletic and boyish in appearance. His unlined face was slightly cherubic. Sy Rosen had been married to the same woman for nineteen years. They had three children, girls, and his marriage was a happy one. He had arranged it that way.

Nothing about Sy Rosen's office was different from any of the other agents who worked for him. It was no larger, nor did it have any special furniture or a private john. Those things weren't important to him, and he insisted on the appearance of total equality among his people. His desk was the same dark burnished wood, and the chairs were done in the same overstuffed upholstery as the rest of the imitation American colonial offices.

Sy Rosen never raised his voice when he disagreed with one of his people at a staff meeting. He didn't have to. Even before he cleared his throat, his employees were attuned to hearing what he would say, how he would decide. He made those decisions in what seemed to be a tentative, halting way. He would couch them in a language full of expressions like "Perhaps we ought to," or "What would you gentlemen think if we tried it this way?" There was never any disagreement. Sy Rosen was almost always right, and when he was wrong he was the first one to blame himself—and he was right about that as well.

As head of IA, Sy Rosen controlled over forty agents in the L.A. office and some twenty-five in New York. There was an eight-man office in London, and once, when the picture business was important in Italy, an

office in Rome. Including the young men in the
mailroom, secretaries and bookkeepers, there were
over two hundred souls in the IA empire.

Despite its small numbers, IA had an enormous
control over major talent in the entertainment field.
They had competition. The William Morris office was
larger. The Creative Management group—now International Creative Management, due to a merger with
International Famous Artists—was fighting hard and
very competitive, but through the force of Sy Rosen
and his keen sense of the needs of the industry, IA was
the key agency in the business of representing talent,
the toughest contender in a very tough field.

In the past, IA had been known for double-dealing,
sharp practice and generally sloppy followthrough.
That was years ago when they were much smaller. Sy
Rosen had taken a small, second-rate agency of ten
people and converted it to the mammoth power it
presently was, changing its image from a shyster
operation to the multimillion-dollar organization that
represented some of the most important actors, actresses, writers, directors, musicians, singers, variety performers and sports figures in the world. The combined
yearly income of the people who were represented by
IA was a closely guarded figure, but it was in excess of
250 million dollars, and IA—as agents—received ten
percent of that income.

Sy Rosen had not only led his agency into that role of
extraordinary affluence, but apart from the huge sala-
ries that he paid himself and the other mainstays in the
agency, he had invested the agency's money in Nevada
real estate, Florida citrus groves, a large toy manufacturer, office buildings in L.A., Phoenix and Tucson,
and all of those investments made money as well.

The long-term agents who had been with Sy for most
of his twenty-five years at IA were all millionaires.
Their fate was so inextricably tied up with IA that in
order to derive all of the benefits from IA's profits and
investments, they had to retire at an advanced age. This
deferment plan left IA free of the usual agent's

ambition to take his personal clients with him and start his own agency. Sy had invented this "golden hand-cuffs" system which prevented his best people from straying.

Stevie sat in the talent mogul's office, dressed in a beige linen suit, holding a Gucci handbag on her lap. Her extraordinary blonde hair hung loosely over her shoulders as she sat in a very uncomfortable colonial chair. She had wanted to look attractive, and yet not overdo it—businesslike, not flashy. She did not want to call attention to her beauty. She even crossed her legs carefully to ensure enough skirt to cover her knees. She was twenty-four and she had been through some rough times.

What kind of fortune had it been to meet Sy Rosen? Stevie had first worked as an agent in partnership with a man once well-known and respected in the field, Morrie Amster. Theirs had been a tiny and intimate enterprise, struggling and succeeding, bit by bit. Then quite suddenly Morrie died and Stevie was back at ground zero. Yet it was Sy Rosen who held her hand warmly at Morrie's funeral. That had set the scene for this meeting, but it could end right there, with another sincere expression of his sympathy.

Stevie had no idea thus far how the interview was going. Sy Rosen was not a man you could easily read. Stevie had been in his office a half hour, and half of that time Sy Rosen had been on the phone with "emergency" calls.

He was concluding a conversation now, and Stevie made up her mind how to approach the rest of the interview. She thought she had a bead on this man, and her instinct told her she could get the job. Stevie crossed her fingers, out of his line of sight.

Finally Sy Rosen hung up from that last interminable call. He buzzed his secretary.

"No more calls. Absolutely." Then he turned to Stevie. "You've been extremely patient, Miss Tree, and I appreciate that. Part of the problem about your working here is that we don't employ many women."

Stevie smiled. "There's a cure for that disease, Mr. Rosen."

Sy Rosen smiled. "I admit we've given some thought to having a woman in the agency. I mean, potentially as an agent . . . Some of our competition have been very successful with women agents. Believe me—even though we have a very tough reputation, some of the women agents are a lot tougher than I'd allow our people to be. Don't get me wrong, Miss Tree. I have every respect for some of the women in the field."

He smiled. "We've tried to get some of them to come our way, without success for the moment, but the whole business makes such demands. It's my experience that women won't stay with it long. They look for the easy way out—marriage, a studio job. Of course, there are some New York ladies—in the legitimate theater or literary agents. But Hollywood is where the action is. It's a place that separates the men from the boys."

He looked at Stevie earnestly and seemed to be preparing for a final warm handshake in a moment or two. "Let's face it, Miss Tree. Hollywood is run by men. It's just easier to deal with your own sex."

Stevie smiled. "I suppose your mother was a man."

"*Touché*, Miss Tree . . . and I suspect that a boy shares more confidences with that woman than with anyone else." He continued, as he appraised Stevie's looks, "But no one in my agency could ever confuse you with his mother. I'd like to do something for you, Miss Tree—particularly since Morrie Amster was a dear friend. Before we met at his funeral, I had learned all about you. One thing I pride myself on is staff work. I know all about the people I deal with, *before* I deal with them."

Stevie gritted her teeth. She sensed that she was losing headway, and the next thing she would hear would be Sy Rosen's continuing sympathy, and his promise to call her if anything ever came up. Things *never* came up.

"I appreciate your desire to help me . . . if it only

could be translated into fact. You see, after Morrie died, I did consider continuing with the clients we had. As I figured it, there would have been enough to cover expenses and to build on, but I couldn't do it—for other reasons."

"What were they?" Sy Rosen was interested.

"I associated the entire thing with Morrie. Morrie had befriended me in a way that no other human being has ever done. He rescued me from the physical and financial pits. He made me conscious of myself in a form other than my face and my body . . . as a thinking, growing creature. Morrie felt that I could be an important agent in the industry. I want to do that for his sake, as well as my own."

Sy Rosen was softening perceptibly. "But working in IA is very different from working in a small agency, Stevie. Take—as an example—we seldom put anything on paper. It takes a trained mind to master all the details in his head. The reason we don't put things on paper is habit. It used to be that the business was full of mobsters and ruffians. Many of our early transactions were with the Mafia and hoodlums. That's the way it was during Prohibition. Unfortunately, there are still those kind of influences in Las Vegas and elsewhere . . . and so we got used to dealing with those elements carefully, by not putting anything in writing that we don't need. And then I discovered that it was enormously beneficial to train our people in the details of every transaction . . . I mean *every* one, without using files and documents as a crutch. I will tell you this, that's one of the reasons we use male secretaries a lot . . . each of them has an earpiece to listen to important conversations and then commits them to memory—in case there should be a slip-up by an agent. Now a woman couldn't handle all that."

"Sy—and I'm using your first name for the first time, because I want to get your full attention—I've been sitting in your office. I've been nervous and anxious. I've paused for a sip or two from the coffee your secretary brought me. The total elapsed time I've been here has been thirty-five minutes, and you've been on the phone for about twenty of those minutes. You made three calls and answered two. The first call was to someone named Jeremy. Now I assume, even though you never used his last name, that it was Jeremy Gordon, who is the president of Eagle Films. Your discussion was as follows." Stevie uncrossed her legs and recrossed them, feeling the sweat behind her knees. "You had been insistent on maintaining the deal for your client, whose name you didn't mention, but since he was a director and it was for an Eagle film, and since you were asking for a $750,000 director's fee, it must have been Franklin Pierce. The film is one that Eagle canceled six months ago, and was in need of recasting after their star took sick. It is called *Dark Start,* although you didn't mention that either. Now you wanted Pierce to be guaranteed his usual ten percent of profits, but you also wanted to have the studio commit to buying out his interest in another picture—again not mentioned, but since it was an Eagle picture, it could only have been *The Pity*—for a half million dollars. The money would be paid over a period of five years, in installments of $50,000 per year for the first years . . . and then $250,000 for the last, the fifth year."

"That only adds up to $450,000, Miss Tree."

"I know, Sy . . . and I thought about that. Either you had made a mistake, or you were giving the customer an edge for a particular reason. In any event, it was not up to me to comment."

Sy Rosen took a deep breath, "Can you do the same with my other calls?"

Her eyes sparkled, and she felt a high-voltage intensity. She knew she was winning. "Yes, I can."

Rosen stood up. "Stevie . . . forget what I said before. We'll work out the money when you start. Welcome to IA."

"Sy, I thank you very much. But let's work out the money now—while the fish are biting."

Sy Rosen laughed.

"Of course, you know, Stevie, that you'll be in

training for a while, and it's going to cost us money to have you around."

"I know, Sy, the question is how much?"

"What would you say to fifteen thousand?"

"I'd say the same thing that I'd say to twenty, Sy."

"What's that?"

"I'd say that you were getting me cheap. The only question is how cheap."

"Of course, in time, Stevie, there will be increases—and then in time you'd be part of our profit-sharing plan, based on the amount of business you bring in. It's all computerized."

Stevie smiled broadly. "I'd rather deal with you."

Stevie would start the next day as assistant to Jerry Fentris in variety entertainment.

Jerry Fentris showed up at the offices of IA at ten-thirty that day. He and Stevie were introduced right after her coup at the interview. Rosen buzzed Fentris on the intercom, then walked around his desk and took Stevie by the hand, leading her over to the French doors that overlooked the ante-bellum garden of colonial IA.

"It's something special to be with IA, Stevie."

"Yes, I understand."

"I wonder whether you do, not meaning any offense, that is. We have a reputation for hard dealing, representing our clients in the most direct and honest way. Our word is our bond. A customer can always count on us to deliver what we commit to. And sometimes that's not easy. Some of our biggest clients are like small children. You're going to have to learn how to deal with them. It's our job to lead them out of the burning buildings they always find themselves in. They must learn to rely on us—never themselves. We must make them see that they are only safe when they listen to us—that there is quicksand and danger all around them, except when they do as we tell them to. We train them, you see, so they'll need to hold our hand. My twenty-five years in the agency have been my life. I wouldn't trade any year with IA for ten years in any other life. I set out to do exactly what I'm doing today, Stevie . . . When I was a kid on the Grand Concourse, I said to myself, I'm going to be a success. Today I have an art collection: three Gauguins, four Dufys, two Kandinskys and one Renoir. I jog five miles every day and I haven't put on one pound in twenty-five years. I started out in the mailroom—someday when we have time, I'll tell you what it was like growing and building in the industry."

"I'd love that, Sy."

"As for Jerry Fentris, he's an up-and-comer. You'll like him, and I'm sure he'll like you. He started in the mailroom too."

"Yes, Sy . . . and he's also your nephew."

Sy Rosen took a long look at Stevie. He stared her into the ground, then he smiled. "I'm glad we hired you, and I wonder what you'll be in 10 years."

Stevie smiled. "In ten years, I'll be thirty-three, my teeth will be falling out and my wrinkles will have wrinkles, and I'll still be eternally grateful to you for this opportunity."

The meeting with Jerry Fentris was courteous and brief. Jerry, too, wore the dark blue business suit and black tie that were the uniform of Rosen's army. Jerry was young—he couldn't have been more than thirty-two. He was about five foot six, and Stevie was beginning to come to the conclusion that successful agents couldn't be tall. Trim and athletic, with a very boyish smile, Jerry Fentris was all charm, and Stevie didn't trust him as far as the ladies' room.

Before Stevie left the apartment at the Marina the next day, she carefully considered what to wear. The female secretaries all wore slacks or jeans. They looked neat and trim but very casual, too casual to be aspiring agents. Stevie tried on pants and shirts, and nothing worked. Her bed was a kaleidoscope of silks and cottons. It could have been an artist's pallette. She wanted to look businesslike, but not the counterpart of the blue serge suit. Besides, she didn't have that kind of wardrobe, and even if she had, she wouldn't have liked the Xerox image effect, as if one man had been duplicated a dozen times.

Stevie tried on several dresses. Her light blue chiffon was too frilly. A linen skirt and matching silk top made her look as if she were waiting for someone on the tennis court. She had to consider how to wear her hair too. The blonde length of it was typically *American Girl, Ladies' Home Journal*—the long-legged beauty. Better, she thought, to put it in a bun, but that looked like hell, as if she were auditioning for a lesbian role in a soap opera.

Then she realized that for the entire period she would be in the industry, she would either have to play a role, which would be difficult or impossible, or count on the world simply adjusting to the way she was. And Stevie couldn't live a lie.

Fifteen minutes later, Stevie Tree was dazzling in white linen pants and a turquoise silk shirt, which set off the blonde of her hair, along with a narrow gold belt. She turned in front of the mirror, and her hair flew around her head like a gold pinwheel.

Stevie took another look and smiled to herself. 'Fuck 'em all,' she thought. A good exit line that took her to the Porsche in the garage, which led her to the freeway to Beverly Hills at eighty-five miles an hour, and to her desk at the agency fully one hour before her boss, Jerry Fentris, arrived.

Brenda Johnson, a young, attractive black secretary, introduced herself to Stevie. Brenda was eating a late breakfast of bagels and coffee.

"Have a half a bagel?"

"No thanks, Brenda. I had breakfast."

"So have I, but it gets me into the spirit of the day." Brenda took a big swallow of black coffee and circled an item in the paper she was reading.

Stevie smiled. "A friend?"

Brenda looked and acknowledged Stevie's look. "Nah . . . I go through the trade papers looking for the biggest lie of the day, I circle it and then I scare our mutual boss with the news that I *know* it's true from a girlfriend."

"Really?"

Brenda chewed the last morsel of bagel. "You think that's cruel and unnatural? Wait till you meet him."

Stevie laughed. "I already have."

The two of them had facing desks in the glassed-in cubicle outside Jerry's office. All three of them shared phones with four separate incoming lines. Stevie soon found out that the careful manipulation of those calls was one of the more challenging aspects of an agent's job. As she knew, even from her experience in business with Morrie, an agent's ability to handle the flood of incoming and outgoing calls, the allocation of time for each call, the priorities of callbacks, was part of an agent's lifeblood.

Brenda was slightly aghast when she met Stevie. The idea of a female as an agent's assistant was cataclysmic at IA, where sexism was invented. Brenda was smart. She had a tight, sardonic view of the world, and particularly the white world. She narrowed it down even further as Stevie got to know her. Brenda was very cynical about the white world, the white men in it, the white men who were agents and the white agents who were Jewish.

As far as Brenda was concerned, apart from Jewish agents, there weren't any other. Her first question to Stevie told Stevie all she needed to know. "You ain't no nephew and you ain't Jewish! What you doing here, girl?" Stevie laughed and Brenda concluded, "Excuse the street nigger, Miss Tree . . . I only had three years of Fine Arts at UCLA, a year in Paris, and the money ran out. They pay remarkably well at IA, Stevie . . . and you get all the usual holidays and fringes, plus Rosh Hashanah, Yom Kippur, Purim and the anniversary of the State of Israel."

Stevie interrupted, "and the discovery of chicken soup."

"I can dig it, Stevie."

Brenda handed her the client list, then the book with

the names of the clients, together with their assignments, the terms and conditions and prices they received and a notation if they were currently on assignment.

Brenda showed her the file of negotiations in process: under each heading was the customer's name, the offers, the counteroffers, together with dates and comments.

Stevie stopped her. "I thought that nothing was put in writing here."

"Oh, don't listen to that bullshit, Stevie. The agents can't read or write . . . just us lowly persons have to keep notes. Who could remember all this shit?"

Then there was the telephone log with the name of the caller and the time of the call. The subject was listed, and there were boxes to be checked if the calling party was phoned back. In the first part of every day, Brenda and each secretary would transfer to the next day's notebook page all the calls that hadn't been completed the day before. Alongside each name and number would be a priority number for the day's calls. Yesterday's page was filled to capacity.

Then there were the wheeldex files of all the listed and unlisted numbers of the clients. No numbers were ever to be given out to a caller. No caller was ever to be put directly in touch with a client. No client was ever to be encouraged to contact a customer without going through the agent. On each index card were listed alternative numbers of girlfriends, boyfriends, hangouts and heavily guarded numbers that would allow an agent to track down a client virtually anyplace but Forest Lawn.

Stevie sat down at her desk and began to study the client list. On a corner of her desk was a two-foot pile of scripts that had been submitted to clients by producers, and before they were submitted to clients, someone at the agency would have to evaluate them. The brief hour together with Brenda reinforced Sy Rosen's dictum that, at whatever cost, the client must look to the agent for everything. The client must never be freed from the obligation of going through his agent. The customer never dealt with the client directly. Even on the merest item of trivia—the notification of a change of time for an appointment—these had to be cleared through the agent.

Stevie wondered to herself whether clients were allowed to pee for themselves, or did an agent have to hold the client's cock for him. But she understood the concept. It was abundantly clear to her. If the agent allowed even one chink in his armor, one incident in which the client found that he or she could shift for himself, there might be a second or a third. From that time, it would only be hours till the client began questioning the agent's judgment, his insolent manner and—most importantly—his commission.

This enterprise, Stevie recognized, was not the American Red Cross. IA collected ten percent of everything the client made on anything, acting, singing, writing, dancing, hopping up and down, in movies, TV, state fairs, Rotary smokers, birthday parties, streetcorner hustling, or singing in the shower, whether the client performed for dollars, kopeks, pizza, electric toasters, kisses or thank-yous.

At ten-thirty as usual Jerry Fentris strode in. He was dressed exactly as the day before. He threw his attaché case on his desk, without even saying hello to either Stevie or Brenda. Instants later, he reappeared and motioned to Stevie to follow him.

Brenda had forewarned Stevie of what came next. It was the daily staff meeting of the agents to discuss problems, to trade information and set up agency priorities and assignments. Stevie, as Jerry Fentris' assistant, would attend all but the most confidential of these meetings and be expected to contribute nothing. Brenda had cautioned Stevie that Jerry's former assistant had made the unpardonable mistake of commenting on the business at hand. He had done it once and was stared at. He had done it a second time and was fired.

Stevie and her boss walked briskly down the hall into

the conference room. All of the key agents, plus six assistants who sat on the outside perimeter next to the walls, were easing themselves into their seats. No one had a cup of coffee or was indulging in a first or second breakfast. No one looked at the assistants or at the agents, except one man sitting next to Sy Rosen who looked familiar to Stevie Tree. He had to be a man of importance, since she saw that the senior members were located near the head of the table.

No one acknowledged her presence. The discussion started at one end of the room. As if programmed, each agent reported on deals in progress and activities at studios or networks that would be of interest to other agents, then discussed any serious problems with talent or customers, and then it was on to the next dark-suited man.

Stevie sat listening. Then the man next to Sy Rosen turned around slowly and stared at her. His face was familiar.

The third and then the fourth agent reported. The man near Sy Rosen turned around again. And then he returned to the business at hand and ruled on some point in the discussion. He showed no deference to Sy Rosen, who seemed to acknowledge his right to make decisions affecting the agency.

When Stevie heard his voice, she knew who he was, and she caught her breath. She had been with this man during a weekend in Acapulco when Morgan Oliver had "loaned" her out as the best piece of ass in Hollywood. She recognized him by his voice, because—as she now remembered—he conducted business on the telephone from the hotel bed, as he was lying naked and Stevie was giving him very expert head.

2

"Here at IA, we have a reputation for hard dealing and honest representation. Our word is our bond, and a customer can always count on us to deliver what we commit to."

Those were Sy Rosen's words to Stevie the day she was hired and appointed an assistant to Jerry Fentris. Fifteen minutes after the staff meeting, when Stevie returned with Jerry to his office, those words rang a little hollow. Stevie didn't have time to inquire about the identity of her Acapulco lover. She would ask Brenda what his job was at the agency. Stevie didn't even have time to sense disaster approaching, the accidental discovery of part of her past life—her first day on the job. Stevie very clearly understood that her job at IA could end almost as fast as it began. Surely this man would not be willing to associate the IA name with an agent whose colorful lovelife could serve as an embarrassment all around town.

It would never do for her to walk into a meeting at one of the networks and find someone she had been "loaned out" to by Morgan. What if there were two or three? How would that influence the negotiations? Surely she would be the only person in the room who knew in fine detail the bedroom habits of the man she was talking to. It might be reassuring over lunch to know that you were now with a beautiful lady who could validate you as a stud and who turned lovemaking into a three-ring circus. But what would happen if the event hadn't come off like gangbusters, or if the guy was married and didn't want to remember an early dalliance?

Stevie felt sick at the prospect and was certain that any moment she would receive a call from Sy Rosen, coupled with regrets. She didn't have any time to reflect. When she reached the office, Brenda was holding the phone and motioned to Jerry, "It's Mirsky."

As Jerry sat down at his desk, he picked up the phone and motioned to Stevie to pick up the earpiece on the "dead key" instrument across from him, which would allow her to listen without any disturbance on the line.

"A.J. . . . I've been trying to get you for two days now."

"Bullshit. My phone is not out of order, young man. In the worst case you could always send me a bouquet of flowers, red for yes or white for no. I am not in the habit of waiting this long for someone to pick up an offer."

"A.J., I've been trying to get hold of Randy for three days now. I've checked his house every half hour, his lawyer, his dentist—even his proctologist . . ."

"That's not funny, young man . . . I have had a lot of trouble down there myself . . . and I for one don't think that's a funny remark."

"Excuse me, A.J. . . . I mean that I've checked everywhere."

"Fentris, let me state my case, once and for all. Randy Davis has been a feature at the Vegas Palace for five years. I personally have paid that no good son of a bitch over one million dollars a year for the past five years, for four weeks of work each year . . . now that's when he's sober. I get less when he's drunk."

"He's over the drinking problem, A.J."

"Bullshit. I'll believe that when Arafat pledges to U.J.A."

"Seriously, A.J."

"To continue . . . and your client . . . your esteemed client owes the casino slightly less than $150,000 in gambling debts . . . which I'm fully prepared to forgive . . . just tear up . . . and all that I'm asking is for him to live up to his contract and give me the two weeks that he owes me at Christmas . . . for which, if you'll deliver him, I will also buy some of your lousier and overpriced lounge acts."

"Royce and Baskin were terrific in the lounge."

"I'd rather have Baskin and Robbins."

"By the way, A.J., their price is up this year. It's now twenty-five thousand dollars."

"For what? Per lifetime? That's too much for those no-talent boobs."

"No, of course, you're kidding . . . twenty-five G's per week, and they want a suite, no more double rooms."

"Listen, you . . . no, never mind. OK . . . now go ahead and nail down Mr. Randy Davis. Find him, goddammit. I've got advance bookings . . . I've got ads to place . . . I've got a hotel to fill."

"Oh, A.J., Randy wanted ten complimentary rooms for his friends for the whole Christmas week. That'll be OK, won't it?"

"Goddammit—find the cocksucker!"

He hung up the phone and Stevie looked at Fentris.

"Shall I try to locate him, Jerry?"

"No, don't bother . . . Mirsky is good for one more push before I speak to Randy. When Mirsky calls again, I think I can push his offer to $300,000 a week."

So much for "our word is our bond," and it was only fifteen minutes into the workday.

A light on the phone blinked. Brenda buzzed and Jerry Fentris called out, "Keep them on hold. I'll tell you when."

Stevie leaned across the desk. "Jerry, is there anything you want me to get started with?"

"Yeah . . . call my tailor Eric Ross—he's in the wheeldex, and tell him I got a spot on the sleeve of my tan cashmere sports jacket. Should I give it to my cleaner, or will he take care of it for me? Tell him I think that it's cocktail sauce . . . and then phone my barber—he's at Hillcrest—and find out if I can come by for a light trim right after my tennis lesson at nine tomorrow?"

Stevie murmured to herself, So this is how it's going to be. "Should I go to my desk for these things or do you want me to stay in here with you?"

"I don't care where you make the calls. Look, figure these things out for yourself."

Brenda called out, "It's the 'Tonight Show,' Jerry."

He picked up the phone. "Hi, baby . . . long time no see. Hey, did you hear what happened last week at Caramia's place?"

"What, Jerry? . . . I haven't spoken to Ted in a while. Got to get him on the show as host when Johnny goes out of town again."

"Yeah, he'd be great."

Jerry leaned back in the black swivel chair, simultaneously pulling a nail clipper from his desk drawer. Cradling the phone against his ear, he proceeded with the never-ending task of trimming his nails. "Well, Caramia had this creep in from New York, Burgess something or other—very big in investment banking and all that shit—and he's after Ted to headline some kind of cockamamy charity event . . . you know, for some goddam disease or other. That's all that Ted Caramia has to do. Well, this turkey never tried coke before . . . and when the stuff got passed around, he decided to try some. He must have blown a grand's worth of the stuff in the course of the evening, and he never came down. Talk about a coke freak . . . so he calls Ted the next day and wants to buy some to take home to his girlfriend in New York."

"Wonderful, Jerry. Give my best to Caramia when you see him and tell him I'll be calling him."

"Look, baby . . . you can do me a favor."

"Yeah?"

"You know this act . . . Royce and Baskin?"

"Yeah . . . they're turkeys, Jerry."

"I've seen Steve Martin bomb. Rich Little, David Brenner . . . everybody takes his turn in the barrel."

He laughed. "Nobody's perfect—except you and me. Use them on the show. What can you lose? Hey, I got a great number for you. I tell you, this one is the greatest in the sack you ever had."

"But their material stinks."

"Baby—they've got brand-new material, been working on it for a month, and they'll use the best of it on your show."

"No shit, now."

"Honest. I've never crossed you."

"OK, I've got a spot they can fill a week from Tuesday. New material now."

"Absolutely—you got it. See ya . . . say hello to Johnny for me."

"Jerry, before you hang up, gimme that phone number—"

After he hung up, Jerry called Stevie in. "Phone Baskin and Royce and tell them to dig up something new for the 'Tonight Show' even if they have to steal it, and give them the date . . . and call my goddam tailor like I told you to."

When Stevie walked out of Jerry's office and sat down across from Brenda, she had a page of notes given to her by Jerry Fentris.

Apart from the call to Royce and Baskin, there were a host of personal errands he had charged her with. Any incompetent secretary could have handled them. Stevie had her work cut out for her. It had nothing to do with the job, and everything to do with whether Jerry Fentris would allow her any responsibility. Stevie had a certain notion that she had been hired over Jerry's objections, that he would play the game out, and at the end of a decent period of time, report to Sy Rosen that she couldn't cut it.

Stevie sat down to call Eric Ross about the stain on the cashmere jacket. Brenda interrupted her.

"Stevie—you have to go around and see Fred Wine. He wants to see you right away."

Stevie recognized the name. It was the man who had stared at her in the staff meeting, the man with whom she had spent the weekend at Acapulco.

Stevie walked down the corridor toward Sy Rosen's office. Directly to the right was Fred Wine's door. She announced herself to his secretary, waited for five minutes and was told to enter. Fred Wine's office was slightly smaller than Sy Rosen's, but impressive and replete with good modern paintings. Pictures of stars represented by the agency were on the wall, as well as photographs of Fred Wine with major world figures and citations and honors given to him by civic organizations.

"Sit down," Fred Wine ordered.

Stevie sat, silently. She adjusted the turquoise blouse nervously.

"You know why I wanted to see you."

"Mr. Wine, there could only be one reason—but why don't *you* tell me your way."

"I have nothing against you . . . nothing at all, but I have a loyalty to IA, and you don't belong here. You can do yourself a favor by resigning, say at the end of the week. We'll arrange to give you a month's pay, and we'll call everything off."

"Is that the way Sy Rosen wants it?"

"That's not important."

"Mr. Wine . . . you have no idea at all about me . . . none at all. You are basing your decision on a weekend together in Acapulco years ago, and anyway I believe you had a good time."

"Look, Miss Tree, or whatever your real name is, the simple fact of the matter is that this is a town where you can buy anything, any time, and I'm not about to let 'Miss Blow Job' of Hollywood work here."

Stevie sat there. She had expected something like this, but not such anger. It had to happen sometime. Hollywood didn't forgive and it didn't forget. Wherever she went, she might see her past mirrored in the eyes of one of the men she met. Those who knew would never forget what she had been.

Fred Wine continued, "I spoke to Morgan Oliver not more than ten minutes ago. We talked about you."

"What did he have to say, Mr. Wine?"

"I won't go into that."

"Did he say that he passed me around from man to man—to friends of his, to men he didn't even know? Did he say that he was my pimp, Mr. Wine?"

"Let's not continue with this anymore, I've got important business. Just get out. Morgan told me all about you. He said that I ought to get you out before somebody caught something from you. Look—I'll send you the money in cash." He leaned forward, his hands on the desk, but Stevie wasn't going to let him intimidate her into leaving his office or IA.

"I'm not going, Mr. Wine."

"What are you talking about?"

"Mr. Wine, why can't you forgive me? Forget who I was, what I was? I'm not the same person. I have respect for myself now. I had none then. I have hopes for the future. Please give me a chance." Wine turned away from her gaze.

"Miss Tree, I don't have any more time to talk."

"One more minute, Mr. Wine. You haven't discussed this with Sy Rosen, or he would have fired me, or Jerry Fentris would have. You offered to give me a month's pay in cash. The agency wouldn't pay me in cash. The money must come from you. You're afraid of me, Mr. Wine." Stevie looked directly at him.

Fred Wine stared. He was barely keeping himself under control.

"It's not your wife. Lots of men play around. I know what it is. It's you. It's those pictures and plaques on the wall. The photo of you and Billy Graham. The picture of you with Rosalynn Carter. You're frightened that your image would be tarnished if anyone knew. They wouldn't care, Mr. Wine, but you would. You've taken too many bows as a moral upstanding type. What would happen to you if you ever admitted you were human?"

"Miss Tree, you are trying my patience."

"Mr. Wine, I've asked for your forgiveness—but I don't even think that's necessary. I slept around—big deal! I was young. I was stupid. I was human. Why can't you accept that as a fact of life and begin accepting your own humanity, too?"

"I really don't need a sermon, Miss Tree, especially coming from you."

"I tell you what, Mr. Wine. Let's both of us go in and see Sy Rosen. He knows nothing about this. He doesn't know what I used to be. He doesn't know that you and I were once involved. I'm willing to trust his forgiveness for both our indiscretions. If you're willing to level with him, so am I."

Stevie sat there counting her pulse beats. There were too many. Fred Wine took a pencil and turned it over, end on end. The intercom buzzer rang and he picked up the phone.

"Yes, I know that I'm late for an appointment. Tell him I'm just leaving now." He hung up the phone and looked at Stevie. "Get back to work, Miss Tree."

Stevie stood up and walked out the door, avoiding eye contact. If she could get out without his saying *one* more thing, she would win.

On her way out, Stevie passed Fred Wine's secretary and offered her hand.

"I'm Stevie Tree . . . I'm new at IA."

"Hi, Stevie. I'm Gloria, Mr. Wine's secretary. He's a wonderful man, don't you think?"

Stevie smiled. "He certainly is. I'm going to enjoy working with him. By the way, you didn't buzz Mr. Wine just now, did you?"

Gloria smiled. "He has one of those gizmos under his desk so he can buzz himself. But don't let him know I told you."

Saturday Morning—8 A.M.

Fred Wine made the arrangements with a Charter Air Service for Jerry Fentris and himself to fly to Palm Springs to meet with Sy Rosen. The Charter Service had been used many times by the agency for rock acts and superstars who liked its availability and the privacy of flying when and how they wanted.

The Lear Jet was five minutes away from the Palm Springs Airport and the time was eight in the morning.

The flight had lasted only fifteen air minutes, but it was enough time for Jerry Fentris and Fred Wine to catch the first bit of sleep they had in twenty-four hours. The entire night had been devoted to setting things straight.

Nicholas Long had been much less of a problem than they thought he would be. Jerry Fentris had expected a struggle to get him to cool his fever for revenge and replace it with something that would be more malleable for I.A. It helped, of course, that Melinda, his sixteen-year-old daughter, had been in and out of very serious trouble for many years. Though the thought of a daughter violently dead would be enough to chill a parent, Nick Long was ready to accept the fact that Melinda would inevitably have come to a bad end.

"OK, Jerry . . . look, she wasn't the best, and she was a lot of heartache, but she was my daughter . . . and Morgan Oliver had no business being involved with her . . ."

"Nick . . . you know how things are in this town . . ."

"Yeah . . . but Oliver was working for me . . . on a picture, and he had a responsibility . . ."

"Nick, I admit it . . . the man played the wrong card . . . but with due deference to Melinda, she wasn't inexperienced . . . and maybe she led him on."

"So what?" That left a silence as thick as night.

"Well, after all, Nick . . . a guy can't be responsible if a gal shows him where to park it . . ."

"I don't like that kind of talk, Jerry . . . cut it."

"OK . . . I'm sorry . . . I overstepped. You have my sincere apology. . . . Nick, tell me, do you accept it? It's important for me to know. Your friendship means more to me than the whole damn picture, more than Morgan Oliver . . . There are things in this business that you can't put a price on, and one of them is friendship."

Nick Long turned to look at Jerry Fentris. "What do you think this will do to the picture?"

Without a moment's pause, Jerry replied, "Kill it . . . destroy it . . . and it's too bad. It's a masterpiece—not only the finest thing you've ever done, Nick, but a landmark picture, the kind of thing that film historians will write about . . . the first of its kind."

Nick Long stared at Fentris. "You know it came in right on budget . . . even with all the trouble that Morgan caused."

Fentris whistled. "Jesus, Nick . . . they ought to put up a monument to you at the studio."

Nick Long sighed. "No chance of that. Christ, you know what this business is all about, Jerry. This picture might have gone through the roof . . . and even if it had . . . Christ, the studio would steal me blind on the accounting, and it won't make a goddam bit of difference when I come up with another project to show them."

Jerry Fentris knew he had him. The rest of the transaction was simply an endgame position of closing the deal.

"Nick, listen to me."

"Yeah, what is it, Jerry?"

"Nick . . . if I say something . . . promise you won't take it the wrong way? Can I say something to you that I wouldn't want repeated, wouldn't want you to take offense? We've known each other a lot of years . . ."

"Yeah . . . go ahead . . . what is it?"

"Nick . . . the Melinda thing could be an accident . . . she had a heart attack . . . and it makes everything work . . ."

"Oh, come off it, Jerry . . . my God, even if I would buy that kind of deal . . . this is something for the police. It'll be over every radio, TV and paper in the country in twenty-four hours . . . and that's the end of it . . ."

"Nick . . . listen to me."

Nick Long sighed. "If you make sense."

"Nick . . . it's a good shot. The doctor who's coming is a pal. I mean *really*. He supplies . . . man, he

supplies half the rock acts we have in the agency . . .
and a lot of the stars. We're good for a quarter of a
million dollars a year to this guy . . . in *cash*. You
know what that means in after-tax money? Christ, a
guy would have to earn three-quarters of a mil a year.
You know how many doctors would give their left nut
for that kind of a setup? Let me tell you . . . dozens.
OK, listen. I *know* he'll call it a heart attack . . . and
that means no cops . . . no papers."

Nicholas Long turned his full attention to the conversation. "OK, so that's the doctor, if you say so, but do
you know how *many* people were here tonight? Any
one of them could blow that sky high. Look, and there's
Valerie . . . I admit there's no reason why this
wouldn't be helpful . . . But Christ, how are you going to shut the rest of these people up? Remember
Watergate?"

"Yeah, Nick . . . I remember Watergate . . . and
the answer to that was there wasn't enough in it for
enough people. It's simple."

"You say." Nick Long looked very faraway.

"No, Nick, I know!"

"Go ahead . . . show it to me."

"Let's say by way of example that I gave you Morgan
Oliver for another picture . . . at the same price you
paid for this one. All I'd want would be a little more at
the back end of the deal . . ."

"How much of the profits?" He felt the old stirrings.

"Christ, I haven't even given it any thought. What
did he get on this deal? Five percent of the gross?
OK . . . easy . . . just ten percent . . ."

"Yeah . . . I'm listening."

"As for Zelma . . . I don't think she knows a goddam thing . . . but Sy Rosen has her by the nuts and
she'll forget what day it is with the right word from Sy."

"What about Randy?"

"Listen . . . Randy needs a picture bad . . . he has
all the money in the world, but he just broke up with his
last wife and he wants to work. He'll swear that I'm the
Virgin Mary if we get him a picture, and we do that by

laying off the next Nicholas Long Production starring
Morgan Oliver at a studio . . . and for that privilege,
they turn out a quickie private-eye caper with Randy
. . and look, Nick, if you want to produce that
one—just for the fee—it's a snap."

Nick Long was no longer lethargic. He was listening
intently. "What about Walker Perkins?"

Jerry smiled. "I have Walker Perkins sewed up with
a deal I can work with a little faggot friend of
his . . . and whatever way the faggot turns, that's the
way that Walker will turn. Nick, you've got to understand that everybody wants it to be a heart attack.
Everybody. All I have to say is that the doctor said it,
and they can have seen her hit by a truck and they'll go
our way."

"The projectionist?"

Jerry smiled. It's all done. Ten grand." He put his
arm around Long.

"What about Valerie? . . . Christ, Jerry, I can't
deliver my wife—even if you can make all the rest of
this stuff happen."

Fentris squeezed Nick Long's shoulder. "Nick, don't
worry about a thing . . . I didn't say anything about it
first . . . but I expect that you wouldn't have any
objection to our representing you on these deals . . . I
know you never needed an agent before . . . but I
think you could use one now."

"Sure, Jerry . . . that's OK with me."

"OK then . . . revered client . . . just leave Valerie
to me. Sometimes things work better through a third
person. OK?"

"OK . . . it's in your hands . . . Say, do you think I
could up Morgan to two pictures?"

"Christ, Nick, as your agent, it would be to my
advantage too. Don't worry about a thing." Jerry
Fentris gave Nick Long another squeeze.

Valerie Long was next on Jerry Fentris' list. Jerry
walked out of the room and ran into Fred Wine,
coming from the direction of Melinda's bedroom with a
gray-haired man Jerry knew to be the agency doctor.

Fred Wine introduced the two of them. "Jerry, you haven't met Dr. Randolph . . . he works with some of our people." The two shook hands. Fred Wine motioned Jerry into a guest bedroom with the doctor and then closed the door.

"Jerry . . . there are some complications. Dr. Randolph can sign a death certificate only if Melinda Long has been a patient of his before."

Jerry turned to go. "OK, so she was a patient."

"No, Jerry . . . there's more to it than just saying so."

Dr. Randolph cleared his throat. "What I'm doing is very irregular."

Jerry Fentris looked bored. "OK. We know that. How do we make it work?"

Dr. Randolph continued. "You see, there are laws concerning this whole thing . . . There have been doctors conspiring, covering up murders . . ."

Fred Wine interrupted. "Christ knows that's not this case, Doctor. She OD'd. Nobody killed her. It was an accident."

The doctor continued. "Yes, I know. And that's the reason I'm prepared to help you . . . to save the family embarrassment . . . but unless I can *prove* that she was a patient of mine, and that I diagnosed her ailment sometime before, then I can be leaving myself open to criminal charges . . . and, of course, if there is an autopsy . . ."

Jerry Fentris interrupted. "There won't be . . . and why can't you do some examinations for her file right now? We can get you all the stuff you need. She's been away at school for three years . . . I know for a fact that she hasn't seen a single doctor in that long. Your records could pick up anytime in those three years . . . you can do that."

The doctor nodded. "Yes . . . I suppose so."

Jerry Fentris cut him short. "Look, Doctor . . . if you'll excuse me . . . you have things to do and so do I. I think we can work it out . . . Look, it's for the family."

The doctor nodded and left the two of them there.

Fred Wine broke the silence. "How did you know about her being away at school?"

Jerry Fentris replied. "What school?" Then he left the room to see Valerie Long.

As Jerry Fentris strode down the hall to Valerie's bedroom, he passed a gurney taking the covered body of Melinda Long down the hall toward the stairs, to the station wagon and the funeral home. He paused for a moment in silent respect, and then as the two men passed he continued his errand.

Valerie and Nicholas Long had separate bedrooms and separate lives. Jerry Fentris closed the door behind him softly in her bedroom.

Valerie Long was lying on a chaise in the distant corner, a bony scion of privilege. Her long, dark hair hung over a topaz embroidered dressing gown. Her slim figure reclined in just the proper attitude to demonstrate poise, cultivated for years. The slight moisture in her dark brown eyes shone from a face that had been cared for, attended to, caressed and adored by the most expensive practitioners to the rich in Beverly Hills. Whatever grief Valerie Long suffered, it was fashionable.

"Jerry . . . thank God you were here."

"Thank God for me too, Val . . ."

"Jerry . . . I'm going to say something terrible."

"Val . . . you can say anything you want to me . . . we've been friends for twenty-five, no, thirty years . . . Christ, your family and mine lived on the same block in Beverly Hills . . ."

"Jerry . . . Melinda is gone . . . she's gone. Maybe it's for the best . . . but Jerry . . ." Valerie sobbed and leaned forward to nestle her head on his shoulder. "Jerry . . . this scandal will kill me. . . . My family is *important* in this town . . . Jerry, what can you do? Can you do *anything?*"

Jerry held on to Valerie for a long moment and then grasped her around the shoulders. "Val . . . what I'm going to suggest is a little irregular . . . and it would need Nick's cooperation . . . but if you were behind me . . . and the two of us worked it together, I think there's a way to hush the whole thing up."

At eight-fifteen, the Lear Jet landed at Palm Springs Airport. Jerry Fentris and Fred Wine got into a waiting taxi and rode the thirteen miles to Sy Rosen's modest home. By any standards, Sy Rosen was a multimillionaire, but he believed in a quiet display of wealth, meaning no display at all.

When the taxi arrived at the house, Sy Rosen met them at the door. He was in a thick white terrycloth robe and sandals. His hair was faultlessly combed and he sported a healthy, light bronze tan. He ushered them into the house, hung up their jackets in the hall closet and led them to an outdoor patio next to a small swimming pool. The table on the patio was set for breakfast for three. Sy Rosen had already been in for a morning swim.

"Fifty laps today . . ."

"That's terrific, Sy . . . You must feel back in shape."

"Fred, I feel like a million dollars . . . The doctors say that I'm as good as new. The operation was a complete success." He laughed, "Don't know why anybody would want a prostate anyway."

Sy motioned to them to eat the half grapefruit that sat at each place. "I've had my breakfast, but you boys must be starved. I understand we have a little problem."

Over the grapefruit, scrambled eggs, toast and coffee, Fred Wine and Jerry Fentris outlined the events of the night before, the matter of the doctor's participation and the reactions of Nick and Valerie.

Sy smiled. "I've known Valerie Long for thirty-five years. I knew her folks. Good people. I'm glad that we could work this out for her." He poured coffee for the two of them from a thermos.

Sy Rosen had not failed to recognize the business advantages of this complex transaction, but he had chosen to observe it as a charitable undertaking meant exclusively to rid good friends of needless suffering.

Jerry interrupted Sy's reverie. "I think that we can control it, with the family and all that . . . but there are those other stops we've got to make—Randy, Walker, Zelma and her black boyfriend—and then there's the matter of the deals. We've got to deliver these deals immediately. If we don't, Randy is gonna talk to someone and that someone will talk to someone else . . . and the Nick Long deal has to be made . . . and Morgan has to be brought into line . . . not to mention Stevie. She's a big problem because of her past relationship with Morgan."

Sy thought for a moment. "The last item that we have to worry about is Stevie Tree. The first is the deals. From that, people make money and see their faces on the silver screen. So if my guess is right, then I should call the head of the studio, Ralph Stanton, and say something like this, 'Ralph, I can deliver Morgan Oliver for another picture . . . and the director . . . and the producer . . . and we want a picture commitment for Randy Davis . . . and a couple of other things that I'll mention.' I think I have a pretty good idea of the numbers involved, and I'll push for a substantial deal . . ."

Jerry Fentris and Fred were finishing their second cup of coffee.

Sy continued. "Now I think that Stevie will be on the phone to me in a little bit. I won't be too easy to find. I'll be in town . . . and then I'll be resting . . . and finally I'll talk to her. I'll listen to everything she has to say. That's what I should do as head of the agency. Now what you gentlemen should do is make sure of your other people . . . and it would be a good idea if the funeral for the poor child were tomorrow. Sunday is a good day for a funeral. It shouldn't be too large—a simple small thing appropriate for the loss of one so young."

The two of them nodded at the correctness of Sy's judgment.

3

At the age of eleven, Stephanie Tree witnessed the murder of her mother and her mother's lover. The killer was Air Force Sergeant Ray Tree, Stevie's father.

She stood by the bloodstained bed, silent, transfixed, her blue eyes wide open. Stevie was in shock.

But she didn't cry.

Moments after the double murder in the bedroom, when neighbors rushed up the stairs of their tiny house on the Air Force base, she was dragged away from the horror scene.

The neighbor's wife carried the young girl in her arms. "Don't look, honey. Promise not to look." When the two of them descended the stairs, they heard the screams of Virginia, Stevie's nine-month-old sister.

Another neighbor lifted the tiny child from her carriage and the four of them departed the murder scene, leaving the figure of Ray Tree, still sitting on the bed, holding his spent .45, staring at what he had done.

Stevie's father went quietly and willingly with the Air Force police who showed up soon after. He was taken to the orderly room where the provost marshal had him removed to the prison stockade.

The provost began the laborious task of interviewing witnesses and building a file on the case that would go to the court-martial. Ray Tree readily admitted the facts. Under questioning, he admitted that he knew that Stevie's mother, Audrey, had been unfaithful to him for years. The circumstances were more bizarre, since in a diary that Ray Tree kept, he had marked down names of some of her previous lovers. What had he kept them for? He didn't know. Why had he killed this particular one, and his wife, on this particular day? He had no answer for that, either.

Audrey Josoff, a pretty but shy girl, had been working at the post exchange at Andrews Air Force Base when Ray Tree met and married her. She was a virgin. On their very first date, eleven years earlier, she had become pregnant. Stevie was born shortly after their wedding.

Audrey grew up quickly. She came to understand that Ray was a bad bargain. He drank excessively and beat her frequently. Fortunately, Ray Tree was often on extended overseas tours as a member of an air transport crew. During those years, Audrey developed relationships with many men. It was an answer to the loveless life she led with Stevie's father.

Audrey often thought of leaving Ray, but was never able to steel herself to that decision. Then, in one of their few occasions for sex, Audrey became pregnant once again. Virginia was the result. Fate in the form of another child had once again conspired to bind Audrey to a man she didn't love, couldn't abide and couldn't leave, except in death.

Within days of the event, Ray Tree would be a forgotten man. His buddies and his commanding officer would remove him from their lives and the Air Force would go on.

It was the same with the girl, Stevie. The small figure in a borrowed, flowered organdy dress went to the funeral service, organized by the Air Force, with a chaplain provided by the Air Force, to see a casket provided by the Air Force lowered into the barren Midwestern ground.

Apart from Stevie and the chaplain, there were only five others at the graveside—some curious neighbors —and the sixth the driver of the hearse.

In that way, the body of Audrey Tree was put to rest.

Stevie's only living relative, an aunt who lived in Illinois, had been difficult to locate, and for the next few days Stevie returned to a neighbor's house and sat in front of the small television set, leaving only for occasional trips to the cupboard for food.

Wanda Josoff, at forty-one, ten years older than her sister Audrey, was secretary to a bank manager in Urbana, Illinois. When the Air Force officer who located her told her the news, she inquired whether there were any alternatives to her taking the little girl. She was a single woman. She lived alone. She worked. She had no experience with children, nor did she want any.

Wanda would take the older one, Stevie. Virginia, the dark-haired baby, would be too much trouble. She would have to be put in an orphanage.

The wood-frame house in which Wanda Josoff lived was off Main Street in Urbana, a sleepy college town containing the University of Illinois. The house had a single story which held a small kitchen, covered with peeling linoleum, featuring a kitchen table with tiny rosebuds painted on the wood. A living room with a worn couch and chairs separated the kitchen from the main bedroom where Aunt Wanda slept. A tiny breakfast nook next to the kitchen had been fixed up with a cot for Stevie. Stevie's room had one window that looked out over the back stairs.

Slowly, Stevie settled into the local school and found a few friends. She was intensely shy, but her teachers liked her.

Stevie entered Urbana High when she was thirteen and although she had menstruated at twelve, she was so little developed and so tall and thin that she felt awkward and ill at ease.

Stevie was five foot seven, as tall as she would ever get. Her ash-blonde hair was long and excessively fine. Her features were regular but without any distinction. Her breasts had not even emerged and her pubic area was virtually without a whisper of hair.

Still, high school was a great awakening. The girls spoke openly about sexual feelings. There were older boys she could observe and fantasize about, and most importantly there was a drama club to which Stevie was immediately drawn.

In her private moments in the wood-frame house, Stevie would sometimes put on her aunt's clothing and pretend. She would look at photos in *Life* and dwell on the glamorous movie stars, the Janet Leighs, the Liz Taylors, the Doris Days, and arrange her hair with rubber bands to strike a similar pose in the mirror.

At first Stevie got parts in the singing chorus. She had a thin but true alto voice. Although her height made it difficult, she began to get leading roles in the holiday shows the drama club was forever preparing for assemblies.

Stevie took to staying late at school. Miss Turner, the drama coach, found Stevie a more than willing and surprisingly apt pupil. Stevie was willing to help Miss Turner in her assigned class of freshman English, grading papers and sorting homework, in exchange for additional help in coaching. With the passage of time and the sense of achievement in the school plays, Stevie became more outgoing in school. The drama club members became friendly. But Stevie felt out of things because she didn't have much spending money to buy records or hang out and have a burger and a Coke with her schoolmates. She brought her lunch to school, and it was a rare treat for her to go to a movie. Stevie would babysit for neighbors whenever possible and the few dollars she made went for magazines and other small treats.

After a period of time, Wanda announced that she was going to get married. Bertram Spinner, her husband-to-be, age fifty, quiet and graying, had suffered a permanent disability as a result of falling from a Post Office truck.

Since Bert didn't work, he was home almost all the time. From time to time he did help with the breakfast dishes, and occasionally he would exchange a word or two with Stevie. His entrance into the life of the house was a welcome event for the young girl, because it diminished her aunt's concentration on her. Thus it allowed Stevie to retire to her tiny room alongside the kitchen and shut the door. The first week of Bert's presence in the house went by without any incident.

The first night of the second week Stevie heard the heavy sound of bare feet on the kitchen floor in the middle of the night. A crack of light appeared at the bottom of the door and Stevie listened to the sound of drawers being opened. Then the refrigerator was opened and closed.

She lay there awake, waiting for Bert to leave so she could go back to sleep. She looked at her clock. It read one-fifteen.

The knob on her door turned and the door opened to reveal Bert standing in his pajama bottoms with his back to the light. He came in and sat down on the side of her bed.

"Hope I didn't wake you up."

"It's OK, Uncle Bert . . . It's OK."

"Want something to eat? I got a baloney sandwich."

"No thanks, Uncle Bert. I just want to get back to sleep."

"Stevie," he droned on, "I think you're a nice girl, and I didn't want to say anything to your Aunt Wanda, but someone stole twenty dollars from my wallet."

"Who took it, Uncle Bert?"

"I think you did, Stevie—and I want you to put it back, or I'll have to tell your aunt." He put his hand on the blanket covering her leg.

In the light of the half-opened door, Stevie saw that the fly front of Bert's pajama bottom was wide open. His penis hung outside the opening. As he talked, he started to fondle it absently.

"I didn't take your money, Uncle Bert. I promise you."

"There's been other things missing, too. You'd better give me my money, or I'll tell your aunt. I guess she'd have to send you away. You wouldn't want that." He smiled soothingly.

Bert's penis began to get hard and Stevie grew frightened. She started to turn away, but Bert held her there.

"I'll tell you what I'll do—just to show you that I don't hold any grudge, just touch my johnnycake here, and wish him good night and we'll forget all about it."

Stevie struggled, and thought to cry out. She tried to move away but he held her there.

"It's no big deal—just wish him good night. It's only friendly."

He took her hand and guided it against his hard penis. The touch repelled her and she pulled away, but his hand forced hers back.

"Please, Uncle Bert. Let me alone."

"Just wish it good night."

He forced her hand around the hard shaft and pulled it to the knob end. Putting his hand around hers, he slowly pulled it down and up again. Despite herself, she couldn't pull away. There was a pounding in her heart that she had never felt before.

"Uncle Bert," she cried. "Please let me go."

In a hoarse voice he rasped, "Just a little more time."

With a convulsion, he came all over her hand. His hand and hers were held together with his grasp and the stickiness. Stevie sobbed.

"I'll help you wipe it up. Don't worry. Nobody will ever know."

Stevie didn't get to sleep that night. She cried into her pillow and when Bert and Wanda came into the kitchen for breakfast the next morning, Stevie had already left.

That night at dinner, the three of them sat around the humming television set listening to the canned laugh track of the Dick Van Dyke Show and occasionally looking up from their food. Stevie was even less noticeable than ever. Bert looked over at Wanda and back at Stevie, who saw him in a corner of her eye.

"Did I tell you, Wanda, I found that twenty-dollar bill I lost? It was on the dresser under your scarf."

"I told you to look around before you accused

someone. Stevie—stop playing with your food. Bert
and I paid good money for it. Eat it."

That night Stevie put her bed against the door, but
there was no sound in the kitchen, no disturbance of
any sort. She relived the night before. Should she have
screamed? What would have happened? Would Bert
have hurt her? Would Aunt Wanda have believed her?

The next day the rehearsal for the school production
of *Our Town* had been called off, and Stevie walked
home from school. It was October and an autumnal
feeling had been in the air for a week or more. The
slanting afternoon sun was golden against the trees,
which were a crisp orange and gold in the stark light.
The quiet town was stiller than ever. The dust on the
side of the road was dry and it kicked up a little trail
behind her as she walked. Looking up in the sky for a
moment or two, Stevie stopped occasionally to re-
hearse her lines in the play. Finally, toward dusk, she
approached the house and walked up the back stairs
into the kitchen. The kitchen door slammed behind her
and she stepped into her room to deposit her books.
Uncle Bert was lying on top of her bed, with his pants
and underwear off. His body hair was dark against his
pale aging skin. He was casually moving the tips of his
fingers along his stomach down through his darker
pubic hair. He got up off the bed, and closed the door
behind her.

"You liked it the other night. I could tell. You did it
so good."

Aunt Wanda was still at the bank and wouldn't be
home for at least an hour. Stevie's heart was pounding
both from fear and an inexplicable tension. The feeling
in her head was as if the insides had bulged out and so
shut off sounds and vision. She saw but didn't see. She
heard, but didn't hear.

Somehow she sat down on the bed with Bert holding
both of her hands in his. She grasped his penis, first
loosely and then tighter, and began to massage it. Bert
guided her hand to keep the movements steady and to
prevent her from pulling away. When he was sure

Stevie wouldn't stop, he reached his free hand and slid it up her dress. Stevie recoiled and stopped. She murmured, "No . . . please." Bert moved his exploring fingers inside her thighs to the crotch of her cotton panties. He began to rub her gently. The tightness of Stevie's body was intense. Bert slipped a finger inside the elastic of her underpants and felt her young smoothness. His exploring finger found the little button of her clitoris and gently fingered its dryness. Stevie's body relaxed its stiffness and seemed to embrace the big hand inside her panties.

When they were finished, Bert dressed and left the room. Neither of them said a word. Stevie sat there on the coverlet as he dressed, not daring to breathe, and as he left the room she plunged her face into the pillow and cried.

Many times in the weeks that followed, Stevie sat with her aunt and Bert at the table. She wanted the words to escape. She had to tell someone what she was doing. But Stevie couldn't summon the resolve.

As the months went by, Bert's sexual demands increased, and Stevie did whatever he asked of her. Her enormous feeling of guilt was compounded by the terrible fact that she couldn't stop.

Stevie found herself skipping drama rehearsals to rush home to Uncle Bert. On the way home, she would half walk, half run, with her heart pounding so hard in her chest that she couldn't think. In her room Bert would be waiting for her. And when it was over, she was always overcome by an incredible sadness. If it made her so unhappy, she thought, why couldn't she stop?

At school, Stevie's work was suffering. Her participation in the drama club became less, and her interest in the goings-on of her schoolmates, boys and girls, became almost nonexistent.

Yet, during these months, Stevie began to blossom as a young woman. Her flat and boyish figure began to develop curves. She wore no makeup and the plainest of dresses, while the rest of her classmates were aping the fashions on TV and in the movie magazines. Yet unmistakably Stevie was becoming womanly.

There were moments of deep depression when she thought of telling all to Miss Turner, who was the only adult she trusted. Stevie would stay after school, fully prepared to describe the worst of her relationship with her uncle, and beg for Miss Turner's help.

On one occasion, she steeled herself to do it. As the time approached for her to say something, Miss Turner looked at her quizzically and asked her if Stevie had something on her mind.

Stevie broke into tears and ran out of the school, all the way home.

When Stevie was sixteen, she was already beautiful, with the promise of becoming even more beautiful in time. Her eyes, a dark blue, were framed in a perfect oval face. The depth of their blue color had only recently become apparent to others. Her hair, blonde at birth, had remained ash blonde and accentuated the dark of her eyes. Her neck was long and in perfect keeping with the long line of a graceful and supple body. At five feet seven, with a lovely but smallish bosom, she was finally at home in her body. The willowy quality that was her hallmark in later years was already there for others to recognize.

That year Wanda took sick with the grippe and remained home for a week. Her illness was not thought to be serious, and only when she appeared to have difficulty breathing did Bert call a doctor. Her aunt had pulmonary pneumonia, usually simple to treat. However, at the Urbana Hospital where she was taken, further infection developed.

The second time Stevie came to the hospital was an hour after her aunt had died. Stevie didn't shed a tear then, nor did she cry at the funeral. It was a warm spring day, and the small knot of friends and mourners, most of whom were co-workers at the bank, came to the cemetery during their lunch hour. It was precisely for this reason that the interment was set for noon.

It was a long walk home from the cemetery for

Stevie. She had refused a ride with some of the ladies at the bank, who were returning to town. Stevie wanted to be alone. The day was strikingly beautiful. The temperature was warm. Dogwood and cherry trees were beginning to bud on the front lawns of houses she passed. There was a smell of bone meal fertilizer in the air that gave promise of the lush green lawns of summer. The sun was shining brightly at just after one in the afternoon, and the three miles back to her house were full of little pleasures. She felt no sadness at Aunt Wanda's death, just wonder as to what it would mean.

Stevie walked in the front gate and around the back to the kitchen steps. As she walked up the steps she looked through the window of her room and saw Bert lying on the bed. His pants were off, as were his shorts. He was fondling his penis.

Stevie looked through the window, unobserved. She stood there for several moments looking at the very familiar scene.

She turned slowly and quietly, and making no noise, she retreated down the kitchen stairs, past the front stoop and out the gate, and never looked back.

4

Promptly after she got off the bus from St. Louis, Stevie Tree made her first Hollywood contact.

Stevie managed to hitch a ride with a Chinese lady who was picking up her nine-year-old son at the bus station. The boy, James Po, had traveled on the bus with Stevie all the way from St. Louis, and after three days of close contact the two of them were friends. They had shared Twinkies, *Playboy* and opinions about the Beatles over the course of a 2,000-mile trip.

The boy's mother and father worked, as a couple, in the beach house of an unemployed Hollywood producer, and the son was coming for a short visit. The producer had been unwilling to let the couple keep their child—he even had an aversion to his own children—but he did permit visits for the youngster at Easter and Christmas.

James Po took the separation gracefully. He lived with an aunt in St. Louis who owned a grocery store, and his mother accepted the occasional visits as a matter of course. Mrs. Po was not an expert at the wheel of the producer's ten-year-old Rolls Royce, but on the drive from the bus station at Cahuenga and Hollywood Boulevard, she proved herself an expert tour guide to the sights of Hollywood Boulevard—the Walk of the Stars, featuring the names of prominent entertainment figures engraved in bronze on the sidewalks of the boulevard, and Grauman's Chinese Theater with its garish and ornate gold-trimmed, red lacquer front, shaped like a Chinese temple.

"There," she said proudly, "Chinese Theatre, you

51

see footsteps and hands in cement, of big Holly-wood stars—Clark Gable, Shirley Temple, Spencer Tracy . . ." she droned on as they passed. "My boss, famous movie producer. Two years ago he produced *Beach Party Roulette*. Big hit. Now he write script for bigger studio, Paramount. Good script. All need is proper casting."

"I saw that movie, it was a piece of shit," James Po remarked.

Past the Chinese Theatre, the woman headed the Rolls south and drove along Sunset Boulevard. It was a four-lane road of no particular distinction, occasional palms lining the side of the streets. Small, one- and two-story buildings housed banks, supermarkets, retail shops and motels, a uniform cement street border.

As if answering an unspoken question, her driver commented, "This part nothing. Rich people live in Beverly Hills or like boss, in Malibu. You want to go to Schwab's Drug Store? We pass by. You an actress, maybe? Maybe you be discovered in Schwab's, like Lana Turner. You pretty girl. You be discovered, I betcha."

Stevie decided she might as well. She had to go to the bathroom, and the lady's driving made her nervous. She hardly ever looked at the road as she leaned over to nudge Stevie and point out another landmark. Stevie figured it was time to get out or die.

The car slowed to a stop and Stevie got out. She started to wave to James as the Rolls pulled away, but he had turned to talk to his mother. Now she had no one. Stevie looked up at the street sign on the corner, Laurel Canyon Boulevard and Sunset. Across the street the long, low pink building had a huge sign on the front that read, "Schwab's Pharmacy." She stood waiting for the traffic to thin so she could cross Sunset.

When Stevie first walked into Schwab's, it was twelve-thirty and the lunch crowd had assembled. Schwab's at lunch resembled a railroad club car in which the passengers were going nowhere, but endless-ly congregated to pass the time and gossip.

Inside the front entrance was a newspaper and magazine rack. Oddly dressed types pored over copies of *Variety, Hollywood Reporter* and *Casting News*. The readers appeared to have a special stance, feet spread apart, elbows extended, so as not to be dislodged by others who wanted free library privileges. Aisles of shelves extended toward the rear with selections of deodorants, mouthwash, toothpaste and the like. More expensive items were enclosed in locked glass cases. In the rear, pharmacists busily mixed prescriptions to minister to the hurts, pains and torments of a vulnerable clientele.

Opposite was the portion of Schwab's that provided the highest decibel level, the famous soda fountain. Here, legend had it, movie starlets had been discovered. Next to the counter was a separate room filled with luncheonette tables and very unconventional people. The noise, the gaiety and the action would have done honor to a bon voyage party.

Stevie was transfixed by the sight. She continued to stand openmouthed in the entrance.

Many of the girls were young and beautiful, 'models or actresses,' Stevie thought. 'Some were young and not so pretty, probably the production assistants and secretaries.' An elderly couple wandered in. They were obviously from out of town. It seemed to Stevie worth your life to be in Schwab's at feeding time. The old folks were casually ignored, while the native group kissed the waitresses, hugged each other, yelled across tables to newly arrived friends, drank endless cups of coffee and chatted animatedly.

The need to pee interrupted her reverie. The cashier pointed her to the back.

As Stevie came out of the ladies' room, she passed the four pay phones that hung on the wall, and overheard a fat man in his thirties, dressed in scruffy, faded blue jeans and an embroidered Western shirt, yelling into the mouthpiece of the phone. The other phones were in use, but the conversations were more subdued. On one phone, against the wall, a very pretty girl in her twenties, dressed in a pair of gaucho pants and boots with a thin nylon top that accentuated her nipples, was calling her answering service for messages. The other two phones were booths, so the conversations inside were private. One of the doors opened periodically to expel the cigarette smoke from the cabinet and invite some fresh air from the outside. Each time the door opened, the mumbling became clear and profane. The man in that booth inspected Stevie to see if she were interesting, decided against pursuing it and went back to his conversation, closing the door again.

Stevie stood for a while before reentering the central part of this wonderland. She paused, as if to inhale enough air before going under again.

A corner stool at the near end of the counter was empty and Stevie sat down. A waitress came up to her and stared.

"That's not your seat."

"Why not?" asked Stevie. "Are they reserved?"

Stevie was making a simple inquiry but the waitress took it as a statement of territorial imperative. She handed Stevie a menu and was gone for ten minutes. She came back and asked haughtily, "Have you decided?"

"What's a tuna melt?" Stevie inquired.

The waitress turned away, astounded by the girl's stupidity. A thin little man stood behind Stevie and whispered to her.

"That's my seat you have."

"Oh, I'm sorry. I'll move."

Stevie moved to the adjacent seat, now available, and the little man who had dispossessed her picked up several packages of blank luncheon checks from the counter and proceeded to write on them. Stevie looked over at him. He was writing "Beverly" into the space left for the name of the waitress. By the time Beverly returned, he had filled in half a book of checks.

"You're late, Smokey. I ran out of checks."

"Sorry, Beverly. It won't happen again."

The waitress, identified as Beverly by the lunch checks and by the name tag on her dress, proceeded to pour Smokey a cup of coffee, served him a French cruller and then started to walk away.

Stevie called after her, "Beverly, please may I have a tuna melt and a vanilla malt?"

"You're from out of town." It was her neighbor's voice.

"Yes . . . I'm from Urbana, Illinois. It's near St. Louis."

"I like your hair. It's your best feature, along with your eyes."

"Thank you very much. Do you know where I can find a place to live?" Unconsciously she touched the straight blonde hair. At least she still had that.

The little sharp-featured man paused in the middle of his printing, chewing on his pencil for a moment. "Right near the phones in the back. Sometimes people put up notices of things like that. You might take a look."

On the mirror behind the counter a sign read, "Limit—one half hour per cup of coffee." Stevie glanced at the clock. She couldn't stay at Schwab's forever. She needed to find a place to live.

As soon as she finished her lunch she walked to the rear and saw the same group on the telephones that she had passed over a half hour ago. The smoke in the booths was denser than before, but miraculously, she thought, the people were still alive. Next to the phones, tacked on the wall, were business cards, scraps of paper with notices on them and notes written on index cards. Stevie studied them slowly. Script typing, little-theater auditions, cars for sale, dogs lost, first names of girls with phone numbers, and finally a few apartments to rent. There was nothing of interest except a card that read, "Let me practice on your hair and you can stay at my pad." It was signed "Jon" and underneath were the words: "Hairdresser to the Stars of the Future" and the street address.

Stevie unpeeled the card from the wall. Pleased, she

smiled to herself and walked through the store and out to the street carrying her small valise.

The black parking-lot attendant pointed her toward Fountain Avenue, and Stevie turned right at the corner and walked a block down the hill, looking for the house number. She found a small apartment house set back from the street, over a four-car garage. In the garage, a young man, dark and muscular, dressed only in jeans, was polishing the chrome on a white Mercedes 190 convertible. Stevie waited for him to come up for air, then showed him the card. He pointed with his elbow, simultaneously chewing the end of an unlit cigarette between his teeth. Stevie was startled for a moment— She had seen him on *television*.

She walked up the stairs and rang the bell. The door opened, and a slight young man about twenty, with bleached blonde hair, peeked out. He was wearing only the thinnest black nylon bikini underpants.

"I saw the ad in Schwab's," Stevie stammered.

"What was that, sweetie?"

"About my hair . . . you remember? Jon, that's your name, isn't it?"

The young man laughed. "Oh, my *Gawd*. That was when I was studying. Do you mean that you came here to let me work on your hair?" He opened the door and stared at Stevie's serious face, framed by gleaming blonde hair. She seemed on the verge of tears.

He smiled an impish grin and invited her inside. "Welcome to Casa Grande." There wasn't a stick of furniture in the entire apartment except for a bridge table in the center of the living room. Jon followed her gaze. "Isn't it terrible? He took the TV and everything. There really wasn't much, just some beanbag chairs. But can you imagine, after all we meant to each other. Did you by chance see some lump of turd downstairs polishing a car?"

Stevie nodded.

"That's him . . . that's Brad. Two years, I worked myself to the bone supporting him, being here when he needed me and then he gets that part in that *dreadful*

TV show, and now he thinks he's a goddam star. As far as I'm concerned, bad rubbish. I have part of a Pepsi left. Want some?"

"He was your roommate?"

Stevie didn't understand the significance of the situation.

"He says he's bi, but don't you believe it. Wait till that no-good tramp from across the hall finds out what he really wants, then she'll kick out Miss Thing . . . and it'll be his own damn fault."

Stevie still didn't understand. "Bi?"

"Who are you? Fanny from the Farm? Look, if you haven't any place to stay tonight, you can sleep on the floor."

Stevie looked momentarily uncertain.

"Silly, I won't touch you. Stay if you want to. I've got to get dressed to go out."

With a turn of his tiny ass he marched into the bathroom, shut the door and turned on the shower.

5

For the next two years Stevie lived with Jon De Lisle, nursed him through love affairs, terrible head colds, hours of deep despair, took care of his laundry, cleaning and endless messages from former lovers, would-be lovers, and voices in the night.

Jon was a hairdresser in The Broadway Department Store in Hollywood, and was forever falling into bad relationships that appeared to offer suicide as the only solution. Stevie had to spend long hours consoling, advising and enduring his torment.

During those two years, a progression of lovers—some one-night stands, some lasting a couple of weeks, sometimes a group of three or four—occupied the bedroom while Stevie slept in the living room.

Gradually Stevie was able to convince Jon to furnish the small apartment with castoffs from garage sales and Goodwill Industries. There was now an old brown corduroy couch for Stevie to sleep on, and she began to think of Jon as a member of her family. She had no one else.

During Christmas, Stevie was able to get part-time work in the packing room at The Broadway, then occasional work in a telephone answering service and waitressing at various restaurants in Hollywood. Stevie taught herself to type and earned money typing scripts. Little by little she felt at home in Hollywood and comfortable with Jon and his gay friends. She also accumulated enough money to afford acting school. Stevie tried to get any kind of work in the business—

commercials, extra work, modeling. Sandwiching all of these activities in between the task of staying alive.

Stevie discovered that there were hundreds and hundreds of women just like her, wanting to be in the business but continually being rejected. Any occasion when she could get a job as a nonunion extra on a low-budget film was like a trip to paradise. She forgot the endless boredom of standing around the set waiting to be shepherded from crowd scene to crowd scene, in the exhilaration of being on a movie set, with movie people, eating a soggy and barely digestible box lunch and collecting the magnificent sum of ten or fifteen dollars for the day.

At Schwab's, Stevie had become a regular and began to make friends with some of the other regulars. Stevie was especially intrigued by an actress named Loretta Danger. Danger was her stage name, and if not mesmerizing, she was interesting.

"My name is just OK, huh?" Stevie said.

"I don't know, baby . . . Stephanie Tree. It sounds . . . floral."

Stevie laughed. "No . . . it sounds like . . . forests."

Loretta lit a cigarette and sipped her cold coffee. "Nobody will pay attention to a name like that. You need something exciting, something that will make people stand up and take notice."

"Got any ideas?"

"Christ, kid . . . just look around. I won't even tell you what other names I had . . . dozens of them until I found this one, 'Danger' . . . I thought and thought, but then I saw it on an elevator shaft, and I said to myself, who could ever forget a name like 'Danger' . . . Why you get free advertising all over town. Everything spells 'Danger'—and that's me, kid."

Loretta was in her late 20's and lived with her boyfriend in Laurel Canyon. Together the two of them had a small house on Laurel Vista, just three blocks north of Schwab's. Her boyfriend was a rock musician, and Stevie was told that he was waiting for a spot with

Jagger and the Rolling Stones. Loretta had once been beautiful, but had hardened in a way that made her look ten years older than her twenty-seven years. Her five-foot-three frame was seven or eight pounds too heavy. Her face was thickly powdered and her eyes were painted on with liner. Her breasts were too large, and her pants suits were always too bright and too tight. Early on, when Stevie talked about acting school, Loretta laughed and said that she was wasting her time.

"Learn how to give good head. Fuck the rest of that noise, honey."

Almost two years to the day from the time that Stevie moved in as kid sister, mother and pal to Jon de Lisle, she was evicted. Jon's erstwhile lover, the dark, handsome TV actor, was returning. They had made up and were in love again.

Jon was sad when he explained that he had asked Brad to let Stevie remain in the apartment, but Brad wouldn't consider it.

She sat on a stool in Schwab's, eating breakfast at noon next to Loretta. Stevie explained her predicament. "Don't worry," Loretta said, chewing on a hamburger. "You can put up with us for a while."

Stevie moved her things that afternoon and found herself in a new world.

The center of life in Laurel Canyon was the Country Store, which stood in the middle of a plaza by the side of the Canyon Road. If you had money, you could buy almost anything in the way of groceries or household goods inside, or if you were just hanging out, there was always company. Bikers would drive up the canyon road, see other bikes parked in the plaza and pull over. The Country Store was a waystation for travelers on the road, heading from Baja up to Bakersfield. On the bulletin board you could see a cluster of hastily scrawled notes for other bikers known to be coming this way in the future.

The regular residents of Laurel Canyon found it tough to get into the plaza parking place, and if they

were able to thread their way through the rows of
bikes, then they had the additional problem of the
congregation of silver-studded black leather jackets
leaning against the entrances. There were never any
serious incidents of violence between the wayfarers and
the locals. A kind of truce existed. It was a sample of
the permissiveness of Laurel Canyon folk that they
accepted this additional hazard to life with good grace.
After all, they were doing their thing, too.

Days turned into weeks before Stevie realized she
had moved in permanently with Loretta and Jimmy. It
happened casually, like Stevie's first steps into the drug
world. At first, the continuing use of wine and grass was
strange, as was the easy way that Jimmy had with
nudity. He took any opportunity to remove his clothes.
His favorite roost was a mattress in the center of the
living room, and his favorite occupation was scoring
weed and smoking it.

Stevie had no idea how Jimmy and Loretta supported
themselves. There was always money for dope and for
the luncheon meats, cheeses, bread and juice they kept
munching between highs. Loretta was frequently out
on auditions for commercials, but the jobs appeared to
be few and far between. Stevie realized that certainly
didn't bring in much money.

A long extension cord allowed Jimmy to lie on the
living-room mattress like a naked pasha and conduct
business. Stevie heard one particular call, and that was
all she had to hear.

"Hi, David . . . glad you called." Jimmy relit a joint
as he talked.

"Yeah, I'm still thinking about it . . . What do you
mean? . . . I go into the shitter, not *you.*"

Stevie was listening as she fixed herself a cheese
sandwich in the kitchen.

"Come on, David . . . the real reason is the bread
ain't enough . . . I go risking my neck to bring the stuff
in . . . and . . . this one's a big mother. Do you know
what I'll get if I get caught with that much grass?"

Stevie bit into the day-old bread and finally got

through to the cheese, as she walked into the living room.

"OK . . . that's better . . . I knew you'd come through, David. See you on the Strip tonight."

Jimmy hung up and smiled at Stevie. He was very pleased with himself. "Got the son of a bitch to come up with a better split." He grabbed Stevie by the hand and pulled her down on the mattress.

"Hey . . . I'm still eating my sandwich."

"Fuck the sandwich . . . got something better for you to chew on."

Stevie laughed and kept it between her teeth as she slipped out of her clothes. She kneeled and softly caressed his chest and gently flicked the tips of her fingers under his balls and smiled up at him. "Here . . . you have the sandwich," she murmured.

Jimmy had initiated casual sex with Stevie when Loretta was out of the house. Most of their afternoons were spent getting high, and then Stevie went through a long and satisfying daily ritual for Jimmy. As with her "uncle" Bert, Stevie had learned how to control and tantalize a man. It meant nothing to her. No excitement, no pleasure, nothing more than a way of paying her dues. A way of staying alive.

That night Stevie and Jimmy were standing outside Pandora's Box on Sunset. Loretta and Jimmy had had a fight. She had accused him of having sex with Stevie, and threatened to throw her out of the house. Jimmy denied it vehemently. Stevie was quiet. In his anger, Jimmy decided to take Stevie along with him that evening. On the drive, Jimmy explained that David financed the buys for smuggling grass out of Mexico. The meeting tonight was to firm up the details and get the cash. David—no one knew his last name—had many of these operations going. For that, David took fifty percent of the profit.

Stevie and Jimmy had been standing on the Strip for half an hour when a young man in his late twenties, with curly black hair, trim and well dressed, came over to them, tapped Jimmy on the elbow and led him away. The young man had the elegance of a prince, although his upturned nose gave him the look of a pixie. It was David.

Jimmy came back in a few minutes. "It's OK. He wants me to meet him at his house in half an hour and he'll give me the bread. I asked him if I could bring you. He said, 'Sure.' I think he likes your looks."

"What else is new? Where does he live?"

"I'll show you. It's quite a pad."

David had disappeared as mysteriously and silently as he appeared. In about twenty minutes, Jimmy grabbed Stevie's arm and led her to the car. They proceeded to enter Laurel Canyon Boulevard from Sunset, driving up the twisted road, deserted at that hour, passing the Country Store with its rows of bikes in front. In the light of the store interior, dark-clad bikers looked like a tableau of black, ghostly silhouettes. Then the car mounted higher, onto Wonderland Avenue, and after a left turn they entered a small dead-end street. Jimmy pulled his car into the port, next to a Rolls Royce. He and Stevie walked up the stairs of a beautiful house, small but tastefully constructed in a refined style of modern architecture.

Stevie entered the house and instantly saw a haven of grace and luxury that she had never encountered before. There was a teakwood staircase to the left of the hall that rose to a balcony with rooms leading off of it. Directly facing her was a two-story living room, chastely but exquisitely furnished in huge, dark leather pieces in warm tones of brown and orange. The walls were beautifully decorated with a combination of modern paintings and Mexican folk art.

At the far end of the living room, a huge picture window, extending the length of the wall, looked out on the entire sprawl of Los Angeles. The lights of the city at night were almost too beautiful for Stevie to stand. Something inside her was touched by the luxury and tranquility of the room and the excitement of the view. It was all that she had ever dreamed about—the sense of being apart and yet close to the heart of a great city, with all its excitement and wonder at one's feet, ready to be explored from a protected perch that was like a nest overlooking a densely populated forest.

David walked into the room, dressed in white slacks, white loafers without socks and a black silk shirt. He was as good-looking and graceful as Stevie had first thought. He invited Jimmy to pour himself a drink and one for Stevie. He lit a cigarette and looked at Stevie measuring her thoughtfully, and then at Jimmy, who interpreted the look as an invitation to speak.

"This is the first run with a plane . . . I'm not sure it's the best way. I can still get through the Federales. I know them."

"It's not the Mexicans that bother me, Jimmy. It's our own Border Patrol. In the past month I've lost a bundle on three runs that got busted. I'm a business-man. I'm used to taking risks, but this kind of thing is bullshit. Until someone can make the right connections with our Border Patrol, we've got to find other ways to bring in the stuff. This pilot I've got you has made a couple of runs before, all small stuff, but he's got a bigger plane for this run, and it's faster, surer. I'm willing to put down some more bread on this one to bail me out for some of my losses."

"I don't know the pilot."

"He's OK, a little strange, but he's a pro."

"You're sure?"

"Of course, I'm sure. It's my bread."

"It's my ass."

"Jimmy, between the two of us, we both know which of those commodities is more important."

Jimmy and Stevie had sipped their drinks and Jimmy stood up to go. David sat there musing into his drink.

"Whatever your name is . . . don't go. Stick around."

Stevie replied tartly, "I've had better invitations from rapists."

"I'm sorry, Miss . . ."

Jimmy interrupted and put his hand on Stevie's. "Her name is Stevie . . ." and addressing Stevie, he murmured, "Honey, do yourself a favor—stick around. David is a very good guy."

Without a further word, Stevie put her feet up on the coffee table to signify that though she was staying, she was going to do it on her terms, whatever that meant. She wasn't sure, but she felt something between herself and this very attractive young man. After Jimmy left, David returned and sat down in a huge chair directly opposite Stevie. He put his feet on the coffee table as well. Stevie laughed. She understood that he understood.

"I'm sorry, Stevie. Sometimes I get confused as to who I'm talking to. You're different."

Stevie replied instantly, "No, I'm not, David . . . I'd just like to be, but I don't know that I'll ever make it."

"That's the first sign of wisdom . . . and if there are others, then you might just."

"One can always hope. This is not a city that prides itself on being different. It kills you if you don't conform. Do you want to fuck? Or do you like getting head better?"

"Stevie, I appreciate your directness, but you've got to understand that I'm an old-fashioned boy who likes to ask a girl. You'll find that I'm not afraid to ask for anything, when the time is right. Would you like another drink?"

"Yes, please . . . I'm sorry, I just thought that you wouldn't like to waste time . . . After all, you're a businessman. You said so yourself."

"Touché. I dig. You know, Stevie, bullshit aside, you are probably one of the most beautiful girls I've ever met, and there is something decidedly special about you."

"Like what?"

"Like the element of confusion in you that doesn't know whether the center of your world is your face or your pussy. I think you'll always be confused until you realize that there's a better locale in your case."

"Where?"

"Your brain! You're a smart young lady . . . and I won't begin to ask you what you're doing with an asshole like Jimmy Moffet, but I don't have to ask that, you've already asked yourself."

"He's not all bad."

"No, he's not mean . . . but the one secret ingredient I've found to be the most important between a man and a woman is something that couldn't possibly exist between the two of you."

"What's that?"

"Appreciation. Stevie, come upstairs with me, and let me appreciate you. I have a feeling you deserve it."

Stevie smiled warmly. He had asked, and he had asked nicely, very nicely. She stood up and took his hand as he led her upstairs to his bedroom.

It was a huge room on the second floor, with its own picture window over the city. With the curtains open as they were, there was an even more magnificent view, since they were now fifteen feet higher than the living room. The bedroom was all tans, beiges and grays. A huge canopy bed was in the center of the room, on a pedestal above the floor. The pillows and linens were in brown and white geometric designs and the cover for the bed was a dark luxurious fur. A mirror covered the ceiling over the bed, and an entire wall was mirrored closets. A small couch and chairs were set in a corner, alongside a bar and refrigerator.

Stevie sighed, "Will *Playboy* photograph the screw?"

David smiled as he took off his shirt. "No, but you may wish that *you* had." She threw her hair back over her shoulders defiantly.

The first night that Stevie spent with David brought a stream of emotions that she had never experienced. The first step that Stevie made with David felt like rejection. She knelt down on the carpet in his bedroom and proceeded to perform for him. But he stopped her. He led her over to the bed and slowly took off Stevie's shirt and jeans. He lay down beside her and gently touched her face. Then slowly he moved his fingers down her body, past her nipples to the little swell of her stomach. As he did this, he smiled and talked.

"You may think it's strange, Stevie . . . but I think

that this is the first time for you. I think it's the first time
that you had anyone ask you . . . the first time you're
with someone who wants to please you . . . as much as
you want to please him."

For some unaccountable reason, Stevie closed her
eyes as David began talking. She felt a wave of
nervousness, as if she had never been naked before,
never been caressed, never involved in an act of love.
Stevie relaxed her closed eyes for the first time in as
long as she could remember and curled her body into
his exploring hand.

"A girl like you thinks only of giving, Stevie . . ."
David continued, softly touching her cheeks with the
tips of his fingers, "giving her body . . . giving her
lips . . . because that's all you think you have to give.
Can I make you understand that a man who is worth
anything wants to give as much as a woman?"

Stevie turned on her side, then onto her stomach.
For a moment she seemed ready to fall asleep, but then
her body came alive and called for his exploring hand,
and the beginnings of small kisses that he lavished on
the back of her neck and the curve of her arms and
beyond.

"You're going to ask me how I know this. You're
going to think that it's just a line to get a lady into
bed . . . but, Stevie, you *are* in bed, and I know what
I'm saying, because I've been looking for a long time
for someone who really wants to give everything she
has . . . not just a body . . . not just a mind . . . but
her soul as well . . ." And David whispered hoarsely,
"I want her to come out even. You're that kind of girl,
Stevie . . . and I know I'm that kind of guy."

Stevie turned over on her back. Her eyes had tears in
them, and she reached over to David and embraced
him with such force that it surprised him. She hugged
him and kissed his cheeks, his eyes, his ears, and let
herself be his.

Making love was almost the least important part of
the evening after that, though it went on for hours,
though Stevie did experience her first orgasm. The

lovemaking was in those first minutes when he told her that he understood her for wanting to please. No one would ever understand, Stevie thought, that she had to please to exist. She was only alive because she gave pleasure.

The next morning, Stevie was exhausted. She had no idea whether or how often David had come. She had no idea how often the two of them dozed off, only to find themselves making love once again. She had no idea, except that it melted into a new part of her life that was warm and safe and wonderful.

6

Stevie didn't set foot out of the house over the next few days, nor did she come downstairs from the bedroom when David had people over. She waited in the bedroom for any moment that he could find free to give her, to be with her, fondle her, laugh with her. She found herself awake during the night, hoping that he might awaken too, to make love, realizing how selfish it was of her, but not really giving a damn.

David was helping her find out who she was. In bed together, before making love, he began to instruct.

"Stevie . . . a man's cock isn't a weapon . . . it's a paint brush."

"Paint me some more, darling," she sighed.

"No, seriously . . . I want you to be the kind of woman you can be . . . fantastic . . . to get and to give pleasure . . . so, let me show you a few things you might have missed in your early years."

"If a guy starts out stiff, it's gonna be soft in the sack . . . either between times or just lying there . . . a nice thing that a girl can do is to keep in contact with him . . . all the time. You can just keep the palm of your hand over his balls. A fellow appreciates that kind of thing . . . and one more thing, for tonight, a nice thing guys like is the sight of a girl playing with herself. Now don't do it as if you were stroking a guitar. It has to be soulful and slow . . . and tuned in to the guy she's with. No obvious fantasy trip-outs—look at his dick, or his lips. Let him see you're looking at him . . . and that's the reason you're playing with yourself—because you're waiting for him."

Then they would make love.

Another time he said, "Baby . . . when you come . . . it's like an eruption . . . but when there's an eruption and nobody hears it, there's no applause. Now, I'm not saying fake it . . . because some guys can spot it . . . and even if they can't, then the girl knows it, and that's degrading. But, if there's a hint of it coming your way . . . help it along. Get in the swing of it . . . A little crying out, a little moaning . . . and shaking never hurt anyone . . ."

And they'd make love. Then another day he said, "Baby . . . after a guy comes, some women have a trick they do with their vagina that's special. You can contract that little work of art on command—anytime you want to. Practice it when you're peeing. Try and hold it in, and then let it out . . . and then hold it in again. You can practice while you're doing nothing too. Nobody can see a damn thing while you're practicing. Try it . . . we'll both like it."

And they'd make love some more.

One might have thought that Stevie would have been angry at hearing David's thirty-day program for brighter and more rewarding lovemaking, but Stevie thought it was the funniest and most glorious thing that she'd ever heard. In the kitchen, when she'd make David breakfast, she'd call to him.

"Baby, do you want fresh squeezed oranges or fresh squeezed pussy for breakfast?"

Stevie understood from the very moment that David put her at rest in his bed the first night they were together that he was teaching her for many reasons . . . for him, but more importantly for her. For some strange and unaccountable reason, he wanted to bring Stevie a knowledge of loving that was his, a kind of legacy for reasons he didn't understand.

David lay in bed that afternoon after one round of lovemaking.

"Baby, let's see how many positions we can get into without my ever coming out of your pussy. I'll count."

Stevie laughed. "I'll keep count . . . you'd cheat, motherfucker!"

She sat astride him, poised on the balls of her feet and took his hands while she deliciously sat down on his waiting cock. Then she laughed and slid slowly on her side. They laughed some more . . . and then on her stomach, with David on top of her . . . and she pushed her small ass in the air and he kneeled behind her . . . and then . . . and then . . . they lost count, and they broke up laughing.

"Stevie . . . baby . . . it should be funny, too."

How in hell this twenty-seven-year-old knew all he did was a question that Stevie never asked. It didn't make any difference to her. She felt the birth of a freedom of body and mind.

On the morning of the sixth day, Stevie sat on the edge of the bathtub while she watched David shave. In the middle of the process, he stopped and turned to her.

"Stevie, I love you. I never want you to leave me . . . and whether you like it or not you're gonna marry me."

Stevie broke into tears. David helped her up and she kissed him until neither of them could breathe, and both their faces were white with lather. When they finally broke apart they looked in the mirror and roared with laughter. David said they would be married in the fall. He wanted to take her back to meet his family in New York.

The next weeks were the happiest that Stevie had ever known. She was totally in love with a man who loved *her* totally. They shared every intimacy as if they were afraid of losing each other if they left each other's sight. Full of pride, David took Stevie shopping. Hand in hand they romped through the boutiques in Beverly Hills on a Saturday afternoon, while David indulged Stevie's every fantasy, and his own as well.

David's action on the Strip had quieted down. The two of them liked nothing more than staying home in the evenings watching TV and smoking grass. Jimmy and Loretta had dropped out of her life, not through Stevie's wishes but because of the very negative vibrations she got from them. Stevie was upset. They had been good to her and given her a place to live when she needed it.

"Honey . . . it's a little of the green god of Envy. Face it, and forget it," David explained.

"But why, David? Jimmy was the one who introduced me to you."

"Stevie, Jimmy's thought was that it would be a one-night stand . . . but when it turned out the way it did, they lost you. They want you to be *with* them, and *of* them. You're a different person now—not a girl, playing house with a pair of overaged hippies. You're a woman."

Stevie smiled. David was right.

Evenings, some of David's street friends dropped by—musicians, dealers, many of them black. David rejoiced in the company of his black friends, and they responded to him with equal affection. David tuned into their bravado, their soulful lust for living and their struggle to make it in a white world. Their love for each other was very unusual.

Charlie Prince was the essence of the street. He was immense, coal black, with a huge smile and a soft, mellow voice. Not possessing any real education, he loved to read. He devoured books on history and biography. In keeping with his profession, he wore a green silk bandanna on his head, huge gold and diamond-studded jewelry on his hands and wrists and a single gold earring. Charlie dealt in hard drugs. He had been in prison for other crimes, too—armed robbery, confidence games, bad checks, but he had great respectability in the black community of East L.A. He was a highly successful dealer. Charlie Prince was totally without pretense. His "rap" was continual, and David was never sure whether it was a con, but it didn't matter. He was funny, and he was gallant to Stevie in quiet and gentle ways.

A dozen times Charlie offered to have David come into drug deals with him, to have David finance buys in cocaine. Each time David refused, the terms got better. It was clear that Charlie wanted David in not for his money, but as a gesture of his affection. Then Charlie introduced it another way.

"David . . . you don't want to put up money till I deliver. OK, I understand. Tell you what—on my next deal, I'm gonna put twenty grand in for you. I'm gonna pretend it's your money. That way, only I lose . . . and you can only win."

Days later, when Charlie came by to give David his share of the profits, David turned it down.

"Give it to the Red Cross."

And Charlie did. Eighty-five thousand, in cash.

David gave Stevie a beautiful red Porsche. Her eyes brimmed with tears as she walked around the car for five minutes, thrilled at the prospect of driving it, stunned at the prospect of owning it, and not sure she had the right to. She smiled at David, as if to get his permission. He moved to kiss her, always understanding how she felt.

Fifteen minutes later, she peeled out of the showroom, shifting and maneuvering as if the car were a part of her body. Stevie began the game of timing herself on the drive up and down Laurel Canyon from Schwab's. Her best time to Schwab's was two minutes and fifty-three seconds. Up the canyon took longer. She never broke four minutes. The gang at the Country Store knew her and her fire-engine-red car, and waved as Stevie cornered, downshifted and passed them at sixty miles an hour.

David was pleased when Stevie returned to acting. She was a completely different person when she appeared at auditions. Expensive clothes and beautiful jewelry were only part of it. The sense of being loved and cared for gave Stevie enormous self-confidence. As a result, she looked absolutely stunning. Her smile and her eyes, happily flashing, melted even the most corrupt casting directors, although she was totally unattainable.

On one audition, Stevie met Cindy Warren, a statuesque brunette. Cindy had been Miss Tennessee six years ago, then a Playboy Club bunny and a

Playmate of the month. The two met in the ladies' room of a Hollywood commercial studio. Cindy was drying her hands. She looked in the mirror as Stevie walked in.

"My oh my . . . aren't you pretty."

"Thanks." Stevie smiled. "Are you here for the P&G commercial?"

"Yes, I am . . . but I don't think I have a chance. I used to be a Playmate. June of 1974. They don't like to have pictures of your boobs floating around."

Stevie looked admiringly at Cindy. "You've got nothing to be ashamed of. My name's Stevie Tree."

"Cindy Warren. 'Course that isn't my *real* name. It used to be Mary Lou. I don't tell that to everyone."

"Cindy . . . how would the P&G folks find out . . . I mean, about your boob shot?"

Cindy looked astounded. "How? Why, I *show* everybody the picture. I'm very proud. They only take twelve girls a year—to go along with the months, that is. Would you like to see it? I have a copy right here in my portfolio."

Cindy's Southern accent was charming, but prevented her from getting speaking parts and at five foot nine she was too tall for most commercials. When all else failed, Cindy modeled for mail-order houses. Sears, Roebuck and Montgomery Ward were always looking for new faces and full bodies to model underwear in their glossy catalogues. As much as Cindy hated it, her lifeline to eating was girdles and brassieres.

On her rounds, Stevie met Cindy once or twice a week and the two of them became friendly. Cindy would whisper to Stevie as the casting director or the agency man walked through the waiting room, "I fucked him . . . he's a number three . . . I fucked him . . . he's a seven. I balled him . . . really a disaster, he's a two and a half."

Cindy had slept with almost every casting director or agency producer in Los Angeles. Some of them remembered her, but the sadness of it was that most of them didn't. Sadder still, the evening's entertainment with most of them didn't provide much employment. Screwing to get a part frequently didn't work. Most of the girls did the same thing. But if everyone screws, then the marketable commodity is the girl with the concrete cunt, the one you can't get into. At any rate, it was a problem that Stevie didn't concern herself with, since she got just as many commercials as the girls who slept with any and all comers, and Stevie was very content for the protection and security that being with David gave her.

Sometime later, Stevie was called to read for a part at the Columbia Studio on Gower Street. She could play any age from fifteen to twenty-five, and this particular part was for a high school picture. Stevie dressed for the audition. It was supposed to be a '50's film, and Stevie wore a long skirt and bobby sox, a sweater and a scarf tied around her hair. Stevie looked every bit of fifteen. Flushed with the pleasure of giving a good reading for the director, Stevie knew that she would get a callback, the next step to getting the part.

Stevie walked outside the director's office and, as she did, she caught her watch on the door and it fell to the floor. She stooped to pick it up and as she did she heard footsteps behind her and a voice, "Cute little ass, honey . . . pick up your skirt and you can make ten bucks easy."

Stevie stood up, flushing, and saw a tall, dark-haired man coming toward her. She recognized him.

"Go fuck yourself." She bit off the words, one by one.

He laughed. "Why bother, when there's so much cheap ass around?"

The man walked on down the corridor. Stevie knew him, and so did everyone else who went to the movies. He was Morgan Oliver. Everyone recognized him from his movies and his widely publicized lovelife. This was Stevie's first meeting with a man destined to play a crucial role in her life.

Morgan Oliver was the brother half of a brother-and-sister acting family. The sister was a television personality, Bebe Connors, pert, freckled star of her own variety series, a pixie with close-cropped hair and a grin, much loved by television audiences. Bebe Connors had been a musical comedy star, then followed it with a movie role that she had initiated on Broadway. Finally it led her into a weekly TV series that used her talent as comedienne, singer and dancer. Morgan was a younger brother. The two of them had been extremely close, until Morgan's escapades and narrow escapes with women made their relationship a difficult one. Morgan was part of a rat pack of new Hollywood stars who would not conform. Not only was their refusal to bend to Hollywood authority a badge of office, but they felt so much a breed apart and so worthy of special attention because of their talent, that they felt they were entitled to do as they damn well pleased. This small group of successful Hollywood actors, directors, writers and producers made their own rules, and broke even those rules when the spirit moved them.

Beautiful—and he deserved to be called beautiful—Morgan Oliver was at the hub of this small group. He exuded an extraordinary amount of control, which came from the quiet assurance of his own appeal and the knowledge that no matter how badly he misbehaved, someone would fix things for him. Morgan Oliver was uniquely spoiled.

When Stevie told Cindy Warren about her meeting with Morgan, she said, "I balled him . . . he's a nine."

Stevie looked at her. "I'd rather screw King Kong, and he's only an eight!"

They both laughed.

Stevie didn't get the part in the '50's picture, but it wasn't a matter of life or death. She was working. She got a day on a TV game show, three days on a feature film and a voice-over for a commercial. Stevie felt delight and satisfaction in showing her paychecks to David.

When Stevie was working, David spent occasional afternoons with Charlie Prince. Charlie gleefully drove his huge white Caddy convertible up to the house on

Laurel Canyon and the two proceeded with Charlie's rounds. David was clearly seduced by the excitement and the danger. Driving through Watts, David saw the remnants of the riots and the sullen poverty of the community. But Charlie—Charlie Prince was a street king of the ghetto. Kids would scamper out to his parked car. Dudes chatting on street corners would make their way over to pay their respects. Charlie was a sight, all 240 pounds of him, spectacularly tailored in his white linen suit and white buck shoes. His trademark, the green silk bandanna tied in the back, gave him the aspect of a pirate.

Charlie carried huge amounts of cash with him, sometimes fifteen to twenty thousands dollars. Part of it was from collections, and some of it he used as payoffs. He would park the car near a grocery store or poolroom, disappear inside and go through the back door to the alley, either to collect from someone or hand some over to the cops. Never at any time that David knew did Charlie carry dope. All of the transport was made by people Charlie controlled.

Stevie listened to the stories David told her about these afternoons. Stevie didn't like it, but as fearful as she was, she realized it was a necessary part of David's life.

"What's the matter, Stevie?"

"David—I think that Charlie's a terrific dude, but he's into stuff you wouldn't touch, would you?"

"No way, baby. As a matter of fact I'm thinking seriously about producing a picture or two. I told a few agents to send me some scripts. There's so much shit now, I don't think that I could do worse."

"You could be terrific, honey."

"If I gave you a part in one of my movies, could I get you to fuck me?"

"Try me, David."

And he did.

Their lives went on happily in their accustomed loving way. Then a few days later, Stevie was shooting a commercial at the Peterson Studios on Vine near

Sunset. The TV spot was for a beer and they needed a
lot of good, clean American-girl types going on a picnic
with good, clean American-boy types, while in the
background a team of horses and wagons would give
the product its thematic identity. Everything was going
wrong on the shoot. It was only a thirty-second spot.
The "typical American" girls, or at least half of them,
had gotten the commercial by sleeping with the agency
producer. Half the "typical American" boys were gay,
bitching to each other between takes and making phone
calls to boyfriends that delayed the shoot. In addition,
the horses were misbehaving. One horse relieving
himself is an acceptable hazard. Two is too much, and
three is a catastrophe keeping stagehands hopping and
performers dodging nature.

That afternoon Charlie drove David to Compton, a
black community in East L.A. Charlie wanted a favor
that had to do with Charlie's fifteen-year-old sister,
Melodee.

It came as a shock to David to learn that Charlie had
family, and he knew enough about the customs of the
black community to realize what a gesture it was for
Charlie to ask a favor of a white man. Melodee was
hoping for a part in the road company of *The Wiz*.
David offered to call an agent he knew to arrange an
audition. This afternoon was important to Charlie. He
wanted to reassure David that Melodee had talent.

The young girl lived with an aunt and was very shy in
the presence of her brother and his white friend. But
when she sang her self-consciousness disappeared.
David was delighted. He would gladly make the
introduction.

On their return, Charlie had to make a stop. They
came to a poolhall, where David had been other times.
David remained in the car while Charlie went inside. In
the back alley, as Charlie emerged, he asked three
young teenagers, who were drinking wine, the where-
abouts of the man he was to meet. They didn't know.
The oldest of the three, not more than fifteen, asked

Charlie for money. Charlie said no. The teenager
pulled out a switchblade and held it at Charlie's throat.

Charlie reached into his pocket for his money. He
would give it to them. It would be very easy to find
them another day. Life was too short to fuck around
with drunken kids.

Without another word, the fifteen-year-old stabbed
him once, then time after time with vicious glee.
Charlie fell to the ground bleeding. The twelve-year-
old wanted to leave, but the others wanted to strip the
body of jewelry. The proprietor heard the fight. He
stepped out as the teenagers raced away. The man
would normally have avoided trouble, but he had seen
David with Charlie previously, and he raced outside to
tell him.

When David arrived in the alley, Charlie was dead.
The poolhall owner phoned the police. As David
returned to the car, he saw a black teenager across the
street. He was wearing Charlie's green silk scarf around
his neck.

David ran toward the teenager, not knowing what
he would do when he caught him, but convinced that he
had to catch him, had to get Charlie's killer. David
grabbed the boy from behind and wrestled him down.
The youngster was suddenly a massive force of violence. David called a passerby to help. No one listened.
The two young friends standing across the street rushed
to help the boy. The fifteen-year-old with the switchblade plunged it into David's chest.

They heard the police siren in the distance, and the
three teenagers fled.

The cast and crew went into a dinner break without
completing the shoot for the commercial. The agency
producer and the production assistant had computed
the cost to them if they went into meal penalty and
completed the remaining shots, or if they gave everyone a meal break and brought them back for a
completion. They went the cheaper way and let everyone off for a half hour.

Stevie went across the street on Vine Street to a taco stand and ordered some Mexican food. Cindy Warren was in the commercial, too, and Cindy was seated at the table when Stevie went to the phone.

The phone rang at the Laurel Canyon house several times more than usual. Finally someone picked it up.

"Hello, David?"

A strange man's voice spoke, "Who is this calling?"

"Do I have the right number?"

"This is Officer Renquist of the Hollywood station. Who is this?"

"I'm Stevie Tree. What's wrong? Where's David?" Stevie felt a chill. There was panic in her voice. Her shoulders shook.

"You're a friend of David Winter?"

"Yes," Stevie said. "I live with him."

"In that case, I think you ought to meet me down at the Hollywood station, Miss. Ask for me or Sergeant Thomas. Mr. Winter has met with an accident."

Stevie screamed into the phone. "What happened to David? Please tell me—is he all right?"

"He was killed this afternoon. He and another man, a black man named Charles Prince. Don't worry, Miss, we've got the youngster who did it."

Stevie dropped the phone, leaving it swinging from the cord. Cindy was at her side as Stevie began to cry. "David is dead."

There was silence, then Cindy spoke. "Stevie, what can I do?"

Saturday Morning—10 A.M.

Stevie took a Seconal when she got home from the Nicholas Long screening. Nevertheless, she spent the better part of the night watching the late night movies. Her eyes stared, barely in focus, and her ears were not sure about any of the dialogue as she sat in her spacious living room on Laurel Canyon. Despite the drug, she was still unable to sleep. The view of downtown L.A., beyond the wall of picture windows, was a smog-free expanse of twinkling lights. Finally their hypnotic quality made her drowsy and at four A.M., she went back to her bedroom and fell asleep.

When Stevie awoke, she went to the front door to retrieve the delivered copy of the L.A. *Times*. She scanned the front page and the inside pages to see if there was any mention of Melinda's death. It was unlikely, she thought, since it wouldn't have been reported to the police until after midnight, too late for the morning papers.

Drinking her coffee in the kitchen, she read the paper and listened to the all-news radio station. There was no mention of the incident.

As Stevie showered and dressed, she considered the situation. There was no likelihood, in her opinion, that Fentris would be able to convince Nicholas and Valerie Long to go along with his scenario. It was unthinkable for a mother and father to conspire to save the neck of someone who helped lead their daughter to death. Even if Nicholas Long *could* be convinced to hush up the matter, there was still his wife and a half-dozen others at the screening.

Stevie decided to phone the producer. She wondered what she could say to him. She could inquire about the funeral arrangements. That would lead naturally to the answer she was searching for.

His telephone rang repeatedly. There was no response.

Stevie redialed and waited. Still no answer.

Stevie phoned Jerry Fentris' house. She was angry. What would Fentris say to her, or she to him? This was the end of undeclared war at the agency and the beginning of open hostilities. They would start for real on Monday. The telephone rang endlessly. There was no answer there either. Finally the service picked up.

"Mr. Fentris' residence . . ."

"Where is he?"

The service continued its chorale. "I'm sorry. Mr. Fentris is not at home. Would you care to leave a message?"

"Do you know where or when he can be reached?"

"He left no forwarding . . ."

Stevie hung up.

She reflected. Two "no answers" and it's easy to be paranoid. She reflected further. Sometimes it's not paranoia, but the real thing, and with that she picked up the phone and asked the operator for the Los Angeles Police Department.

"Sergeant Driscoll."

"Sergeant, would this be the place that would be called in the event of an accidental death?"

"Do you wish to report something, Miss?"

"No. I'm a writer, doing a script for a TV series . . . and I'm stuck . . . maybe you can help me, Sergeant Driscoll."

The sergeant warmed up. "Sure."

"Well, in this script, this party dies from a drug overdose . . . and the story takes place in Bel Air . . . just so that I can get my facts right, I wonder who you would call?"

"It's us, lady—the number you dialed."

"Well . . . then it would be on your message pad . . . or whatever record you keep, correct?"

"Sure, lady . . . just like I'm keeping a record of your call . . . Lady . . . are you still on the phone?"

Stevie thought for a minute. "Officer, I don't know why you would do this for me, but was there a report of such an incident last night?"

The sergeant took a different tone. "Please state your name, lady."

Stevie hung up.

She thought for a while and dialed another number. It was Walker Perkins, the director of *Young Dillinger*. Someone answered.

"Walker? Stevie . . ."

"Christ, Stevie . . . you're up early. This is Saturday. Don't you agents ever sleep?"

"Walker, please be serious. I'm concerned about last night."

"Stevie, what about last night?"

"Walker, talk sense. A teenage girl OD'd on heroin and the star of your picture gave her the dope and was nude in the next room."

There was a long pause.

"Stevie . . . that wasn't the way it happened."

"What do you mean, Walker?"

"Look, I don't know where you got the idea that Morgan was in the house. He left during the first reel. He had a date in Hollywood. I know the people he went to see."

"Who were they, Walker?"

"Some people on the picture . . . What difference does it make?"

"Walker, the girl, Nick Long's daughter, OD'd."

"Stevie . . . come on now. She had a congenital heart condition. Valerie told us. A brave lady." He paused. "The funeral is tomorrow."

"Walker, this is important. Are you saying that the girl had a heart attack and suddenly the rest of this doesn't exist?"

"Stevie . . . look, I don't know what you're smoking this early in the morning. I know you're not a fan of Morgan's. He *was* truly difficult on the shoot, but I for one wouldn't mind doing another picture with him. He's going to be a huge success after this picture comes out . . . and yours truly, Walker Perkins, isn't going to be a slouch either."

"Walker."

"Yes, Stevie."

"Please let me know when the funeral is supposed to take place."

"You're going, Stevie? I wish I had time, but I've got to take a run up to Santa Barbara. Bye, Stevie."

He hung up. Stevie waited a moment and direct-dialed Palm Springs. A Spanish maid answered the phone and told Stevie that Mr. Sy Rosen was at the hospital having tests. She had no idea what hospital, what tests or when he would return.

Stevie had a problem.

7

David Winter's older sister, Mrs. Harriet Daniel, flew in from New York the night he was murdered. She took a taxi straight from Los Angeles International to the hospital. A Los Angeles lawyer she had contacted after Stevie phoned her had already set matters straight with the police. David's sister, a woman in her late thirties, tight-faced and grim, took complete charge and made all the arrangements to have the body sent back to New York by plane. David was to be buried in a family plot in New Rochelle, beside his mother and father. The sister glanced at Stevie in passing, but said nothing to her. The sister planned to spend the night at the Beverly Hills Hotel and return to New York the next morning on the same flight with David's body.

The Los Angeles lawyer would arrange to close up the house, inventory the belongings for the IRS, sell the house when suitable, and report to the sister that all had been accomplished with a minimum of trouble —to her.

David's sister was dry-eyed throughout, but openly bitter about her brother who had gone wrong years ago and brought this disaster on himself.

Stevie couldn't stop crying. Her tears were quiet but continuous. All she held of David were her memories, and perhaps one more night in the house on Laurel Canyon.

But even that was denied her. As a result of instructions from David's sister, the lawyer accompanied Stevie back to the house on Laurel Canyon and

waited while she packed. He had been instructed to
stay lest Stevie walk off with something of value. She
packed her bag with silent tears, standing in the
bedroom they had shared. She paused for a few
moments and moved to the huge picture window,
looking out below at the lights of Hollywood, and
promised herself that she would live in this house once
again. Somehow, she whispered to herself, she would
come back.

For now, she zipped up the soft leather valise, threw
the clothes on hangers over her shoulder, went down
the stairs to the hall, took another look at the view of
Hollywood at night, and closed the door behind her.

David had given Stevie title to the Porsche and she
had some money saved from what she had earned from
time to time. The only jewelry she was allowed to keep
was what she wore. The lawyer said that she could not
take the other pieces David had given her that were in
the house. Stevie knew he was wrong, but she refused
to argue.

Late that night after she left the house on Laurel
Canyon, she drove down the familiar road into the
parking lot at Schwab's. At the pay phone in the lot,
she called Cindy Warren.

"It's Stevie."

"Oh, honey . . . I'm so sorry. I don't know what to
say. I never know what to say at a time like this. Can
you forgive me?"

'For what?' Stevie thought to herself. 'Life goes on.'
"Look Cindy, I don't have any place to stay. Would it
be OK if I stayed with you?"

"Stevie . . . that's the least I can do. That's what
Southern hospitality is all about."

"I'll be right over." Stevie hung up and thought,
Cindy really didn't know what to say at a time like this.
About that she was right.

So Stevie moved to Cindy's small apartment farther
south on Laurel Canyon, a building called the Laurel
Vista, on Selma. That night Cindy and Stevie cried
themselves to sleep in each other's arms.

Cindy had not known David, but the emotion of the moment was contagious. It made Cindy feel good to feel bad for a friend.

On the outskirts of Beverly Hills near Bel Air is Holmby Hills. In that section of the world stands the Playboy Mansion West.

To keep the mills of fun grinding, the Mansion demanded a nonstop flow of new and hopefully fresh female talent. If it wasn't fresh, if the faces were almost interchangeable, if the tits were almost identically shaped, and other distinguishing physical characteristics similar, and if the names were pretty much the same, Debra, Cindy, Patti, Lori, etc., etc., the search must still go on.

To fill the larders, most particularly on Sunday afternoons, when the preliminary ceremonial took place with a buffet and then a movie in the screening room, additional talent was necessary. A secretary in the Playboy empire was detailed to make up the complement of Mansion regulars and those who represented interesting prospects to be invited.

Somehow the mechanics of the Playboy empire kept track of every pretty girl who came to Los Angeles, who had been a beauty queen or a campus lovely of spectacular proportions. Cindy Warren made that list as a former playmate.

That Sunday morning Cindy said, "Listen, I'm going up to Hef's this afternoon. You want to come?"

And Stevie said, "Yes." The David experience had left Stevie remarkably untouched, or so it seemed. It was more anger than sadness that made it impossible for her to have a decent period of grief.

Stevie was angry that she had done nothing to protect David from his involvement with Charlie Prince. She was angry that she hadn't spent more time with David and told him small intimate details of her life that she would like to have shared with him. Yes, she had for the first time in her life communicated with a part of her that allowed her to experience love and to feel passion, but she was angry that she hadn't learned more about David, how he had become so decent and so loving. She wished that she had told him of her mother and the event she remembered all too clearly, the murder. She wished that she had told David about Uncle Bert, not only about the years when she had sex with him, but how she felt about it. How the guilt of it was engulfed by the overwhelming desire to participate in it, all of which made her feel even more guilty. She knew that David would have understood, that he would have held her and loved her in spite of it. And he would have explained it all to her. And it would have been all right.

Everything would have been all right.

But the thing that made her most angry was her inability to express how angry she *was* at the missed chance that she knew was gone for good. And she hadn't even said goodbye to him.

Cindy had cleared the invitation with the Mansion and that Sunday they drove west along Sunset and took a left turn at Charing Cross Road. A few hundred yards from the turnoff was a huge iron gate crowned with a television camera which recorded the visitors. When a button was pressed, a telephone connected the visitor to a person in the main house familiar with every name on the OK list. If your name was on the guest list, the gate would spring open and you could drive through. Frequent visitors at the Mansion knew to wait on the inside of the gate until it closed to prevent crashers and celebrity gawkers from slipping through on someone else's entry.

The drive to the huge Tudor mansion led up an incline to a circle where only a few cars were parked. The one most in evidence was the huge black limousine that waited for Hefner endlessly, either to take him or a favored guest somewhere, or to go on an errand to pick up a Detroit paper at the newsstand on Las Palmas, or an elephant sandwich, if the master wished it, provided, of course, that the complete and twenty-four-hour-a-day kitchen didn't already have a quarter of an elephant hanging in the pantry.

Stevie looked beautiful that Sunday. Her dark azure eyes had rescued the light that had been lost since David's death. Her ash blonde hair was short and curled, crowning her face like a pale wreath. Young ladies she saw standing and chatting in the great hall of the Mansion had breasts of such prominence and kinetic potential that one would be fearful of the cannonading if their buttons failed to hold.

Stevie wore white linen pants and a matching tailored overblouse, and around her throat a turquoise and white Hermes scarf that David had given her. She wore a small gold Van Cleef bracelet, another present from David. She didn't have a bag with her—just a penny for luck. Stevie didn't wear makeup. Without effort the sun had found her, radiant in white, imparting a glow to her skin that accentuated her natural beauty and youth.

Dozens of attractive men and women stood and chatted in the great hall. Black-suited butlers quickly and efficiently kept the drinks replenished. The animation and the noise level of the guests was at a high decibel count, as if to prove to everyone how much each person was enjoying himself. To Stevie it looked like a giant casting call for beautiful extras to create atmosphere for a glamorous party picture.

"I said to Dennis, 'Look, I'll play the part, even though it's a piece of shit . . . but I want my own Winnebago.' Now my agent tells me that Redford has his own specially fixed-up Winnebago that he takes with him all over . . . and if Redford can have it . . ."

"Baby . . . look, I don't have all day to screw around. I want the key back to my apartment, either that or I'm gonna have the locks changed and I'm gonna throw your clothes out in the street."

"What do you mean, what do I mean?"

Cindy had left Stevie's side and was in deep discussion with another beauty, another past Playmate, and Stevie continued to walk slowly and deliberately through the playing fields of the lord.

Outside was a huge expanse of lawn, sloping gradually away into trees. At the end was a small hill and a tiny stream in which flamingos waded, flashing their pink feathers. Birds and monkeys chattered, parrots let out occasional screams, and a small pool was full of huge, magnificent fish. Alongside was a wooden barrel, and a man's form was absently dipping a hand into the barrel and feeding the fish. As Stevie walked over to the barrel, the form turned to her and stared.

"What happened to the bobby sox?"

It was Morgan Oliver, his dark handsome face framed in a wry smile. It was the smile that he turned on for his film close-ups that seemed to drive women crazy.

"I gave them to Goodwill Industries . . . for a tax deduction."

"Are you in a high bracket? Ninety percent, eighty . . . ?"

"If you're from the IRS, I want you to know I gave at the office."

Morgan warmed, sensing more than just a uniquely pretty girl. And Stevie felt a distinct quiver that said, 'I dig him.' She laughed, and it was at once spontaneous, musical and enchanting.

He reached for her hand and shook it. "I'm Morgan Oliver. I'm an uncouth prick."

"I'm Stevie Tree. You're absolutely right."

They laughed.

"This is my first time here. It's quite a place."

"It's what God would have done if he had money. Come on, I'll show you around. Would you like a Jacuzzi?"

"OK—wrap it up and send it. How much?"

Morgan led her to the hill, covered by rocks and alongside a pool with a waterfall, which curtained a large door opening on to a cavelike interior.

Mellow rock music filled the air alongside the spray from jets streaming water into pools of different sizes. "If you want to change, there's a bathhouse." It seemed to Stevie that no changing was necessary, only the dropping of clothes. Several stunning young ladies were caressing themselves in the sprays. They and others sitting nearby were naked.

"Do you think you could learn how to fuck here?"

"If you don't know already," Stevie replied, "the geography won't help."

Morgan continued, "If you'd like to change . . ."

Stevie brought her finger to his lips. "I've changed already. I like you . . . I think I could like you a lot. What did you say your name was?"

Morgan laughed and they walked back to the main house. When they got there, Hefner had finally descended. It was six o'clock and it seemed as if he had just awakened. He was dressed in bathrobe and pajamas, and when he caught sight of Morgan, he walked over to him and clapped him on the shoulder.

"How're you doing? Missed you on Wednesday night for the fights."

"Sorry, Hef, something came up." Morgan paused and turned to Stevie. "I'd like you to meet Stevie Tree."

"Nice to know you, Stevie. Is this your first time here?"

Stevie thought, Doesn't he know who anybody is?—and she replied, "Not really, Mr. Hefner. My family was part of the Arapaho tribe. Where your Jacuzzi stands, my great-grandfather fought and scalped twenty settlers and sold them to Gucci for loafers . . ."

Hefner laughed. "I love it. I love it. You've got to come here all the time. And don't bring this donkey." He hugged Morgan. "I like your girl."

Morgan looked at Stevie, and Hefner retreated to another area of the action.

Stevie gave him a long look. "I'd like to be your girl."

Morgan stared at her and then turned to the butler to order another drink. Hefner, circulating among the crowd, was calling, "Movietime everybody." The regulars stayed on into the night, while the Sunday-only

crowd drifted away. The movie was being shown in the
huge living room. The room was huge, with darkly
paneled walls, and deep red pile chairs and couches.
Wordlessly, Morgan led the way with Hef to the center
couch. Stevie sat down beside him. Next to her was a
beautiful Swedish girl, Miss February, who had the
favored position for the screening, sitting next to Hef,
cuddling up against him and warming him through a
terrible movie.

In the dark, Morgan whispered to Stevie. "Do you
like movies?"

Stevie whispered back, "Not this one."

"Do you like guys?"

"Yes," Stevie said. "I think the word is yes."

"This one?"

"Yes. The word is very much yes," she replied, and
Morgan reached out and held her hand.

At the end of the picture, Hef said goodbye to his
guests.

"Make sure we have your phone number," Hef said
to Stevie. "You've got to come by a lot." And to
Morgan he said, "Treat her right, and see if you can
come by Thursday night. Got some things to talk to you
about."

Cindy had been following Stevie with her eyes
through the late afternoon, and into the evening. With
any other girl but Cindy, seeing Stevie in the center of
all the action, on *the* couch with Hef, with *the* heart-
throb of movies, Morgan Oliver, it might have pro-
voked all the envy in Christendom. Not Cindy. She was
an extraordinarily decent girl, and when Stevie left with
Morgan, Cindy whispered to her, "Remember, he's a
nine. You heard it here first." Stevie left her Porsche
for Cindy, and accompanied Morgan in his Rolls along
Sunset to the Beverly Hills Hotel, where he lived for
the moment in a bungalow. Morgan was between
pictures, between houses, and between girls.

The first night that Stevie spent with Morgan was the
beginning of a new cycle in her life. When he walked in,
the phone was ringing. As he strolled over to pick it up,

Stevie gazed around the living room at the accumulation of newspapers on the floor and spread out over the couch. A pile of scripts was on the coffee table, along with a partially full basket of fruit provided by the hotel. Several trays, that had not been returned to room service, were on the carpet near the color TV, the remains of various meals still on them. The set was on, and obviously had been on for the entire day. Morgan picked up the phone while Stevie turned off the TV and sat down on the couch, idly thumbing through *Playboy* while Morgan talked.

"Just got in." Morgan grinned at Stevie and listened.

"Look, I can't see you now. What difference is it where I've been? If you must know, I was having a script conference at Malibu, with this writer. No, I didn't go to Hefner's." He tensed while he beat his fingers on the table.

"Look, you can't come over. I'm beat. Emotionally drained. Call me tomorrow."

Morgan hung up the phone. Neither of them acknowledged the phone call. Stevie looked at him and smiled.

"Sit next to me, Morgan . . . and let me tell you a story."

He reached down to the coffee table and opened a small black box. He took out a small plastic bag filled with white powder, and as he sat down on the couch, he picked up a tiny gold spoon that was at the bottom of the box. Stevie watched while he filled the spoon with coke and sniffed up one nostril, and then after a second dip, the other. He offered the spoon to Stevie. She waved it away. Morgan leaned back into the couch and put his feet on the coffee table. Stevie placed her fingertips along his temple and rubbed her hand lightly against his forehead. He closed his eyes and listened.

"In the palace of my father, the King of Kabul . . . ruler of all the lands to the east, north, west and south, the young princess waited for her prince." Stevie continued, "The princess was of inestimable beauty, much to be admired for her wit, her charm and her musical ability. It is said that nightingales paused in flight when they heard the princess sing her refrains. They were of such sadness they brought tears to the hearts of even the wicked."

Stevie stopped rubbing his temples and turned to look at him. Her dark eyes were mysterious and troubled. Morgan murmured from the pleasure of her touch, "Don't stop."

"Waiting for her prince . . . Oh Morgan, I don't know what I'm talking about. I've never felt so little and vulnerable before. I'm scared to death . . . and Morgan, please take me into the bedroom to that unmade bed covered with scripts and make love to me. I'll be good for you."

And he did, and she was, because Stevie wanted it more than anything she had wanted since David died. The loss to her of David's caring and loving had hurt more than she realized, and perhaps she understood that making love to Morgan now was paying her dues to David for having shown her the way to feeling. Stevie thought that she could show Morgan that same way, show a man who could and did have every woman he wanted. She wanted to show a man how much a woman could give, with a man who could fully accept her loving, as she had David's.

'God, I pray that I can get through to him,' she thought, as they walked into the bedroom. 'God, I need this man. Please God, let him love me a little. Let him be good to me, just for a while. I need him so.'

And Stevie made love to Morgan in a way that Morgan had never known. Stevie was the best. David had shown her how.

8

"HI, THIS IS STEVIE. I'M OUT NOW. BUT YOU CAN LEAVE A MESSAGE AND I'LL RETURN IT. IT'S BEAUTIFUL MONDAY IN L.A. WAIT TILL YOU HEAR THE BEEP."

"Hi, Stevie . . . gee, you sound fantastic. Call me when you get in, I've got the greatest news. In case you don't recognize my voice now that I'm rich and famous, it's Jon De Lisle, your favorite hair stylist extraordinaire. Have I got news for you! I can't wait to tell you, I'm out of that tacky place in Tarzana. I met a friend who can get me into Saks in Beverly Hills! You can make a lot of loot with those Beverly Hills broads, and I've got to tell you they're a better class of people than those yechh Valley types . . . so call me, I start today . . . and by the way, a little bird told me that you were with somebody very macho last night . . . and you wound up at the B.H. Hotel. I'll bet his initials are M.O. Isn't he divine? Call me, Stevie, for shit's sakes, I hope you're not running out of tape."

Stevie went to Schwab's for breakfast early that Monday morning. She hadn't gotten back to the apartment on Laurel until eight A.M., and Cindy was sleeping. Stevie thought about going to sleep and canceling the audition that she had at ten, but she decided that she was too excited to sleep. Morgan Oliver had gotten up early for a seven-thirty call on the set. The hotel operator had phoned at six-thirty, and he had risen and dressed. Stevie heard the sound of running water in the bathroom and the sound of the toilet flushing, and he went out the bedroom door while Stevie drowsed. She heard the front door close and went back to sleep. An hour later the phone rang again. It was a London call for Morgan. Stevie told the operator that he had left. Finding it impossible to go back to sleep, she got dressed herself.

Next to her clothes, which were spread out on the sofa in the living room, she saw a fifty-dollar bill sticking out of her purse.

Stevie looked around the living room. In the light of morning, the pile of scripts, newspapers, photos made the place look like a warehouse on moving day. Stevie went back into the bedroom and opened some of the dresser drawers. They were almost empty. Where the hell did he keep his clothes? She opened a closet and there were two suitcases partly open, bulging with dirty laundry. "That's where he keeps it," she laughed. Morgan had asked her to give him a call later at the hotel. He didn't know his plans. Stevie looked at the king-sized bed with the sheets hopelessly entangled. It had been a wonderful night. Stevie left the same way Morgan did. She had the doorman get her taxi and she used part of the fifty to pay the cab fare. Stevie thought he had been very thoughtful to leave her the money.

Stevie stripped and as quietly as possible walked past Cindy and into the shower. The water felt glorious, the soap fantastic. Never had there been a lather as creamy and foamy as the shower that Monday morning. She reached down and massaged herself with a loving tenderness that was not so much playing with herself as it was a means of recreating the memory of a love-filled night.

Cindy would inquire what Morgan's score was. Was he a nine? Was he a nine and a half? She really had no answer for Cindy. She would have to just smile, and let Cindy imagine for herself. Surely, Morgan was goddam good in the sack—but David was better. Morgan was less intent on giving pleasure than David, although giving pleasure *to* Morgan was pretty damn nice. He didn't respond as David had, but all men weren't the

same. Was it because Morgan was a star that it had a
special quality? Was there an edge that was indefinable
and special in star-fucking? Was it enough for the
star-fucker to know it herself? Or was there some kind
of badge you could get at one of the novelty stores on
Hollywood Boulevard that said "Star Fucker to the
Stars," or should it be "Star Fuckee"? Stevie smiled.
Morgan was special. It *really* wasn't the fact that he was
a star. He would have been a star even without his
movie career. There was an indefinable quality to his
whole personality that made you want to be around
him. 'Holy Christ,' Stevie thought to herself. 'Here I
am playing with myself. The water pipes clanged and
cut off her reverie.' Stevie rinsed off the soap and
stepped out of the shower to towel herself dry.

When Stevie pulled into the parking lot alongside
Schwab's, there was a space directly beside the entrance. She wouldn't even have to walk. She got out
and greeted Cliff, who was unpacking his shoeshine
gear and passing out claim tickets for people he didn't
know. The mark of a regular at Schwab's was the fact
that you *didn't* get a parking check for your car. Stevie
bought the trades at the counter and moved inside to
one of the tables in the restaurant portion. The
breakfast crowd was very noisy. Stevie recognized a lot
of them. They waved and greeted her.

Stevie unfolded a letter that she had received a few
days ago from her sister Ginny, who was still at the
orphanage. It was printed on one page. "Dearest
Sister. I am well, and I like getting all your postcards
and letters. I'm going to be an actress like you when I
grow up. Keep sending me stuff. Do you meet stars?
Please get me some autographs. Your sister, Virginia.
P.S. I liked your picture. Here is mine. It was taken
about three years ago."

Stevie stared at the photo of a pretty girl, tall for her
age. The picture was out of focus. Stevie promised
herself she would write tonight and tell Ginny about
Morgan Oliver and the Playboy Mansion. Surely every

twelve-year-old girl would be thrilled to hear about *that*.

"Hey, Stevie . . . what's cooking?"

"Nothing much, Lenny . . . Taking it slow."

"Hi, Stevie . . . you're looking good."

"Thanks, George . . . had a facelift last week."

"Hi there, Stevie."

"Good to see you, Sylvia."

Stevie waited for a booth for two, not daring to occupy a booth that seated four. Some of the regulars could get away with that, but not at Gertrude's station. Gertrude, the tall, middle-aged German waitress, was variously known as "The Nazi," "Ilsa Koch" or "Ms. Hitler." All were variations on the theme compounded by Gertrude's preoccupation with telling her customers what to eat, how to eat it and when to get out. The latter bit of information was more difficult to impart except in the subtle way of presenting the check a second time, after the first time failed to move the customer.

"Did you get your check?"

"Yes, Gertrude . . . I'll have another cup of coffee," said the customer.

The coffee never came, indicating displeasure with the customer's behavior.

"I asked for more coffee."

"Are you sure I didn't give it to you?" Gertrude inquired.

"I'd know if I drank it."

"I'm not so sure."

Stevie left Schwab's and went to her ten o'clock. The audition went well, but there was no way of telling how well. If the director really liked her, she would get a callback through her agent. Which reminded her that she had better phone her agent and check her phone messages. Stevie had a gizmo that allowed her to beep into the telephone recorder in her house and pick up her messages from wherever she was. It was a lot surer than some of those idiotic answering services, and a lot cheaper. David's answering service had always screwed up and switched messages or never delivered them, but he had never changed. It must have been a status thing, she thought. Between the end of the audition and going to the parking lot for her car, she looked at her watch. It was eleven—a decent hour for her to call Morgan. She had been thinking about him all morning, so she went back into the building and cajoled a secretary into letting her use the phone on her desk and placed the call to Morgan. Stevie noticed that when she mentioned Morgan Oliver's name, the secretary, who was doing a crossword puzzle, looked her over. The switchboard at the Beverly Hills Hotel asked who was calling. Celebrity guests always had their calls announced, so they could be in or out to whomever they wanted.

"It's Stevie Tree."

"Would you say that again, please?"

"Miss Tree . . . the first name is Stevie." Stevie glanced at the secretary. What was she thinking?

"Hold on just a minute."

The silence felt long and deadly, long enough for the secretary to finish her crossword, Stevie thought. "Yes?"

"Mr. Oliver is not in. Would you care to leave a message? Please hold and I'll connect you with the message operator."

Stevie left her home phone number, and then she phoned her number and got Cindy on the phone. Cindy had just awakened and yawned into the mouthpiece until she remembered to inquire about Morgan Oliver.

"OK . . . let me hear it."

"Ten plus."

"No kidding! How many times . . . I mean . . . did you do it all night?"

"We did it in the bungalow, then on the tennis court and then in the lobby of the hotel, and then for breakfast in the Polo Lounge while we were eating French toast . . . and then."

"OK . . . I get it. Skip the details."

Stevie laughed. Cindy gave her Jon's message, another call from her agent, an actor who wanted to borrow her cassette player, a director in from New York who wanted to know if she was busy tonight and three hangups.

Stevie tried the Beverly Hills Hotel once again. There was no answer at the bungalow, and she asked to speak to the message operator.

"This is Miss Tree. Did Mr. Oliver pick up my message? I called earlier."

"Just a moment, please. No, I still have your message here, Miss Tree."

"Is it possible that he missed it?"

"No, Miss Tree. We have a lot of messages for Mr. Oliver that he hasn't picked up yet. We deliver a copy of each of them to his bungalow."

"Please leave another message . . . I'd like him to have my home number."

"I'll be right back. I have another call. Please hold on."

Stevie hung up. She realized that she was being an idiot. She had come on to Morgan and she never stooped to that. "I'd like to be your girl." What kind of stupid kid stuff is that? Even the kids in Urbana High would be too hip to throw that to a killer like Morgan Oliver. Of course, she had been fantastic last night. She wasn't counting on too much. The chickens *had* hatched—She could count them. He would call.

At seven o'clock that night, Stevie stopped at a pay phone in Hollywood to call the Beverly Hills Hotel. She announced herself to the operator who tried the bungalow. Morgan Oliver couldn't be reached, she said. There was a "Do not disturb," on the phone line to his room. Stevie asked for the message operator and again left her home number with the operator. Then she went home.

Stevie tried the Beverly Hills Hotel again at midnight. The operator came on the line and reported, "There's no answer in Mr. Oliver's bungalow. Do you wish to leave a message?"

"Thank you, no," Stevie said, as she hung up and went to bed.

9

Stevie wondered what the hell was happening to her. She knew all the guidelines that any sensible young lady follows in playing the game with men. A girl, particularly one as beautiful and desirable as Stevie, shouldn't make herself too available. "Don't break a date with one man to make a date with a second . . . and, if you do, don't let the second man know that you've done it." Stevie had broken a dozen dates with guys around town in the last months to be with, or just to be "available" if Morgan should call, or if he should want something. "Don't get emotionally involved. More importantly, play it cool and don't let the man know if you feel very deeply about him."

Stevie was turning into a faucet. There had been at least a half-dozen times in the last months when she dissolved into tears, twice in Morgan's presence. He knew what it meant. She passed it off as a secret sorrow, a death of a friend. How many friends have to die as excuses for uncontrollable tears, before you know that you're behaving like a fool? But equally bad or worse, and she didn't really know which, was the life that she was living. She had really turned onto stuff. All kinds of stuff. Coke, quaaludes, uppers, downers. She carried three tabs of ludes with her to get her through the day. She promised herself never to take them when she was working, but she broke that promise. She found that she needed an upper to start the day and a downer to nod off a bit, to get her down when she was too high. She had lost five pounds and she wasn't happy with the way she looked. Not much could dim the loveliness of her skin, the dark blue eyes that were her trademark—darker and bluer than other eyes because of some trick that worked in the shadows. But she looked ten years older, and at twenty-two, that was not only a crime, it was a disaster.

The other part of it—the sex part—started very soon after they met.

Stevie discovered to her horror that life chasing Morgan Oliver wasn't pleasant. Morgan had a way with the telephone and with messages that could drive you crazy. He would tell you to call him at a certain time, and he wouldn't be there. Trying to track him down was like running an obstacle course. There were a half-dozen places that he might be: his agent's, a friend's house, the studio, another friend's house, the Playboy Mansion. If he *was* there, and she saw it happen when someone else called, he would tell the party answering the phone to tell the person calling that he wasn't there. It gave you little bumps of pain when you saw it happen to others. It was gruesome when you knew it was happening to you.

His friends. Morgan knew everybody, and it was a thrill for Stevie to be with him as his girl in the company of others. Face it, Morgan Oliver was one of the handsomest men in the world. He was either number three or number four on the list of the ten biggest male stars in the world, voted by the theater owners in America every year. Just behind Redford and John Wayne some years, and in front of Wayne this year. That wasn't anything to make a girl vomit, that kind of rub-off. Cindy said so herself, and Stevie saw it wherever she went. Even if Morgan separated himself from her at a party, and even if no one saw them come in, by some curious kind of jungle drum that works in society, everybody knew that she was Morgan's girl, and that she was with him (at least for that night). There was a quiet buzz that surrounded her, of people looking at one of them, and then at the other. They were a beautiful pair. The others were jealous. Cindy wasn't, though, or at least she didn't give any indication of it, except by the insatiable demand that she had to

live each and every minute with Stevie. Stevie first
thought that it was a delight, sort of the pleasure one
has out of twice-told tales, the historical reporting of
each and every detail of an evening out with Morgan, a
party they went to, a screening they attended. Then it
got to be a problem, because she found that she
couldn't tell Cindy about the details. She wasn't proud
of them.

When Morgan was busy or out of town, he would
arrange dates for her with one or another of his friends.
Stevie first imagined that it was meant in a spirit of
closeness that he wanted her to feel with the gang he
palled around with. Even that started out as fun, too,
because Morgan knew everybody, and most of his
friends were celebrities. Hollywood knew that they
were friends of Morgan's, ergo it only made it more
obvious that Stevie was Morgan's girl.

But that was not the way it really worked. Morgan
was just pimping for her.

It took her about thirty minutes on the first date to
realize what was happening. The first setup was with a
handsome Italian movie star—a world reknowned
figure who had Stevie meet him at his suite at the Bel
Air Hotel. Stevie had been under the impression that
the Italian was an old and good friend, but that was not
the case. They scarcely knew one another. They had
met at a party in Rome, and that was that. The Italian
had ordered food and drink from room service before
Stevie arrived. The conversation was limited, due to
Stevie's lack of Italian and his sketchy knowledge of
English.

The nature of the party was made clear when the
Italian told her that "his good friend Morgan" had told
him how passionate a woman Stevie was, and then told
her how much he "adored American women" for their
fresh, spontaneous and frank ways. After his room
service order was delivered, Stevie recognized that she
was not destined to leave the suite. She considered
telling the Italian "in her frank American way" to get
lost, but she realized that it would be an embarrassment

to Morgan. Stevie was looking for ways to bring them closer, not further apart. She sighed and thought, 'I'm not a virgin. The food looks good. He's an almost friend of Morgan's. OK. Where do you want my ass?'

As far as drugs were concerned, Morgan didn't take anything but coke. An occasional quaalude perhaps, but it was very simple, very early to see how very committed Morgan was to the white stuff. Morgan's friends, the Hungarian director Manny Maya, the actor Flip Christopher, and the producer Harry Cantor were equally into coke. Among those in the frozen-nose contingent, those who sniffed or snorted enough of it to freeze up, some made the solemn vow never to use it while they worked. Others could only work if they snorted. Morgan and his friends could take it or leave it at work, but they took it, not only because it helped get them through the day, but because it was a power trip. It was a way of showing the people on the set, the director and especially the studio, that the stars were in control. Morgan and his friends would take the studio's money—these men were some of the most highly paid actors, directors, and producers in a high-paying town. Yes, they would take the money, and then show the studio heads they hated them for paying it. It was simple rebellion.

Stevie discovered that coke was better than eating, better than sleeping, better than fucking, better than everything. The rush she got—the immediate sense of power and the sharp focus—was beyond anything you could get from anything straight. Since David, Stevie had not only enjoyed fucking, it had been a pursuit with her, both for the pleasure it gave her and the sense of accomplishment. It was like being a homerun hitter. If you were one, you loved to play the game. Stevie knew she had become one—a star on the pussy parade. It was something she took for granted, but wished she could share only with someone she cared about. But it was also part of the game of survival, to put out for men. You couldn't be a hermit. You had to show appreciation. You needed company. Someone had to buy you

dinner when you didn't make a lot of bread, and you
were always looking for a contact to give you a part in a
commercial or a TV show. It was expected; it was
essential to life. Besides, Stevie began to like the look
of wonderment that came over men when they discovered how good she was.

The men Morgan turned Stevie over to were tough,
cynical and sexist. There wasn't even a pretense that
she was anything more than a convenience. In her
heart, Stevie understood that it was nothing more than
these brittle and powerful men wanting a part in her
reputation—the "best piece of ass in town." Most of
them, the smooth, silken darlings, gave Stevie "taxi
money." It was a way of signaling to her that she was
nothing but a whore.

Stevie took the fifties and hundreds. She needed the
money for drugs and an occasional new dress, so she
looked good enough to appear in public for the few
moments before her "dates" took her where they
wanted, to do what they wanted, in private.

Morgan became less and less interested in making
love to Stevie or anyone else. It was the coke. With
others, coke was not a substitute for screwing, it was a
way of getting off twice over. But Morgan became quiet
and dispirited. As Morgan's girl, Stevie found herself
fucking everybody but Morgan, rich fools, some of
whom didn't remember her name during the course of
the evening.

Morgan had moved out of the Beverly Hills Hotel
and taken a house on Mulholland Drive in the Hollywood Hills, just a few blocks off Laurel Canyon
Boulevard. Stevie became only an occasional guest in
the house. She could never drop in unannounced. She
had tried once. When she rang the bell, Morgan came
to the door in his robe. He told her that he was
sleeping, that he had been on a night shoot. He yawned
and left her standing at the door at two in the afternoon
feeling stupid. Obviously someone else was inside, but
goddammit, the day before he had told her to come.

At night, there was never anything that resembled

being alone at Morgan's house. Friends always dropped
by. They brought other friends with them, and in the
course of an evening as many as twenty strangers were
wandering around the living room talking, smoking and
drinking or disappearing into bedrooms. There was
never a shortage of grass or coke at any of Morgan's
parties. A few of the guests brought their own, but it
was usually the host's place to supply the coke. In the
Hollywood fraternity, the measure of one's importance
is marked by the amount of coke one has at his
disposal. It is also generally very bad form to inquire of
someone where he or she gets his drugs. You had your
own contact, and the mystique was heightened and the
kick intensified in proportion to the illegality of acquisi-
tion. Some of the guests had obliging doctors who
prescribed for affluent members of the Hollywood set,
which allowed the "patients" to have their pills delivered minus any fear of narcs. Others had contacts in the
rock world, where part of any top record contract is the
assurance the record company will provide all the drugs
the act needs while they're in L.A. For that matter, if
the act is important enough and the record company
has worldwide distribution, the coke or pills can be
delivered to their door anywhere in the world, like the
New York Times.

Morgan kept the coke on the coffee table in a huge
white mound, the size of an upturned mold of Jell-O.
Silver spoons were on the dish for those who used
communal utensils. For those who brought their own
spoons, gold or inlaid or diamond-studded, it was still
the proper kind of hospitality. Morgan's coke was the
real thing. His supply represented a four or five
thousand dollar centerpiece.

One of the regulars at Morgan's was a talented young
Hungarian director, Manya Maya. He made his reputation in Hungary for powerful and original films featuring violence and the grotesque. Manya was tiny,
ferretlike and given to outrageous behavior. He had a
vile way of talking to everyone, imperious and commanding, lofty and dictatorial. Once in Hollywood, he

made his mark with a horror classic, featuring acts of brutality that had never been seen before in a major picture with major stars.

Following that success, Manya was on and off more picture assignments than some directors get in a lifetime. That he was talented provided the assignment. That he turned out to be an unmitigated pain in the ass, irritating studio heads, producers and actors, provided the opportunity to fire him.

He once walked into the dressing room of a major female star and pissed in her sink, meanwhile carrying on a discussion about her failings as an actress. At first, it had been regarded as a crude and tasteless joke, but she heard within days that he had boasted about it all over town. Manya's explanation was that it allowed him to communicate with the actress on an open and more honest level. The lady's agent got him thrown off the picture. If this had been anything but a practical joke, then one would have to wonder about Manya Maya's sanity. It was a practical joke that had been concocted in Morgan's living room. After Manny was thrown off the picture, he commented, "The script needed work anyway."

Harry Cantor was another of Morgan's friends whom Stevie got to know. Heir to a prominent motion picture fortune derived from two generations of leaders in the business, he had made his own fortune producing several hit television series. One was the first of its kind in the 1960's, a series about a pair of youthful wanderers, whose exploits filled a TV hour every week in a different small town in America, saving one or more good townspeople from the perils of one of the local heavies. The title of the series was "U.S. One," after the highway of the same number. Immensely popular, the series was followed by a number of special programs for holidays that featured motion picture stars celebrating patriotic events in communities throughout the country.

Having amassed a considerable amount of money, Harry Cantor, who had propagandized in favor of traditional American values in traditional American ways, proceeded to aid and abet those who would plow them all under. Harry Cantor was largely responsible for bringing leaders of every faction of the New Left into the mainstream of Hollywood. No one in Hollywood under the age of fifty had anything good to say about Nixon or the war in Vietnam. Lyndon Johnson was a matter of considerable hatred after his vendetta against Bobby Kennedy, and his record in Vietnam. By 1973, the very tip of the Watergate iceberg had surfaced, but in Hollywood, where hating Nixon was as much in vogue as Gucci loafers, no one suspected what would surface shortly after.

Hollywood had been rocked by the assassinations of Jack Kennedy, Martin Luther King and Robert Kennedy, but the group that Harry Cantor championed considered even those liberal leaders reactionary.

Evenings spent at Morgan's house would sometimes be spent in propagandizing for the Weather Underground. (Harry Cantor had a pipeline, he said, to Mark Rudd and some of the other fugitives.) Jerry Rubin and Mark Lane were favorites. One evening Abbie Hoffman (wanted by the FBI) surfaced and was a guest for a very small but very select group of Harry's buddies. Harry always suspected that the FBI was monitoring all of his phone calls and mail, and their surveillance was a perfect insurance policy, or so he thought, against his ever getting busted for drugs. The way Harry explained it, the FBI had so much going in its phone taps and other investigations of him that they told the Narcotics Enforcement folks to cool it. Cantor was their pigeon, he went on to explain. Let the narcs pick on some of the *schwarzes* and hippies. Leave the Jew millionaire to the FBI.

Some evenings the Black Panthers dragged their Fritos in Harry's cheese dip and had the munchies along with the white intellectuals. Eldridge Cleaver was a frequent visitor and so was Huey Newton, whenever they could tear themselves away from the saber rattling in northern California, or the cocktail party circuit in New York and Washington. Substantial amounts of money were raised for the Panthers in Harry's living room. A lot of grass was blown and a lot of coke snorted. Some of the Panthers developed quite a liking for Nate and Al's delicatessen. Harry always ordered more than enough. What they didn't eat seemed to vanish with one or more of the Panthers as they brown-bagged it back to Oakland.

But all the time there was fucking.

There was occasional business talk about which pictures were making it and which weren't. There were frequent critiques of movies and directors and studios and agents.

But *all the time* there was fucking.

Stevie tap-danced through the months of being "Morgan's girl." Her life was a routine now. There were Sundays when they went to Hef's, but not many. Morgan had too many other commitments. During the week, Stevie kept phoning him endlessly, getting no response. She had long since been able to work out a deal with Morgan's phone-answering service to override their policy of reporting all calls—even the hang-ups, the "never minds," and the wrong numbers.

The frequency of Stevie's calls was too embarrassing for her, and she was able to convince the ladies in the service not to mark down the ones that inquired, "Did he pick up the message that I left for him?" She had little enough pride now.

Stevie was still going out on jobs and working enough to pay her share of the rent to Cindy. She still had a few thousand dollars left from the gifts that David gave her, and of course the Porsche. She had never realized how expensive it was to doctor German cars. They were always sick.

Then there were the passoffs. There were the messages on Stevie's service that a friend of Morgan's would call, or that Stevie should meet Morgan at the party of a Beverly Hills attorney or a Bel Air producer. Almost always, Morgan wouldn't show. Almost always, he wouldn't even call.

And there were the drugs. Morgan might have had some idea how deeply Stevie was into drugs if he had seen her much, but he didn't. Cindy might have understood, had she been more sophisticated and knowledgeable. But Cindy Warren, Miss Tennessee, was still small-town and wide-eyed on most of the issues Hollywood was about. Nobody really knew how dependent Stevie was on pills to get her through the day and on coke to get her through the night.

If Stevie knew that there would be coke at a party, then that was where she needed to be.

And all the time there was fucking.

The whole town knew, and Stevie didn't really care. They knew that she could be had for a dinner or a snort. They knew that she was "Morgan's girl" mainly in the sense that Morgan had complete control over when and whom she slept with. The only thing Morgan didn't share was the proceeds. Morgan didn't get any part of the taxi money.

Stevie found herself crying frequently and without control. Her eyes, those blue diamonds in the crown of her beautiful face, were red and puffy. Stevie began to wear dark glasses day and night, in or out, to hide her eyes.

"THIS IS JON AND AS YOU CAN TELL I'M NOT AT HOME. PLEASE LEAVE A MESSAGE. WAIT FOR THE BEEP."

"Jon, this is Stevie . . . you've got to do my hair tonight. I've got this big party to go to at Morgan's and I look a mess. Please call my service and tell me when I can come over to Saks. Or if that's not convenient, can you come over to my place on your way home? Please, Jon . . . I need you." Suddenly Stevie broke into tears. "Jon, don't pay any attention to me. I haven't the vaguest idea why I'm crying. I wish I could wipe this message. Oh, Jon, please call me."

That night at Morgan's house on Mulholland Drive, Stevie had never looked better. Somehow Jon pulled her together. With loving attention to her ash blonde hair and a thoughtful and expert touch to her makeup, Jon recreated Stevie's youthful radiance, which had vanished almost a year before.

Stevie hadn't seen Morgan in almost a month and hadn't spoken to him in three weeks. She called his message service endlessly. A new operator, unaware of her unique deal with the service, informed Morgan of the dozens of calls. When Stevie heard from one of the other girls what had happened, she broke into tears.

But tonight was going to be different. Stevie was stunning. Her face and hair glowed. She wore a very expensive, flowing chiffon gown of pale green. The dress, at $300, had depleted her savings. She would have to skimp until the next check came in for some residuals from a commercial. But it was worth it. The softness of the line, the sheer gossamer of the dress and the pale green against the dark blue of her eyes made Stevie look like a dream. She was twenty-three and beautiful.

The party was under way when Stevie got there. It was the first planned party that Morgan had given in a long while. She hadn't known that it was for someone, but when she got there it was clear that it was in honor of a French movie actress, Denys Dubois, somewhat known in Europe but not particularly known in the U.S. Denys was in her early thirties, pretty and petite, but very much in charge of herself and men. She had a flirtatious air, which was replaced moments later by a steellike determination. Morgan had met her at a dinner party a week earlier, and she had attached herself to him like glue.

Stevie had never seen Morgan so surrounded, and all it took was a five-foot-three French coquette with a will of iron. He appeared to want to escape from her, but Denys had her hand on his arm, and when she saw that irritated him, she ran the tips of her fingers on his chest. At another time, Stevie would have walked over to Morgan, planted herself in front of him, put her arms around him and kissed him, but she hung back. She thought Morgan looked at her out of the corner of his eye, but she wasn't sure. 'Play it cool for once, Stevie,' she thought. 'Circulate. Undulate. Copulate.' She smiled to herself. Most of the men in the room weren't strangers to her, at least not in bed. 'Jesus,' she thought, 'there's that Italian actor friend of Morgan's.'

"Hello, Angelo . . . How have you been?"

"*Comé?* I'm sorry, I don't know you."

"Stevie Tree . . . I'm a friend of Morgan's . . . we had a date, about six months ago . . ."

"Stevie Tree . . . I'm sorry, I don't remember. That's an unusual name. You're a pretty girl. Why don't you phone me at my hotel? I'm at the Bel Air."

Stevie looked at his back as he moved to another corner of the room. "I know," she muttered.

Beautiful people were here tonight. Movie folk with their supertans, and their thin, thin watches, their thick, thick gold chains. More bare flesh appeared on the men, with their shirts open to the waist and skin-tight pants, than on the beautiful and faceless models and starlets who came with them. And there were others, millionaire actors and producers, who wore scruffy jeans, tennis shoes and workshirts. Their hair was frizzed, bobbed, crimped and babied. Endless effort went into making them look like boyish runaways from a prison farm. Endless time was spent in having hair stylists turn their looks into something teenagers achieve by never combing. And their watches were thin, and gold was everywhere.

Harry Cantor walked over to her, accompanied by a tall black woman in a simple dress.

"Stevie, do you know Angela Davis?"

"No, I don't, Harry."

"I'm sorry, I didn't get your name."

"I'm Stevie Tree. I'm a friend of Morgan Oliver."

"Wonderful man."

Stevie looked at her back as Harry and Angela turned to the center of the room. "You know it," Stevie murmured.

The hi-fi spun Miles Davis and cool jazz. In the corners on tables there were some chips and some dip and pretzels. (Morgan never put himself out to provide anything much to eat—just to snort.)

Stevie went over to the coffee table for a hit. She

stopped. I want to be *in* this party, she thought, not out of it. I want to be really around. She went to the bar and poured herself a tall scotch. Stevie didn't usually drink. When she did, it was white wine. But tonight it would be different, and whiskey had never affected her, only drugs.

The noise level of the party got higher. More people came in and made their way over to Morgan to say hello, giving him a hug or a kiss. Denys still had him locked up, but instead of fighting it Morgan now appeared to be pleased.

Stevie walked over to a director friend of Morgan's, Newton Jones. Newton was talented, but not very attractive.

"How did you ever get a name like Newton Jones?"

"I never thought you'd ask."

"OK," Stevie continued, "I'm asking."

"Well, my mother was passionate about Fig Newtons while she was carrying me, and decided to name me after her favorite cookie."

"Next case."

"Would you buy it if my name were Oreo, or Lorna Doone? You wouldn't be such a smartass then, would you, Stevie Tree? What kind of a *fakokta* name is that?"

"My mother comes from a long line of botanists."

Newton looked at her and smiled. "You're not stupid, young lady."

"Who said I was?"

"Nobody really. But if you're so smart, what are you doing with this crowd. You're too nice. It isn't the booze that's making me say it, and it's not that I want to get into your pants . . ."

"You don't?"

"No . . . well, maybe . . . well yes, but something tells me that I pressed all the wrong buttons." He looked quizzical.

"Look, Newton . . . or chocolate chip . . . or just plain cookie . . . we're both here as guests of a damn nice guy—Morgan—and I for one am not going to say anything bad about him, and I'm not going to listen to anyone saying . . . so you can go fuck yourself, Mr. Marshmallow." As she spoke, Stevie wondered why she was coming down so hard.

Six beautiful young ladies were standing alone in one corner, looking at each other disinterestedly, and gazing back at the men languidly. The men were talking to each other.

A black man came over to the tallest and prettiest blonde and picked up her skirt. "Just wanted to see," he said. She said nothing, did nothing. When he left, she turned back to the others.

A man in jeans climbed up a bookcase to retrieve a pile of scripts that were lying up there. The scripts fell from his arms as he climbed down. He muttered, "One of these scripts is mine."

In the kitchen, two very young girls, no more than sixteen, were rubbing each other's crotch. One of them placed her hand inside the fly of the other. A well-known director came in, saw them, turned away and proceeded to get some orange juice from the fridge, drank from the bottle and returned to the living room. The young girls continued moaning with pleasure.

Back in the living room, Stevie picked up a glass full of amber liquor, sniffed it, and tossed it down her throat. It was somebody else's scotch, but it was easier than pouring her own.

Stevie was drunk. It wasn't the liquor. It was the reds she had taken before coming to the party. That plus the alcohol were a combination she hadn't counted on.

Stevie walked over to Harry Cantor, who was changing a record on the hi-fi.

"Want to change your luck, Harry?"

"What do you mean, Stevie?"

"Don't you fuck any *capitalists*, Harry? How do you get your cock in when the chicks you screw have a red flag up their twat?"

"You're drunk, Stevie. Morgan isn't going to like it. Why don't you go into one of the bedrooms and be a good girl and lie down?"

"Fuck you, Harry. Nobody takes me into any fucking bedroom without giving me taxi money first."

"See you around, Stevie." He dismissed her with a quick nod of his head.

She walked slowly and gingerly out of the living room aiming for the bathroom. Down the hall in Morgan's bedroom was a black man making a phone call from the bed. He had the phone cord pulled out along the side of the bed and was fingering it as he talked. Noticing Stevie, he put his hand over the mouthpiece.

"How's it going, sweetmeat?"

She stared at him, as disdainfully as her drunken state would allow.

"Shove it, pigmeat."

He laughed and went on with his conversation.

Stevie walked into the bathroom. The door was ajar and the light was on. Manny Maya was taking a leak. Stevie started to leave.

"Stick around, Stevie, you can blot it dry for me . . ."

"No thanks, Manny."

"Then let it drip dry and you can blow me. I'm told by the Friars Club and Hillcrest Country Club and the YMCA that you are one grand banana eater."

Stevie walked out and slammed the door behind her. She heard Manny laugh and then flush the toilet.

Stevie came back from the hallway into the large room. The noise level was higher, and the music louder. Now it was Quincy Jones on the hi-fi. She made her way over to the bar and refilled her glass. The room had the effect of a prism, the scenes refracting and glittering in her unclear vision.

Out of the corner of her eye she spotted Morgan and haltingly made her way over to him. He saw her and held a false smile. The French actress was still with him. The two of them were talking to an English actor, whose name Stevie never knew.

"Hello, Morgan . . . You remember me?"

"Hi, Stevie. Denys, this is Stevie Tree."

Stevie held out her hand to shake Denys', but the

move was so tentative and uncertain that their hands
never met. Stevie turned to look at the Englishman.

"Do you want me to fuck him, Morgan?"

Morgan took it without missing a beat. "Sure."

The Englishman broke the awkward pause. "Don't I
have anything to say about it?"

Stevie took his hand, turned it over and looked at the
palm. "It says here that you have a two-inch dick,
which when aroused becomes a three-inch dick. It says
also that you take it out of your pants to have it
photographed and that it can sign autographs and
contracts, but it's shy of fucking. How do you train a
dick to sign contracts? Is that dickwriting?" Stevie's
eyes were glazed oceans.

The Englishman walked away. The French lady tried
to move Morgan away. Stevie held him there.

"Morgan, why is it I never see you? Why won't you
ever talk to me? I love you. I shouldn't have said
that . . . forget what I said, Miss French cunt, forget
what I said . . . Please forgive me, Morgan. I do
whatever you ask me . . . I'm the best, and you know
it."

Denys broke in. "I think you've had too much to
drink, *chérie*. Why don't you go home?"

Stevie smiled and spilled her drink. "Understate-
ment of the year."

Morgan turned to go. "Get lost. Leave me alone."
The two of them linked arms and walked away, leaving
Stevie bewildered and helpless.

Stevie wandered through the hot crush of the crowd
and out onto the terrace. She had always loved this
house. There was a brilliant view of Hollywood on one
side and the San Fernando Valley on the other. At the
top of Mulholland, the height allowed almost a 360-
degree span. At the back, it dropped off into a deep
ravine that washed into the darkness of the gorges
around it. The air was cool. The dark soothed her.

She looked again at the view. It was the same as the
vista from the house she had shared with David. Why
had he died? If he were still alive, things would be so

different. She needed someone. She had torn it for good with Morgan. Now she would be alone. The Englishman came out on the terrace. He looked at her and turned to go.

Stevie intoned, "I'm truly sorry . . . Can you ever forgive me?"

Stevie went up to him and tried to kiss him.

"Please let me go, Miss. This is no concern of mine. Let's forget the whole thing."

Stevie reached down and picked up her pale green chiffon skirt. She lifted it above her waist. She wasn't wearing underwear.

"Stick it in. I'm the best. Anybody will tell you. Shit. *Everybody* will tell you. Go ahead, fuck me. Maybe you're a faggot, but I'll turn you on . . ."

The Englishman pulled himself free and walked quickly back into the living room and over to Morgan.

"Dear fellow. You've got a problem on your hands. That young lady outside on the terrace is absolutely out of control. I think you'd better do something."

Morgan walked through the crowd. The moment carved a hollow stillness into the party. The hi-fi was silent, almost cued for his exit. Morgan moved out onto the terrace. Stevie was standing on a bench overlooking the deep black drop into the gorge below.

"Morgan . . . that French bitch will have to go."

"No, Stevie, you have to go . . . You get the hell out of here and out of my life."

"I was never in your life, Morgan . . . Why won't anybody fuck me? Is that Englishman a fag?" She swayed back and forth on the stone bench.

"Come down from there," Morgan commanded.

Stevie looked at him and then below into the darkness. She swayed unsteadily. "If you don't fuck me, Morgan—I'm going to jump. I mean it."

Morgan turned. "Who gives a shit? Jump!" His words felt like ice.

Stevie jumped without another sound.

The next moments were panic. No one but Morgan

and Stevie had been on the terrace. No one knew of their conversation. The English actor might be a witness. She fell. Still there would be a stink, because there always was.

Morgan was struck by a thought. Was she dead or alive? He didn't really care. It would be unpleasant either way.

He walked into the living room and muttered that there had been an accident. He grabbed Harry Cantor and told him to call an ambulance.

"Maybe I should call the Fire Department."

Morgan disappeared into his bedroom. He told the black who was still on the phone to get out. He hung up, muttered and left. Morgan dialed his agent.

"Bernie, it's me. I'm in a spot."

"Yeah, Morgan . . . What time is it?"

"Shut up and listen. Some dizzy broad . . . Let's start again. I'm having this party with a lot of people and some dizzy broad gets out of control and jumps off the terrace."

"Any witnesses?"

"No . . . just me."

"She fell," he concluded matter-of-factly.

"Yeah, she fell . . . and someone is calling the ambulance or the Fire Department."

"Who's there?"

"A lot of people . . . some you know and some you don't."

"Any political types?"

"What do you mean?"

"You know what I mean . . . any commies, or any Panthers or any fugitives. You know what I mean."

"Who knows?"

"Get them out. What are you serving? The usual?"

"Yeah."

"Get someone to take all that shit off the premises, pronto."

"Yeah, yeah . . ."

"Look—do it. I'll have one of our lawyers up there in fifteen minutes. Now hang up and get that shit out of

the house and the pinkos as well. It won't look good in
the papers."

He clicked off, and Morgan came out of the bedroom. There was a stir in the main room. They had
heard what happened. Harry Cantor came up to him.

"The ambulance will be here, and I guess the cops
and the Fire Department, whoever comes to stuff like
this."

Morgan had Harry get the cocaine and the grass out
of the house. People were leaving on their own. There
was no need to tell them to go.

Denys Dubois rushed over to Morgan.

"Oh, that poor girl. Suicide. She must have cared for
you a lot, *chérie*."

Morgan was noncommittal. "She fell."

"Of course, *chérie*. Don't worry. I'll stand by you.
Denys will stand by you."

The sound of the ambulance siren was audible in the
distance as it sped up Laurel Canyon.

The Los Angeles Fire Rescue squad was quiet and
efficient. Three men on the team surveyed the location
with powerful searchlights, and in the middle of the
brush, approximately sixty-five feet below the terrace,
they saw the pale green of Stevie's dress. One of them
went down to the floor of the gorge, linking a line to a
tree below to set up a pulley. The remainder of the
rescue was by the books, as they transferred Stevie to a
basket which could be pulled up the steep side of the
canyon, then toward the ambulance.

Seven minutes after the ambulance arrived, a black
and white squad car from the L.A.P.D. pulled into
Morgan's driveway. Two officers saw the rescue in
progress and walked into the house. They found
Morgan and a half-dozen others sitting on couches and
easy chairs. Morgan's feet were on the coffee table and
he was sipping cognac from a brandy snifter. He rose
when he saw the officers, and sat them down while he
arranged himself to answer questions.

The officers were extremely polite. They realized
that they were in the presence of a lot of Hollywood

muscle. They knew there had to have been drugs. They knew that something had to have been amiss. They sensed it. The firemen had almost completed the rescue and they had everyone's names and the pertinent facts—and by Christ, thought one of them, Morgan Oliver is one lucky son of a bitch—they get all the chicks.

As the ambulance pulled out and the officers were leaving, a tall, young gray-suited man walked through the door. He spied Morgan Oliver and walked up to him.

"I'm a lawyer from the agency, Mr. Oliver. Is there anything I can do to help?"

Stevie was rushed to the emergency entrance of the Queen of Angels Hospital. She was wheeled into emergency receiving on a gurney and left lying there for ten minutes while the ambulance driver filled out forms for the hospital. Finally an intern gave her a superficial examination. That was the first time in forty-five minutes that anybody had looked at Stevie's face. It was a mass of cuts and bruises. Her forehead was a long, wide gash of blood and her cheek was badly ripped open. There were huge patches of bruised skin where she had fallen and continued to slide. The resident arrived and prescribed whole blood. She received an injection of chloramine for profound shock. There were obviously multiple fractures, and through this all Stevie, still conscious, remained silent, not complaining of pain at all. She had been conscious through the entire rescue attempt.

There was no way of knowing at the moment how serious her internal injuries were. She was hemorrhaging vaginally, and the nurse applied local sponges, as well as cleaning her facial and body wounds. Stevie's blood pressure had fallen to 40 and her pulse rate was at an extraordinary high of 135 and of a weak, thready nature. The next twenty-four hours would determine whether she would ever walk again. The extent of her other injuries would only be known after a complete examination was made, following the treatment for shock.

The resident motioned to a nurse to wheel her into the x-ray room. The nurse grasped the gurney from behind and started to push it down the corridor.

As she rolled the cart, looking down at Stevie's face, she saw the lips move. The nurse bent down to hear.

"I don't want to live . . . Please don't make me live."

And tears rolled down her cheeks.

Saturday Morning—11 A.M.

Stevie picked up the telephone extension in her living room. As she dialed Nick Long's number, she saw the progression of traffic winding up Laurel Canyon. The cars weren't distinct, just flashes through the trees, reflections of sun on windshields and chrome. The trees deadened the sounds of screeching tires as the cars negotiated the turns.

"Nick . . . I hate to disturb you . . . it's Stevie."

"Go ahead, Stevie . . . It's all right. Life must go on."

"Nick, I didn't have much of a chance to talk to you last night, when we found Melinda."

"Nothing much anybody can say."

"Nick, what are you going to do?"

"What do you mean?"

"I mean, about Morgan."

"I don't know what you're talking about, Stevie."

"Morgan killed your daughter. Morgan gave her the heroin, you know that." Stevie stared at the continuous thread of cars out the window.

"Yeah, so?"

She was bewildered. "Nick, you can't let him get away with it." She made a fist with her free hand.

There was a moment's pause, then Nick returned on the line. "Stevie, I don't know what's in it for you. I've never heard such a pitch from an agent. What are you trying to do, sell out your client?"

"I only want to do what's right."

"Bullshit . . . you agents are all alike. Must be something in it for you to want to dump Morgan. Let me spell it out to you, Miss Tree. I plan on doing nothing about my daughter's death. I have it only on your say-so that Morgan gave her heroin. How do you know? Next, I've heard of disloyalty in this business . . . people would kill each other over a deal . . . but I never heard of this kind of treachery. An agent trying to destroy her client."

Stevie tried to reply. "Nick . . . please listen . . ."

"No, I won't. This is the last thing I'm going to say to you—stay out of it. Let the dead rest in peace. Let the living pick up the pieces they can. There's nothing in this for me and Valerie except the good name of our daughter. So keep out." He hung up.

Stevie knew he was lying. That was simple. Nick Long knew what would happen to *Young Dillinger* if word got out. For a second, she considered that she too might play the game and forget it. How could she risk the fortunes of so many, just for the sake of personal vengeance against Morgan Oliver? The point was she knew more than anyone else did about Morgan, more than the whispered talk of her own suicide attempt, more than the whispering now. She had to destroy Morgan Oliver.

That was all that counted.

After he hung up on Stevie, Nick Long placed a phone call to Jerry Fentris, who had just returned by chartered plane from Palm Springs.

"I tell you, Jerry, the bitch will be trouble. I just got off the phone with her."

"Nick, I ask you for once and for all, please let me handle it. Everything has gone fine so far. The doctor did his job . . . and before the day is over you'll have your deal for two . . . not just one . . . but two pictures."

"What about the one with Randy? I thought I'd like to get into that deal."

"Of course, Nick, it's in the cards. I'm not only your agent, I'm your friend. Everything is coming out like I said it would, and I advise you just to ignore Stevie. She had a thing with him, you know. He kicked her out. Women are fucking unstable."

"But what if she goes to the cops?"

"Nick, she won't. Everything is packed, boxed, wrapped and labeled. It'll all be in the bag by Monday morning the latest, I promise you. And that includes Stevie Tree." Jerry stretched luxuriously on the sofa where he'd taken the call.

"Sure?"

"Honest injun. You've got things to do, Nick, and so do I. Call me if anything new comes up. But relax . . . relax . . . you're in the hands of IA."

Nick hung up the phone and Jerry Fentris turned in prone position to look at his wife, who stared at him blankly. Mildred Fentris knew enough not to inquire into her husband's activities.

"Jerry, there's someone to see you in the living room."

"Who is it?"

"He says he was the projectionist at the screening last night."

Jerry reacted. "Why did you let him in, Mildred?"

"Well, you were out of the house, and it seemed to be important. Did I do something wrong, Jerry?"

Jerry walked into the living room and saw the man he had paid to remove Morgan Oliver from the house. In his late twenties, thin and bearded, the projectionist wore a pair of jeans and a workshirt. He was smoking a cigarette and turned to Jerry Fentris as he approached.

"What do you want?"

"It's simple, Mr. Fentris . . . money."

"You got some last night."

"Sure, a hundred bucks. Big deal. Do you know what I did? I saved your ass for you, Mr. Fentris, that's what I did, and I could go to jail for it, and you think that I'm gonna be paid off with a hundred bucks."

"What do you want?" Jerry stared straight ahead at the man's forehead.

"I want a thousand . . . no, two thousand. That's what I want."

Jerry considered for a moment. "You work for the studio?"

"No, I'm nonunion. All the private screening rooms use me. That way they don't have to pay union scale."

Jerry smiled.

"You can't threaten me with blackballing me in no union, Mr. Fentris, 'cause I ain't in one."

Jerry sat down across from the young man, reached for the cigarette box on the coffee table and lit one. This took a matter of ten seconds. Then he smiled again and looked the young man in the eye.

"First you give me your name, and then I'll tell you what I'm gonna do."

The young man was hesitant, but there were so many ways that Jerry Fentris could find out.

"Harry Belson, that's my name."

Jerry drew in some smoke and exhaled. "Well, Harry, from now on you're in the union, and you can get yourself a studio job that will pay regular and more than those chickenshit jobs you have to take for private screenings. What's more, if you want, you can still scab at those screenings. Some of the union boys do."

The young man looked at Jerry. "Do you really mean you can get me in the union? They said it was a five-year wait."

Jerry Fentris smiled again. "Just leave it to me, Harry Belson."

And Jerry Fentris led Harry Belson to the door and closed it after him.

10

"Did you have any dreams last night?"

Dr. Ben Grossman, the resident psychiatrist at the Queen of Angels Hospital, had been seeing Stevie during her stay there at first, daily. Now in its fifth week, a pattern of thrice-weekly sessions had been established and would continue as long as she was in the hospital.

The staff psychiatrist in any city hospital consults with an attempted suicide as a matter of course, but that process must follow the diagnostic and medical phase that begins immediately on arrival in the emergency ward.

Stevie had been examined initially by a neurosurgeon to see if there was any internal brain damage or bleeding. Simultaneously, x-rays were taken. Her hip had been broken and both her legs too. Luckily, she had fallen on her heels. Had she fallen on her head, she would have been instantly killed. Fortunately, too, the spot on the canyon from which she fell was only thirty feet above ground. An additional five to ten feet would have killed her, no matter how she had fallen.

No brain damage was discovered in the twenty-four hours Stevie was kept awake to see whether her reflexes and eyes gave any negative indication. Her bones were set by an orthopedic surgeon and her legs and hips placed in a cast. The doctors ordered her placed in traction.

Stevie's face and body suffered severe multiple lacerations. The body portions were sutured, but her face was a more serious problem. Stevie's jaw was broken, as well as her cheekbone. The area was a huge swollen and discolored mass. Any treatment had to wait a number of days after the first orthopedic operative procedure was complete.

When the broken facial bones could finally be worked on, Stevie was taken to the operating room for the first of several plastic surgery procedures. The initial work was to fix her collapsed cheekbone and then to wire her jaw together. After four and a half hours under general anesthesia, Stevie was returned to her room.

During these weeks, Stevie was like an infant, bathed, powdered, changed, patted dry. The traction and the casts made her immobile. With her wired jaw, she couldn't speak except through clenched teeth. Initially she was fed intravenously after the plastic surgery. Then in the course of the second day, she was fed through a straw. Everything had been pulverized to liquid, but she still sucked it in with considerable difficulty.

If Stevie had been in control of her emotions, she would have wished herself dead. If she had been less than totally occupied with the quotient of being a patient, she might have begun to think about herself. Although she had all the time in the world, the hours were passed in an anesthetized state, helped by the continuing presence of a TV set in her room that stayed tuned to one station day and night. The sound level was low in deference to her neighbor in the semiprivate room, and on the day that Stevie was aware of what it was she was watching on the TV screen, it marked her return to the world around her. She was beginning to recover.

On that day, her plastic surgeon, Dr. Sam Di Benedetto, inserted the first three wooden tongue depressors in her mouth, after he had removed the wiring in her jaw, commencing the laborious and painful process of getting jaws to open again. Each day another tongue depressor would be added to pry her jaws increasingly wider.

Dr. Di Benedetto, the plastic surgeon, had been

businesslike, but gentle with her. For the first time Stevie became aware of him as a man.

She took a good look at the doctor who had been fooling around with her mouth, her cheeks, her skin, her bones, her teeth, and saw a tall, dark young man in his thirties. His brown eyes danced beneath their impersonal and businesslike demeanor. Stevie took a beat and looked again. He looked like a young Tony Curtis. Through the gritted teeth that Sam Di Benedetto had been responsible for, Stevie managed a weak smile. She knew what the doctors would find out soon. She was getting better. She was interested in a man.

As Stevie began to take notice of the world, she grew sullen and suspicious of Dr. Grossman, and his manner didn't do anything to help. He spoke in a pompous, studied way, emphasizing the pronunciation of his words as if he were giving a sermon. He had the unfortunate habit of using one word (a long one), where two or three shorter ones would do. Stevie thought he was a pain in the ass, at a time when she didn't need any further inconvenience, not to mention any intrusion into the workings of her mind.

Queen of Angels is a large hospital, and although the staff treats thousands, the nurses and doctors that Stevie dealt with seemed genuinely interested. Was that the way everyone handled a suicide? Christ, Stevie thought, what a way to get service! It's almost as if living was so uncertain a gift that the medical profession views it as their responsibility to sell you on it. Stevie surmised that their success at selling people on living was the way they justified their astronomical charges.

Stevie had escaped internal injuries. The vaginal bleeding that first night had simply been her period starting early. If Stevie could have smiled, she might have. That was the one additional thing that she needed to make everything right. What a mess! On some, the birds do shit. For the rich they sing!

When Stevie was first able to communicate, she told the nurse that she was a member of the Screen Actors Guild and was entitled to hospital benefits. It was unnecessary because in the minutes before any treatment the nurse at the admittance office had found the membership card in her wallet.

"Excuse me, Miss Tree . . . I asked you if you had any dreams last night." It brought Stevie back to the present, to Dr. Grossman's office.

"Dr. Grossman, you can see that I am one fucked-up girl. I can hardly talk. Moving my jaw is painful. I'm in a wheelchair, and I can't use my legs. They're in a cast as you can see. I just want to get out of here. And yes, goddammit, I did have a dream, and it's none of your fucking business what it was."

"Why do you feel that way, Miss Tree?"

"My name is Stevie."

"Why do you want me to call you by that name?"

"Because it's my name."

"So is Miss Tree. Is there a reason that you want me to call you Stevie? You call me Dr. Grossman."

"Yes, but I don't like you."

"And if I liked you, Miss Tree, would I call you by your first name?"

"Yes, everybody does. Everybody who likes me. You don't."

The doctor tapped his desk with a pencil. "About that dream?"

"Look, Dr. Grossman. You're only trying to do your job. Let me spend the time here practicing my spelling, or let's talk about the Rams—or let's talk about you. My story is not very interesting. I got messed up over a guy, I had pills and booze and they knocked me on my ass and I jumped. Now, I'm sorry I did it, and I'm going to have to pay the price for the rest of my life."

"Miss Tree . . . how do you feel about being off drugs?"

"Frankly, Doctor, I don't miss them. Maybe I've had too much to keep me busy, and maybe the pain pills that the nurses give me are a replacement, but I don't think that I'll go back to them when I get out of here, whenever that will be." Sheathed in plaster and a white hospital gown, Stevie resembled a grotesque mummified caricature of her former self.

"What will you do when you get out, Miss Tree?"

"I don't know, Dr. Grossman. I'm not fit for anything. My face will be a mess. Not too good for a career as an actress or posing for cosmetic ads. The doctor says that I'll walk, but with some difficulty at first, and maybe I'll always have a limp. They say no, but they lie a lot. So, if you have any ideas about career guidance, let me know. I suppose I could go into brain surgery, or become Secretary of State. Those are good possibilities." She tried to laugh.

"Do you want to talk about your dreams, Miss Tree?"

"No, dammit. I want to get out of here and go back to bed."

They sat in silence for ten minutes. Stevie said to herself that she'd be damned if she'd say anything. Dr. Grossman countered Stevie's antagonism by trying to wait her out. But Stevie was not having any of it. She would not stoop to the nonsense of "being in love with her father," or "wishing she were a man." How could a girl be in love with a father who killed her mother? As for penis envy, "Why not?" What was the expression? "I never met a penis I didn't like."

The nurse finally came and wheeled her back to her room. An orderly assisted the nurse in putting her back in her bed, arranging her stiff white limbs and body in the position most akin to comfort. The trip to the psychiatrist had been exhausting. Stevie fell asleep.

She was awakened sometime later by the sound of a conversation in the next bed. In the semiprivate room the Guild was paying for, the woman in the next bed had a huge family who were continually visiting. The woman was recovering from a gallbladder operation. She was Mexican and loved food and company. The entire neighborhood seemed to take turns cooking and visiting. She was always gracious and friendly to Stevie, offering her Mexican favorites that Stevie might otherwise have tried, had it not been for the ridiculous matter of the way she felt and an immobile jaw.

She heard the sound of curtains being drawn around her bed and the familiar voice of Jon, her hairdresser.

"Some girls will do anything to avoid giving the hairdresser a tip." He grinned impishly, pushing his blonde hair back with his fingers.

"Hi, Jon . . . it was good of you to come. About my eye shadow, do you think I'm wearing the right color for daytime?"

"You're a caution, little Miss Stevie. Love those bruises and black eyes. Très chic!"

"That's what all the boys say. If you don't want to discuss the problem of my eye shadow, perhaps you can advise me on what I'm wearing. You gay folks have such a keen notion of style. Are plaster casts in this year?"

"What happened to you, Stevie? I just got back in town yesterday, and I heard the horrible news."

"Where have you been?"

"I left the morning after Morgan Oliver's party, and I didn't read anything in the papers at all. We didn't get any papers. This friend of mine had the loan of a house in Cuernavaca and the two of us just left town the next day. Did we have a time? I'll tell you about it, but first—what happened?"

"I ran into a door."

"Some door." His mouth took on an expression somewhere between a grimace and a smile.

"Would you buy that a door ran into me?"

"No, I don't think so," Jon mused. "Did he hit you? My boyfriend hits me sometimes."

"No, baby—it was just too much vino, too many pills and I went ass over teakettle from Morgan's terrace into the canyon."

"Nobody pushed you?"

"Of course not. Tell me, what's new?" It was getting hard for her to talk.

"Well, you can guess that I had a lot of explaining to do when I got back from Cuernavaca, I mean at the salon. After all, I did take off without giving them any warning. They were going to fire me. This high-busted queen who runs the shop came over to me and asked me to tell him exactly where I'd been. I told him that there was a death in the family and I was settling my father's estate in Wilkes-Barre. Have you ever been to Wilkes-Barre? I wouldn't take a million dollars to spend four hours there, let alone four weeks. Well, this queen knew Wilkes-Barre and caught me in the lie. Would you believe that?"

Stevie was enjoying herself for the first time in a long while. Jon was wonderful. Perhaps her only true friend.

"So, this queen says to me, 'Sweetie, who were you fucking, and where?' So I took a good long look at Miss Thing, and I told her. Now, I couldn't mention my friend's name to you, Stevie, even though we're the best of friends. He's a very prominent TV actor, and he hasn't come out. Nobody knows he's gay. OK, I'll tell you if you insist. It's Curt Robbins, the star of that big detective series on TV. Well, you won't believe it, but when I told that queen who I was with, she almost shit from jealousy. But you know, she realized that I'm a star—and she said to me 'Go get to work, and don't do that again, without letting me know.' Do you believe it?"

"Jon, I'd believe anything you told me. I'm too weak to put up any argument. What's happening in the business? Any news of Morgan Oliver?"

"My, you're sweet on that one? A friend of mine was hairdresser on his last picture. You know I don't read the trades. It's all lies. I'll try and find out from my friend. Stevie, I've got to go. There's a party tonight at Curt Robbins. Well, I'm taking that queen who runs the salon. Sort of a payoff for keeping her mouth shut. God knows, I always keep *my* mouth open, you never know who you're going to meet."

Stevie fell back asleep. The Chicano contingent around the next bed stayed another hour, but the noise didn't disturb her. She was too exhausted to hear it.

The days continued in uniform color and texture. The visits to Stevie's bedside by nurses, orderlies, doctors and occasional visitors were a welcome interruption from the tedium of lying there. Stevie had been able to arrange herself so that she was able to read. She was given pills each night to sleep, but more often than not, she would take them from the nurse and throw them away. It was almost as if the suicide attempt had cleansed her system of its craving for drugs. Even though drugs might ease her nights and the discomfort she felt, Stevie treated the experience in the hospital as a kind of housecleaning. As if only pain could provide the counterpressure for her anger against herself.

On the first day that the nurse wheeled her into the solarium, she saw the backdrop of dozens of patients in white hospital gowns, sitting or pacing in the large hall, strange soldiers united in a battle against pain. Here was a community that existed beyond the war it fought. Through the windows of the solarium, dirty though they were, was a view of smog-laden Los Angeles that remained as a promised reward to all of departure from the hospital and its world of dependence.

As she sat in the wheelchair, a graying, middle-aged man in a robe and slippers ambled up to her.

"You're new here. I'm Morris Amster."

Stevie looked at him. He smiled. "What's a nice girl like you doing in a place like this?"

Stevie suppressed a laugh, because it hurt. Even though the movement of her jaws was improving, her face, still covered with bandages, felt as if someone had poured candle drippings on waxed paper and was about to peel it apart. It wasn't so much the pain that bothered her, as the anticipation of pain. And Stevie knew that Dr. Di Benedetto had several more bouts of plastic surgery with her. How many more, he wouldn't say. It depended.

Morris Amster pulled up a chair and sat down next to her.

"The nurse told me who you are, Stevie. I read about your accident in *Daily Variety*. Tough break."

"Yeah . . . what are you in for?"

"I had a heart attack. It was my second . . . they put in a pacemaker. I'm OK now, better than ever . . . but they say that I need the rest."

"So do I," Stevie said. "Could you ask the nurse to

wheel me back to my room? Nice to meet you, Morris."

"My friends call me Morrie. I'll see you again."

That afternoon in Dr. Grossman's office, Stevie started to cry uncontrollably. It came about after a lapse in Dr. Grossman's usual procedure of noninvolvement with his patients. He was on the phone when Stevie came in. Later, Dr. Grossman would blame himself for the breach of conduct, but it was an inadvertent blessing.

Dr. Grossman was talking on the phone, and as the conversation continued Stevie realized that he was talking to a young girl, his daughter. He concluded the conversation on the phone, "Susie . . . I love you very much. There isn't a thing that you could do that would surprise me or make me stop loving you. Don't worry, honey. We'll work it out. I'll see you tonight."

He put the phone on the hook and looked self-conscious when he saw Stevie. The nurse had wheeled her in quietly. Stevie felt ill at ease. She raced to say something to cover her embarrassment.

"Dr. Grossman, what can I do when I get out of here? I'm not trained for anything except acting. I can't type and I can't take dictation. I can't even become a hooker—with my face."

Then Stevie exploded in tears. For five minutes she continued to cry. The doctor came around the desk and handed her several sheets of Kleenex. Then he retreated to his chair and waited.

"It isn't that," Stevie said. "That's nothing new. I've known all along that I'm in for a very tough time when I get out of here. I don't even want to think about that. I guess what set me off was that conversation you had with your daughter. That was your daughter, wasn't it?"

"Yes, it was. It was very unprofessional of me. Excuse me."

"Maybe it was, but it made me see a side of you that . . . well, I've told you that my mother and father are both dead. That's not so . . . my father's in jail, or somewhere, I don't know. He killed my mother and her lover. I was there at the time. *I saw him* . . . oh, Dr. Grossman, why did I jump off that terrace?"

"It seems to me, Miss Tree, that there were at least a few reasons you might have. Can you think of any?"

"Yeah, I was spaced out."

"But you've been spaced out before and you never tried to kill yourself."

"He told me to jump. Morgan told me to."

"Well, that's a possibility. You may have wanted to please him. Does that ring a bell?"

"No . . . I hated him at the moment . . . and I hated what I had become, because of him . . . you can't have any idea what it's like. He was pimping for me. He had me screwing all over town. And I was into drugs so much, I couldn't get through a day without pills."

"Did you blame your father for killing your mother?"

"Of course I did. My God, Dr. Grossman . . . the man killed her right in front of me. Oh my God . . . and her lover."

"Did she have many lovers?"

"Tons. All the time . . . all the time. I used to keep count of all of her friends. I've never told this to anyone . . . who could I tell? There were over twenty-three lovers she had that I knew about when I got old enough to catch on."

"Would you say, Miss Tree, that you had that many lovers?"

"I can't count high enough . . . but my mother was married—she had a child, me. She was nothing more than a prostitute."

Dr. Grossman sat there, tapping his pencil.

"And what you're saying, or not saying, is that I was one—correction—am one too."

"Correction, Miss Tree . . . *was* one, but only in *your* eyes . . . and that may have been the person who was no good, the bad person who was the prostitute, the bad person who had no use for herself, for her body, for her spirit, who had no self-respect."

"And that's who I tried to kill?"

"It's very possible."

"But I didn't . . . that's the joke. I'm still here."

"You are, Miss Tree. But, in my opinion, the person who you felt deserved to die is lying at the bottom of Laurel Canyon, gone forever, and what is left is a young lady, hurt and in pain, but neither destroyed, nor without hope, and certainly not without friends."

"Like who?"

"For one, Miss Tree, me."

Stevie sucked in her breath. It was a lot to digest. It was too much to digest. It wasn't enough to digest. She cried again, but this time quietly.

"Can I tell you about my dream, Dr. Grossman?"

"If you'd like, Miss Tree. We still have twenty minutes."

Over the next week, Stevie became funny and loving and receptive with a host of people who before had been gray faces in the hospital. She found herself becoming very flirtatious with Dr. Sam Di Benedetto, who also found frequent excuses to drop by Stevie's bed to pass the time of day, even apart from the surgeon's need to check on his patient.

"Dr. Di Benedetto . . . do you do silicone jobs, too?"

"Certainly, Stevie . . . would you like a third breast, or your left one larger? We have a special this week."

"Could I get a third breast, a nose job and a tattoo? What's your price on that combo?"

"Of course, and in the case of that much work, we give green stamps, and a money-back guarantee. If you're not completely happy with the third breast, we'll continue to add another, and another, until you're pleased."

Stevie smiled. She really liked him.

"Now as to the tattoo. What would you like that to say?"

"Just that I'm very grateful to you, Doctor. I know how hard you've been trying to make me look like what I was . . . and how very decent you've been about my bill . . . and well, several other things."

"Another time, we'll talk it over. You're going to look beautiful. That's what I specialize in, turning drab young ladies into raving beauties, then I send them to Tangiers, or I marry them."

"How many?"

"In Tangiers, hundreds—in marriage, another question. I'll see you tomorrow." He turned to leave.

"OK . . . if you say so, Doctor."

"Call me Sam . . . all my deadbeat patients do." With that he was gone.

The next morning, Stevie was wheeled into the solarium. She felt good enough to stare out the window at the gray city in the distance. It was the first day that she could contemplate the future. It was hard to discern one, incapacitated as she was and without the certain knowledge of when she could leave the hospital.

What would she do when she got out? Maybe pose for before and after pictures? She'd have to specialize in the "before."

"Did you read the trades today?"

She looked around and saw the same graying, middle-aged man she had seen several days ago. He was still in his hospital robe and slippers. He had a copy of *Variety* and *The Hollywood Reporter* in his hand.

"Morrie Amster . . . we met the other day—and you're Stevie Tree. I like that name. It has a kind of poetry, and a kind of style. I'm willing to bet that's your real name, not a made-up name. It goes with you."

Stevie looked at him and smiled. It was good to hear that kind of talk. She looked him over, carefully. Morrie Amster was of medium height and plump, with a soft and childlike face. He looked warm and friendly. "Are you trying to flirt with me, Morrie? If you're not, please start, and if you are, please don't stop."

"Of course I am. I've always been a lech for a pretty face. In my time, I had quite a reputation as a ladies' man."

"Try again," Stevie laughed. "I believed everything up to the part about the pretty face."

"As a man who has seen them come and go," Morrie

continued, "I know pretty. Now would you like to find
out what's happening in Tinseltown, the destination of
a thousand souls, the target of a million dreams, the
goal of a zillion heartbeats?"

"No," Stevie smiled, "just read me the daily lies.
And see if anyone is planning a remake of *Scarface*. I'm
perfect for the part."

Morrie laughed. "But *Scarface* was for a man—it was
played by Paul Muni, who I might add, used to be a
client of mine."

Stevie looked at Morrie with new respect. "*Scarface*
. . . starring Paul Muni and Ann Dvorak . . . directed
by Howard Hawks . . . the year—now don't tell me—
1932."

Morrie Amster looked surprised, then smiled and
laughed. "Young lady, I have a distinct feeling that you
and I are going to be great friends, despite the fact that
I usually like younger girls . . . I used to be an agent
. . . As a matter of fact, I still am. First, you're going to
tell me how you knew that."

"I like the movies," Stevie said easily, "and I have a
pretty good memory for facts."

"Then," said Morrie, "in that case, I'm going to read
the trades to you, although you appear to be smart
enough to read yourself . . . and *then*, you and I are
going to talk and become very good friends . . . very
good friends."

"I think you're right," Stevie said simply.

11

At Stevie's request, Cindy Warren had been sending her copies of the trade papers—*Variety* and *The Hollywood Reporter*. They had accumulated during the first few weeks in the hospital, when Stevie had been too tired to read.

Cindy had gladly obliged even though it was expensive, because she substituted this favor for visiting Stevie at the hospital. On her last visit she had nearly fainted from the hospital smells, the sights of the forbidding stainless steel equipment and most particularly the sight of Stevie disfigured and encased in the bed. Cindy put her head between her knees, and with the nurse's help, slowly recovered from her fainting spell.

Included with the trades were two letters from Ginny, which the nurse read to her. Enclosed in the second was a photo of a beautiful fourteen-year-old girl with dark hair and a full bosom. On the back was written, "I really like boys, Ginny."

The letter described Ginny's school, her best friend, and was full of questions about Morgan Oliver. Everyone at the orphanage loved Morgan Oliver. Ginny had seen every one of his pictures at least twice. Ginny concluded the letter, "Gee, am I jealous. Maybe someday you can introduce me to him. *Would* you?"

What Cindy had not told Stevie was that in order to pay her rent in the apartment off Laurel Canyon, she had taken in a roommate, and Stevie's clothes were packed away in a suitcase waiting disposition. Cindy had quickly decided that it was not only out of the need for another paying roommate that she wanted Stevie out. Blame her or not, she couldn't stand the thought of being with a sick person, and Cindy had no idea what Stevie would look like when she came out of the hospital. She knew about the scars and she understood that plastic surgery could work wonders, but one couldn't be sure.

A week's collection of trade papers is a lot to digest. By the time Stevie was ready to start reading, almost a month's worth had accumulated in a pile in the corner of her room.

Initially, Stevie was concerned about keeping up. She read every item in the papers, even news that couldn't possibly have anything to do with her career. *What* career?

And then she saw a short piece about a film starring Morgan Oliver that had recently opened (as of the date of the newspaper) in London. The story gave the first week's box-office gross in English pounds, and Stevie did some quick arithmetic to convert the figure to dollars. It said in the article that it would be held over another week. She looked at the following week's *Variety* and located the story about the London results. She compared the box-office gross for that week against the previous week. Stevie took a nail file from the top of the night table and carefully removed both clippings.

In another issue, Stevie found a piece in Army Archerd's column describing a recent Sunday afternoon party at the Playboy Mansion. She looked at the date on the top of the page, wrote the date in pencil on the clipping and tore it out.

Stevie continued reading. In addition to information of a general nature, she found nine other mentions of Morgan Oliver—new projects he was considering, a piece that mentioned him at a party in company with Denys Dubois, more box-office grosses on his recent film. Stevie tore them all out of the newspapers, an eccentric collector with a singular passion.

When Cindy phoned, Stevie asked her to buy a small copy book and send it to her along with a roll of scotch tape. The supplies arrived, and Stevie inserted the clippings in the book in chronological order. Above each clipping, she wrote the date. With each succeeding week, the clippings and reports of Morgan Oliver's activities grew in her notebook.

During the nights, when Stevie found it difficult to sleep, she took the scrapbook off her night table and pored over the clippings time and again. Stevie had quickly exhausted the pages in her first notebook, and was well into the second. She devoured each issue of the trades to find news about him, then read it several times and finally immortalized it in her scrapbook. If someone had asked her to repeat, word for word, the contents of each and every one of those clippings, Stevie could have. She was becoming the master authority on Morgan Oliver.

Each week the hospital mail brought another statement of hospital costs. Two weeks earlier, Stevie had exhausted the amount of hospitalization the Actor's Union would pay for. There was the possibility of going to a city institution, but that would mean that she would have to abandon the care that she was getting from Dr. Di Benedetto and from Dr. Grossman. No more work was required on her bones. They were healing, and although the surgeon wasn't certain, he thought that in a while, Stevie would be able to walk without a limp. It would take time to recover the full use of her legs, and considerable exercise.

Stevie's greatest concern was about the plastic surgery. She talked about it with Dr. Di Benedetto.

"Sam, what will I look like when you're through with me?"

"Well, in the first place," he remarked with a smile, "I'm going to turn you into a small boy. Chinese, I think."

"Please, I'm serious, Doctor. You've been wonderful. I've paid you only one bill. Rather the union paid it, and I guess I owe you at least ten thousand dollars. How long can you go on? I mean, you don't owe it to me. Will you throw me back into the water in a while? When you're finished being good to me?"

"Actually, I'm the real son of Howard Hughes, and medicine is one of my hobbies." Then his smile faded. "Stevie, I'm interested in your case. I only do work that interests me. I have a good reputation in my profession. I'm young, or rather I was until I had the hospital food for lunch, and my only concern is what I can do to make you whole again. You'll pay me. I don't care when. I really don't. Perhaps when you're out of the hospital, you can wash my car, or something like that, to make up for it. As for what you'll look like, you'll look fine. You're covered up with bandages, and you're still swollen and healing, but you'll be beautiful."

Stevie smiled. "Please go on. I think I like this conversation."

"Well, you can never improve on nature, and you were a very pretty girl. You will still be a very pretty girl when you leave this hospital, but you'll owe me a lot of money—and my car always needs washing."

Stevie couldn't say anything. She took the doctor's hand in hers and brought it up to her cheek. She kissed it and held it there for a moment. Gently the doctor pulled away.

"The most important thing is to heal the scars inside. I'm a terrific outside man, but you'll have to do the inside work."

With that, the doctor left. His assurance of patience in connection with his bill was fine as far as that went, but it didn't satisfy the cost of the hospital care, which was staggering. Like it or not, that had to be paid.

Stevie decided to sell the jewelry that David had given her. Stevie had no idea how much that would bring, and although she still had the Porsche, she was reluctant to part with it yet. Though chances were she would have to. But not yet. Maybe there would be some other way. Stevie had no idea what that would be.

Cindy reluctantly came to the hospital to collect the few pieces of jewelry Stevie was wearing the day David died. In Stevie's room, she tried to avert her eyes, and

it was only with insistence that Stevie got her away from
the window to come over to her bed.

"Stevie, you know I can't stay long. I have a
reading."

"I know, Cindy. Could you reach into my purse. The
pieces I'd like you to sell for me are in there."

When Cindy opened it, she sighed. "Not that
beautiful Piaget watch. Gosh, I wish I had the money,
I'd buy it from you myself. How much do you want?"

Stevie sighed. "There's a silver compact, too . . .
and that heavy gold link bracelet from Van Cleef's
. . . and the gold chains. Could you find a place to sell
them for me, Cindy? And could you do it soon? I really
need the money."

Cindy looked at the jewelry in her hand. "Hmmm
. . . the only thing I'd want is the watch . . . you don't
suppose you could sell it to me on time?" She hurried
to complete the thought. "No, I suppose not . . . I'll do
what I can, you know that. Hmmm, I really *do* like that
watch."

Cindy had sent her the check from the jeweler, and
the barking dogs at the hospital accounting department
were quieted. She still owed several thousand dollars,
but she'd worry about that later.

Stevie rolled her own wheelchair into the solarium
each morning and afternoon. She was proud of her skill
in getting around. On every occasion she looked
forward to her talks with Morrie. If something held her
up, or if he were late, she would be unhappy. Once,
when Stevie was too tired to push her chair, Morrie
came to her room, saw she was asleep, and left. Stevie
found herself talking to Morrie on the most serious of
subjects, without any fear or hesitancy. She was
surprised.

"I suppose men are men . . . and the casting couch
routine is ugly but natural." Stevie continued thoughtfully, "I've never examined the possibility, but if
women were in charge, I wonder if they wouldn't be
involved in the same kind of blackmail men use."

"It doesn't have to be that way, Stevie. I've been in

the business for over thirty years, and I've seen good and bad—and the good ones were power-hungry, but they used it for the perfection of their work, not to get some girl to go to bed with them."

"I understand what you're saying, Morrie . . . but my feeling is that the important people, the stars, are so fucked up today that they don't know when to use their power, and when not to."

Morrie looked at her. "I agree with you, Stevie . . . but please don't use that word."

"Which word is that?"

"You know which word . . ." He looked disturbed.

Stevie laughed. "Oh, you mean fucked up. Morrie, you're very old-fashioned."

Morrie smiled. "And you're a very nice girl. Nice girls don't use that word."

Stevie smiled.

One week later, Morrie left the hospital. What had preceded his leaving had been dozens of very pleasant and intimate conversations between the two of them. Stevie heard endless stories of Morrie's childhood and dozens of anecdotes about his life as an agent. For her part, Stevie was frank with him (not in the same way that she was with Dr. Grossman, but frank just the same). What was even more important was that it was the first time she had ever analyzed her own thoughts about people. It may have been a result of her sessions with the psychiatrist, but Stevie found herself giving thoughtful judgments about life around her. It pleased her to sound so adult. God knows, she thought, I don't have the vaguest idea of what to do with my life, but here I am sounding off about everyone else.

The day that Morrie left the hospital, Stevie cried. He told her that he would be coming back two or three times a week to visit her. Stevie didn't believe him. Morrie looked very different in his loungewear suit and sports shirt. He looked younger and in a way sadder. It was as if the hospital was a natural place for him to be, a place in which there would be people to care for him. Now he was going back to his apartment at the Marina alone. Stevie found herself feeling sorry for him.

A few days later, Cindy came to call on her. And not at Stevie's request. Cindy looked like a fashion ad. Not the least of the items that added to her appearance was several thousand dollars' worth of new clothes. Stevie recognized the stylish cut of designer sportswear, and was knocked out by the sight of a cabochon ruby ring on Cindy's middle finger.

"OK . . . what liquor store did you rob?"

"Stevie . . . I had to come see you. You know I hate hospitals. It's just my way. I have such a delicate stomach, and I can't stand the sight of pain . . . but anyway, I wanted you to be the first to know. I think I'm in love."

"Is that where you got the goodies?"

"How did you know?"

"Put it down to woman's intuition. Come on, Cindy. Who is it?"

"You promise you won't say? You see, he's married and it would absolutely destroy him . . . what with community property and all."

"Cindy. You're driving me crazy. Who is the lucky son of a bitch?"

"Randy Davis. What do you think?"

"My God, how did you snare him?"

"Well, it all happened the day I sold your jewelry for you. I went to this Beverly Hills jeweler . . . he was recommended by a friend . . . and I spent a lot of time getting the best price I could for you, 'cause I know how much you needed the money . . . and after the jeweler gave me the money and I was about to leave, in walked Randy . . . you know how much I like his TV show. I watch it all the time . . . and so, while I was waiting for the jeweler to write out the check, I just went up to him and told him so."

Stevie was drinking it all in. "How old is he? He looks almost sixty. Is he that old?"

"No, of course not. Later on, he told me. I wouldn't ask, of course, and he told me that people think that he's older than he really is. He's actually forty-seven, and very well preserved . . . I mean *very* well, if you get my meaning."

"You mean he fucks a lot."

"Stevie. I wish you wouldn't talk that way. It's one of the only things that I didn't really like when we were living together."

"OK, I give up, little Miss Muffet. Keep going." It seemed as if everyone was getting on her case about her language.

"Well, he thought I was pretty, and he said so . . . he's so charming, and when the jeweler came to give me a check, he thought that I was hard-pressed and had sold *my* jewelry. He told me later that before he made it, he had gone through the same kinds of things. But that was years ago. Now he's a multimillionaire. At any rate, he offered to buy me lunch and we had a divine lunch at the Bistro . . . on Canon Drive . . . the most expensive lunch I ever had. I started with vichyssoise. That's pronounced *vishy-swoz*."

Stevie laughed out loud. "Cindy, you're wonderful. You are really an original. OK, I now know how you met, thanks to me, or to my jewelry, or rather ex-jewelry, and I know that you now have some of your own, and some clothes that must have cost a fortune."

"Randy took me shopping in Palm Springs when we went down there for the weekend."

"When did you go away for the weekend?"

"Right after lunch at the Bistro."

"OK . . . right. That's where those big shot entertainers go for dessert . . . . Palm Springs, bingo, then a shopping spree. Tell me, Cindy. We've never discussed it, but are you good in the sack?"

Cindy stammered. "Stevie, you are my friend, but there are some things that people, even good friends, don't talk about."

When Randy Davis walked into that jewelry shop on Rodeo Drive in Beverly Hills, he was ready for something. He didn't know what. When he walked out with Cindy, he had acquired something. Typical of Randy, when he found a thing he liked, he bought it.

It wasn't always that way with Randy Davis. As a matter of fact, there wasn't always a Randy Davis. He was born Antonio Sarafino in the year 1918 in Brooklyn. As the first child of the Sarafinos he was doubly welcome. First, he was a male heir, and second, he kept his daddy, Louis, from going into the army.

Louis Sarafino was the proprietor of a small shoe store on Columbia Street in Brooklyn. Columbia Street was a tiny enclave near the docks of the East River, a largely Italian community. Louis' shoe store wasn't particularly successful, but he gradually built up a clientele of longshoremen who came for shoes, and who would exchange stolen goods from the docks for shoes for themselves and their families. Louis found it easy to sell off these items to other shopkeepers, or other customers, and it made an unsuccessful shoe store into a successful enterprise dealing in stolen goods.

Louis was not a Sicilian, but he did favors for the families of small-time gangsters in the neighborhood. Soon it became known that his shoe store, which now had blossomed into a small department store, was run by a "friend," and that the prices were fair and the treatment was good.

Antonio was part of the tiny Italian contingent at the parochial school, which had many more children of Irish descent. Although his father was perhaps more well-to-do than the Irish families, the Italians were always looked upon as second-class, and Antonio had serious problems dealing with the prejudice of the other children.

Antonio was a confused victim of a lot of kid jokes among the boys in Holy Name. When the boys changed clothes to exercise in the yard, they would spot Antonio's unusually large penis. As a boy of eight, when other kids were underdeveloped and hairless in their pubic region, Antonio was abundantly gifted. They called it "Sarafino's Jungle." And his cock was an object of awe.

The gift had been noted with pleasure and embarrassment by his mother, when the substantial size of his genitals was evident from early infancy. Marie pointed with pride to her husband and whispered an embarrassed joke, although no one but her husband could hear it.

Initially, Antonio felt freakish and an object of ridicule. The youngsters kept referring to his penis by a lot of names. One of the kids called it "La Tosca." "Would you like to play with his twelve incher—La Tosca?" "Hey, Dickie . . ." "Hey, Louisville slugger."

Antonio's mother, Marie, was a quiet and unassuming woman who doted on her son. The boy was handsome. The dark good looks of his father's side and the soft eyes of the mother made Antonio a considerable favorite among the young girls in the neighborhood. Antonio was no longer a virgin at the age of ten, finding a willing teenage girl and later many more among the Irish girls in the neighborhood. It would have been unthinkable for him to have fooled around with the Italian girls. Even as independent a young man as Antonio was, that was against the rules. The girls in the neighborhood were spoiled for life by Antonio's cock. In later years, they never forgot it.

Antonio's sexual activity got him in a lot of trouble. Provided he didn't get caught, it was OK to screw all the twelve- and thirteen-year-old girls in the neighborhood. It was also OK to do the same to their mothers, particularly if you did get caught by their daughters.

When Antonio was nineteen, he decided what he wanted to do in life. He wanted to become a singer.

His mother, ever adoring, was perfectly willing to accept this decision and—surprisingly—so was Louis. They had never paid much attention to their son's talent, nor had he, and they felt that they could indulge him in it. Louis Sarafino was well-to-do and had only one child.

Antonio decided to change his name, and became Denny Davis, after the fashion of the Irish tenors of the day. He changed it a month later to Randy Davis, and it stayed that way.

Randy was able to get club dates in neighborhood
Brooklyn cabarets through his father's contacts. The
passion in music at the time was for crooners in the
style of Russ Columbo and Bing Crosby, and Randy
found that he got a fair amount of local acceptance
doing Russ Columbo songs in the Russ Columbo
manner.

Later, Randy's career languished after the war until
he played an engagement over the Fourth of July
weekend at The Morningside, a Catskill Mountain
resort.

At the Morningside he met a young Jewish comic
named Joey Morrow. Joey was several years younger
than Randy, and specialized in impressions of Jimmy
Cagney, Clark Gable and other stars of the period.
During the course of the weekend, Randy and Joey
shared the loving attention of one of the female guests,
who kept them both busy while her husband was
playing cards. When they discovered they were only
two of a three-man running game (the third person who
serviced the oversexed lady guest was a bellboy), they
enjoyed the joke, had a few drinks on it and became
friends. They decided to work out an act together,
which became, from that weekend, the comedy team of
Morrow and Davis.

The pair were extremely suited to one another.
Randy was the diffident lover with the mellifluous
voice, crooner and straight man, indulgent with the
brash manners of his partner. What they were on stage
was precisely what they were off.

In the early days of TV, the team of Morrow and
Davis were stars and headliners. But not only in TV
was the pair famous. They played Las Vegas, and had a
successful transition to motion pictures. Their slapstick
comedy was hugely popular.

At the height of their popularity, the team broke up,
and each of them went his separate way. Everyone
tried to figure out why, but there wasn't any more
important reason than the fact that the two of them
were bored with each other. Each of them felt that the

other wasn't pulling his weight, and the point of the
matter was that neither of them was. Joey was worrying
about everything else but show business, investments,
politics and self-improvement, and into new passions
all the time. Randy was drinking heavily and only
interested in exercising his cock.

Joey Morrow continued his career as a motion
picture producer and comedy star in simple-minded
movies that did very well at the box office, and Randy
Davis took it easy, and amazingly his popularity grew
along with his increased reputation for booze and
broads.

Famous legends abound in show business—the size
of Jimmy Durante's nose, the amount of booze that W.
C. Fields could drink, but there was no legend more
useful than the one that surrounded Randy Davis'
cock. In the booze palaces all over the U.S., the game
rooms in Las Vegas, and thinly veiled in gossip
columns, the legendary proportions of his tool were
noted time and time again.

Some had said that he had to have it strapped down
to the side of his leg so that it didn't show in
performances. Some said that he wore a metal cup to
keep his perpetual hard-on in place. Some said that he
had to get laid three times a day, otherwise he would
have severe migraine headaches.

The truth was that Randy had some time earlier
stopped functioning very well with women who weren't
patient and paid for. He had a big reputation among
very expensive call girls as having one of the laziest
pricks in showbiz. Big but lazy.

Randy was bored except in the company of his
compadres. His friends didn't have to be Italian, but it
helped. They did have to be fun-loving, hard-drinking
and enormously successful. He preferred the company
of his buddies to any woman, but his yearning to be
youthful and vigorous made him continually search for
the right combination of soft, firm yet yielding flesh that
would make him fifteen years old, fucking everything in
South Brooklyn, time and time again. That was the

secret—the fucking time and time again, not just
rationed portions for a nearly sixty-year-old man
having a tough time getting it up.

In that particular jewelry store on that particular
afternoon on Rodeo Drive, he found such an experience awaiting him. Cindy Warren, Formerly "Miss
Tennessee," made Randy Davis feel very young again,
and that first weekend that the two of them spent in
Palm Springs was like Brooklyn in 1943, or The
Morningside Hotel in the Catskills with fucking around
the clock, and a cock that didn't know the words "no"
or "maybe."

Tomorrow might never come for Randy Davis, but
with "Miss Tennessee" his cock was fantastic today
. . . and that's how love came to Cindy Warren, once
an impoverished resident of Laurel Canyon.

After Stevie hugged Cindy goodbye, she had lunch
and waited for Morrie's visit. She got a phone call from
him instead, saying he'd come tomorrow. He was busy.
Stevie was disappointed and suddenly she felt very
alone. She hadn't realized how much she depended on
his company.

When Morrie showed up the next day he was smiling
and appeared so pleased and self-satisfied that Stevie
was annoyed.

"OK . . . who did you kill? And why didn't you
come yesterday? I was lonely." It was the closest she
could get to being demanding.

"I had something very important to do . . . Stevie,
you're moving in with me."

"Next case!"

"I have a little money, you know . . . I saved quite a
bit over the years, and I have this condo at the
Marina . . . it's really very nice . . . one bedroom and
a terrace . . . a full kitchen. Well, I had the idea
several weeks ago that you don't have anyplace to go
when you get out . . . no money . . . and no job . . .
and I thought that I could help you on some of those
points. Yesterday, I sold the condo . . . and rented a

bigger apartment, with two bedrooms . . . and two baths. It has a terrace overlooking the Marina. You'll love it. No demands, if you understand what I mean."

Stevie was struck dumb.

"And then I was thinking—I'm still an agent. There are some of my old clients who would come with me in a minute if I went back in business . . . and, Stevie, you could help me. You're a smart girl and you know the business . . . and you're good with people . . ."

Stevie just stared. Life was coming back to her.

"Another thing . . . and I hope you won't mind. I paid the hospital what you owed them. You don't owe them a thing . . . your doctor, Dr. Di Benedetto must be crazy . . . or crazy about you. That's what it is. He wouldn't accept my money for his bill. He said something to me about the deal you have to wash his car. Nuts. All those Italians are nuts. Hey, Stevie . . . you're crying."

"Well, wouldn't you?" Stevie asked as she reached up and kissed him.

The day before Stevie left the hospital, she had a final session with Dr. Grossman.

"Miss Tree, I know that you're leaving tomorrow, and I want you to know that you can phone me anytime if you have something that comes up you'd like to talk about."

"Thanks, Dr. Grossman. I think these sessions have been very helpful . . . but you know, the more we talked, the more I discovered there was to talk about."

"When you begin to be more in touch with yourself . . . that can cause new and different problems. You've repressed these emotions so long that you've defended yourself against everything. It's become a habit with you."

"My dreams have started to get violent, Dr. Grossman. I'm a real killer now—and a bloody killer at that. I'm tiny in most of them. Big cars, big houses, big everything, and the people are all giants except me."

"That's the way it appeared to you as a child."

"Yes . . . I know . . . and I know why I've been

keeping that scrapbook about Morgan Oliver. Dr.
Grossman, I have three books of clippings about that
man. I've changed my mind about him—he destroyed
something in me—not only my face. I know Dr. Di
Benedetto says I'll look OK . . . but it was my self-
respect he destroyed . . . He made m‿ want to kill
myself, even if it was the bad part of m‿ . . . Morgan
Oliver is in those scrapbooks . . . and when I look at
them, he's all mine . . . and I'm not going to stop. It
may sound silly, Dr. Grossman, but I'm going to know
more about Morgan Oliver than he does himself . . .
and someday"—her eyes were blue ice—"I'm going to
destroy him. How does that grab you, Dr. Grossman?"

Dr. Grossman didn't say a word. He stared at her for
a moment or two, and then stood up. "Our time is up,
Miss Tree."

With that, Stevie walked slowly out the door. She
needed her cane, but she felt stronger than ever. The
next day Dr. Di Benedetto came to her room. When he
lowered the shades to darken the area, she waited
breathlessly while he carefully removed the bandages
on her face.

When it was done, he handed her a mirror.

Stevie waited a minute. "How do I look?"

The doctor replied, "I'm partial. I like my work and I
like the girl."

Stevie looked.

For the second time that week she cried for joy. She
hugged Dr. Di Benedetto, still crying. The nurse left
the room.

"Just a few tiny scars . . . after all that mess . . . oh,
Doctor, if I do get it together again, it will be you who
made it possible."

"Now, Stevie . . . you do have to continue to see me
for treatment . . . and then there's my car to wash
. . . and I intend to see a lot of you for personal
reasons, too, Stevie Tree."

One hour later, Stevie was dressed. There was
nothing she could do to her hair. It was flat from lying
on it. She was pale and thin. She had lost ten pounds,

and her eyes were red from crying. She walked slowly down the corridor toward the exit. The nurses and patients she had known, the ones who remained behind, were at the end of the hall to say goodbye. They had given her a farewell party the day before in the solarium.

The elevator arrived at the third floor and Stevie got in. The door closed and it descended to the hospital lobby. Morrie was there to meet her, in a sports shirt that was far too loud. He had a grin on his face. Morrie took Stevie's suitcase and the two of them walked to the hospital exit, and out the door to his car.

In a few more months her limp would be unnoticeable. Her tiny scars would all but disappear, and Stevie was starting all over again at the very beginning.

12

It was the third date that Sam Di Benedetto had with
Stevie that month. For every time that Stevie accepted
a date with him, she turned down one, and for every
invitation that she received from him there were at least
two phone calls inquiring about her health.

Sam Di Benedetto was falling hard for his patient
Stevie Tree.

They were drinking at Jack's at the Beach, overlooking the Pacific. The doctor had arranged to meet early
for dinner, so they could sit in a booth overlooking the
water and watch the sunset. It was nearly six and the
sun was still high, making a metallic mirror of the
surface of the water. There was a gray plastic curtain
over the expanse of glass, which made the blinding light
bearable. However, in a few minutes, the vista would
change and the mountains of the Santa Monica range
would be free of the glare. The slanting rays of the sun
would make the sun gentle, drifting into a warm red
sunset . . . The day would be at its most intimate, most
romantic hour . . . and San Di Benedetto thought
—maybe, just maybe.

Stevie moved her long, lean body into the booth. She
was late. She had worn sunglasses to fight the bright-
ness on the drive to the restaurant, and they compli-
mented the oval of her face, with her ash blonde hair
cascading over a white silk blouse. She wore a thin gold
chain around her neck with a tiny pair of green dice
hanging from it instead of a locket. They were the same

dice she had been given by the young Chinese boy James Po on the bus from St. Louis, years ago.

"Sorry to be late, Sam . . . there was some business that came up at the last minute. Morrie was out and—why are you looking at me that way?"

"What way is that, Stevie? Surely, an intelligent girl like you has seen the awed stare of an ungainly eleven-year-old admiring a very beautiful woman. What passes on my face for stupidity is, Stevie, apart from that possibility, a sense of admiration for one of God's loveliest creatures, wearing an outfit suitable for an angel, or a devil. Perhaps you are a witch." His eyes glowed at the prospect. "Help me out," he laughed. "I'm lost in my words."

"You should be an agent." Stevie smiled. "That sounds like the kind of doubletalk I give someone when it turns out what I just sold him I don't even own."

"You look great."

"Thanks to you. I said that before . . . and I mean it, not only because you repaired this monster of a face, but because you've given me confidence in myself."

"That monster of a face you're talking about should be in pictures. You could go back, Stevie. The scars are minimal, and time and makeup would cover them."

"I couldn't go back, Sam. I just couldn't. What you don't understand is that for the first time I've turned into a person."

"What were you before, a rabbit?"

"No . . . I'll tell you, but first, order me a drink."

The waiter arrived and took their drink order. The sun had just turned from white to orange. 'The time of the day was perfect,' thought Sam. 'Jesus Christ, here we are, and we're going to be talking philosophy and bullshit, and all I want is to wrap her in my arms and hold her, and—hold it, you are behaving like a jerk.'

The waiter brought the drinks.

"Sam, it's difficult to explain. You know about me. As a doctor you had to. You saw me at the worst time in my life for me, but you saw me at a time that was the best for you. You were my lifeline. I don't think that I'll ever be the way I was in the hospital."

"Not unless you fall out of an airplane."

"Dammit, Sam. You know I jumped . . . but part of me ended that night in the pits of Laurel Canyon, and part of me was born the next day. You might say that I presided at my own funeral."

He smiled. "Just so long as it wasn't mine."

"It's a very heavy number I'm trying on for size, but I've got to tell you that I've never been happier, never been more content with my lot, never worked harder, and I love it."

"How's Morrie?"

"He's wonderful, Sam. He is a saint. We're getting new clients all the time—not big ones, but some good character actors that are always in demand. We're making a little money. You know it seemed crazy, trying to run a talent agency from Morrie's apartment in the Marina, but our clients don't seem to mind. They deal with us on the phone, and if there's something they want to see Morrie or me about, they get out to see us on the freeway, and they like it—the notion that there's some stability to their agent. It's as if seeing us in the place where we actually live means that we're real." She moved her hands in eloquent gestures to punctuate her comments. "Instead of the usual Hollywood rat race, they're into the Marina rat race."

Sam put down his drink. "Stevie . . . let's go to my place," he said and immediately regretted his awkwardness.

"If you want, Sam." She tried to lighten this new turn of events. "Tell me, do you fool around?"

"Only with my patients, my ex-patients, and my nonpatients."

"I think I fit into all three categories." Stevie felt good about herself. In the time since she'd left the hospital, she felt as if she'd lived a lifetime, and a lifetime in which she'd built a new world and a new Stevie Tree to live in that world.

They laughed, and Sam moved closer to her in the booth, motioning to the waiter to bring the check.

In the six months since Stevie had left the hospital with Morrie, a flower had blossomed, and reached a state of vigor that defied logic. She had grown stronger and her strength came as an outgrowth of her efforts to make the agency go. It was an act of God, thought Morrie, it couldn't have happened any other way. To have had a second heart attack, to have faced the bleak recovery period following the operation for his pacemaker and the certainty of returning to the solitary life he knew in his apartment in the Marina, was all that appeared certain. What was uncertain was how long he would live. How close was he to another heart attack, possibly fatal? The prospect of the certain and the uncertain made for a very bleak outlook indeed. But then he met Stevie, and somehow he knew that his future was to be involved with this remarkable young lady. The days in the hospital, when they talked, made him more certain. He needed her essential goodness, her vitality and her youth. He needed more than that. He needed to be useful to someone in the waning days of his life. He had no family, no attachments. He had built no relationships in which the warmth of his friendship, the gift of his spirit could be imparted to anyone. And then there was Stevie. The solution was incredibly simple. Once he realized what needed to be done, it was easy. It seemed very possible that he could build an embryonic talent agency once again from his apartment. It was insane, but what isn't?

The first steps were faltering. Morrie made innumerable calls to some of his former clients. They were commercial actors, variety performers, club acts, animal acts. All of them were pleased to hear from him. Some were represented by agents and were happy. Others said that they would consider coming along with Morrie, if he could find them work. At present they found their own jobs.

After several days they had a list of talent available

for representation, but they would make no commitment until there was some indication of Morrie's being able to do something for them.

"It's like the chicken and the egg."

She stopped and thought. "Morrie, why don't we give them a free sample of our skill as agents?"

"What do you mean?"

"Say to them . . . sign with us, and it will be subject to cancellation on thirty days' notice . . . If you sign, then we'll get you the first job free of commission."

"That's not very good business, Stevie."

"Morrie, I know it isn't, but it's a way to get some merchandise in the store. Actors will believe us when we tell them that. We'll be putting our money where our mouth is, and they'll like it—I promise you, Morrie . . . and while you're doing that, I'll sell them. I have an idea—what if we decided to find a way not to sell them one at a time, but, say, all together?"

"For what, Stevie? Cattle fodder?" He admired her spunk, but Stevie was talking more than a little crazy.

"Morrie, listen . . . I know I can do it . . . I wish to Christ I were strong enough to get out and make the sale, but Morrie, I promise you. Get the merchandise, because I'm gonna sell it by the carload."

Morrie was skeptical. He didn't think Stevie knew what she was talking about. She had no experience, but by God—this was the most fun he had had in fifteen years, and he had made it happen by convincing her to move in. If he could do that, well, maybe there was a God, and if there was a God, then it might just be possible for the two of them to succeed. But how? What's the difference? he thought . . . I'm having the time of my life. Stevie retired to a phone.

"Yes, operator . . . I want Battle Creek . . . the number is 987-6000. No, I don't have a particular party . . . I'll speak to anyone who answers."

"Good morning . . . Consolidated Foods . . . start the day the Consolidated Way!" The operator's voice was bright and cheerful—like breakfast food, Stevie thought.

"Can you tell me who is in charge of your advertising department?"

"Is that advertising for our breakfast cereals, our coffee division or our cake mixes?"

"For your breakfast foods."

"Mr. Fred Benson is senior vice president of the breakfast food division. Reporting to him is Clark Janson, who is marketing manager of the grain and cereals division."

"Yes, please go on."

"Mr. Janson is out of town right now, but he has an assistant, Mrs. Barnett. She's conducting a marketing seminar in Cleveland. Would you like to speak to her secretary?" The voice buzzed with professional courtesy.

"No," Stevie said. "Please let me speak to your president."

"Charles Caroll is the president of Consolidated Foods."

"Yes, that's who I want."

"Hello, Mr. Carroll's office."

"Good morning. My name is Stephanie Tree and I'd like to speak to Mr. Caroll."

"Will Mr. Caroll know what it is in reference to?"

"Without a doubt."

"Please hold a moment."

"OK." Stevie could hear the hold button click, then the secretary was back on the line.

"I'm sorry. I've checked . . . and Mr. Caroll says he doesn't know you. Would you like to write Mr. Caroll instead?"

"No . . . just mention the following to Mr. Caroll . . . Tuesday, May 13, six o'clock."

"Please hold on a minute."

"OK."

"Hello, Charles Carroll speaking. What is this about Tuesday, May 13th? Is this some kind of game, young lady? We have lawyers in my company to deal with this kind of blackmail."

"May 13th, 6 P.M. was the time I was born, Mr.

Caroll . . . and if we have a successful conversation,
I'm going to give myself a wonderful birthday present.
If not, I may hang myself." She heard a chuckle at his
end.

"I've been through days like that before. I like your
approach. What are you selling, Miss Tree? You're not
related, are you, to the Philadelphia Trees . . .
Marietta and that tribe?"

"Are they rich and successful?"

"Oh, very."

"Mr. Caroll, you check with them, and if they say
we're related, it's fine with me."

He laughed. How many times during the course of a
day does the president of a billion-dollar corporation
deal with a bright, funny, sexy-voiced young lady, who
sounded like she must be pretty.

"You're calling from Los Angeles? I get out there
every so often. How can I help you?"

"Mr. Caroll, I'm a talent agent, and as everyone
knows who looks at a calendar, this is 1974. In two
years, America is going to have the biggest celebration of its life, its two-hundredth anniversary. Now I'm
sure you and your people have been racking your
brains to find a way to tie in your products with the
spirit of America. If you find a way to do that, then not
only do you have your own advertising to work for you,
but the billions of dollars that the country will be
pouring into the festivities will be working for you,
too . . . and if that isn't enough, then you can identify
your company with the spiritual and moral values of
America—at no cost to you."

Charles Caroll thought to himself, 'Not one idiot in
my marketing division has been giving any thought to
the Bicentennial, and we're coming out with a new
breakfast cereal in a few months.'

"Miss Tree, what would you, a consumer, think
about something called 'America's Breakfast,' the
patriotic way to begin a day?"

"Mr. Caroll . . . that's fantastic. Is that from your
advertising division?"

"No," he said proudly. "I just made it up. After all, I am the president of this outfit . . . and I've got to be good for something."

'She sounds like a terrific girl,' he thought, 'young, bright . . . wonderful voice . . . I'll bet she *is* good looking. The bright ones usually are. And I do get to California often.'

"Miss Tree, you don't get to Battle Creek very often, do you?"

"No, but I'm sure you get to California, Mr. Caroll."

"What is your idea?"

"We represent some of the most entertaining variety performers in America—worthwhile, wholesome entertainment—with the kind of traditional values that 'America's Breakfast' has . . . I thought we might design a series of commercials, beginning with perhaps twenty seconds of entertainment, leading into your commercial. It would be in your image. It would deal with the history of entertainment, everybody's favorite business—and would be an absolutely different pitch from any other breakfast-food maker."

Caroll caught the spirit. He was enjoying himself. "How about 'Entertain yourself, America'? We'd show the entertainment and then show the dancers or jugglers for twenty seconds . . . then say something like 'Entertain yourself at breakfast with America's Breakfast, two hundred years in the making . . . and blah, blah . . .'"

"Mr. Caroll—you're a genius. You give me goose pimples."

Stevie knew she could do no wrong now.

He continued, "I really like it, too. You aren't just saying you like it to make a sale, Miss Tree? You wouldn't fool an old man?"

"Honest injun, Mr. Caroll, and you sound like a man in his late thirties, awfully young to be running everything."

"Miss Tree . . . now you hold on . . . I'll put my secretary on the line, and I want to get your name, your company's name and all of that . . . I think you've got

something, really something. I thank you on behalf of
Consolidated. Do I sound that young? I'm a couple of
years older, but you'll see for yourself when I get to
California. Now, hold on, Miss Tree . . . my secretary
is going to pick up. Don't hang up now."

Stevie whistled under her breath. 'I'll hold on
forever,' she thought. 'Mr. Caroll, you great big
billionaire, you. I'll even eat your cereal.'

The man's voice came back on the line after his
secretary got the information.

"I'm glad you called us first, Miss Tree. We've got all
the information we need for the moment. You'll be
hearing from us."

Stevie hung up the phone and looked back at Morrie,
who was staring at her, shocked and bemused. "What
was that all about?"

"I don't believe it," she said, "I actually spoke to the
president of that huge company . . . after I couldn't get
anybody else."

Morrie was bewildered. He listened to what Stevie
told him, but he didn't understand how anything would
come of it. He had already made a few calls to clients
and explained the "free sample" notion, and they had
readily accepted the idea. It's not very good business to
work for nothing. That much Morrie understood. He
imagined that Stevie would learn that in time.

While they were considering what to do next, the
phone rang. Stevie picked it up.

"This is Mr. Bruce Thompson's secretary at
D.D.&O. May I speak to Stephanie Tree?"

"This is Miss Tree."

"Can you hold for a moment for Mr. Thompson?"

"Gladly."

"Hi, Steffi . . . Bruce Thompson, here."

"It's Stevie . . . hi, Bruce." Stevie was beaming.

"Say, Stevie . . . thanks for correcting me . . . we're
the advertising agency that handles Consolidated . . .
we don't handle all of their business, don't get me
wrong, but we do have a very big share, all their
breakfast foods, some of the instant coffees. I was

talking this A.M. to Mr. Caroll, you know, C.C., about some ideas that the agency has been putting together for the last year on the Bicentennial celebration, you know, two hundred years of America and all that . . . and C.C. thought that I ought to give you a call, seeing as you might have some ideas we could tie into."

"I'm pleased you called, Bruce." She had certainly pushed the right domino the right way, judging by how fast things were happening.

"Are you a personal friend of C.C.'s? Not that it makes any difference."

"I'd rather not answer that, Bruce, for obvious reasons."

"Oh, of course . . . what with Mrs. Caroll . . . I mean . . . never mind, you know what I mean. In any event, would it be convenient for you to come to the agency and talk this over? You're at the Marina . . . strange place for a talent agency, but I guess we could come out there . . ."

"Of course we'll come to your offices, Bruce. My associate Morrie Amster and I. How would it be for eleven tomorrow?"

"Good . . . Oh! Just a second. Miss Jensen, excuse me a moment, Stevie . . . I just want to check out my secretary and see. Miss Jensen, cancel everything for tomorrow morning . . . and I want all the right people lined up for eleven A.M. to discuss a major promotion for Consolidated . . . Are you still there, Stevie? OK, eleven it is . . . and save time for lunch afterwards, say, at Perino's? See you tomorrow, Stevie . . . Bye."

"Bye." He sounded like an ad man, slick and well-packaged. Stevie tried to visualize how he would look, but put it out of her head.

Morrie had been further bewildered by the second phone call and now was hopelessly enmeshed in an arena of business he knew nothing about. He understood the buy and sell of a TV variety show. The show had fifty-four minutes to fill. The star would do fifteen minutes, and the key guest up to ten. That left about thirty minutes to fill with acts, and if you had a name they would pay so much, and if they had overspent their budget they'd *hondle* a little. And you'd *hondle* back, and then you'd send a case of whiskey to the booker for Christmas, his birthday, and maybe his wife's birthday, and you'd get your share of business. And that was that.

This was very different. Two phone calls. One to the president of a billion-dollar company, and the second a call from his advertising agency, and if what Stevie said was accurate, everybody was hot for something that nobody understood. What gives?

Stevie tried to explain. "Morrie, it's the Emperor's new clothes approach. The emperor, that is Mr. Caroll, is in love with an idea. I'd like to think that it's my idea. Frankly, when I first called him on the phone to speak to the advertising manager, I had one idea, but when I started to speak to Mr. Caroll, I cooled it and let him tell me his idea. Now, Mr. Caroll has the money to promote his ideas, and that's all there is to it. If we let him tell us what he wants, he'll buy what we've got to sell."

"I don't believe it. I don't believe it." Morrie continued his phone calls to line up the talent.

The next day Stevie and Morrie drove down into L.A. to the West Coast headquarters of D.D.&O. in her red Porsche. She hadn't driven it in a long time, but Morrie had kept it cared for and garaged. Morrie held his breath as he watched the speedometer hover at 80 along the freeway. Stevie cut in and out of lanes with one hand on the wheel, pausing to wave to other Porsche owners in the great club of German autodom.

Stevie had spent an hour deciding what to wear and another half hour changing to something else. In the final analysis, she had decided to play the part of a young lady, who just might be the California girlfriend of the president of Consolidated. It would be wrong to lie directly (unless it were absolutely necessary), but if such status should be inferred, well, what the hell.

To look the part, she had to figure what sort of man Charles Caroll was. She had very few clues except that he was self-conscious about his age. Therefore Stevie tried to look her oldest. Charles Caroll would not want to be seen with jailbait.

He obviously had some fears about Mrs. Caroll, too. Bruce Thompson had said as much on the phone. Therefore, Stevie tried to look like someone Caroll might pass off as a professional person (not a professional hooker, of course). And so, Stevie decided to look very businesslike, very New York, very professional and somewhat severe.

In her less than well-to-do days, Stevie patronized a secondhand store that specialized in selling the designer clothes of the very rich. With an eye for style, Stevie had wandered through the shop, amazed that in one place she could see, touch and feel Balenciagas, Chanels and leading American designer clothes. She had bought a beige Adolfo suit, trim, tailored and very expensive in its first incarnation. Luckily Stevie had a pair of expensive tan shoes that would work, and a matching handbag. That, plus a beautiful green Hermes scarf, with its brilliant print of Paris, completed her look. (If only she hadn't been forced to hock her jewelry.) The scarf Stevie tied casually around the strap of her purse, and when she presented herself to Morrie, Stevie knew it was going to work. The way he looked at her made Stevie realize how every other male pair of eyes would look, and apart from that Stevie felt she had a hot hand.

Morrie wore his full leisure suit, light blue acrylic and a bright orange sports shirt, open at the neck. Stevie knew it was a different uniform from what they would meet, but she knew that Morrie's amusement park colors would not make or break the deal.

On the drive downtown, Stevie worried more about her face than Morrie's appearance. The scars were visible. They weren't pretty, she thought, but on the other hand she was looking *for* them. What would others see in her face? Would they see a marred beauty? She hoped they would concentrate on her dark blue eyes, particularly brilliant this morning. She hoped that they would be looking at the hair that flowed over her shoulders and shone particularly now.

People have looked worse, she thought, remembering Quasimodo.

The reception area of D.D.&O. was exquisite. Brass and copper rectangles framed the mirrored walls, and the solitary receptionist sat at a marble-top desk. The furniture was rich brown leather, and the carpet was specially designed with the initials of the firm repeated as a pattern.

'What God would have done if he'd gone into advertising,' thought Stevie.

The receptionist announced them, and moments later a tall, beautiful blonde secretary entered from a corridor. When she spoke it was with an English accent.

'Who God would have hired if he'd needed a secretary,' Stevie's private monologue continued.

Morrie and Stevie were ushered into a conference room, huge and extravagantly furnished. A solid, thirty-foot marble slab served as the table, around which were fifteen plush chairs on plexiglas frames. The walls were suede and chrome-trimmed. At the far end was a projection booth, and drapes could close off the room for a screening.

The six people scheduled for the eleven A.M. meeting were already seated around the table. They stood up when she came into the room, and the cast of characters was introduced to her by a thirtyish, good-looking man, trim, Gucci-loafered, wearing a $500 cashmere jacket and fawn-colored slacks. He was Bruce Thompson.

Stevie was introduced, and Morrie was introduced, and the names were all a jumble to Morrie, but Stevie remembered every one of them, instantly repeating each name to herself and grabbing it forever.

Bruce Thompson opened the discussion. "Stevie, do you have a film to show us?"

"No, Bruce . . . what I've got is a concept that has to be molded by you gentlemen. Morrie and I felt that we would be wrong to try to immortalize our thoughts without getting an exchange of thinking from you."

Stevie wondered if this dialogue was her own or did she see it in *The Hucksters*, a Clark Gable movie with—who the hell was in that movie?—Sydney Greenstreet, and it was produced in 1946 and it was directed by Jack Conway.

Bruce Thompson replied, "Good thinking . . . when things get stuck in concrete they lose the freshness that makes magic. Another thing, our agency boys are no slouches creatively . . . and when a project gets locked in . . . then, where can you go?"

Morrie sat there in utter bewilderment.

Another man, Stan Latham, passed around some cigarettes, the manufacturer of which he identified as a client of D.D.&O. He picked up a phone near him and buzzed, and then looked over the crowd.

"Who wants coffee? Anybody for tea or a diet drink?"

He took the drink orders and while they waited for refreshments the conversation continued on a more personal level.

Stan Latham took Stevie's suit collar in his hand. "It's an Adolfo . . . I recognized it right away. Wonderful designer. It's all my wife ever wears."

"Stevie, do you get to Battle Creek very often?"

"Not as often as I'd like to." She tried to smile at the group in general.

"I tell you, I *like* that town. There's not an awful lot to do at night, and the Holiday Inn isn't the Beverly Hills Hotel, but the town has character. It's America."

The secretary pushed open the door and wheeled in a cart with the beverages. When they were served on fine white china and the silver service of sugar and creamer were passed around, the conversation swung back to business.

"Stevie," said Bruce Thompson, "tell us about your discussion with C.C. and that Bicentennial thought you had."

Stevie paused for a moment, thinking how to begin.

'Here,' she reflected, 'is where the bullshit stops. The whole nonsense about her getting to speak to the president of Consolidated was a freak happening. The input from Bruce Thompson and the characters at this table had been charming but nonsensical. Or perhaps here is where the bullshit starts. Maybe everything has been a preliminary to bigger and bigger hype. Maybe the only thing that these guys will understand is doubletalk that they can interpret any way they want to. Fuck it,' she thought. 'If that's what you have to do to sell something, who needs it? That's not what I was reborn for in the pits of Laurel Canyon. That's not what I spent a year in the hospital to find out, that I'm a fraud and a poser, and that I'm a phony. I'm for real, so here goes.'

"Gentlemen, I have an idea . . . it's very loose, and I don't even know if it's any good. My associate and I are here to sell you talent, some of whom we don't even know, or even control. But . . . the notion about doing something with the American Bicentennial is a good one. Mr. Caroll, whom I have *never* met in my life, and whom I spoke to just once, has an idea that it could tie into a new product he's created—America's Breakfast. Now that sounds nice, and maybe it will even sell."

So far, nobody had left the room. Nobody jumped out of the window and—more to the point—nobody pushed her out.

"My associate and I come in because we can coordinate this project for you . . . for a fee . . . not high, not low . . . not a commission such as you would have to pay us as agents, but as experts in dealing with other agents who, along with ourselves, will have all the talent you need. We'll be a liaison of sorts. Now, gentlemen, if there's any more hot coffee, I'll have some to hide my shaking hands . . . and if you fellows can convince each other that the project has some promise, my associate and I will handle the talent side for you."

Stevie filled her cup with a trembling hand and added two sugars and cream. Bruce Thompson broke the ice.

"What do you say, guys?"

Stan Latham responded for them all. "I think it's great, Stevie. Glad to have you aboard. We'll send it back to Battle Creek with our total recommendation."

Stevie looked around, slowly putting her coffee cup down. The saucer rattled and the coffee spilled over the rim of the cup.

"Can anyone direct me to the ladies' room? I used to get this way in Vincent Price movies, too."

They all laughed. They loved it. They loved her. And she hadn't pulled any punches, and she'd used her own style.

On the drive back to the Marina, Stevie kept the Porsche at 45 miles an hour. It was below the speed limit, a crime against the power of West Germany. Men in Valiants and Mustangs honked at her. Even driving in the right lane of the freeway, she was obstructing traffic. Stevie didn't care. She was so deep in conversation with Morrie that only subliminally did she see the road. The two of them were buzzing like magpies.

"Did you see the look on his face when I told him that I wasn't going to tell him how often I went to Battle Creek to meet C.C.? He wanted to know how often the old man and I were fucking."

"Stevie!"

"Sorry, Morrie . . . and then that whole routine with my Adolfo suit, and the business of coffee in those fine cups . . . and the dumb, dumb conversation."

"So when did you decide to level with them about your one call to C.C.?" Morrie had been awed by her frankness and control.

"I guess that when the chips were down, I couldn't lie my way into a situation. I've never done it . . . and even though it was important that we make the sale, I couldn't do it there . . . and when the words started to form in my mouth, I couldn't say the lies that were there waiting for me."

"I'm proud of you, Stevie."

"Oh, Morrie . . . I'm proud of myself too . . . This was the first time I ever did something like that—and all on my own. It felt wonderful to be at the center of all those men . . . with them waiting for me to tell them what they should do, how they should do it. I really got started at lunch, didn't I? I almost talked their heads off."

"That was some lunch. Some fancy restaurant, huh?"

"Do you think I'm losing my touch, Morrie? Not one of them asked me for a date."

"Stevie, I think you've found your touch. They were thinking about you in a way men haven't before. You were giving them good advice and leads that—if you'll excuse the expression—you were saving their ass."

"Why, Morrie . . . such language, before a lady."

And with that, Stevie put her foot on the accelerator, floored it, and went through fourth and fifth gears until she got the Porsche up to 90. It was more her speed.

David flashed through her mind. He would be proud of her. He had told her she was bright and now she was confirming that for herself. Of course, it didn't hurt to have Morrie believe in her either.

On the night of the dark red sunset at Jack's on the Beach, she felt that the pieces of her business life were clicking into place, but she wasn't so sure about the pieces of her shattered personal life.

Sam and Stevie had left the restaurant holding hands, but on the ride home both were absorbed in their own thoughts. As Sam exited the freeway at Santa Monica Boulevard, proceeding north to Beverly Hills, he realized that he was very much in love with Stevie Tree. He had behaved like an idiot up to now. How could he change? This was no way to catch girls. He'd never messed up a relationship as badly as he had this one. Sam, at thirty-three, was tall, dark, with Dr. Kildare good looks, and although young, he was enormously successful in his medical career. He could have any girl he wanted. Any girl—married, divorced, single, black, white or green. Apart from the fact that he was handsome and successful, his being a plastic surgeon

was like catnip. Even beautiful women who had no
reasonable need for plastic surgery had a secret concern
that they had to share with him, some little formation
of flesh that might be in need of improvement. For any
and all, Sam was a magician, like the Merlin of old,
changing old for new, beautiful for ugly. And they were
sure as well that he had the secret, not only the secret of
beauty, but also the secret of life that he could entrust
to them. They were sure that trust would never be
broken. It wasn't any wonder that Sam could catch
many ladies. He was used to it. It was commonplace,
and expected. Why had he messed up so badly with
Stevie? He looked at her, but she seemed far away. He
sensed the dread she felt at the prospect of making love
to him or to anyone. Sam couldn't figure it out. He had
been infatuated with women before. There had been a
few he was even passionate about, but Stevie was
special. Sam had never met anyone like her. If it was
possible, the imperfection of the tiny scars on her face
gave her a dimension of mystery that was even more
captivating. He had met no one more beautiful than
Stevie, and her quality of inner grace Sam had never
met before. 'I can think of a thousand reasons why I'm
hooked,' he thought. 'The problem is that there only
needs to be one, and whatever that is, I don't know
what to do about it.'

Those thoughts ended his drive, but Stevie's thoughts
were still flying as he parked the car in the underground
garage. For Stevie, there had only been one man,
David. There had been the disaster with Morgan
Oliver, but that had to be dealt with in the same way
one would exorcise a demon to destroy it. Before
David, there had been emptiness. There had been sex,
but no enjoyment. There had been the dutiful servicing
of men to stay alive in Hollywood, without pleasure,
without emotion and even without appreciation by the
men she gave pleasure to.

And the man who had started her passionless
performances had been her Uncle Bert, the years of
enslavement to his body, doing everything to him and

with him. Those times had been an erotic nightmare she had both dreaded and loved, a sensual torture she had hated herself for and that had degraded her. Even to Dr. Grossman, Stevie had not mentioned one word of her four-year relationship with her uncle. And tonight, for the first time since the suicide attempt, would be an occasion for sex, the first time in a year. 'My God,' she thought, 'what kind of woman am I?'

Sam escorted her from the elevator to his apartment. Stevie had no doubt that Sam would want to make love to her, and she couldn't say no. There were a thousand things she would rather have done, including going to the guillotine, but she would function; she would perform. She knew every move, and yet in her view Sam was a marvelous and charismatic man, who deserved more than just moves. Stevie's problem was not that she didn't want to give him more; there *was* no more. Stevie was biding time, and she didn't know if there ever would be a time when her emotional life would recharge, a time when she would be able to feel anything in the way of passion. And she certainly had no idea of who it might be who could press that button.

"Here it is, Stevie . . . all that Mom and Pop worked their lifetime to provide . . . a son, a doctor and a doctor's apartment."

Sam opened the door and reached inside to flick on the lights. In the subdued light, Stevie could make out a huge piece of sculpture, bathed by an overhead light, directly facing the door, and tiny recesses of light coming from the bookcases around the room.

In the living room there were huge couches over-stuffed and covered with pillows, pulled up around a fireplace. A handsome antique Oriental rug covered the center of the floor, and a glass and chrome coffee table held Indian objects. On the walls, Indian blankets and in other recesses, small Mexican figures. Opposite the entrance was a large picture window and the entrance to a terrace, with a magnificent view of the lights of the city.

"Sam . . . it's beautiful."

Stevie walked around, taking in the details. Sam looked pleased.

"I'm glad you like it. I take the blame for everything you see. I like it. The credit I share with a lot of artists in the past, rug makers, sculptors, Indian artisans."

"I adore it." She meandered back to the center of the room. "Say, do you have anything to eat? Bachelors usually don't."

"Of course I do. I have a whole half a pizza which I didn't eat two days ago, and all that it needs is reheating, and I have some very good chilled white wine. Let's face it, I usually eat out." And for a fleeting second he remembered the dinner reservation he had not canceled.

Stevie followed Sam into the spotless kitchen and helped him heat the pizza and uncork the wine. Together with pretzels, potato chips and wine, they returned to the living room. Stevie picked the largest couch that looked out over the city and began to munch on the pizza.

"It isn't half bad, this pizza. Can you tell me what kind it is?"

"You mean what flavor?" he inquired.

"Mmm, yes . . . I taste tomato and cheese. I also taste tuna fish . . . and cornflakes. Am I right so far?" Stevie was ravenous.

"Holy shit . . . I forgot. Everything fell on the pizza the other night. Look, Stevie, it's no trouble to send out for another one."

"Sam, please don't. I'm enjoying this immensely . . . now the wine . . . that was just opened, so I know that nothing fell into that. Or am I wrong?"

They both laughed.

"Stevie . . . a toast, to bigger and better pizzas."

"I'll drink to that . . ."

"Can I talk to you frankly?"

Stevie reacted as if she were stung. "Of course."

"Well, as you see, I'm not much of a housekeeper . . . but my taste is excellent . . . you said so yourself. What I mean is that I generally leave my clothes in pretty much of a mess, and I didn't even make my bed this morning . . . and the maid only comes every other day . . . and so, even though I'd like to show you my bedroom, Stevie . . . I'm afraid it's off limits for tonight."

Stevie drew in a breath. What a relief, she thought. "Yes, I understand, Sam . . . cleanliness is next to Godliness. I do understand."

"Really, what I wanted to do was be away from the kind of artificial places we've seen each other in, Stevie . . . to be in a place in which we're the only people we need to know, or need to deal with."

"Sam . . . you know . . . I had prepared myself to come here and be raped by a stranger. Now, since I'm to be deprived of that pleasure, I want you to tell me something more about yourself, so I'll at least know who you are."

Sam dug himself into the sofa. He took a bite of the pizza and some of the sauce landed on his chin. "What do you know?"

"Well, first, with the name Di Benedetto, you're Italian."

Stevie wiped off his chin with her napkin.

"Wrong . . . I'm Jewish."

Stevie laughed and handed him a napkin. "Christ, not you, too."

"Yes, baby . . . my pop is Italian and my mom is Jewish. According to the ancient Hebraic scrolls, which I can read if pressed, the child takes his religion from the mother. Frankly, I swing both ways. Next?"

"Well, you're unmarried . . ."

"Wrong . . . I'm married, and have been for ten years."

"You're married? I would never have guessed it."

"No, and neither did I. My wife and I were married when I was in med school. She was, and is, a nurse. Marriage was a stupid idea. She's a terrific person, and I wish her the best of everything . . . but we stayed together a sum total of three weeks and then each of us was bored to death."

"It's tough to come to that conclusion after only three weeks."

"No, we had been living together for two years and it was terrific . . . but marriage changed things. Neither of us was prepared to grow up and be a husband or a wife."

"And now?"

"Well, neither of us wants to remarry . . . and we've both been too busy to get a divorce. I speak to her often. You see, they're out here in L.A., and I see our daughter Laurie whenever I can . . . and whenever either of us wants to be free, we are . . . so there's no rush . . . It's a protection for both of us and it may be good for Laurie."

"Sam . . . I didn't know."

"I know that, Stevie . . . I know more about you than you think."

Stevie started once again. The pincers on her stomach grabbed her and the pressure in her chest indicated the panic she felt at his words.

"I know how tender and loving you would be if you ever had the chance. I know the corner of your eye that tracks a secret sorrow while the rest of your eye is smiling. I know your sense of honor and the trust that you give anyone who would let you share his honor and his trust. Those are all the things I know about Stevie Tree."

In the gentle light of the room and the reflection of the terrace window, Stevie felt vulnerable. And there were small tears, the tears of acknowledgement that someone has said precisely the thing you secretly hope is true but have been incapable of believing.

"Sam . . . please take me to bed. Take me into your bedroom. I want to make love to you."

"I want it more than you know," he said. "But I want you more than just for tonight. I want to hold you, Stevie . . . for a very long time. There's a lifetime ahead of us to make love, but first there's the time to show love."

And he held her tight, and that was all that Stevie really wanted of him.

Saturday—1 P.M.

Stevie remembered that one of her clients had been story editor of a TV series that had secured the cooperation of the D.A.'s office in Los Angeles. The man assigned to serve as liaison for the D.A. was a young law school graduate, Henry Borris, and Stevie had met him during the production of the series. Borris had risen in importance in the three years since. Stevie found his number listed in the L.A. directory and phoned him.

"Mr. Borris, you may not remember me, and I'm sorry to disturb you over the weekend. My name is Stevie Tree, and I was agent for . . ."

"And you're beautiful, blonde and five foot . . . don't tell me . . . six . . . or seven. I couldn't forget you, Miss Tree."

"Well, I hope you mean that, because I have a problem, Mr. Borris."

"Henry, OK?"

"Right, Henry. You impressed me as being very smart."

"Flattery will get you anywhere."

"I think I was a witness to a felony death . . . that hasn't been reported."

"Go on."

Stevie took a deep breath. "Let me describe the circumstances. A young girl died from an overdose of drugs—heroin—I'm sure, and instead of calling the police, a private doctor was brought in to certify the cause of death."

"What did the doctor do?"

"To my knowledge, nothing . . . he was instructed to report the cause of death as a heart attack."

Henry broke in. "That, in addition to the heroin, would be two separate felonies. Please continue."

Stevie breathed deeply. "Well, the people involved are pretty important."

"Where did this young girl get the heroin?"

"From a very important person . . . an actor . . . Morgan Oliver."

"Could you testify to that?"

"Yes . . . but wait a minute . . . let me tell you the rest."

Borris' voice had a colder tone. "When did this take place? And where?"

"Last night . . . at around ten . . . in the home of Nicholas Long. He's a producer."

"I know who he is. And why have you waited so long to report this, Miss Tree?"

"Well, I thought that the people involved would . . . but they haven't. And the girl is being buried tomorrow."

"Look, Miss Tree, give me your phone number. I have a few things to do, so give me the phone number and address of Nicholas Long, and any other details you can think of that are pertinent. I'm asking you once again, clearly . . . will you testify to these things?"

Stevie breathed very deeply. "Yes, I will." She proceeded to give the assistant D.A. all the information he requested.

In Palm Springs, Sy Rosen phoned the compound in Palm Desert where Ted Caramia held court. A giant patch of cultivated green stood like a blossom in the middle of the arid hillside. Around the oasis was a huge fence, continually patrolled. Ted, now retired, had been hugely successful as a singer, actor, friend of presidents, and now a multimillionaire distributor for America's most popular beer.

Randy Davis was in Palm Springs, Caramia's guest for the weekend. Sy Rosen had invited Randy for lunch earlier that morning, and Randy was unusually prompt. Sy was a powerful man. As successful and rich as Randy was, Sy Rosen could make things happen in Hollywood. In addition, Randy was upset by the screening Friday night at Nick Long's and wanted to talk to Sy about it.

When he heard the sound of a car door open, Sy met Randy at the door.

"Randy, please come in. I can't tell you how grateful I am that you made time for an old man."

"Come on, Sy, cut the crap. You're younger than I am."

Sy smiled. "You're as young as you feel, Randy, and today I'm a little on the Methuselah side. Come on in. My wife is at the supermarket, but she laid out a little lunch just for the two of us. Do you like shrimp salad?"

"Whatever you're eating, Sy." The two of them walked through the house and out to the pool. Sy looked at Randy. For a man near sixty, Randy looked very fit. A little jowly, and a little too much to drink. Strike that. Way too much to drink. Randy's trouble was that he liked booze and broads too much. Sy could never understand how a man couldn't discipline himself to stay with one woman and away from alcohol. He had seen brilliant careers ruined by one of those pursuits, and together they were killers. But Randy was still in demand, singing in Vegas, entertaining on TV specials, and he was profitable for the agency. But, good Lord, why did people do that to themselves?

Sy pointed Randy to a chair.

"Sy, what's the problem?"

"Randy, you're on top of things, and I like that. Everything is out front with you. Randy, the agency has a problem and we need your advice."

"My advice?"

"Certainly, you're a man of the world. You've seen a lot. This is a thing that you could help me in. Would you be willing?"

Randy said nothing and gave no indication of saying anything, and Sy Rosen chose to accept that as agreement.

"Good, Randy. Now let me ask you a hypothetical question. Just consider the situation of a family, in which a child—in this case a young teenage girl, falls in with bad people, and that girl accidentally, again just accidentally, passes away."

"The Nicholas Long girl, Sy. Please. Come off it. I was there. That guy Oliver gave her the dope."

"Randy, please, no personalities . . . hypothetical now."

"Yeah, hypothetical." Randy took a forkful of the shrimp salad.

Sy continued. "I think you'll like the shrimp. My wife goes very light on the mayonnaise. So, in the goodness of charity, it appears that if certain people who were in a position to say one thing would forget what they saw, then that hypothetical family could live in peace . . . could hold its head high in the community . . . could continue to contribute to the betterment and the welfare of our industry."

"Look, Sy, I've got too much money, and I've been around too long for this kind of bullshit. I don't give a rat's ass for that guy Oliver. He's a no-good guy, and I don't give a damn what happens to him. But I do give a damn what happens to me. I don't want problems, and when the cops come to call, I don't want to commit perjury, and I don't want to have any part of a cover-up. I'm clean, and I want to stay clean."

Sy smiled. He continued. "Hypothetical is always better, Randy. Just suppose that one person who could be helpful to heal this hurt knew what it was to have trouble . . . trouble like having beaten up a hooker in a hotel in Las Vegas in September of 1971 . . . September 12th, I think it was . . . and that some important friend of his managed to hush it up . . . and how when the time came several years ago to avoid a Senate Committee that was looking for the connection with entertainers and the Mob, some friend of this hypothetical person was able to get the senators to forget about Mr. Hypothetical . . . and how this same person was witness to a number of criminal conspiracies with associates in Chicago, Asbury Park, Las Vegas, while he wasn't so rich, and he wasn't so famous . . . and he wasn't so Mr. Clean. What about those friends of his in the past who were always there to help him? When a favor was needed, it always was there . . . always."

Randy stopped eating. He stared at Sy. Sy chose to take the stare as continued agreement and he pushed his salad away to concentrate more fully on his speech.

"Furthermore, that Mr. Hypothetical, as a result of very serious efforts on the part of his agents, will, this Monday be offered the starring role in a new movie . . . a detective mystery, which will be produced by a major studio, and which will show Mr. Hypothetical as the young, virile, courageous and *loyal* person he really is."

Randy picked up his fork again. His look said it all.

Sy smiled. "Randy, my wife will be so happy you like her shrimp salad."

13

At the end of each day, Stevie and Morrie sat out on the outdoor terrace of the apartment at the Marina to unwind and review the day. The pace was increasing as their business grew. Now they were representing several lounge acts that played Las Vegas and Lake Tahoe, and they were booking comics for guest spots on TV variety shows, but the big growth was in producing entire shows for industrial clients. Stevie was becoming somewhat of a specialist in the introduction of new lines of lingerie, vacuum cleaners, termite control, office supplies and such. Sales departments of these companies could be convinced to put on shows for dealers, with music, dancers and special material, including songs that extolled nonrun panty hose, easy-to-empty vacuums, the joys of ridding one's home of roaches—in fact, anything that was for sale.

It meant securing talent from every phase of the business, and it meant a continuing set of nightmares. Stevie had to mother-hen each and every production. To someone else, it might have been a burden: to Stevie it was a blissful means of forgetting. The only tranquility she seemed to find was in the privacy of her room, staring at the scrapbooks devoted to the life and career of Morgan Oliver—as if by looking hard enough she might find an answer to it all in the yellowing clips.

Each time Stevie read the trade papers and extracted an item having to do with Morgan, for that moment she was in control of a life. Her anxieties could be cut, pasted and bound up in the volumes that rested at the bottom of her closet.

Stevie dreaded the moments of silence, the periods of inactivity. Sunday was painful for her because there was no business to occupy her mind or fill the time. The end of a day brought depression, and only because Morrie was close and business discussions continued, could she calm the inexplicable fears that overtook her. Somehow Morgan still had power over her, and the only magic Stevie had was to contain him somehow in her volumes of clippings. She was captive and captor both.

In her closet, in the six overflowing scrapbooks, the demon was alive, but quiet.

The sun was setting and Stevie went to the terrace overlooking the yacht basin. It was a view that always pleased her, the end of a day and the low sun casting long shadows over the small boats tied at the docks. There were hundreds of them. Across the way were other buildings like their own, peopled with young couples either married or living together, stewardesses pooling their money for rent on an apartment near the fun of the Marina, bachelor singles getting ready for a night of making the rounds. The Marina had all the marks of a small community given over to physical pursuits, sports, sailing, drinking and lovemaking.

Stevie had continued to see Sam. On two occasions they had made love. Sam had been attentive, tender, accomplished and unstinting. Stevie had made all the appropriate moves. She had sighed the perfect sighs, made the pluperfect moans, twitches and convulsions. For the first time, Stevie had *really* faked it, and faked it with one of the most wonderful men she had ever known, a man so decent, so considerate and good that she was repulsed by her own deception. And Sam knew. She knew he knew. Another man might have counted the night as a triumph. Sam had viewed it as an exercise willingly engaged in by an expert who wanted nothing more than to sit on the sidelines, not get into the game. Every move had been considered, and that was what had made it bad. And it was with Sam, a man she owed so much to, a man she would have loved— that is, if she could love anyone.

The second occasion was a duplicate of the first. Stevie smoked some grass to ease her through the barrier to pleasure. It hadn't helped. From that time on, though the two of them saw each other, it was accepted without a word that they would not go to bed. Stevie pushed the matter aside. She rejected all thoughts of sex before they even entered her mind. Stevie's sexual drive was virtually nonexistent. An effective rampart had been built. And worst of all, she wasn't even unhappy about it.

Morrie was still speaking—under the misapprehension that she had been listening.

"It's been unbelievable, Stevie."

"What has?" she asked, coming back into the room and dropping into a chair.

"Frankly, you have. You have an extraordinary head on your shoulders, young lady."

"Morrie . . . I'm learning a lot."

"You are learning so goddam much, so goddam fast that you scare me."

"It's just fun."

"That's the best way to do it . . . the best way. I never thought that I'd have so much enjoyment out of my life. Stevie, you'll make this old Jew die very happy."

"Cut that out, Morrie." But Stevie knew he was joking, was in his own way knocking wood and assuaging the angry Hebraic God. He had never been fitter, never happier, never freer from pressure. They were making money, and the prospects were very good for the future. True, their sphere of activity was small, and they were only representing small acts—but the Consolidated deal had not only been profitable, it had established them as part of a new kind of talent agency. Small, but smart.

Morrie continued, "I've seen all the great agents in

my time, and you've got the same stuff they have, Stevie. But you've got it different. All the greats have it in a special way."

Stevie listened, but her mind was wandering. She looked out the window. The sun was golden pink. It would be night soon. A pair of stewardesses appeared on an adjacent terrace, fixed flowers on a bridge table and arranged candles and silverware. They were expecting company.

Down below, a couple walked arm in arm to a boat tied to the dock. The man, who was carrying a picnic basket, boarded first, then lifted the girl into the boat, set her down and kissed her.

Stevie got up from her chair. In her white jeans and tight-fitting white T-shirt, she looked very pretty, even after a tough day. She adjusted her blonde hair in the magnifying mirror on her desk. Stevie never wore makeup, only some mascara. She reached for her purse and walked toward the door.

"I'm going out for a while, Morrie. Don't wait up for me. I may be late."

"OK, Stevie. Have fun."

Stevie closed the door of the apartment, walked down the corridor and took the elevator down to the street. The sun was setting over the water. It was a short walk to Donkin's, a singles bar in the Marina. Cocktail hour. The place would be jumping, with men and women sizing each other up and trying to connect. She had never been there before, and it might be a total disaster, but after so long she suddenly wanted to feel another body next to hers, wanted to make love. She hoped he would be nice. She hoped he would be gentle.

She hoped he would say, "I love you." But that might be too much to ask.

Stevie took a look at the entrance to Donkin's. Every night of the week, the place was crowded. Tonight, Friday, it was particularly full. Even in her earlier years in Hollywood, she had never gone to a singles bar. It hadn't seemed necessary. There were always calls, dates to be had just for the taking. Some of the out-of-town directors and producers who came to Hollywood to shoot commercials talked about the "great places" all across the country where a stranger in town could always find a little action. According to these "experts," Donkin's was high on the list and worth the trip out to the Marina. A lot of "stews" hung out there, and it wasn't overrun with married ladies out to cheat on their husbands. Not that married ladies weren't goddam good in the sack, said Stevie's knowledgeable friends. Frequently, they were friskier and more willing to experiment than younger girls. Some of them brought their own poppers and ludes. The problem was that once you scored with a married lady, it was tough to keep them off your back. They kept phoning, sending you presents and birthday cards and little notes that always read the same: "When are you coming out to L.A. again?" Stevie's friends said those letters and phone calls were a drag, especially when you had a gal or a wife, back wherever, who opened all your mail.

Stevie entered and went to the bar, which overlooked the yacht tie-up through a large picture window, the pinpoints of lights glittering like expensive jewels one might covet, set in a purple night. The bar was three deep. Everyone was in animated conversation. The disco beat of a huge sound system seemed to overwhelm the room and it was difficult for Stevie to concentrate. She wondered what the hell she was doing there. A seersucker jacket containing a sport approached.

"Hi, my name is Martin . . . What's yours?"

"Stevie."

"You're a pretty girl, Stevie. Were you named after your father?"

"No, after my mother. She was Robert Louis Stevenson."

"Oh, *excuse me*. That's not very funny." The seersucker was looking for sincerity, not jokes.

"I didn't think so either." Martin disappeared, and a new man took his place. This one wore rings and chains.

"Can I buy you a drink?"

"If you'd like. I'd like some white wine."

"Why is it you chicks are only into white wine? What the hell happened to rum-and-Coke and Seven-and-Seven and all those fun drinks?" He motioned to the bartender and ordered a glass of white wine.

"My name's Stevie . . . What's yours?"

"It's not important . . . Are you into threesies?"

"Right here?" she inquired wryly.

"No, I don't mean here, for Christ's sake . . . If you've got a friend, why don't the three of us leave and go to your place? I mean, right after you finish the wine. You've got cute tits."

"We don't have to wait for the wine . . . We could leave now. My friend is a guy and he's black . . . but if you're into threesies, you won't mind."

The bartender handed Stevie the wine long after Rings 'n Things had disappeared.

"Bartender, did that fellow pay for the wine?"

"No . . . it's a buck and a half." 'It figured,' she thought, as she reached in her pocket.

An attractive redheaded girl came up to Stevie as she sipped the white wine. She must have lain down on the floor to get into her jeans.

"You busy?"

"Who, me?"

"Yeah . . . Look, I've got two real cute fellows and we need another girl. We're ready to split. One of the guys has some coke. I haven't seen it, but I don't think he's shitting me . . . We're all going to his place out in the Valley. You wanna come? We could all play house. You into that?"

"Yeah, but not in the Valley. I get nosebleeds going over the pass."

"Well, fuck you too, Miss Smartass. That's the best shot you're going to get all night."

A good-looking man in his late twenties came over to Stevie. He was tall and had dark, classic good looks. He was smiling.

"You're a real sharpshooter."

"You caught my act."

"Not easy to miss. You are one killer lady. Did you lose an election bet?"

"I think we all did," Stevie said. "We wound up with Nixon."

"My name is Ed Holmes. I live in Westwood. What's your name?"

"It's Stevie . . . just plain Stevie."

"You're a little on edge."

"You've noticed."

"You're also a very beautiful girl, and you obviously don't want to tell me your name. This man Holmes you are looking at is a real nice type. He's warm, friendly and affectionate. Given half a chance, he will be loving and gentle."

Stevie looked in his eyes, placing her hand on his arm, and said her first honest words since she entered the bar.

"Ed, take me out of here. I just pray that you're not lying to me."

Stevie was just emerging from the bathroom of Ed Holmes' apartment. Except for one, the lights in the bedroom were out. Ed Holmes had thrown a red shirt over the lamp to create a kind of whorehouse sexy quality in the room. On the bedside table was a tape deck and the music coming from it was Mantovani playing "Music For Lovers" (so it said on the cover). Stevie was naked. She had deposited her clothing on the shower curtain rod.

It had been a fifteen-minute drive from the Marina. There had been virtually no conversation in the car. Ed had started to ask questions and Stevie had parried them all with nonsense answers.

"Ed, let's just forget the small talk. I came into that place to meet a man—to get laid. That's all."

"If that's the way you want it, OK, but you're an interesting girl. You don't have to meet men like that."

They were driving along the Santa Monica Freeway, and Stevie was silent. Ed wouldn't give up.

"Are you married? Is that it?" he urged.

"Please, mister, no more questions . . . I don't want to know where you went to school. I don't have any interest in your church affiliation or whether you like your job or your chances of improvement."

He looked hurt and Stevie could tell that she had been too rough. "Look," she continued, "I think that you're an enormously attractive man, and I'm a healthy woman—so why shouldn't we just make the most of the time we have together? Tomorrow may never come."

He leaned over to kiss her, causing his car to narrowly miss another car.

Stevie took his exploring hand out of her crotch.

"Later . . . when we get there."

They had been at the apartment less than half an hour. As Stevie surveyed the prepared site of the red-tinted bedroom, heard the Mantovani, saw Ed standing in front of the bed in a short robe in acceptable *Playboy* fashion, she thought to herself, Spare me the peanut butter cookies that he prepared for after fucking.

She moved gracefully over to the bed and took off his robe. He stared at Stevie, unbelieving. Her long, willowlike body was spectacular. Her ash blonde hair fell down below her shoulders and the tiny waist accentuated the full richness of her hips. She kneeled down on the floor and took his cock in her mouth. It got hard swiftly and she guided them to the bed. She felt with her fingers in her vagina to see if she were wet. With David, Stevie had been instantly wet, after even the merest contact. Tonight she was dry. Ed began the conventional foreplay, kissing, caressing, sucking on her nipples. Every move he made seemed like an intrusion on her body. What was worse was that he had no idea that nothing was happening. She felt his stiff cock with her hand, and it was as if she were in contact with a garden tool. She stopped his action and leaned over to suck him again. He responded excitedly to her tongue and her mouth.

She felt herself again. She was dry.

"Ed . . . just fuck me, baby . . . Don't think of anything else . . . and don't let me think of anything else."

She turned over on her back and guided his cock, wet from her saliva, into her dryness. Stevie wrapped her legs tightly around his waist. She squeezed him. He let out a little groan and began to rock back and forth. He was huge inside her, and still Stevie couldn't feel a thing. Moments later, he stopped, still hard inside her.

"What's the matter? You frigid or something?"

"No . . . Ed . . . just that I got bad news from home tonight . . . I'll be OK . . . just fuck me, darling. You're the greatest."

It satisfied him, and Ed Holmes went back to his moves by the numbers. Fully ten minutes after he started plunging in and out, Stevie began to gasp and to roll, breathing heavily and making passionate noises.

Later, when Ed finally came, Stevie faked orgasm again. Then Ed got out of bed to offer her a choice of vanilla or chocolate chip ice cream. She hadn't felt a goddam thing.

Next morning, when Stevie left the apartment, Ed was still asleep. Before her return to the Marina she stopped at an all-night diner for a cup of coffee and picked up a paper. The L.A. Times had a small item that captured her horrified attention. A man of fifty-five had been robbed and beaten by a group of teenagers. The man, identified as Morrie Amster, had died at the hospital.

14

The first few weeks after Stevie joined IA were a contrast of abject terror and sheer boredom. Nobody, especially her boss Jerry Fentris, had the vaguest interest in explaining what needed to be done. The boredom consisted of tedious phone calls to clients to remind them of appointments, to obtain tickets for sports events, close up houses, rent houses, obtain plumbers and listen to endless complaints of the most intimate and childlike nature.

The panic came on the few occasions when Jerry Fentris would dash out of his office on his way to a squash game, or a lunch or a haircut and yell on the way out, "Tell Franken it isn't enough" or "Find me that contract for that *fakokta* lounge act that played that week in . . . wherever the hell it was" or "Get the info to Sy Rosen's office right away on the payment schedule on what's-her-name."

Even Brenda, who was of considerable help, had difficulty deciphering this shorthand, especially when most of the information that might have been in a file was secreted somewhere beneath a pile of papers on Jerry Fentris' desk. That litter included personal bills, love letters from ladies he was having affairs with, undeposited checks for clients, and folders for vacations in Aspen, Palm Springs, plus junk-mail letters of inducement to purchase rare stamps, diamonds and second mortgages. Jerry's organizational ability was nonexistent.

Occasionally, walking through the hall, she passed Sy

Rosen or Fred Wine. Neither took note of her existence.

At night in the apartment at the Marina, Stevie spent the better part of a month with lawyers and accountants settling the business she and Morrie had shared. She spoke to each of their clients, who regretted her decision to abandon the operation. But the most wrenching part was going over the files and the accounts—the history of a moment in time that had saved her life. That, and wrapping and packing all of Morrie's personal effects and forwarding them to his brother in Cleveland.

A month later all vestiges of his life had disappeared, and she was alone in the Marina apartment, frightened by the solitary nature of her life, the angry and foreign environment of International Artists, and the sense that once more she was walking alone down a lonely lane, the only accompaniment the gentle footfall of her own tentative steps.

Then one day, not more than five weeks after her start at IA, things began to catch. It was as if she had been plunged into a household of children speaking a foreign language, who couldn't care less whether she understood a word they were saying. Suddenly, as if a veil were lifted from her eyes, she began to act. Perhaps that was what they had in mind all along.

The most serious problem Stevie now had was Jerry Fentris, whose playboy approach to business required someone who would constantly pick up after him.

Jerry Fentris began enjoying life when he was three. He was a beautiful child, beloved by his mother and father, his grandparents and neighbors. He was beautiful, and he had the gift. The gift was the ability to get what he wanted at all times, to manipulate his parents, his grandparents, his teachers, and in later years his girlfriends, his wife and his clients.

Jerry married the right girl, lived in the right neighborhoods, joined the right clubs, met the right

people and was on his way to becoming a successful
agent. The intervention of his uncle Sy Rosen was more
than helpful, it was essential, since even with all the
right elements working for him, Jerry was very much a
lightweight.

Jerry was too good-looking, too much enamored of
the impression he was making to want to get his hands
dirty as a dedicated and hard-working agent. Although
initially he had resisted the idea of a woman assistant,
when his uncle hired one, he quickly discovered that in
Stevie Tree he had struck gold.

Stevie was quick and intelligent. She anticipated
Jerry's every need and those of his clients. Where
Brenda had seemed barely capable of handling the
correspondence and phones before, with Stevie's en-
couragement she developed a huge appetite for work
that made her oblivious to coffee breaks, long lunches
and early departures.

The clients that Jerry represented began to gravitate
slowly to Stevie for answers to questions. Stevie
returned every call on her call sheet, every day, even if
it took her late into the night. If she didn't have the
answer, she got one the next day and phoned again with
the information.

Casting people, producers and directors liked to talk
to her as well. They preferred her to Jerry Fentris.
They didn't get doubletalk. They didn't wait around
endlessly for answers. She began to negotiate deals
with them without subterfuge. When she said that she'd
recommend a deal to a client, she would spend an
inordinate amount of time with the client showing him
why the deal was right. The deals almost always held,
and the producers began to feel that when Stevie said
that she thought the deal would work, it did.

The huge pile of scripts that Stevie had seen on
Jerry's desk, untouched and unread, were part of the
submissions that producers made in good faith to
clients of Jerry's. Jerry had never taken the time to read
any of them himself or have one of the readers

associated with the agency read them and report back. Consequently, unbeknownst to the agency heads, many picture opportunities that might have gone to IA clients went to the clients of other agencies.

One of the many producers who met Stevie for lunch summed it up, "Stevie . . . if you haven't done anything else for me from IA, you've given me 'no' answers when the best answer I got before was the sound of being put on hold."

At staff meetings, Stevie was quiet and unobtrusive. She still sat in a chair by the wall, although all the agents clung around the huge table each morning, sharing information and reporting on problems.

More and more, when asked, Jerry Fentris would turn away from the table and ask Stevie to give the answer to a question posed to him by Sy or the other men around the table.

Sy Rosen stopped Stevie on her way out of one staff meeting. "Stevie, I made the right decision on you. We all like you. I wanted you to know that."

Jerry Fentris was having trouble at home. He had always had a girlfriend on the side, and Mildred, his wife, either didn't know about it, or knew and didn't care. This time it was a black singer, Donna Lally, and Jerry had abandoned all pretense of discretion.

In establishment circles, one-night stands with black chicks were OK, but a relationship with a black girl was bad. Jerry's white buddies wouldn't have cared for it, and blacks don't like white men involved with their women. Jerry was very much alone, and his isolation from his family, his friends and his business associates was becoming more and more obvious.

Stevie and Brenda were continually required to cover for Jerry around the agency. When he wasn't playing tennis or taking three-hour lunches, he was with Donna in an apartment he had rented for her in Hollywood.

Finally Stevie managed to get Jerry to lunch with her at the Brown Derby in an out-of-the-way booth. Jerry had consumed a double martini and was ordering a second by the time Stevie arrived.

"Sorry I'm late, Jerry . . . they had me on the phone."

"Who?"

"NBC . . . they accepted the deal for those specials."

"What specials?"

"I put together a package of Coleman Flack to direct, and Frank Flaherty to produce. It's a summer series of three shots."

"I don't get it."

"We talked about it the other day. The package price is $175,000 apiece. I sold three of them."

"Yeah, but what do Flack and Flaherty get? Remember, young lady, we commission our clients. That's how we earn our living."

"I know, Jerry . . . but I worked out the deal so it's their package. They get their usual fees, plus any profits, and we get to commission the package—10 percent of the total cost."

"You're kidding."

"No, the deal memo will be over this afternoon by messenger. And NBC thinks it may become a regular series if the concept works."

"What concept?"

"I told you, Jerry—it's a salute each week to a different American city."

"That's a shitty idea."

"Thanks."

"It was yours?"

"Yeah."

"It's still shitty," he muttered.

"They bought it, Jerry."

"Where the fuck is the waiter? Are you gonna have a drink, or are we gonna order?"

"Jerry . . . here's the waiter. Captain, I'd like a glass of white wine and my friend will have one more of the same, and can we have some menus? We'll order right away."

"Stevie . . . I'm not happy with your work."

"OK, Jerry, I'll quit."

"No, goddammit . . . it's just that you're forgetting who you are and what your job is. Those deals of yours are OK, but you shouldn't be making them. I should."

"I agree."

"The clients call in, and when I pick up the phone they want you. That's wrong."

"I agree . . . here's the waiter, Jerry. What will you have?" Stevie felt like a camp counselor placating a recalcitrant camper.

"I don't give a shit . . . Order for me, and bring me another martini."

"Two Cobb salads, waiter, and another drink for my friend."

"What do you say to that, Stevie Tree?" he mumbled.

"I say that you're drunk, Jerry, and I say that you're getting ready for a fall, and I say that I have been breaking my ass and Brenda has been breaking her ass to keep your department going and to cover for you. Jerry, you're gonna get in a pot of trouble."

"Stevie . . . you're a woman. What can I do? What am I gonna do?"

"Jerry, marry the two of them."

"Stevie . . . I can't get it up anymore."

"Ever?"

"I mean, with anyone else except my girl."

"You mean just with your *wife* or everyone else?"

"Everyone."

"That's inconvenient."

"Inconvenient, my ass. What would my friends think if they knew?"

Stevie had to stifle a laugh.

"There's no need for them to know, unless you're planning to fuck *them*."

"Yeah, but it gets around." Jerry looked morose.

"So do you, Jerry."

"What do you mean by that?"

The waiter, blessedly, arrived, put down the Cobb salad in a wooden bowl on the serving stand, and began to toss it. Jerry looked grieved and impatient. The waiter performed his functions without regard for the inconvenience of his presence. He finally finished and disappeared.

Stevie thought, 'How much is he saying because I'm a woman, and a woman doesn't mean a damn thing in this town. How much is he saying because he knows what I've been? One of the women in Hollywood who hardly count for anything, the easy lays, the party girls who count for zero.'

Jerry stopped in mid-forkful of Cobb salad and broke into tears. "Stevie, you're the best friend I ever had . . . the only friend . . . Say, we would split and maybe get into the sack and I could try you out. You're a terrific dish."

"Thanks a lot, Jerry. If it worked I'd want more. If it didn't I'd be disappointed. Better not to know."

"Yeah . . . I guess you're right."

"Jerry, I'm going to New York over the weekend. There's a singer I saw a tape on, who I think has promise. I'd like to sign her."

"Stevie . . . look, I think of you as a friend. What am I gonna do?"

He wasn't even listening.

"Jerry . . . there was a doctor who helped me through a rough time myself, when I was in the hospital."

"I won't see any shrink."

"Think of him as a golf pro . . . someone who can improve your *putz*."

"For a *shiksa*, you know the right approach."

"Jerry—what you've got is the right approach, but poor followthrough . . . You pay for lunch and I'll see you on Monday. I'll write down Dr. Ben Grossman's name and number and put it on your desk before I go. Good luck."

During the time after Morrie's death, Stevie had been working on a personal project.

For over three months, a New York attorney whom Stevie hired ploughed through the paperwork to get her sister Ginny out of the orphanage. Finally it was accomplished, and the TWA plane carrying her was about to arrive at Los Angeles International Airport. During the intervening time, Stevie had spoken on the phone to Ginny. Now waiting at the gate, she was amazed to see a tall, statuesque brunette walk directly toward her. The young lady looked nineteen or twenty, with long flowing black hair, dark eyeshadow and lots of lipstick. Under her jeans jacket was a soft cotton T-shirt, outlining rich full nipples when the jacket fell away. The girl's waist was trim and her long legs were snugly covered by tight-fitting jeans.

Stevie knew it was Ginny, but she wasn't ready for a sixteen-year-old who looked like a Las Vegas showgirl. 'My God,' she thought, 'what have I gotten into?'

"Ginny? . . . Guess what, I'm your big sister."

"Hi there, Stephanie. What a fucking trip!"

Stevie said to herself, 'Orphan Annie was never like this.' Without waiting for any further exchange, Ginny handed Stevie two baggage claim tickets.

"I sat next to this creep on the plane . . . He was black. Christ, I know I shouldn't feel that way, but I do . . . ugh, and he started hitting on me. I mean, really. Here is this guy old enough to be my father and he's trying to make out with a kid."

Stevie and Ginny walked away from the gate together and down a long corridor to the baggage area.

"Ginny . . . it's a free world, all you had to do was tell him to cut it out. I must say, though, you look a lot older than sixteen."

"See, he kept following me to the bathroom, to trap me inside. He offered me money. He wanted a quick blow job, you know? So where's your car? What kind of car do you drive anyway?"

"I've got a Porsche . . . It's a couple of years old, but I like it. It's in the parking lot. As soon as we get your bags we'll go out to the apartment. It's at the Marina, near the water, but I'm thinking of moving." She didn't know how to talk to Ginny. They were as different as their hair color, and she sensed hostility.

Ginny picked up the step to get a Skycap. "Why don't you give those checks to him and we can stop for a drink."

Stevie looked surprised. "We can get a drink when we get home." She handed the claim checks to the Skycap and lucked out. The baggage arrived promptly.

When they got home, Ginny deposited her baggage on the bed in her room at the apartment and joined Stevie on the terrace. It was four o'clock and the sun, changing from gold to red, was beginning to dip behind the Marina. Ginny fixed herself a drink and sat down on the edge of the railing.

"Hey, man . . . you do have a view. But I guess you can afford whatever you want, can't you, big sister?" Ginny's tone was icy and snide.

"Look, Ginny, I know that it's going to be difficult . . . We haven't seen each other in fifteen years and each of us is a different person. Take some time and just let's get to know one another. I want you to know that I'll do my damnedest to be a sister to you, to help in any way I know how."

Ginny looked at the boats and slowly turned around to stare at Stevie coldly. "You've got a lot of making up to do, sister of mine. You went with a family. I went to the fucking orphanage. You're living in the lap of luxury, and I'm lucky to get chicken on Sunday. You're Miss Rich Bitch. Yeah. Go ahead. Do your damnedest."

Ginny walked back into the apartment and Stevie heard her fixing another drink, then the sound of a door slamming as Ginny disappeared into her room.

Stevie hated to leave Ginny that first weekend but she had no choice. Ginny had made some friends at the Marina and was more than happy to be on her own. It made Stevie realize that Ginny should be doing something—school or a job. That could wait a little while, Stevie thought, but not too long. When she got back, it could be settled. But it was a bad time to have to go away, she admitted. It wouldn't bring them closer.

On the American Airlines flight to New York, Stevie luxuriated. She had always loved plane travel, particularly since she had come to work at IA. The travel agency that booked for IA knew all the peculiarities of IA family seat preferences, and their connections with the airlines were so good that they could invariably get space at the last moment, when no one else could, and obtain the seats the agency regulars wanted. On the 747's Stevie liked to sit in the first row window seat. It gave her the most leg room and allowed her to put a case full of papers in front of her and have five uninterrupted hours catching up with scripts, paperwork or a book that she wanted to read.

As soon as the plane leveled off and the seatbelt sign blinked off, Stevie ordered a scotch and opened her attaché case. It was Friday evening, and although *Weekly Variety* was published on Wednesday in New York, the West Coast didn't receive it till Thursday, and Stevie regularly read it on the weekend. Generally, there wasn't much in *Weekly Variety* that Stevie didn't already know. The agency intelligence service at her daily staff meeting was weeks ahead of the information in the trade paper, but occasionally there was something of interest.

Stevie first turned to the grosses of the top fifty pictures and noticed with satisfaction that clients of the agency were represented in many of the films that were doing the most business.

From the days of Stevie's recovery in the hospital after her suicide attempt, she continued to maintain her scrapbook of the developing history of Morgan Oliver. In the two years that Stevie had been out of the hospital, that first scrapbook had expanded to six. The detail was enormous. Every article Stevie saw that mentioned his name was included. Every mention of the grosses of his pictures was clipped out and inserted. Almost every gossip column in which Morgan Oliver's name appeared was sequestered in the scrapbooks too.

In those two years, Morgan had lived through the disaster of the movie *Colorado Fever*, which had been

number one on the New York and L.A. critics' "Worst
Pictures of the Year." He had made all the newspapers
with the story of the lawsuit brought against him by
Denys Dubois. Denys had claimed half ownership of a
company formed for a three-picture deal in which
Morgan would star. In an unusual moment of generosi-
ty, he had given Denys a half interest in that company. That fact was recorded by Denys and signed by Morgan in a contract that he later conveniently forgot.

One of the pictures contracted under that partnership was *Colorado Fever*, and as a result of that disaster
the picture company bought its way out of the other
two. Consequently there was very little to divide after
the huge legal fees they both incurred. What remained
was a host of intimate details that reached the press as a
result of the animosity between the lovers, since
Morgan and Denys now had a conscious desire to
destroy the other.

Denys was painted as a money-grubbing, venal shrew
who stole silverware and dishes from the hotels where
they stayed. Hardly an item of much concern, but
typical of the kind of slights each was dealing the other.
Morgan was pictured as childish, given to tantrums,
addicted to dope, a rutting stud, vile-mouthed and
violent. To Stevie and the Hollywood community, that
was nothing new. After months of haggling, the case
was settled out of court, and Stevie discovered that
Denys had possession of shares in an oil well that
Morgan's accountants had written off as unproductive,
two cars, a Rolls and a Lamborghini, and fifty thousand dollars a year over the next five years. From the
settlement, Stevie clearly knew that there would be
continuing litigation between them. The cars might
run, but Denys would soon find out that she had been
duped on the oil well, and knowing Morgan as she did,
Stevie doubted that he would ever make the first yearly
payment to her. That was precisely what the two of
them wanted, Stevie realized, the opportunity to
continually get at each other, like a hateful brother and
sister.

Stevie never faltered in her obsession. At first, it was simply curiosity she felt about someone to whom she had been unnaturally attached, a man who had used and abused her. But Stevie also realized that she had been a willing dupe. No one had drugged her and forced her into white slavery or shipped her to Tangiers to stock a North African whorehouse. She could have stopped any time. No, but could she? The way she did stop was to attempt to kill herself. The words of Dr. Grossman had become clearer and clearer with distance. It had been the bad part of Stevie Tree that she had attempted to destroy that night in Laurel Canyon.

And yet something about Morgan kept nagging her. It was the undefined reason that Stevie continued to search out every scrap of information about him. She reveled in the knowledge that he would be dumbfounded if he knew about her scrapbooks—as a matter of fact, if anyone knew. Why was she keeping them? It was essential to have complete intelligence about one's enemy. Each time Stevie pored over the scrapbooks or inserted another clipping, it filled her with quiet satisfaction, as if each addition to the wealth of information about him was another armored division, another airborne assault outfit, another nuclear weapon that could be used—no, *would* be used sometime. Morgan Oliver, Stevie concluded finally, didn't deserve to live, and somehow, Stevie finally realized, she had been collecting all of this material with the solemn conceit that one day she would use it to destroy him—for all time. But curiously, Stevie noted with satisfaction, he didn't seem to be in need of her help. He was doing a good job on himself.

Stevie took another sip of scotch, read further in *Variety*, polished off two scripts, the correspondence that had accumulated, devoured a typical airline dinner of overdone steak, dozed for a half hour and finally awoke when the announcement came over the speaker that they were about to land at JFK.

IA maintained an apartment at the Sherry Netherland for the use of West Coast or foreign-based agents on their trips to New York. If the apartment were being used by one of the senior people, it would not be available to Stevie. When she asked Brenda to make her travel plans, she knew Brenda would inquire about the availability of the apartment at the Sherry. Had Stevie not merited VIP treatment from the agency, even if it were empty she would never have been allowed to use the apartment. This privilege was accorded to her by Sy Rosen. Showing IA's confidence and respect for her.

A more tangible indication had taken place six weeks ago, when Stevie was accepted into the IA profit-sharing plan. Ordinarily only full-fledged agents were eligible, and Stevie had been the first exception. When she inquired how much it was worth, Jerry Fentris was somewhat vague, so she asked the head of business affairs. Stevie's share was small, but by computing last year's results and projecting them to this year, she could reasonably expect sixty thousand dollars as her profit share over and above her salary, to be paid on December 31st, only three months away. Stevie, overwhelmed, made it her business to thank Sy Rosen personally. Sy accepted the thanks graciously and told her that the suggestion had come from Fred Wine.

My God, she thought. Fred Wine tried to fire me on my first day in the agency! Yet Stevie realized that with each passing day, in each passing staff meeting, it was Fred Wine who gently brought her closer and closer to the mainstream of agency power. It seemed like a small thing, but one day months ago there was suddenly room for Stevie at the conference table for staff meetings, and she no longer had to sit back next to the wall. She suspected that somehow Fred Wine had something to do with it, but at the time she dismissed it as impossible.

Stevie had pondered what to do. How could she acknowledge it? How could she thank the man without embarrassing him? And how had she turned his hatred of her into generous friendship?

Stevie finally realized that she shouldn't try at all,

that it was important she treat the matter in as
businesslike a manner as possible. Stevie also realized
that Sy Rosen would tell Fred Wine of her appreciation
and repeat his remark about who had been really
responsible. Then the light finally dawned on her. She
realized that in IA there were no secrets. Sy Rosen had
known that Fred Wine was going to fire her the first
day, and why. Dammit, she thought, how could I be so
stupid? Fred Wine wouldn't have made that decision by
himself. Sy Rosen had wanted her out, but the position
that she had taken in Wine's office had changed Fred's
mind, and he in turn had changed Sy's and now, a year
later, they were saying that they were pleased about it,
that they felt that she was one of the family.

These thoughts came tumbling out on the cab ride. It
was one in the morning. The driver took the route from
JFK over the Triboro Bridge, across the East River into
Manhattan. The view of the city driving west across the
bridge was spectacular. The lights of the huge skyscrap-
ers were ablaze. The route continued down the East
River Drive, past the luxurious apartments of the East
Side, and when you turned west, past Bloomingdale's.
Young people were strolling out of the colony of movie
houses on Third Avenue. The cab proceeded to Fifth
Avenue and 60th Street, where the Sherry Netherland
stood—perhaps the best location in all of New York.
Like a grand duchess, regal and correct, the Sherry
faced the southeast corner of Central Park across Fifth
Avenue and the Plaza Hotel beyond.

The desk clerk, cool, precise and respectful, escorted
Stevie up to the IA apartment. He remarked that the
maid had filled the kitchen with the usual. When Stevie
asked what "the usual" was, the desk clerk smiled,
took her into the kitchen and opened the fridge. Inside
were a smoked turkey, cold Piper-Heidsieck, Danish
beer, Perrier, Tiptree jams, imported foie gras,
Jarlsberg, Swiss and Camembert cheese, Russian pum-
pernickel, croissants, bagels and Lindt chocolates,
without end.

Stevie was dumbfounded. "I've never seen so much

of such wonderful things to eat. It was sent from heaven."

"No, Zabar's," he said and left.

Stevie unpacked and undressed. She sat up in bed watching a late night movie and munching a good deal of the contents of the refrigerator. The food was delicious. The movie was Jimmy Cagney's *White Heat*. She yawned and looked at the clock. It was three in the morning New York time, but only midnight in California. Even so, it was late, and tomorrow would be busy, with two very important appointments.

Stevie fell asleep with the TV on, and the last words she uttered before sleep were the names of the director—Raoul Walsh—the production year and the supporting players.

That same weekend Randy Davis flew to Palm Springs with Cindy Warren in his Lear Jet. The airplane was kept at Van Nuys Airport and made the trip to Palm Springs in twenty minutes. First, however, it took a half hour in traffic to get from Randy's estate in Holmby Hills to the airport and frequently there was a delay in takeoff because of clearances and restrictions. The Lear Jet cost over a million dollars, and the upkeep on it was close to $200,000 a year, including the cost of two pilots' salaries, maintenance and hangar rental.

When they were airborne and lying on the bed in the private bedroom, tiny but neat and cozy, Cindy cuddled after sex.

"Randy, you are the best. What can I say, but wow!"

Randy smiled. "There's a lot more where that came from, honey."

"I love it so-o-o much. You're all man and my favorite man. Randy baby, isn't it going to be a drag, I mean this weekend with all those famous people . . . I mean . . . after all . . . Ted Caramia. I'm a little nervous, I really am."

"Baby, he's just another guy. He's a buddy of mine. After all, he buttons his pants the same way I do . . ."

Cindy purred, "Yeah, but you've got a lot more to button up than he does . . . more than anybody. Let me kiss him some . . . let me just lick him some, Randy. I just love him so-o-o."

"And he just loves you so-o-o, too, baby."

The Palm Springs home of Ted Caramia was as special as he was. He had had a lifetime of success as a singer in radio, TV and motion pictures. When his career faltered in one medium, he turned to another and became an even greater success. When he tired of singing, he turned to acting and became a movie star. Ted made millions when taxes were more favorable, and had had the greater good fortune to invest in California real estate. Ted Caramia's wealth was a legend.

At fifty, there was a lifetime of turbulent relationships behind him. With women (he had been married five times), with managers and agents (he had too many to count), with studio heads (he wound up owning a studio). It made Caramia think in terms of the Imperial "we." Caramia's compound in Palm Springs was ducal, secluded and protected.

It was twenty minutes after midnight in Palm Springs, and Randy had just demolished half of a large pizza that Caramia's chauffeur had brought to his bungalow. Randy had buzzed for someone on the house intercom and a half hour later the chauffeur found an all-night pizza joint in Palm Desert and brought it back, still hot.

Randy and Cindy spread the pizza box over the huge bed and began to wolf it down. Cindy was nude and so was Randy. He had just fucked Cindy for the third time since ten o'clock, and right after the pizza, he thought he might try for one more.

Randy went to the kitchen, came back popping the tops of two cold cans of Fresca, walked to the bed and sat down.

"Baby . . . I've decided to divorce my wife . . . and

then you and I are going to get hitched. How do you like that?"

"Oh, Randy," Cindy cooed. "I love you so-o-o much."

Randy's cock stood quickly at attention, and he looked down at it joyfully.

Cindy completed the discussion. "And he loves me too."

Randy put the rest of the half-sausage, half-regular on the floor and Cindy lay comfortably and happily back to receive her intended.

15

It was Saturday morning and Stevie left the blue and gold Sherry at ten o'clock to travel to Brooklyn. Her appointment was for eleven and she had no idea how long it would take a cab to get to Eastern Parkway. She figured she should give herself an hour. "You can get to Chicago in an hour," was her rationale.

The cabdriver was unusually talkative. He said that he had lived in that neighborhood as a kid, but it had changed. Once Jewish, he said, now the *schwarzes* and the Puerto Ricans had moved in. The Jews, like him, had moved to Queens. And on and on and on. The conversation never ceased, and as they drove over the bridge to what he said was Brooklyn, Stevie was finally able to tune him out simply because he turned on the radio for the news.

The video tape she had seen, which sent her on this trip to New York, was of a local talk show. The tape had come to her attention when the show's emcee moved to California two weeks ago and was looking for an agent to represent him. On that tape, young Zelma Hurwitz, not more than twenty years old, had a spot as a guest. Zelma was a singer, appearing at a small club in the Village. She was beginning to make a name for herself. The young girl had a Barbra Streisand quality to her. Zelma was small and plump with a full face. She had a voluptuous figure, but the first striking note was the force of her personality. Her eyes lit up when she talked. Her responses to questions were charming and funny. She moved her body in a provocative way, and her frizzy red hair was the perfect crown for an adorable pixie.

Stevie was intrigued with the girl, and she decided to watch the rest of the show to hear her sing. After the first four bars, Stevie became so excited she stood up in front of the monitor and nearly tried to reach through the TV screen to grab the girl. Zelma's voice was as rich and commanding as Streisand's, but throatier. Like Billie Holiday, Stevie thought. Zelma's presentation was extraordinarily sure for an inexperienced performer, and her voice was compelling.

Stevie quickly discovered the necessary information to contact the girl and kept the tape, guarding it in her office over the weekend, lest the emcee show it to another agency. Stevie couldn't hold onto it indefinitely. She checked with the emcee. He had shown it to no one else, he said. Stevie looked at him and wondered whether he was lying, but it wouldn't make any difference if she acted immediately.

Zelma Hurwitz received Stevie's phone call with caution. "I hope you're not coming to New York to see me," Zelma sighed into the phone.

"No, of course not, Zelma . . . I have to be in New York on other business . . . and if you have the time, perhaps we could meet for a drink."

"Oh," Zelma replied, "I don t know whether I can do that. I have a kid brother I have to take care of. He's a brat, and my mother and father are leaving for a wedding in New Rochelle and they need someone to watch Bernard."

Stevie got an instant picture of what she should say. "Maybe I could come to your house, before they leave for the wedding, so I could meet them too."

"I guess you could do that. You're sure it's not taking you out of the way?"

"Not a bit," Stevie lied.

Stevie's watch said eleven o'clock, as they hit Eastern Parkway, a gray victim of city blight. The remnants of old and stylish apartment houses and substantial private homes were reminders of a more solid past. Black mothers stood by as their children played in front of buildings. Young kids ran boisterously down the street. It was Saturday morning and religious Jews with skullcaps on their heads were walking from neighborhood synagogues.

In the grimy lobby of the old apartment house a cracked glass covered the entrance to the elevator, which bore a sign marked "Out of Order." Stevie walked up the three flights, passed other people on the stairs carrying laundry, shopping carts and kids, found the door to the Hurwitz apartment and rang the bell. The door opened and the pert gamin face of Zelma Hurwitz gave her a shy smile.

"You must be Miss Tree."

"Zelma, it's Stevie, and I'm very glad to meet you."

A voice emerged from another room. "Who's at the door, Zelma? Answer the door."

Zelma called, "It's for me, Ma . . . I got it."

A small boy appeared in pajamas, carrying a tiny yellow blanket. He stood directly in front of the pair, and Zelma picked him up. "This is Bernard. Say hello, Bernard." She put him down, and Bernard returned to the room he had left.

"He's only seven. He was an accident."

A tall, dark, heavy-set man in his forties came out of the same room. He was tying his tie. "Zelma, how does this go with my shirt?"

"Fine, Pop. Stevie Tree, this is my father."

"Glad to meet you, Mr. Hurwitz."

Another voice sounded—this time a woman's. "Get the lady a bottle of soda or a cup of coffee."

Zelma picked up the cue. "Can I get you something to drink? A Diet Pepsi?"

"That would be terrific."

When they were seated in the small, old-fashioned living room, sipping Pepsi, Zelma started the conversation.

"You really like my singing?"

"Yes, Zelma, I did. Did you study with anyone?"

"Nah . . . I don't have the time. I have this job in the

Village . . . and I'm taking this computer programming course so that I can get a job. I've got aptitude for computers, they tell me, and then my Ma and my Pop both work. They have a delicatessen in the neighborhood and so I have to take care of Bernard some of the time. I don't have too much time for studying."

"Zelma—do you want a career?"

"Yeah, I think I can do good in computers."

"Have you talked to any agents or anybody who has encouraged you to think of a career in show business?" Stevie held her breath, now knowing what answer to expect.

"Oh, yeah . . . especially in the last week. You see, I was on this local show, here in New York—Oh, I forgot, you saw the tape—and the emcee must have shown the tape to every agent in Hollywood. Let me see, I have some of their cards right here."

Stevie's heart sank. *That son of a bitch. He told me he had shown it to no one.*

Zelma reached over to the coffee table and picked up a purse and extricated some business cards. Stevie flashed on the names of a few of IA's major competitors. *Jesus Christ,* she said to herself, *this girl has heard every sales pitch in the book.*

"How much more time do you have in computer school, Zelma?"

"Well, it should be another year . . . but frankly I don't have the money for another year yet. Maybe if the place I'm singing in in the Village does good, they'll keep me on and I can save enough."

"Why were you on that local show, Zelma?"

"Oh, I guess you didn't see the end . . . I do charity work for the temple my Pop is head of. It's right here in the neighborhood and we're looking for clothing donations for an auction. The emcee of the program made me sing and talk about myself . . . Say, Stevie, you don't have any nice clothes you could give us?"

"Perhaps," Stevie said. "I'll look around when I get back to California." Stevie was almost grinning. The ingenuous Zelma Hurwitz was an original.

"Those agents who talked to me," Zelma interjected, "they say crazy things . . . about making thousands of dollars a week . . . and making me a star. They say I could be another Barbra Streisand. Fat chance—me another Streisand, imagine! It just proves show people will lie to you."

"I know what you mean." Stevie felt a warm kinship with the young girl.

"Like your coming here today to see me. All the way to Brooklyn. What are you doing in Brooklyn? Nobody comes to Brooklyn."

Stevie caught her breath. It was now or never.

"Zelma, I made this trip to New York to see you. I work for the best talent agency in the business, IA. We're not magicians, but we are smart, and I may be one of the best people in that agency . . . but it's early, and time will tell. I'd like to represent you, and I think that you could have a career in show business that would be fun and would make you money."

"Could I make thousands of dollars a week?"

"Zelma—the answer is yes, but that's not the most important part. You have a God-given talent, your personality, your looks and your voice."

"Look, Miss Tree. I'm a nice Jewish girl. I don't like to take chances. I can sing a little, and I like it, but it's very risky. I don't have a boyfriend now, but you can never tell when you're gonna meet Mr. Right . . . and if he needs some help or something, to get started, like if he's going to be a professional person, if I have a steady job, then it'll make things a little easier."

"Zelma, I have a suggestion. I'm just an employee of a big talent agency, but I think I can get them to pay your tuition in the computer school for the next year, just to make sure you have something to fall back on."

"You could get them to do that?"

"Yes, I know I can."

"It's only fair to warn you that it's $1,500, plus $250 more for books and supplies. Is it still a deal?"

"Okay, but no more than two thousand dollars total." Stevie had added that line to keep Zelma's ideas down to earth. 'My God,' she thought, 'I think I'll land her.'

"Now, OK. It's a deal . . . your agency. No, make that you, Stevie. I like you. You'll represent me and you'll put up two thousand dollars for my tuition."

"No, Zelma," Stevie interrupted, "up to two thousand dollars."

Zelma smiled. "Thought I'd try and pull a fast one, but you're smart. I like that in an agent—my agent. You wouldn't have a contract with you, by any chance, Stevie? I believe you, but I'd rather have it in writing, if you know what I mean."

Stevie did have a contract, and carefully she wrote in the additional clause about the computer school, and Zelma Hurwitz signed the contract, and Stevie Tree signed the contract, and Bernard came out of the bedroom with his yellow blanket, just as Ma and Pop Hurwitz left to go to New Rochelle. First, though, they all had a toast with Diet Pepsi to the new relationship of Zelma Hurwitz and her agent Stevie Tree ("And what kind of name is that for a girl?" said Mrs. Hurwitz). Stevie was shaking with excitement. She had to go to the bathroom, and when she got to the john she was too excited to pee, but it wouldn't do any good for the Hurwitzes to know that, since the bathroom was next to the living room, so she ran the water briskly in the sink.

When Stevie came out, Mrs. Hurwitz was just completing an intimate conversation with Mr. Hurwitz in Yiddish. *"Zie pisht vie ein ferd."* English translation: "My God, Ben . . . that girl pisses like a horse."

Before Stevie left Zelma's apartment, she arranged for publicity photos to be taken and gave her the name of the man in charge of New York's IA office, should she need anything. Stevie kissed Zelma. Zelma cried. She knew that it would be good luck today. She had read her horoscope in the *Daily News*.

During the ride back to the hotel, Stevie's heart was outside the taxi, soaring a thousand feet above the vehicle. It was swooping like a kite held out an open window. Stevie couldn't stop making all sorts of inane conversation with the cabdriver, a quiet, morose Puerto Rican. He wanted nothing more than to listen to a Spanish station and have his passenger shut up. Stevie finally got the message and hummed to herself till she reached the hotel.

One more thing to do in New York City—a phone call to Mrs. Harriet Daniel.

"Mrs. Daniel?"

"Yes, who's calling?"

"My name is Stevie Tree. I was a friend of David's . . . You may not remember me . . ."

"Yes, I remember you. You were living with my brother when he was killed. I don't want to talk to you."

"Please, Mrs. Daniel. I know that you still own the house on Laurel Canyon . . . and that it's for sale."

"It's not for sale to you, Miss Tree. David was in with bad company."

Stevie let that pass. "Miss Daniel . . . I have something of David's that I want to show you. Can I come and see you?"

"Why should I let you?"

"Because you loved your brother, Mrs. Daniel."

"You have my address. Come by at five o'clock."

The line was dead at the other end before Stevie rang off. It was two in the afternoon and Stevie realized that she hadn't eaten anything. All she had had since breakfast was a Diet Pepsi and she was hungry. Stevie left the hotel and walked toward Lexington Avenue. She had dreamed of what Bloomingdale's would be like, the legendary New York store that was the passion of the native New Yorker and nirvana to the out-of-towner.

Stevie stopped near 59th and Lexington at a coffee shop that had formica tables and smelled like cabbage. She wolfed down two franks, potato salad and an orange drink. Then she plunged into Bloomingdale's, heading directly for the housewares department. On one floor Stevie ogled the myriad glistening dishes, utensils, gadgets, pots and pans. If she could get the Laurel Canyon house, she thought, it would be a way of reliving the extraordinary times with David. She hadn't loved since then. She hadn't even felt. Once in Laurel Canyon she had been alive. Perhaps the house had magic, and perhaps she could furnish it with Bloomingdale's wonders.

After an hour and a half of near mystical communion with the enchanted land of imaginative housewares, Stevie realized she would have to rush to keep her five o'clock appointment.

After ten minutes of waiting on Lexington, Stevie gave the cabdriver the Park Avenue address. When the taxi came to a stop, it was in front of a beautifully maintained prewar apartment house on the corner of 84th Street. The doorman announced Stevie over the intercom in the lobby and when she arrived at the tenth floor the door to the single apartment on the floor opened. A tall, dark-haired woman in her late thirties stood in the doorway, and Stevie held out her hand to greet Harriet Daniel. The hand was ignored and Stevie followed the woman into the huge foyer, then into the living room, luxuriously furnished in shades of blue. Mrs. Daniel was a very wealthy woman. Stevie sat down in a large chair opposite her.

"Mrs. Daniel . . . I want to thank you again for giving me your time."

No answer.

"The situation we were in years ago was one of the great tragedies of both our lives, Mrs. Daniel. I haven't gotten over it."

Stevie was cut off. "You're alive, young lady, and you appear to be thriving. My brother is dead."

"There was never any chance for him, Mrs. Daniel. He was living the life that he chose to live. I tried to get him to stop."

"I don't believe you, miss . . . If you really cared about my brother, you would never have gotten involved with him in the first place. It was people like you who got him into drugs and God knows what else.

He would never have been associated with your type if he'd stayed where he belonged. It may be a very difficult thing for you to understand, but I loved my brother . . . and I'm sure he loved me."

"I have a letter, Mrs. Daniel, that your brother wrote to me when he was out of town. It says just that . . . and it says something else."

"Yes, I know what it says . . . David wrote me once about you and how he associated that house with you and his happiest memories."

"It says more, Mrs. Daniel. It says that he was going to bring me to New York to meet you, and we were going to get married."

"Miss Tree . . . I don't care what it says. I only asked you to come here so that I could take a look at you, and what I see makes me realize that I was right. I don't like you . . . and I never will. If it weren't for you, my brother would be alive today."

"My God, Mrs. Daniel . . . how can you believe that? I loved him. I still love him."

Harriet Daniel stood up. "And so do I, Miss Tree. Goodbye."

When Stevie arrived back at the Sherry Netherland, there was a telephone message for her. It was from Ginny, and when Stevie called the Marina apartment, a girl answered the phone, saying she was a friend of Ginny's. Ginny, she said, was in jail. She had been picked up by the vice squad for soliciting.

Stevie hung up the phone slowly, then made a phone call to Sam Di Benedetto and packed her bags to catch the next plane for California.

16

When Stevie arrived Sunday morning, the apartment at the Marina was in complete disarray. Empty glasses and liquor bottles were all over the living room. A quarter of a dried pizza lay in its box on the coffee table. A chair was overturned and the drapes were blowing through the sliding doors that opened on the terrace.

Stevie walked to the door of Ginny's room and opened it. She was asleep. It was ten in the morning, and Stevie decided not to wake her. Stevie had flown all night and was exhausted. She would take a shower, clean up the mess and face the problem when the problem awoke.

Stevie was luxuriating in the warm shower when she heard the phone ring. It continued to ring and the answering service didn't respond. She got out of the shower, tucked a towel around her and went for the phone.

"Hello."

"Is this Ginny?" It was a man's voice.

"No, this is her sister . . . can I take a message?"

"No . . . no message . . . is she home?" The voice was guarded.

"Yes, but she's asleep."

"Can you wake her?" the voice inquired.

"No . . . if you leave your name and number, I'll get her to call you."

"Well, tell her to call Frank from last night . . . and tell her that I got the stuff."

"What?"

The voice concluded. "Forget what I said. I'll call back. Just forget it." The phone clicked off.

Ginny came out of the bedroom, wearing only a T-shirt. Her dark hair tumbled down over her shoulders, and despite her youth, there was about her a sense of unbridled sex. Stevie got a sinister sensation from her near nakedness. Ginny's heavy sensuality was like the pungent aroma of cheap perfume.

"Ginny . . . I'd like to talk to you." Stevie didn't know how to start.

"OK," she said and sat down heavily on the couch and put her feet on the coffee table. "Shoot."

"That man in the plane . . . the black man you mentioned."

"What black man?"

"The one you said tried to get you into the washroom. Did you approach him? Did you ask *him* for money?"

Ginny looked at Stevie. "Yeah . . . why not?"

"Did you bring men up to the apartment while I was gone?"

"Yeah . . . what does it look like?"

"Ginny . . . I've played around too."

The younger sister looked at her nails and lit a cigarette. "Is that how you got those scars on your face?"

"Yes."

"OK, continue. You're about to read me a sermon." Ginny let smoke out. "Let me say a few words to you, before you steam yourself up. I play around a little . . . so what? That's all there was to do at the home . . . you dig? We got into each other's pants a little . . . to keep warm, while you and all those like you were getting off on Mom's apple pie and all that shit."

"Ginny, it wasn't like that at all." Stevie sounded almost plaintive.

"Don't give me that stuff. You had a family, man.

All we had was cutting class and walking the street, and getting a little kick from some john who liked a little young meat . . . what's so bad about that?"

"Ginny . . . please listen to me . . . you don't have to do any of that stuff anymore."

"Who says? My loving sister, who has this beautiful apartment . . . drives around in a fancy foreign car, dresses like a million bucks . . . lives like a queen, fucking movie stars, while her kid sister sucks her thumb in a shitty orphan home . . ."

"Ginny . . . please listen." It was obvious Ginny had built a barbed-wire fence to keep Stevie out.

"No, sister . . . you listen to me. I deserve something. I deserve a lot, and I'm gonna get it. You've had it all, and I've had nothing . . . and I'm gonna catch up, that's what I'm gonna do."

"It wasn't the way it seems, Ginny."

"Bullshit, sister of mine. You don't know what being grown up is all about . . . you with a trunk full of clippings about the love of your life, Morgan Oliver . . . goddam trunkful of clippings I found in your closet. What's the matter? He brush you off?"

"That's not your business." This was not only getting her no place, it was making everything worse.

"Fucking well right it's not my business . . . yet. Tell me, Stephanie . . . is he good in the sack? Don't bother to tell me, I'll find out for myself. Now, what's for breakfast?"

Monday morning at eight o'clock, Stevie drove into Schwab's parking lot on Sunset. It was out of her way. The route from the Marina to the agency offices in Beverly Hills didn't take her anywhere near there. Stevie had taken to having breakfast meetings at the Beverly Hills Hotel, in the Lanai alongside the Polo Lounge. The Beverly Hills Hotel, a queen in its time, now faded and seedy, was still where the action was in the morning. Stevie on occasion had two breakfast dates, one at seven-thirty or eight, and a second at nine

or nine-thirty. In between, the waitress would clear off
the table, and Stevie would read the trades until the
second breakfast date came along. After a few months,
Stevie was able to get a booth near the door, which
meant that you were an important person. Another
indication was the number of phone calls you received
during breakfast. If you were truly important, you
would get the same table each time you came, the
waitress would bring you hot coffee as soon as you sat
down, and the hostess would deliver a phone to your
table at the same time she announced that there was a
call for you.

That Monday morning, Stevie wasn't up to jokes and
laughter. The situation with Ginny was too explosive,
but when the phone call came through the previous
afternoon from Cindy in Palm Springs, she welcomed
the call. Poor, dumb, sweet, pretty Cindy, the perpetual Miss Tennessee who lucked out, had something she
wanted to talk to Stevie about, and they made a
breakfast date at Schwab's.

Stevie had a feeling that the place had changed.
Either they had redecorated, or enlarged the establishment. But Stevie realized that there had been no
physical changes, just the waitresses and counter ladies.
That had been enough to do it. As she walked to an
empty table, she recognized a number of familiar faces.
My God, she thought, have they been here all along?
Was it possible that the same hands doing crosswords,
the same eyes scanning the trades, the same line of
self-hype, the same whispered gossip, and the same
camaraderie existed that Stevie remembered from
three years ago? It seemed the same; the difference was
that Stevie had changed. The positions had been
rearranged. She had become establishment, while
Schwab's thrived on revolution. Stevie had become one
of the "haves," while Schwab's revolved around the
lives of people fighting the good fight for recognition.
Once she had felt she belonged here. Now she belonged somewhere else. You get one thing. You give
up another.

Stevie sat down at a table, and a waitress came over. She recognized the waitress.

"Hi, Barbara."

"Oh, hello . . . do I know you?"

"Sure, from a couple of years ago. I used to come here every day."

"Coffee?"

"Yes, thanks."

"Do you need a menu?"

"OK . . . I'm waiting for someone."

"Say . . . I remember you. Stevie, that's your name. You look different. Are you working?"

Stevie smiled. She was back home again. At least as far as Schwab's was concerned, what mattered wasn't her health, her suntan or even if she had come into the restaurant bandaged up to the neck and in traction. What mattered was, was she working? "Yes, Barbara . . . I'm not acting anymore. I'm an agent."

Barbara slapped a menu on the table. "That's too bad."

As Stevie looked at the menu, she realized that nothing had changed except the prices. Inflation had not passed Schwab's by. Her eye caught a car pulling in at the entrance. It was a limousine, a gigantic, white custom Mercedes. The chauffeur got out and came around the passenger side, and a familiar face appeared at the door of the car. It was Cindy, her breakfast date. Stevie smiled. Miss Tennessee, no more.

"Stevie . . . I hope that I'm not late . . . After all, you're such a busy person, and all." Cindy was breathless.

"I would have waited for a year for your entrance. Where did you get the pretty car? It's a yacht, that's what it is."

Barbara, the waitress, came over again. She had not noticed Cindy's limousine.

"Are you ready to order now?"

Stevie looked at her. "In a few minutes."

"There are only two of you in a booth for four. You're sure you don't want to order."

They quickly ordered and after the appropriate dramatic pause, Cindy began, "You know that Randy Davis and I have been dating."

"So does everybody," Stevie replied drily.

"Well, Stevie . . . he's decided . . . I mean, we've decided to get married."

"He's already married."

Cindy seemed a little deflated. "I know that, and she's a terrible person, a lush. You know, she drinks all the time and just goes out shopping and plays tennis, and lays around."

"I get the picture." Stevie sipped her second cup of coffee.

"Well, we decided to take the plunge this weekend . . . and he called his lawyer from Palm Springs and told him to get him a divorce. He said, 'Give her anything she wants, but get me out of it.' Can you imagine that? Of course, he told his lawyer not to be too easy on her. After all, they've only been married for eight years, and she does absolutely nothing, Stevie, absolutely nothing."

"Cindy, I'm so happy for you, though I've never met Randy. He's a client at the agency, but someone else handles him and he never comes in."

"That's right . . . Another thing, he said that he's thinking of changing agents . . . all they do is sit around and collect their ten percent. Isn't that terrible? They don't help at all, and they still collect so much money."

Stevie made a mental note to bring the matter up in the staff meeting that morning. The agency would not want to lose Randy Davis. Someone would have to do a lot of hand-holding. She wondered what the key was to keeping him. Not Cindy. She would carry absolutely no weight. Something would occur to someone at the agency.

"Where are you going to live, Cindy?"

"Well, his wife will get the house, but Randy has this ten-acre piece of land on the coast, and he always wanted to build a special beautiful house, not like all the others around . . . but really spectacular, and he's going to get a very important architect to design it, and he's promised to let me help."

Stevie was becoming bored. She didn't think it was envy, just boredom. "Are you going to continue to act or do commercials?"

"No, Randy made me promise that I'd give up my career. Not that it was that much really, Stevie, but I was up for a few big commercials . . . and I still get my residuals, kind of like a little dowry."

"What will you do . . . I mean, with your time?" Stevie was appalled at the thought of that sort of life.

"Oh . . . I guess, take tennis lessons . . . and go shopping, like everybody. I'm going for my first lesson right from here . . . That's Randy's car. I have it all to myself now, except I really don't know where to go with it. Can we take you to work, Stevie? It would be my pleasure."

"Thanks anyway, Cindy. I have my own car. Eat your eggs. They're getting cold." They finished breakfast in silence.

Later, at the agency meeting, Stevie broke the news she had heard at breakfast, about the possible defection of one of their major clients. Sy Rosen decided he himself would deal with the dissatisfaction of Randy Davis. Randy obviously needed high-level massaging and intensive hand-holding. Stevie reported on her signing Zelma Hurwitz that weekend, and was surprised at the criticism when she announced that she had committed "up to two thousand dollars for Zelma's study in computer programming." Stevie didn't believe what she was hearing. It was a curious attitude. Stevie, Sy Rosen had said emphatically, had exceeded her authority. She had no right to commit the agency's money that way. First Stevie was embarrassed, then she got angry and found herself a split-second away from telling them all to go to hell. She knew what she was doing. It was only two thousand. They blew more than that in an agent's monthly expense account. She was angry, but principally about her sister Ginny, and ready to let the anger out any chance she got.

But there was something more to this. She looked at the agents seated around the table, and realized that they were twisting her tail. OK to have the trappings of a star—to make deals and bring in the money and share in the profits, very handsomely—but don't *act* like a star, and particularly don't act like a star if you're a woman. Stevie knew that this was exactly what they meant, and that Sy Rosen was beginning to make his weight felt. This was the first step to seeing the other side of Sy Rosen. The man could be tough. She had heard that about him. She hadn't seen that part as yet. She had the sense that the more successful she became at the agency, the more trouble she would have, most particularly with Sy. So Stevie said nothing. She just took in the situation and recognized that the honeymoon was over. The real reason, she knew, was that she was a threat. Goddammit, she said to herself, that's what it's all about, and it's going to get worse.

By the end of the day, Stevie had set two things in motion, apart from her normal business of the day. She had spoken to Flack and Flaherty about the summer series she had negotiated for them, and informed them gently but firmly that she expected them to use as many of agency clients as they could on the show. She told them she was sending over the tape of Zelma Hurwitz, a singer she felt they would like. The video-tape was delivered by messenger and the boys screened it. Flack and Flaherty were staggered. Zelma Hurwitz was set for their opening show. Stevie recognized that Zelma needed an earlier appearance. She convinced the booker on the "Tonight Show" to screen the tape. She explained that Zelma Hurwitz was set for the opening show of the Flack and Flaherty summer special, and that otherwise Zelma would be exclusive to Johnny. The booker said that if the tape were any good, he would spot her in ten days time. The "Tonight Show" had a spot they needed to fill with a singer.

Stevie had a date with Sam that night and as she rushed from the office to meet him for dinner she thought about their changing relationship. Exactly one month ago Stevie and Sam Di Benedetto drove out to Venice Beach with his daughter Laurie. Stevie had never met the child and was curious. Sam had suggested that they rent bicycles, ride along the beach for a few hours, and have dinner together.

He had periodically mentioned his daughter, but without any details. Stevie knew that he treasured the time that his wife allowed him with her, but this was the first time that she had been invited to share the intimacy of this relationship.

Sam escorted Stevie to his car, and she was introduced to Laurie, a quiet, shy nine-year-old girl with long stringy blonde hair, sitting quietly in the back seat. Laurie, who had huge blue eyes, shook Stevie's hand with a gentle and tentative grip, and then retreated into herself in the back seat.

Stevie tried to make general conversation, addressing many of her remarks to the young girl.

"Do you like to go biking?"

"What grade are you in?"

"What's your favorite TV program?"

All Laurie's answers were polite and softly spoken, but it appeared that she was either painfully shy or perhaps she resented her father's being with a woman other than her mother. Stevie couldn't tell. Perhaps the day was a mistake. It had the beginnings of disaster. Why in hell hadn't she kept to herself this weekend? She really needed some time alone.

Sam cut in on her worrying. "Tell me about the job, Stevie."

"Well, it's wonderful and awful."

"Do you regret working for a big outfit like IA?"

"The jury is still out. The men are tough, really tough. I've never known men the way I see them now. Everything is life or death. There's no perspective about the real values—and there's no humor in their lives. God knows, I'm not the one to teach them. I'm still wet behind the ears. But I guess the answer is that I am glad. I think I have the stuff to make the grade. I think that I can do it, even though women don't count for very much in the business."

Sam was negotiating the freeway. Laurie called out from the back, "Do you know Jerry Lewis?"

Stevie looked around. The young girl's eyes were shining now. "No, Laurie, I don't."

"That's too bad. I want to be the poster girl. I wish someone knew Jerry Lewis."

Stevie turned around again. "What poster girl is that, Laurie?"

"I've got muscular dystrophy—and I want to be the National Poster Child for the telethon, before I die."

"Stevie wondered if she had heard correctly. She turned to look at Sam, who stared impassively at the road. "Laurie's written to the committee and they wrote back that they would consider her."

Laurie interjected, "I'll bet it would help if I knew Jerry Lewis. Do you think that I should have my teeth straightened?"

Stevie's mind raced at a thousand miles an hour. What could she say? How dare Sam not say anything to her about Laurie?

She looked at the tiny face and smiled. "I think that they look fine—very natural, and that's the way they should look."

"You really think so? You're a pretty lady. You would know. Thank you for your honest opinion." Laurie brightened perceptibly.

When they arrived at the bike rental spot in Venice, Sam rented a special bicycle with a two-wheel carrier. With help from her father Laurie got out of the car, walked slowly in her braces, holding his hand, and let herself be lifted into the back. Stevie looked at them both. She saw a father and daughter, but she saw more. She saw herself at the same age, on the Air Force base, a child not much older. She saw her mother's face, pale and haunted. She saw her father's angry expression.

She heard the sound of the gunfire. Once again she saw the murder scene. She felt the loneliness, the fought-back tears, the fright and the desolation of the bus trip to her aunt's house in Urbana. Once again she saw her aunt's new husband and relived her first sexual experience in that tiny bedroom next to the kitchen.

My God, Stevie thought, how can I feel so sorry for myself when I have everything and this adorable little girl, this incredible little girl, wants nothing more than to be on a poster before she dies.

Sam looked at her. "OK, Stevie, move your ass. Laurie and I don't have all day. I hope you brought your own money. One woman at a time is all I'm gonna buy lunch for."

Laurie looked at her and laughed. "Don't believe him. He'll pay for lunch. You're too pretty . . . and too nice. Come on, let's go. I'm hungry. I'm gonna have three quarter-pounders. How about you, Miss Tree?"

"Please call me Stevie."

"You called me Laurie, so that's fair, Stevie."

For his daughter's sake as well as theirs, she had to consider her history with Sam very carefully. The gratitude she felt at having been put together once again in the hospital came first, and *then* the whirlwind courtship that he had started as soon as she came out of the hospital. He was very much in love with her, but where had it gone? She had offered herself to Sam physically, and he had finally accepted, but the times they had made love had been unsatisfactory for both of them. Mechanically they had been perfect, like two sides of an untoasted English muffin, but totally lacking in texture, feeling and form. By unspoken agreement, they now avoided sex completely. What a brother and sister they made—two choice figures, a man and a woman ready for love, but not with each other.

Stevie pulled her Porsche into a spot in front of La Scala on Santa Monica. La Scala, the grandest Italian restaurant in Beverly Hills, very status, very expensive, very good. The proprietor, Jean Louis, took great pride in both his cuisine and his customers. He controlled his chef and selected his customers. The parking attendant came around to her door. "Good evening, Miss Tree." She walked inside and the maitre d'hôtel greeted her, "It's been too long, Miss Tree . . . don't forget us. A gentleman is waiting at your table." The jungle drums had started beating around town. She had a name. They made it their business to remember it. She was important. She had the power, and by God they felt she would be worthwhile remembering—her face and name. It felt good. In fact, it was blissful.

Sam helped her into the booth and kissed her.

"Been waiting long, Sam?"

"No, I just got here. You look absolutely beautiful, Stevie. New dress?"

"Yes, how nice of you to notice. I discovered a crazy place in Beverly Hills near the office. They've got anything you could want there, Sam, and I may have to give up eating, it's so expensive."

After they ordered drinks, examined the menus and ordered, Stevie took Sam's hand. "You know that I'm in love with Laurie."

"Laurie is in love with *you*, Stevie, but she's too young to marry."

"I'm not thinking about marriage. I'm prepared to make you a very good deal to let me adopt her."

"Stevie, I know you agents . . . First you romance a client, get him to believe in you, and them commit to you . . . and then you're off with the next one."

Stevie laughed. "How well you know us. No, it's something entirely different."

"I know what you mean. Laurie is something very special. By the way, you've got to stop sending her presents. It's getting to be embarrassing."

"Sam, those presents are a bonus. Actually I was looking for something to send Laurie and I passed by the window of the store where I found this Adolfo. You can't prevent me from shopping for myself."

"No, of course not," he replied. "It's simply that

Laurie doesn't need that kind of attention. The fact that she's dying doesn't mean that the part of her that's healthy shouldn't be treated just like any other little ten-year-old girl. Stevie, don't do that to her, and don't do that to yourself."

"What do you mean?"

"I mean you can't . . . rather, you shouldn't relive your life in Laurie. She isn't you . . . and she isn't your child. Take it slow. It will be better for you, and for her."

"I think I understand what you're telling me, and I'll try. Sam . . . please tell me. How long does Laurie have?"

"The problem is I don't know. There has been a very slight deterioration over the last six months, but it's a curious disease. There is no way to delay or predict its rate of progress, and one can only hope that it will be slower rather than faster."

"But how long generally?"

"It could be a year. It could be several. I don't know."

Stevie took a beat and started on the pasta that the captain set down before her. "Sam . . . do you know that my friend Cindy—you know, Miss Tennessee—has just struck it rich. I met her for breakfast this morning and she showed up in a pure virgin white limousine, loaned to her by her husband-to-be—Randy Davis." She was trying to alleviate the tension.

"The one with the enormous cock?"

Stevie laughed again. "I didn't think that civilians knew that legend."

"Oh, yes . . . you'd be surprised how that kind of information spreads. Stevie, I have some other news that I want to give you personally."

Stevie looked up at him, sensing danger. "What's that, Sam?"

Without breaking stride, he continued, "Stevie, I'm going back to my wife."

"For Laurie's sake?"

"Not alone, Stevie . . . for mine too. I need Laurie very much, and that's her home, and for Laurie time is going too fast."

Stevie panicked. She understood what that would mean to her. "Will I still be able to see her, Sam?"

"I don't know, Stevie. There is my wife to consider. We'll have to see."

Stevie put her fork down slowly. "Sam . . . will you forgive me if I leave? It's not polite, but I don't want you to see me cry."

"I'm sorry, Stevie."

"I know," she replied as she got up from the table and made her way past the maitre d'hôtel and out to the parking attendant, both of whom knew her name since she was beginning to be a very important person.

Saturday—3 P.M.

After Randy left, Sy Rosen read a chapter from a book he was nursing. At three, he decided it was the appropriate time to call Ralph Stanton, the president of Magna Pictures.

"Ralph . . . Sy Rosen . . . Sorry to disturb you at home, but something came up."

"Never a problem, Sy . . . always glad to hear from you. Have you heard about our picture?"

"It's wonderful, Ralph. It's a testament to your judgment. I've often said to the Board of Governors that there are very few men around today in the tradition of Irving Thalberg and the other industry giants. Of course, I expect that you're too young to have known him."

"Yes."

"Well, he had your vision . . . your feeling for material . . . your sense of the way things come together. I remember Harry Cohn used to judge pictures by the way he felt in the screening room. When his pants used to bind him and he had to scratch, the picture was running too long or going off in the wrong direction. You didn't know Harry, did you?"

"No, Sy . . . I came up on the business side of things . . . Wall Street—you remember us guys."

"And do I? But I'll tell you one thing, Ralph. You must have been born with a flair for showmanship because, Ralph Stanton, you're gonna be right up there with the very important ones."

"That's nice to hear, Sy . . . coming from you."

"Ralph . . . tell you what I called for."

"Shoot."

"One of my people at the agency—and I won't say who—did a bad thing."

"What was that, Sy?" He was becoming wary.

"Well, you know that there's a print of *Young Dillinger* around . . ."

"Sy, we're especially careful of prints . . . the only people who are authorized to have a print are myself, of course, and . . ."

"Well, someone in my shop, and I won't say who, got hold of someone's print . . . and I won't say who to that either, and they thought they could score points with me by getting a fast deal for a hot picture star—Morgan Oliver—by showing another studio just what a great picture it's going to be."

"My God, Sy." Now he was really alarmed.

"Exactly, Ralph . . . my exact words."

"Well, that certain person in my employ negotiated, behind *our backs*, a deal for Morgan, Walker Perkins the director, and Nick Long the producer. You know that's insane because we don't even *represent* Nicholas Long."

"Sy, this is serious. My board of directors will go through the roof. We're counting on this picture. I can tell you that on Wall Street they figure that *Young Dillinger* is going to be worth seventy-five cents a share to this company. Look, Sy, I figured that Magna would have a shot at that combination. I was going to call you Monday. I don't know what . . ."

"Look, Ralph, we have a moral responsibility to you—IA does. First, you should know that the party that was responsible will be asked to resign Monday.

You'll read about it in the trades . . . but I'm going to do something . . . maybe a little unethical . . . but I think that our relationship and our moral obligation is bigger than, well, if you can match the deal that was offered through that other agent, and which she . . . excuse me . . . that person accepted, I'll explàin on Monday morning to this other studio that the person wasn't authorized . . . and the deal will be yours."

"Jesus, Sy, would you stick your neck out like that for me?"

"Yes, Ralph, I would. Say, do you have a pencil nearby?"

"Sure, Sy, let me hear the terms."

Lunch at Ma Maison on Melrose is a heady trip. The most fashionable restaurant in Los Angeles has its regular customers and doesn't rely on having its phone number listed in the directory. If you don't know the number now, forget it, you never will.

Stevie was having lunch with Zelma Hurwitz.

"Stevie, I've never seen you so tense. Come on, lighten up."

"Zelma, there's a lot going on." Stevie found her difficult to talk to.

"You're telling me."

"No, you're telling *me*." Stevie was angry.

"Stevie, what's the big deal?"

"Zelma, you were at the screening last night . . . Has anyone talked to you about it?"

"No, why?"

"Good."

"Stevie, you're driving me crazy. What's the goddam mystery? Please, let's order first, I could eat a horse."

A moment after the waiter left, Stevie continued.

"Zelma, you know, of course, that Melinda Long OD'd last night?"

"OD'd, I thought that she dropped dead of a heart attack."

"No, baby . . . I saw the body in the bathroom. She was nude and there was a busted hypodermic alongside . . . and on top of that, Morgan was laying on the bed outside . . . nude."

"You're kidding?" Could Zelma really not know?

"Zelma, have you spoken to anyone about this . . . I mean *anyone*?"

"Stevie, take it easy. I told you I haven't talked to anybody. Look, when the producer's wife came busting in, my sweetie and I split. We didn't want any part of it . . . so we left. It wouldn't be good for my career to be involved in a death at a screening. Jesus, what kind of stuff is that? The *National Enquirer* will pick up on that shit if you give them an opening."

The waiter arrived quickly with the first course.

Stevie didn't eat. Jerry Fentris had already gotten to Zelma. Zelma continued to eat and afterwards she finished the spinach salad that Stevie ordered.

Stevie drove back to her house in Laurel Canyon and slammed the car door shut. She was frustrated, and if the car hadn't been put together by decent Prussian craftsmen, it would have sprung a hinge. She walked up the steps, and as she put the key in the door she heard the phone ring. She raced to answer it.

"Miss Tree, this is Valerie Long."

"Yes, Mrs. Long . . . I didn't get the chance to see you last night to express my sympathy. I tried to phone your home this morning . . ."

"Yes, Miss Tree . . . we didn't answer any calls, that's why I'm phoning you."

Stevie was wary. "Yes?"

"I thought you might want to know that Melinda's funeral is tomorrow morning. It's sad for a mother to face, but since we're all in the hands of the Lord . . ."

"Where is the funeral, Mrs. Long?"

"No need to concern yourself about going, Miss Tree. You never knew Melinda . . . and it's just for the intimate family."

Stevie waited. "Tell me, Mrs. Long . . . what was the cause of death?"

"You were there . . . didn't you speak to the doctor? The poor child had a weak heart for years . . . It was a heart attack. Nick and I will always remember her just the way she was in life . . . innocent, happy and just a child . . . so young to be taken from us. We'll always treasure her memory. You never knew her, Miss Tree . . . or you'd understand what I mean."

Stevie paused. "No, I never knew her, Mrs. Long."

Valerie Long ended the conversation. "Nick asked me to phone. He thought you'd want to know."

The telephone went dead in Stevie's hand.

17

In the six months that followed Ginny's arrival in California, a strange combination of events took place, which seemed minuscule at the moment of conception, but immense at the time of fruition. It was as if a mouse had given birth to an elephant.

Zelma Hurwitz had appeared on the "Tonight Show" ten days after Stevie signed her to an agency contract. In the history of the "Tonight Show," there had never been a more momentous entrance into showbiz than Zelma's appearance. She was scheduled for the beginning of the show, unusual for a newcomer. Zelma sang "As Time Goes By," with a special arrangement Stevie secured for her from one of her clients.

Johnny had been overwhelmed when he heard Zelma. Her voice was lustrous, loving, deep, profound and sexy. The audience stood and applauded for a full minute. On the spot, the producer threw out the material *and* the guests for the remainder of the show, and for an hour, broken only by commercials, Zelma and Johnny traded jokes and reminiscences, and Zelma sang. She sang with the band when they ad-libbed material she knew but hadn't rehearsed. She sang with a guitar someone handed her when she told Johnny that she knew a few chords. She smiled. She laughed. She cried with happiness. She displayed such poise, such charm, such humor that the program itself became a legend in show business. And at the end of the show she again sang, "As Time Goes By," and the show ran over with applause.

How could one performance on a late-night talk show turn a simple girl from Brooklyn, who hoped for a career as a computer programmer, into the hottest thing in show business? It happens. Overnight, a talent agency that was fully prepared to deal with the ordinary run of the mill found itself with extraordinary prospects for one of its clients.

Sy Rosen opened the daily staff meeting with the general subjects for discussion and was interrupted by Jerry Fentris asking whether they had all seen Zelma. From that moment, the meeting turned into a free-for-all, with asides to each other about the star potential of the girl and remarks about favorite bits she had done on last night's show.

Sy Rosen then asked for quiet. He had thought out this morning, he said, with Fred Wine, how the girl should be handled. She needed careful planning and attention from someone who had dealt with stars at the highest level. This would leave out Stevie Tree, who, he remarked, *had* been the one to bring Zelma into the agency and, after all, he smiled, it was the job of each and every one of the agents to look for promising new talent. He himself, said Sy Rosen, had a remarkable record of finding new talent . . . and he named the stars he had brought into the agency.

Stevie recognized that she was being frozen out, an all-too-familiar pattern, and that this was the declaration of war. She was going too far, too fast, and the forces around her were prepared to put her back where she belonged.

Stevie stayed behind to talk to Sy at the end of the meeting.

"Sy . . . I think that it's a mistake."

"What's that, Stevie?"

"Turning Zelma over to someone else."

"Not just someone *else*, Stevie. I'm going to handle her myself. I see a big future for her, and we can't make a mistake."

Stevie stared at him.

"Stevie . . . don't worry. I don't make mistakes. After all"—he smiled when he said it—"I didn't make a mistake when I hired you. Don't worry." He started to leave.

"No, Sy . . . I do worry . . . and Zelma worries, too. She was very concerned about who in the agency would represent her and she insisted that the contract state that I would."

"I haven't seen the contract; it was handled by Legal."

"Not that you won't be an enormous help to Zelma's career when we discuss it at staff meetings, but that's what you get paid for, Sy . . . and that's what you have the most fun doing . . . supervising the whole agency, not just one client."

Sy paused and reflected. He had seen power plays before. He had initiated many of them. He quickly measured Stevie. Would she, could she pull the plug on this million-dollar talent? He knew that the contract called for Stevie's personal representation. He had remarked on it to one of the agency lawyers. They would have to find a way around it. He wasn't sure whether Stevie would be willing to walk, and if she walked, whether Zelma would walk with her.

Stevie clinched it. "Zelma has been living with me since she came to the Coast. Wait till you meet her. She's really a sweet kid."

Sy turned to leave. "Love to meet her when you bring her in, Stevie. I know that she's in good hands with you—in every way."

She had won this particular skirmish, but Sy wouldn't forget, and there would be another day.

Ginny had waited only three weeks after her arrival to move out of Stevie's apartment. There had been no goodbyes, no conversations, only a note. "I'll give you a call if I need anything. Your sister." Nothing more. Stevie was sure that it wouldn't be long before she heard what Ginny was up to. Hollywood was too small

a town, and Stevie was becoming too well-known. For
the moment, it was a relief to put Ginny out of her
mind.

Three hours after Ginny left the apartment at the
Marina, she was turning tricks on Sunset Boulevard.
On her first weekend in L.A., while Stevie was in New
York with Zelma Hurwitz, Ginny met a pimp named
Frankie Davillo who was living with a seventeen-year-
old named Betty McCord. Frankie was nineteen,
tough-talking and good-looking. He was streetwise and
knew the inside of most of the Hollywood scene. On
that Saturday afternoon, Frankie spotted Ginny clum-
sily soliciting on Hollywood Boulevard. He took her
aside and told her that he could help her get established. Betty, who joined them, was funny and plump.
One wouldn't have thought that she would have gotten
much attention on a street where tall, stacked girls,
both black and white, sashayed up and down the
Boulevard in hot pants and high heels. Betty had a
different approach, which Frankie had taught her and
which he was about to introduce to Ginny. It consisted
simply of standing on street corners with the most
traffic and hitching rides. Ideally, the notion was to pick
the best-looking cars, with single men in them, and
once in the car, it was easy to suggest that the driver
pull into a parking lot or even a side street for a quick
blow job. It was simple and direct, and the best part
was it turned good samaritans into customers. So
Betty's bouncy looks, which gave her the appearance of
a schoolgirl, stopped a lot of traffic.

There was some danger of a driver getting angry and
taking the girls to the police. That happened so rarely
that it wasn't a real problem. Of course, the driver
could be a cop himself. In that case, the way out was to
offer the blow job free of charge and hope the action
was more attractive than the bust. It frequently happened. In the heat of an afternoon, returning from a
tour, cops driving their own cars were not above "one
for the road." The most serious difficulty was the true
samaritan who gave the girls a stern talking to in an

attempt to save their souls. The greatest annoyance was
the square who refused to redeposit the girl on the
street after the shock of the offer wore off, and insisted
on attempting to rehabilitate the sweet young thing in
the course of driving her miles out of her way.

The action in the parking lot of supermarkets off
Sunset on a sunny afternoon was brisk. There were
favorites off the Strip where the girl told the john to
park. He could pull out his cock without interference
from someone with a shopping cart. It didn't take more
than a few minutes. It was neat, didn't disturb a girl's
makeup or hair, and she didn't have to wash up like she
did after screwing. A girl could turn eight or ten tricks
in an afternoon at ten to twenty dollars a trick.

On that first Saturday afternoon, Ginny got picked
up on Sunset near the corner of Highland Avenue, took
the john into a parking lot in the back of an office
building that was closed, gave him head, collected
twenty bucks and, since he was going that way, drove
west on Sunset to the Beverly Hills Hotel. Ginny had a
notion that she had decided to turn into reality. The
mountains of Morgan Oliver clippings that Stevie kept
in her closet intensified her curiosity to meet her sister's
love obsession. She knew that Morgan Oliver occupied
a bungalow at the Beverly Hills Hotel. How she would
approach him she hadn't decided, nor had she figured
out what she would do once she met him. It would take
care of itself. But she knew one thing. She knew that
the sweetest revenge she could invent would be to have
Morgan Oliver.

Ginny's "date" let her out of his car on the corner of
Sunset Boulevard and Crescent Drive, in Beverly Hills.
The huge pink hotel sat in an entire block of elegant
greenery, interspersed with varieties of palms. The
hotel approach was an inclined drive leading to a
portico, protected from the sight of the street. Dodging
an array of expensive foreign cars, driving behind and
past her up the road to the entrance, Ginny finally
stood in front of the grand structure, the color of fresh
Gaspé salmon. Parking boys were rushing to open

doors and whisk away cars, only to be replaced by
equally luxurious Rolls Royces, Mercedes, Ferraris,
Porsches.

At another hotel, Ginny's outfit of faded jeans and a
tight T-shirt, without a bra to conceal anything, might
have caused curious looks from the bellman who
opened the huge bronze and glass doors to the lobby.
The Beverly Hills fraternity of rock stars, producers,
directors and their ladies dressed much the same.
Nevertheless, in respect to Ginny, men in the lobby
turned to stare at her. Not yet out of her teens, Ginny
had a stunning figure, a glorious head of raven black
hair, and the soft, suggestive, petulant look of a
naughty child. A very appealing combination anywhere, and even more in a community given to passion
in perverse sexual games.

Ginny picked up the house phone and asked the
operator to connect her with Morgan Oliver. When the
operator asked the name of the party calling, she hung
up. Ginny walked into the Polo Lounge and asked the
bartender for the number of Morgan's bungalow. She
didn't know that hookers at the bar had an arrangement with the bartender to protect their territory. The
bartender phoned the house detective, who called the
cops, and they in turn booked Ginny for soliciting.

It was a temporary delay as far as she was concerned.
She had found the way out of her sister's custody
through Frankie, who would be her pimp. She knew
where her quarry was to be found, and that he was the
key to settling a score with her sister that was long
overdue.

In the first weeks after Sam Di Benedetto returned to
his wife, Stevie phoned Laurie several times, once
getting Laurie's mother on the phone. Her cold reception made Stevie recognize that she was not welcome,
and so she resorted to sending Laurie presents with
funny notes, not knowing whether the presents would
even be delivered. She spoke to Sam a few times.
Neither she nor Sam made any mention of the gifts.

Mostly the conversations were general, but always Sam would report on Laurie's health. Nothing had changed. It could only get worse.

Stevie began to throw herself more and more into her work. She had decided to submerge her frustrations about her sister, her longing for Laurie and her feelings of being separated from everyone, the men at the agency, her clients, her dates, even herself, with a total commitment to work.

Stevie managed to keep three separate days going, both in person and on the telephone. When she rose early, she made phone calls to New York and Europe, doing business first with London. Since they were nine hours ahead of L.A. in London, when Stevie awoke at six, she could talk to London at the city's return from lunch. With that done, she could begin the New York day; at eight o'clock in California, she could do an hour's worth of phoning before New York went to lunch. Then Stevie could embark on the California day by having a breakfast appointment or going into the agency early. The day would extend to six-thirty or seven, unless, of course, there was a TV show she had a client on or a screening she had to attend. Thus, business could, and did, occupy eighteen hours out of her day. Stevie was busier than ever before, and more miserable, too.

At two o'clock one afternoon Stevie left the IA offices for a hair appointment with Jon De Lisle. Stevie changed beauty salons every six months or more, as Jon moved from place to place. Jon was developing a loyal following, becoming a star in his own right, who could locate at any salon of his choosing. But his elevation on the gay social scene had made him a prima donna with his employers and his clients, and his working relationships were frequently short-lived.

Now Stevie waited impatiently while Jon was having one of his lengthy gossipy chats on the phone. How Jon could talk!

Stevie had met Jon the day she arrived in Hollywood, eight years before, the day she walked into Schwab's

and saw his note on the wall. As friendships go in
Hollywood, it was an eternity, one-third of her entire
life, and yet she was never certain where his allegiances
lay. Stevie had the inner suspicion that she was in a
holding pattern of Jon's friendship, filling a place in the
sky for him that needed continuing traffic of planes at
different altitudes, and that at any moment he might
turn away from her like a radar sweep and find another
plane to track.

As she sat in his chair waiting for him to finish his
conversation, she realized that those feelings were very
similar to the way she felt about everyone lately. She
had initially felt that Sy Rosen would be a father to her,
kind, loving and indulgent. He would be intent on her
progress, and delighted to see her move far and fast.
But that hadn't occurred. She sensed that she had
drawn first blood on Sy with the contest for control of
Zelma Hurwitz, and it was the beginning of a battle
that might mean her future at IA. Why would he turn
on her? What was there about her or about the town
that would make this kind of topsy-turvy relationship
inevitable?

Then there was Sam Di Benedetto. She found *that*
relationship the most confusing of all. Sam had followed every move she made after she got out of the
hospital, attentive to her needs, to her state of mind.
He was the prototype of a man very much in love. So
much that it frightened her. Then as she became more
her own person, stronger physically and mentally, Sam
seemed to drift away. She had done nothing in the early
days to encourage him, but that wouldn't stop a man
who was truly interested. The truth of it, she thought,
was that her strength disturbed him. Like everyone
else, it seemed, he too wanted her to be a piece of
putty, a helpless creature encased in bandages, a
dependent child.

With her sister Ginny, she didn't understand how she
could think that life with her aunt and uncle in Urbana
was better than the company of a group of girls her own
age, who shared a common fate and a common need.

There was companionship, while Stevie had none. She considered telling Ginny about Uncle Bert—the fear and anxiety, the shame and guilt. But she was afraid Ginny might not believe her. Now that Stevie had become self-sufficient and independent, she knew she was a target for Ginny's vilest envy.

The relationship with David had been the only one in her life that had given her any pleasure. It had lasted less than a year, and it had been taken from her by a senseless killing. Even the possibility of keeping the memory green by occupying the house on Laurel Canyon was denied her by his sister. To be weak and submissive meant she would not get the house. By God, she *would* have it, she would not be used as a pawn in the contest over David's memory.

Was there a common thread to it all? Was Stevie just feeling sorry for herself? So what? But those *were* the facts. The elements hung together. When she was weak and tiny and frail, she was adored. It was OK to be a third-class citizen at the banquet. "Women are the niggers of the world." Yeah, man, you know it. But let them raise their heads high and begin to feel that they have a right to be equal, and that's the beginning of trouble in paradise.

Sure, thought Stevie, she was mixing up a lot of things. What the hell did women's roles have to do with her problem with Ginny? No matter. Sure, she thought, it all had to do with her father, Ray Tree, that unfeeling creature whose lack of love and affection had caused her mother to take lovers, and who destroyed their lives by killing her mother, robbing two little girls of a home and a mother. Ray Tree had been undoubtedly screwing every breathing thing in his path, but her mother's indiscretions were worthy of the ultimate punishment. Men's power over women. Fuck that!

And there was Morgan Oliver, the man who had taken everything from her. True, she had degraded herself by being his whore, living out her mother's prophetic fate. Morgan had been the highest-paid pimp in the world. Well, he was slipping badly, but not badly enough. He had been responsible for her suicide attempt, bringing the shame and ugliness of her whoredom to a point where she no longer wanted to live.

She thought of Morrie Amster. He had been the only decent one, besides David. But they both had been taken from her, and all she had left was herself, and now IA wanted to take *THAT* away from her too. She was becoming too successful, too much a threat. How do you get to be the most important woman in Hollywood? How do you get up there with the *big* power, not just as a woman? How do you get there with the most powerful *men*? No woman had ever done that.

Until Stevie Tree. She knew how to get there. She took the measure of the industry leaders she had met. She could handle them. Yes, she knew their strengths and their weaknesses.

Stevie decided at that moment that she would own the house on Laurel Canyon she and David had shared. She could enlist one of her clients to buy it in his name and resell it to her. If it appeared to the client to be a costly and bizarre method of buying a house, so be it. She would do it today.

Jon De Lisle was still talking animatedly to a lover on the phone. Stevie reached over to him and tapped him on the shoulder, and did the unpardonable thing that one must never do to a star—she interrupted him.

"Jon . . . get off that phone. I don't have all day. I have things to do. Get off the goddam phone, and fix my hair, and no shit-fits either."

Stevie had decided to win. She figured that was the only choice open to her.

18

Decisions that involved human life, the future of a talent agency and Stevie's career were way down the line. It appeared that God had given her a sign. After she summoned up the courage to threaten her hairdresser, she discovered that for the very first time, Jon gave her the look, the cut, the feeling that she wanted, without complaining, bitching, or any general distemper. Stevie smiled to herself and realized that all was not lost.

And she had already decided not to lose that fine edge, that nuance of attitude that puts you on top, the perspective of yourself and of others that makes them do what you want. In her mind, Stevie had clearly abandoned the pretense of looking for anything that power could not provide.

It *was* a new Stevie Tree, not different in appearance from the old, but substantially different in attitude, after her soul-searching hair appointment with Jon De Lisle. Only a woman can understand the courage necessary for Stevie to free herself from the tyranny of a hairdresser. Only a woman appreciates the fear and trembling she overcame to be critical and demanding of a hairdresser *before* she put her head in his hands. What might have emerged—a chihuahua?

With this in mind, Stevie Tree acted with a new sureness at the agency. Her first step was to resolve the future of Zelma Hurwitz. All that had happened in her remarkably short history was a one-shot appearance on the "Tonight Show" that had launched her. Zelma had

already taped the special that was to launch the season
for Flack and Flaherty. Stevie had seen it two days ago
when the boys invited her to watch the finished
product.

Freddy Flack, the director of the pair, had done a lot
of ducking and weaving in the production of the
special. He had thoughtfully constructed it to avoid the
traps into which an unseasoned performer could fall.
Having lived through the rehearsals, in which Zelma
appeared as a somewhat hesitant, uncertain performer,
he had given her the protection that he thought she
needed—the long dolly shots that kept away from
closeups, distant enough to miss the lack of stage
presence. With overhead shots, low-angle shots, shots
seen past palm trees in the foreground, singing groups
in the background, Zelma was a captive of production.
When Stevie saw what was happening, she took her
client aside and carefully made her points.

"Fellas . . . you're fucking up." Hardly a tasteful
and thoughtful introduction to any request.

"Stevie," Freddy said, as he got up to leave, "I'll give
you thirty seconds to say goodbye. Agents should be
seen, not heard."

Stevie looked at them both and smiled. "Correction
—*we're* fucking up, but you're fucking up more."

They laughed nervously. Stevie went on to explain
that the very thing they were trying to hide was what
made Zelma extraordinary. They had prerecorded the
vocals and provided a superb sound track. Fine on
records—but that required her to lip-synch to the
playback. As tough as that was to do for someone really
experienced, it destroyed the essence of Zelma Hurwitz. The warts were Zelma, and the audience would
react to her vulnerability. Stevie was certain that as bad
as she was in rehearsal, she would be that great in
performance. Stevie called for the tape of the "Tonight
Show" to review again, and with that as an example the
production team threw out most of what they had done.
They put a microphone into Zelma's hand. She carried
it and stood awkwardly. She tripped on the cord during

the taping, and they left that in. The audio went out for ten seconds and Zelma, not hearing the musical background, yelled out, "God, don't do this to me. I'll have to go back to computer school." The tape was recording during that remark, and they left that in. Toward the end of the taping, the production team was looking for curves to throw at their star, wanting the charm of her ad-libs. When they finished, they had a gem. The program would later go on to win an Emmy in every eligible category, and in the tape editing the producers tried to eliminate the few creeping elements of slickness that had somehow remained.

Stevie, having seen the completed work, realized its extraordinary potential. She imagined that no one at NBC had screened it yet, since it was simply a summer show and the network had other problems.

Stevie's first phone call was to the network vice president with whom she had negotiated the summer deal for Flack and Flaherty.

"Hello, this is Stevie Tree of IA. Can I speak to Brad Michaels please?"

"Miss Tree, he's on the horn with an important overseas call. Can he call you back?"

"No . . . I'll wait, if you don't mind . . ."

The secretary sighed. Her boss had more urgent business than to talk to every agent who called. "All right, but he may be a while."

"Thanks, I understand . . . I have nothing else to do. I'll wait."

Thirty seconds went by and Brad Michaels got on the phone.

"Hi, Stevie . . . how's our little show?"

"Brad, that's why I called you. It's a disaster. I don't want our people to be associated with it anymore. We want to back out. After all, better to know *now* than have egg on our faces later."

"Stevie . . . how bad can it be? I don't have any reports on the show from any of my people. If they're on my desk, I haven't seen them yet . . . but, Stevie, you can't pull out now . . . we need this show for the summer. We have to fill that hole. Granted, it's not an important showcase—not as many people watch the tube during the summer, but we have an obligation to program the network fifty-two weeks a year. Stevie, surely you can control your clients. Really, how bad can it be?"

"Brad, it has more to do with professional reputations. The way it is, unless you and your people can convince them otherwise, they don't want to deliver the show for your summer slotting."

"Stevie—I beg you. It's too late to get anything else. Who gives a shit how bad it is, nobody is watching . . . *nobody*!"

"Brad, the only thing I can think of is to get your people together and screen it. I'll have the boys there . . . and maybe you can convince them."

"Good idea, Stevie. I'll set it up for three o'clock tomorrow. You have them there. I'll have all my people there. Stevie, we can't let this happen. My job is on the line."

Stevie didn't bother to explain the nature of the meeting to Flack and Flaherty. She thought about it briefly and realized that she was trying to pull a very tricky piece of business. If she had partners in the transaction, not only would she have to watch out for herself, but she'd have to be on the alert for them as well. It was her show, and she was playing with fire. Better do it alone.

Stevie knew that she would never have been able to get all the network brass she wanted into one room to view a small summer show, except on the basis of disaster. She also knew that there were two moments in the course of a success to sell something, the first before it happens, and the second after. From the sizzle, you had the input of the customer's imagination working for you. From the steak, you dealt with the fickle goddess of the public, and maybe, just maybe, they were behind in their thinking. Stevie decided that in the case of Zelma Hurwitz, she would sell from the sizzle, from the steak, and even from the stove.

The screening room was luxurious. A single thirty-inch receiver stood in the center of a dozen lounge chairs, carefully placed so that everyone got an unrestricted view, without offending shoulders and heads in the way. Promptly at three, Stevie and her clients walked into the room. The tension was so thick that she felt disaster reaching out to her. Stevie thought that she had truly miscalculated. This was hardly the atmosphere in which to develop a deal. She nodded to the group. Brad Michaels had kept his promise. Everyone important was there, including the president of the network. The power represented in the room was startling. She stood.

"I'm Stevie Tree, for those of you I haven't met—and you may hate me before we're finished." They looked at each other curiously.

Stevie continued. "Brad, your secretary said that you had planned to leave for Europe today and would be out of town when the show hit the air."

Brad Michaels looked at her, questioningly. Stevie turned to another man and continued, "Mr. Sawyer, I know as president of the network you don't pay attention to summer replacement shows. The important money goes into the fall and winter. Chances are you'd never see this program either on or off the air. So, with three strikes against getting you all together, I brought you here under false pretenses. The show you are about to see is probably one of the finest ever produced for TV. If you gentlemen put this show on the air during the summer, it will destroy a golden opportunity. This program, and what it represents, is exactly what you need starting September at eight o'clock on Monday night."

Stevie had their attention, but for what reason she wasn't sure. "I could have waited till the program went on the air, but two things would have happened. First, this show would have been wasted on a small percent of the potential audience, and second, your competition would have had an unfair jump on you, since they would have seen it at the same time you did."

The president, Tim Sawyer, looked at Stevie intently.

"So, gentlemen, it's good to know when to get off stage. I'll wait outside, biting my nails. If I'm wrong, IA will be looking for a new agent."

Ginny Tree made her connection with Morgan Oliver. It had taken a lot of patience, and a hundred and thirty dollars' worth of tips to bellboys and chambermaids at the Beverly Hills Hotel in order to keep track of the comings and goings of her quarry. It was a procedure that had been as carefully planned and executed as a military campaign. In her own way, Ginny was repeating her sister's pattern, whose volumes of clippings on the goings and comings of Morgan Oliver gave her a knowledge that no one else had about him. That discovery, more than any other fact, had set Ginny in the direction of Morgan.

It was certainly true that to a young teenage girl, this enormously handsome and highly sexual star was a fit subject for fantasies. Millions of teenage youngsters were official or unofficial members of Morgan Oliver fan clubs, but the recognition that Stevie Tree had once been this man's lover, and had been rejected by him in some mysterious way, made the chase even more tantalizing. The size of her revenge was directly related to the extent of her sister's obsession with Morgan. She knew that there was no more killing way to even the score than to capture Morgan Oliver for herself.

In the daily battle for survival that Ginny maintained without home and family, she learned quickly to read the signs that would keep her alive. She learned how to ingratiate herself with the Sisters at the home. She had let one of them make love to her and assured her friendly assistance. She seduced one of the Brothers who taught her at the convent school. She understood how to get money from strangers with a sad and compelling story, and she learned how to tease. Ginny knew that she would be able to read Morgan Oliver from her first contact, and she knew, even at seventeen, that she had the gift of making people do what she wanted. That gift had been explored and refined in order to survive.

Ginny now lived with Frank Davillo and his girl, Betty McCord. She knew that most of the money she gave Frank went to drugs for the three of them. Ginny stationed herself on Sunset along the Strip, at about ten in the morning. Any earlier, she had learned, was useless. The drivers might pick her up, but none of them was interested in playing that early in the morning. After ten until sunset, it was just like shooting fish in a barrel. When it got dark, drivers were not anxious to stop, for fear there was a boyfriend nearby who might resort to violence. For Ginny's part, she didn't want to get involved with a crazy after dark. In somebody's car in daylight, if things got hairy, there was always a possibility of opening a door and jumping. In the dark, it was dangerous.

One morning, almost a month after she began her quest for Morgan, she phoned the hotel and spoke to the bell captain. He told her that he had checked in the night before. It was eleven in the morning and Ginny figured that she had about five hours to kill. She got picked up on Sunset near Gower by a schoolteacher from Burbank, who had just deposited his class at the Los Angeles Museum. When Ginny suggested sex, he laughed and continued driving. Ginny began massaging his thigh. She moved her hand to his crotch and felt his cock stir. He belonged to her now. She pointed him in the direction of an office building parking lot on the corner of Sunset and El Centro. Ten minutes later, the schoolteacher drove her out of the parking lot and dropped her off. She popped a red into her mouth, swallowed it without water and waited for her next trick. She had earned twenty dollars and lifted the teacher's American Express card from his wallet.

At three o'clock, Ginny hitched her way to the Beverly Hills Hotel. By this time she had become familiar with the hotel grounds and the various entrances. She no longer had to go through the lobby in order to get to the bungalows. She walked up Crescent Drive and across the lawn directly to a chambermaid who was pushing a cart along the pathways. Fifty dollars in tips had ensured that this chambermaid would let her into one bungalow when the time came. She told the maid that she collected autographs of the stars. No one would ever know how she got into the bungalow. The maid would leave the door open and disappear.

The chambermaid saw her from a distance. She left her cart, walked up the stairs to the bungalow and opened the door with a passkey. She left it ajar and returned to her cart, wheeled it away and disappeared.

Ginny entered the bungalow, closed the door behind her and walked into the living room. Room service dishes were scattered, uncollected, on the table and floor and three suitcases lay by the bed, partly unpacked. There was no one there. Spying a pack of cigarettes on the coffee table, she pried one out of the pack and lit it. The first match sputtered out, but the second lit the cigarette and she drew on it fully, allowing the smoke to escape from her throat. Carrying the cigarette in her hand, she walked into the bedroom. The king-size bed was made up and there was a pile of newspapers in the middle, plus a dozen message slips. A portable radio rested on the night table. Ginny picked it up and walked slowly into the bathroom.

On the sink were Morgan's shaving and toilet articles. A wet bath mat remained in front of the shower. Ginny pulled the bath mat away and threw it in a corner. She put a fresh towel on the floor in its place and turned on the water in the tub. She adjusted the temperature and put a stopper in the drain.

As the bathtub filled with hot water, Ginny took off her jeans and T-shirt. She slipped out of her high heels and sat on the toilet to pee. Then she flushed the toilet and stepped into the tub. She turned on the radio to a local rock station and placed the radio on the sink. The delicious feeling of the warm water moving upward on her body made her lean back in pleasure. She placed her hand on herself and began to masturbate, slowly, luxuriously. In a few moments she came in convulsions, and when the spasms slowed, she looked up and saw the famous blue eyes of Morgan Oliver.

"What the fuck are you doing here?"

"Mr. Oliver . . . I just came to get your autograph."

"Get the hell out of that bathtub, and make it fast."

Slowly Ginny got up from the tub, turned off the faucets and began to dry herself off. Each movement was painfully and delicately slow.

"Get your ass out of here, kid."

"Afraid of me, Mr. Oliver? Afraid of a little teenage girl?"

Morgan Oliver didn't move. He stood looking at the lovely, youthful figure, the tiny hips, the brown, fully formed nipples. She was challenging. She was insinuating. Almost in a flash, Ginny grabbed at his crotch and squeezed his balls.

"Gotcha, didn't I?"

"You little cunt. Get out of here."

She turned around quickly and bent down touching her toes, presenting him with a superb view of her pussy hair and ass. "Nice view, isn't it, Morgan?"

Morgan Oliver swatted her ass a stinging blow, and then he grabbed her around the waist and pulled her moist body over his lap as he sat down abruptly on the toilet seat lid. He spanked her a second and third time. Through his clothing, Ginny felt the hard stirrings of his cock.

It was the ninth time today in which she was certain of herself. At that moment, Morgan Oliver belonged to her, and that was the first step the first time. She knew what to do to make all the other steps work for her.

For now, as his cock strained under her body, she had him where she wanted him.

The next morning, the IA staff meeting started on time, and Sy Rosen opened the discussion after everyone was seated.

"Stevie, I got a call last night from Tim Sawyer . . . He wanted to congratulate me. I asked him why, and he said that you'd tell me yourself. I've known Tim for fifteen years . . . very helpful in getting him his job as president . . . and *he* wouldn't tell *me*." He continued coolly, "OK, let's hear it."

"Sy, I have a deal memo in my hand that represents a firm offer by the network for the Flack and Flaherty series."

Jerry Fentris interrupted. "We already sold that. It's three or four shots for the summer."

"No, they'll be programming reruns for the time period and rescheduling the show in the fall."

"What show is that?"

"The same show, but at a different price tag. The summer shows were at 175,000 apiece. The regular series will be at 350,000."

Sy Rosen interrupted. "Fully commissionable?"

"Yes, Sy . . . fully commissionable. The order is for twenty-six hours firm, which comes to over nine million dollars. Our commissions will come to $910,000." The room was suddenly quiet. Sy Rosen looked as if he had tasted something bitter and unpleasant. Jerry Fentris reached for a refill on his coffee from the carafe, and spilled some on the table as he poured. He grabbed some napkins and mopped up the liquid. Stevie continued.

"I guaranteed Zelma Hurwitz for two out of every thirteen shows."

One of the agents at the end of the table muttered, "I still haven't seen her tape."

Stevie heard the voice and ignored it. All eyes turned to the end of the table. Half of them hadn't seen the tape of Zelma's appearance on the "Tonight Show" either.

Sy Rosen looked at Stevie. "Sounds OK . . . but aren't you selling her too cheap if she turns out to be a real winner?"

"No, Sy . . . that's covered too. I worked in some additional provisions that protect us there. For every Emmy nomination, the network puts up an additional

$25,000, and for every Emmy the show, or the series wins, there's a $50,000 bonus.

"Christ, Stevie . . . Emmy's aren't anything . . . Aren't you selling her too cheap if the show goes through the roof?"

"I don't think so, Sy. If the show, or the series goes over a thirty percent share of audience, there are bonuses worked in that could bring it to another $50,000 per show. If it goes to a forty percent share, there is another $100,000 per show."

Jerry Fentris had now cleaned up his coffee. "Stevie, it sounds OK, but are you committing the girl for life? That's not smart."

"You're right, Jerry. Zelma's commitment is for a maximum of six shows during the first year, and the network has a right of first negotiation for each succeeding year. The network had us in a bad spot. If they put that show on the air, the one with Zelma in it, during the summer, it would have destroyed her career, or at least set it back. She would have been a nowhere lady on a summer replacement show, and she would have lost her virginity for virtually nothing. I had to get them to cancel the summer show."

Jerry Fentris paid attention. "Cancel? We can't let people cancel shows on us."

It seemed to Stevie that she was a kindergarten teacher taking an unwilling class for smallpox injections at the nurse's office. It was terrible, she thought, to have to drag them kicking and screaming. But she realized that this was the way it was going to be. Every step of the way she would have to have answers for *everything*.

"Jerry, rest easy. We've traded commissions amounting to $70,000 for an amount under a million, with the possibility of having the series continue, which would give us close to two million a year in commissions, plus launching Zelma on a career."

Sy Rosen broke in. "It may seem small to you, Stevie, but canceling a show—and our commissions?"

Stevie smiled. "I neglected to mention that I sold them four reruns of that turkey of a film show *Police Target* for the same spot."

Jerry Fentris looked stunned. "You're kidding. That's so old it's in black and white. What price did you get?"

"The same—$175,000 apiece. I tried for more, Jerry, but they explained that no one watches in the summer." Whatever triumph she felt, there were thorns in the laurels, she thought, as she eyed the dark suits that surrounded her.

In a town where royal weddings proliferated, hand in hand, with colossal films, the wedding of Cindy Warren to Randy Davis was in a class that included only epics.

Stevie was the maid of honor. She wore a pearl-colored satin sheath, calf-length so as not to compete with the bride. The ancient royalty of Hollywood was in attendance at Ted Caramia's Palace in Palm Springs, and Stevie looked around to discover that she and Cindy were less than half the age of the average guest. It was a standard Hollywood set. The women wore designer gowns and furs, and their diamonds covered far more flesh than was necessary. And the men wore golf clothes. Caramia wore a baseball jacket, featuring the name of his new Portland team. The wire services and two networks covered the event.

Cindy wore a Georgio gown as white as a swan's breast. The Beverly Hills shop had fitted the yards of filmy lace to Cindy's beautiful shape, as if the dress and the woman were one work of sculpture. Randy's swimming trunks were still damp from the pool, and draped over his shoulders was a huge, black terrycloth towel. In honor of the event, he carried a Bloody Mary and wore sandals.

During the brief ceremony, Stevie thought about the triumph of Cindy Warren. There were a lot of beautiful girls in Hollywood, as beautiful as Cindy, who never made it—either in their careers or in their personal lives. They fell by the wayside, left town, or ended with

small-time men and small-time money in the outback of
suburban living. What an easy way out, Stevie thought,
to marry someone like Randy Davis. Cindy had pulled
herself out of a downward spiral with a blinding kind of
luck.

But it wasn't the luck Stevie wanted. It was a fool's
game, she thought, to be owned by someone. Suicide
was better than being trapped in a bed and on a tennis
court. It occurred to Stevie that she had come some
distance; a week of Cindy's incarceration now and
she'd be climbing the gaudy, wallpapered walls.

The preacher pronounced the couple man and wife.

Randy's accountants and lawyers had calculated the
cost of the wedding. Caramia paid for the refreshments, but the additional help and catering cost him
$20,000 and that was why he wanted to be seen and
photographed in his baseball jacket. His accountants
had said he might be able to charge it all off to P.R.

The rest of the costs were more substantial and borne
solely by Randy. First, the amount that Cindy spent on
new clothes before, during and after the wedding was
$35,000. Randy gave Cindy a diamond ring from Van
Cleef & Arpels that cost $25,000, a new Mercedes 450
SLC that ran to $30,000, since it was a special order in a
non-stock color. Next were the incidental expenses that
Randy incurred getting a divorce from his wife. He had
settled with his wife for a cash payment of three million
dollars, plus the house they owned in Holmby Hills,
plus a yearly payment of $150,000 for ten years, even
should his wife marry again. The amount was substantial but would have been millions more if his wife had
not signed a prenuptial agreement. That called for a lot
less than the amount actually paid, but his wife's lawyer
had petitioned the court to have it set aside due to the
fact that undue pressure had been brought to bear on
her to sign the document before *that* wedding.

The marriage to Cindy Warren (formerly Miss
Tennessee) had cost Randy Davis over five million
dollars, either in payments made, or to be made.
Randy's lawyer had insisted that Cindy sign a prenup-

tial agreement, which Cindy cheerfully did, noting to herself with some thought that she was being put under undue pressure, too.

After the wedding reception and the drinking and eating, Randy and his pals left for the golf course and their respective ladies sat alongside Ted's pool playing backgammon. Cindy was taking lessons in backgammon from a private tutor who came to the house she and Randy were leasing in Bel Air. Plans were being drawn for the new colossal home Randy was going to build just north of Malibu.

The film coverage of the wedding was now safely stored in the vaults of the TV stations, awaiting any update on the relationship—children, custody battles, a wedding anniversary, divorce. For the time being, the happy couple dropped from sight in a flurry of endless spending.

19

At IA, it was business as usual. The jockeying for
position continued to be more important than the quest
and management of business. After all, when you've
got the stars, business has to come your way. Then, on
Monday morning, Fred Wine dropped a bombshell that
demanded everyone's attention.

"Sy . . . I took a phone call early this morning from
the head of Cinema Studios—Charles Goodman.
Camille has been shut down in Rome for ten days now,
and it's costing the company seventy-five grand a day,
with no end in sight."

Jerry Fentris interrupted. "I know all about it, Sy.
It's Diedre . . . that crazy bitch tried to kill herself two
weeks ago, and Walker went bananas."

"How did she do it? Aren't they covered by cast
insurance?"

Fred Wine continued, "No . . . there's no cast insurance on suicide attempts. If she actually killed herself,
they could collect, but on an attempt, then it wouldn't
apply."

"You mean," Stevie asked, "it would have been OK
if she had died?"

Jerry continued, "Oh, yeah . . . and we still would
have been able to commission the amount of her salary,
even if she didn't perform."

Stevie could hardly believe her ears. The discussion
concerned a human being, the possibility of her suicide
attempt being covered by insurance or not and the

prospect of her receiving her full salary whether she died or not.

Stevie tried to hide her reaction. "Maybe she'll try it again and be successful. Could we suggest that?"

Sy Rosen looked her way. He was the only one in the room to acknowledge the grisly humor of her remark. He took charge. "Gentlemen, there's no value in talking about the 'might-have-been.' We've got an obligation to Charley Goodman to get production going again if we can. Jerry, why don't you hop a plane to Rome and see what you can do?"

Jerry Fentris was having very serious personal problems with his black girlfriend and was not anxious to leave town. "Sy, maybe you ought to send one of the other fellows—I've got so much work in town here."

"Jerry, one of the other men can cover for you. After all, Walker is your client."

Fred Wine had a thought. "Sy, what would you think about sending Stevie with Jerry? She's a woman and maybe she can talk to Diedre. It's a thought."

Sy Rosen paused a moment. "I don't like to have two of my people away at one time. What do you think, Jerry?"

Jerry Fentris quickly noted that with Stevie there, any fuck-up would have two parents and, if he played it smart, only one—Stevie. He could arrange an emergency back home that would get him out of Rome in twenty-four hours and allow him to deal with his personal problems. It would make for a lot of air travel in the course of two days, but it was better than being committed endlessly to hand-holding a pair of idiots like Walker Perkins and the love of his life, hopelessly miscast as Camille, Diedre Magee.

Jerry gave an instant readout. "I think it's a good idea . . . and it could get Stevie into a broader agency situation in the picture end of things."

Stevie turned to look at Jerry's face. 'How could anyone talk such bullshit?'

The two of them caught the American Airlines flight

to New York three hours later, connecting with a Pan Am flight to Rome.

On the hour-and-a-half taxi ride in from the Leonardo Da Vinci Airport to the Hassler Hotel, Stevie had a long conversation with Jerry Fentris. She had wanted to talk to Jerry on the plane about the problem they were about to face, but he slept most of the way. There was no way he could sleep in the taxi.

"Look . . . I don't have any more clues than you do. Walker is a strange duck. He was an associate professor of English at some jerkwater school in the East, and he's a film junkie."

"What do you mean by that?"

"Shit, there's not a movie ever made that he hasn't seen . . . I mean it. He could block out the shooting script of every major film that's been made in the last twenty-five years. Who needs that? All that shit is on TV anyway."

"How did he get his start?"

"You won't believe it. He was in the middle of writing some thesis or other on the history of the motorcycle film and he had this date with a guy named Harry Schwartz, who made more motorcycle films in his life than Kawasaki has wheels."

"Go on." Stevie was becoming interested in this strange man, Walker Perkins.

"Well, as I get the story, Walker started telling him how motorcycle films were the true American art form. Not since D. W. Griffith had there ever been anyone more involved in the development of culture than Harry Schwartz and that kind of bullshit. Harry ate it up and he gave Walker a couple of motorcycle scripts that he was considering. Walker read them and gave Harry some criticism, and Harry wound up letting Walker direct the two of them. Of course, Harry didn't pay him a nickel, but the flicks were pretty good."

Stevie nodded. "I know them—*Bike Fever* and *Wheelies*. They played all the festivals, the Museum of

Modern Art included. Wound up grossing substantially all over the world. They're both classics."

Jerry was trying to find a corner of the taxi that wasn't bouncing in order to continue his nap, but the road and the driver wouldn't cooperate. "How come if you know all this, you want to hear it from me?"

Stevie patted Jerry on the head. "There's a lot about him I don't know. It may be tiresome, Jerry—but it also may come in handy."

Jerry seized the chance. "Yeah, Stevie . . . I've got a feeling that you'll be here longer than me. Got lots of problems back home."

Stevie was certain it was more of the same that he had confided in her at the Derby, and she hoped that he would have the sense to keep the latest developments to himself. Jerry, armed with the knowledge that the cable to bring him back to L.A. was already waiting for him at the hotel in Rome, continued the story. "Well, he got a big break from that . . . and every artsy-fartsy studio head in town thought that he was a fucking genius. So they lined up to give him pictures. There was only one problem, every picture he took on to do was a copy of some other picture that was made before by someone else, but goddammit, I'll say this for the bastard—they were successful."

"I read his contract on the plane. He's getting a fortune for this picture—three-quarters of a million dollars, plus twenty-five percent of the profits."

"Oh, yeah, Fred Wine did that deal. Plus he lives like a goddam king! Travels with his secretary, who handles nothing that is related to the picture business, mind you . . . limos all over, suites, Winnebagos, huge expenses, a private chef that's on the budget of the picture. And this guy is five years out of teaching Shakespeare at twelve thou a year."

"Diedre Magee . . . she was in his first two pictures, *The Dollar Club* and *Conspiracy*," Stevie noted. "And they've been together since that time."

"She's OK, I guess. Never acted much before, and

he found her doing breakfast food commercials.
Good-looking dish, cold as ice. Never cared much for
her personally, but that's Walker's business."

"Any notion about why she attempted suicide?"

"Who knows any of that stuff? I think dames try
suicide the same way they try a new hairstyle."

Stevie bit her lip. 'Stupid bastard. She had done it
herself. There was such a short distance between letting
events take their course and living; or doing something
about it and dying. If Laurel Canyon had been ten feet
deeper at that point, she would have done it, according
to the doctor.'

The taxi was taking them closer to the city. The day
was bright and sunny. Sunlight in Rome is golden, and
Stevie marveled at the mustard-seed-colored walls of
the old buildings they passed on the outskirts of the
city.

Motor scooters threaded in and out. Small Fiats
passed in and out of the line of traffic. Stevie inquired
how much longer to the hotel, but the driver didn't
seem to understand the question. Jerry was continuing
his discourse. "This *fakokta* city gives me a pain in the
ass. You can't get a decent steak for love or money
. . . We're gonna be met at the hotel by the producer,
a nice enough guy. Ralph Berlin. He's a glorified office
boy, a regular gofer for Perkins. Perkins is a goddam
dictator on the set. The producer's job is to make him
happy and stay out of the way. *Camille?* Schlemiel,
they should call this opus."

Jerry was running out of steam and the road was
improving, even though the traffic was getting heavier,
when suddenly the city of Rome stretched out before
her, the Colosseum, the Forum, St. Peter's, which
Stevie had only seen in photos. It may have been a
routine for tourists on the part of the taxi driver, or it
may have been a plot to lengthen the fare, but Stevie
couldn't have cared less. For a few brief minutes this
was the Rome of fantasy, and she tuned out the verbal
meanderings of her companion. "Some of the best

hookers in the world—they're terrific. You can have them sent to your hotel, or find them for yourself at any of the best bars. And clean."

Jerry had clearly forgotten that he was traveling with a woman. Stevie couldn't resist a dig in retaliation.

"Jerry, is your flag still at half mast?"

Jerry looked at her. He had forgotten the drunken revelation of his multi-martini lunch. "It's getting better. I had a semi the other day with my girlfriend," he parried.

"I thought that it always worked with your black lady."

"Oh, her . . . she was a pain in the ass, always wanting new clothes and for me to take her out. Imagine what it would look like—me taking her to Chasen's. Why, she's no better than a hooker."

"What's your problem now?"

"My wife. She found out about the black chick . . . *after* I dumped her. Some irony, huh? My wife's got all the bread in the family from her family, so I got a lot of *tsuris*."

Ralph Berlin was in the lobby of the Hassler when they arrived. He had been waiting for the last hour, hoping that some miracle would be transported from the States in the form of Walker Perkins' agent. In five minutes his hopes were dashed. Jerry asked for messages at the front desk as he was checking in. He opened the cable that he had arranged to have sent to himself, with the message he had composed: "IMPERATIVE YOU RETURN TO L.A. IMMEDIATELY. YOUR WIFE MILDRED ATTEMPTED SUICIDE LAST NIGHT. ONLY YOUR PRESENCE CAN INSURE POSSIBILITY HER LIVING THROUGH THE ORDEAL. SIGNED DR. BENJAMIN FOSTER."

Stevie thought to herself, 'What a crock of shit.' Jerry thought his cable was inspired. If one suicide attempt in Rome could trigger a rescue, a fabricated suicide in Los Angeles could counter that. Quickly, Ralph Berlin and the production assistant, who sat by his side, made the arrangements to get him a reservation back to L.A.

"My God, Jerry . . . when it rains it pours," was

Ralph Berlin's inspired remark on the suicide contagion.

Jerry Fentris had figured the connections himself and knew that to get out promptly he could catch a BEA flight that would take him to London, and then over the North Pole to L.A. If he could get a taxi straight out, he could catch the flight. As luck would have it, the doorman and the taxi driver who drove them from the airport were in conversation. Since the driver didn't understand any English, and since he couldn't have cared less, he wasn't surprised to find the same luggage back in his taxi and to receive instructions from the doorman to take the passenger back to the airport. As Jerry Fentris drove off, feigning anxiety about his poor wife and sympathy for Stevie for the job at hand, he was most concerned about whether he could get it up in order to give his wife a long delayed fuck with sufficient sincerity to convince her to stay with him. It would be tough to do, after twelve thousand miles of travel in twenty-four hours. 'Holy shit, the jet lag alone would throw a *zetz* into anyone.' There was a rule in the State Department not to allow their people to do business for a day after a trip lasting longer than eight hours. He wasn't in the State Department, and they didn't have as much at stake as he had. For them it was only the survival of Western democracy. For Jerry Fentris, it was his membership at Hillcrest Country Club and his charge account at Eric Ross.

Ralph Berlin waited glumly in the sitting room of Stevie's suite as she washed her face and changed her clothes. What had seemed like an emotional moment —which he understood—in the love lives of two creative people, Walker Perkins and Diedre Magee, had turned into a nightmare. At forty-six, Berlin had been through a lot of shit in the making of movies. Some of them had been worth it. Most of them had not. He didn't pretend to have the vaguest notion as to whether this film was good or bad. He hadn't known from the script. He hadn't known from the dailies. He hadn't figured it out from the cut sections that the editor put together. The reason he had no opinion was that no one had given him the studio opinion yet. As soon as he got that message, he would know whether the film was OK and would defend that opinion to the death.

Ralph Berlin was technically an expert at the mechanics of crew calls, union regulations, alternative places to shoot when you lost permission at the very last minute, and the matter of meal penalties and overtime provisions when you shot too late. He was also expert in the art of getting the first shot of the day put in the can quickly. He knew that when the studio executives looked at the daily production report, they were most concerned with the time of crew call and the time it took to get the first shot of the day. The way Ralph Berlin solved that problem with a temperamental director was to give the cinematographer a small Aeroflex and tell him to shoot twenty-five feet of scenery. *That* technique was institutionalized by Ralph Berlin and practically patented. More than any other skill, that endeared him to the production executives in the studio. For fifteen years, he had guarded that technique as his own, even though half the industry knew of it. He alone used it religiously. The others thought it too stupid to try. What they didn't realize was that as simple-minded as it was, it continued to get him pictures to produce, while his more sophisticated confreres went without. Now, however, Ralph Berlin was seriously out of his depth. When the work stoppage extended beyond three days, he began to recognize that he no longer could contain it in doctored production reports. Diedre Magee's suicide attempt via sleeping pills was quickly discovered. Within twenty-four hours, she was physically able to continue production. But neither Diedre nor Walker Perkins would see him. Neither would talk to him on the phone. Walker remained closeted in his suite. No one knew what he was involved in. His secretary wouldn't say. The bellboys and room service people weren't allowed in. There were no incoming or outgoing calls. Diedre was

in her suite. She had been released from the hospital
and remained out of touch as well. She was approach-
able, but refused to answer Berlin's simple questions as
to when or even if she would return to work.

What kind of day would it be today? For Ralph
Berlin, it would only be worse than yesterday as the
film fell behind one more day. His ulcer, his hemor-
rhoids and his corns were giving him trouble, but not so
much as the studio would, because today was another
day like eleven yesterdays, in each of which $75,000
worth of holding costs were being incurred while not
one foot of film was being shot.

Not even the first shot of the day—a scenic pan of
wherever they were—twenty-five feet of exposed film
shot with an Aeroflex, totally useless footage that
looked like a million dollars on the production report.

Stevie had just spent an hour with Dimity Edwards,
Walker Perkins' cold-as-icewater English secretary.
She was tall, thin, asexual and an obviously devoted,
totally businesslike young woman. She carefully explained to Stevie that she was Mr. Perkins' private
secretary.

"Miss Edwards, I understand that you have an
allegiance to Walker, and I'm sure you appreciate that
finding a solution to this problem is in his best interest.
The picture has to get back into production."

"You don't seem to understand, Miss Tree, that the
relationship that I have with Mr. Perkins is a very
special one. The working word, here, Miss Tree, is
private. I've been with Mr. Perkins for three very
satisfying years. He understands me, and I understand
him."

Ralph Berlin, sitting on the couch in Stevie's suite,
broke in. "Look, we're not trying to break the bonds of
the confessional. This is not the Vatican and he isn't the
Catholic church. We want to know what goes with
Walker Perkins and when is he going back to work?"

"Mr. Berlin," the English secretary continued painfully, "you've repeated that same query at least five
times in the past hour, and my answer will remain the

same. It is imperative that I keep Mr. Perkins' counsel and his privacy. My profession demands it. My honor requires it. What inner thoughts I may be privy to . . . what secrets of the confessional, so to speak, that I may be privileged to know, I will carry to the grave if need be."

Stevie looked at the ninny and wanted to say, "Right on, motherfucker," or words to that effect, but she realized that it was not the occasion to deal lightly with this lady. If this was the sort of loyalty that Walker Perkins could instill, he must be quite a man. If this was the kind of insanity that Walker Perkins could put up with, he must also be a jerk. Stevie would love to have given Dimity Edwards a kick in the ass.

"Dimity . . . I hope that we know each other well enough to call each other by our first names . . . and please call me Stevie, or Stephanie if you prefer. We are in the middle of a moment of adversity. Surely the way that we handle ourselves in these times will be important not only to the future of this picture, but the history of cinema. I know that I can count on your goodwill and best efforts."

Dimity Edwards looked at Stevie. She thought that this tall and beautiful American lady was totally without culture or feeling when they first met, but on reflection she now suspected she might have been wrong.

"Stephanie, what a lovely name. I had a good friend named Stephanie when I was little. We'll all try our best . . . you can count on me."

Dimity Edwards stuck out a stiff forearm leading into a stiffer hand and Stevie grasped it firmly and pumped away at this first mark of acceptance. With a clear and purposeful look in her eyes, Dimity Edwards turned and walked out the door of the suite, leaving Stevie alone with Ralph Berlin.

"Lovely girl," Stevie remarked.

"British cunt," Ralph Berlin replied.

"My feelings exactly," Stevie punctuated.

Ralph Berlin left. He was resigned to still another day of inactivity, another $75,000 in studio money thrown down the toilet. He mentally figured where all of the money was going and it made him sick. The cast was on standby. All of the crew was on standby as well, since one never knew when shooting would begin, and if they were released then one could never be sure of getting key members back again. There were a lot of films in progress and preproduction in Rome at that particular time. In a month, perhaps, it would be dead, but if one released the camera operator, the key grip, the gaffer and the other members of the crew, then it really *would* be a disaster. Furthermore, the tyranny of the department heads was so effective that even if one kept those people only, and left the other crew members to shift for themselves, the department heads—camera, lighting, stagehands—would refuse to work with any but their own people. Then there was the standby cinematographer that he had been forced to hire to satisfy the Italian union, since Walker Perkins had brought a cameraman from the States, someone with whom Perkins had done all of his films and without whom he refused to work. The Italian cinematographer was having the time of his life vacationing at Capri, while he and his crew were on full salary. The American cinematographer had gotten into a violent fight with Walker Perkins before the suicide attempt, and Perkins had banished him from the set and the picture. In his place, an English cinematographer had been brought in, who came in with *his* crew.

Consequently, on the film known as *Camille*, there were three camera crews being paid in full while none of them worked. The Italian crew was on vacation. The American crew remained in Rome pending the outcome of the arbitration proceedings that the U.S. camera union had initiated against the picture. The British crew, who had yet to turn a crank, were vacationing in Portofino.

Ralph Berlin further considered the expenses that

the cast and crew were incurring. Walker Perkins, while not doing a moment's worth of work on the picture, was ordering suits from Brioni. Angelo of Brioni phoned Ralph five days ago after a fitting in Perkins' hotel suite for eight custom-made suits. It was a normal call, Angelo stated, to confirm whether the suits were to be charged to the picture, per the instructions given him.

Ralph Berlin quietly went up in smoke. My God, the sonofabitch is hustling the picture for six thousand dollars' worth of personal clothing and is not doing a *fucking* thing. Then he realized that it was a tiny matter. If Perkins ever went back to work, it would stick in Perkins' craw. 'What if he goes back to work and says to the studio that the reason he didn't go back earlier was because I was chickenshit about eight suits? What if he doesn't go back to work at all and I can prove that he lifted eight suits from the picture? Maybe I can bring a grievance against him with the Directors Guild. What difference does it make? I hope he's allergic to the fucking material.'

"Of course Angelo . . . anything that Mr. Perkins wants is to be charged to the picture. Thanks for calling."

Stevie sat down at the desk in her suite to write a letter. She thought about dictating it to a secretary, which would make it less personal but more legible, and dammit, Stevie was tired. The thought of handwriting a lengthy plea to Walker Perkins was more than she could stomach. She tried to borrow a typewriter from the hotel by phoning the front desk. It was as if she had asked for state secrets from NATO. They were certain that it could be arranged, Signora, but it would take time. The man who handles such things is sick. His mother-in-law is dying, and the key to the closet where he keeps instructions for handling that particular matter and bombing the Vatican are in his pants pocket, which have been sent to the dry cleaner's who has had a fire. The manager didn't say precisely that, but it sounded like that, and Stevie resigned herself to a case of writer's cramp and pure unadulterated anger.

In twenty minutes she completed the letter and phoned Dimity Edwards. Dimity promised that she would use her very best influence to have Walker read the letter.

"Stephanie . . . I think that you and I understand each other."

"I'm sure we do, Dimity. You're all I hoped you would be for the sake of Walker Perkins, a remarkably gifted filmmaker." Stevie hung up, made a face and phoned the bell captain to have a bellboy pick up the note and deliver it to Miss Dimity Edwards, Mr. Walker Perkins' very private, oh so private secretary.

Then Stevie Tree threw off her clothes, pulled the drapes closed and the covers off the bed and fell asleep. It was her first sleep in thirty-six hours.

The telephone rang and Stevie stirred. She looked at her watch, which she had yet to adjust for the time change, and didn't have the vaguest idea what time it was. The phone continued to ring. She thought of going to the window and peeking out to see if it were day or night, but the phone didn't stop.

"Scusi Signora . . . we have a typewriter for you we can send up."

"Who is this? What time is it?"

"Signora, it's the manager at the front desk. We have a typewriter that we can lend you till tomorrow morning, but the secretary to the Commendatore needs to have it back. There is only one small problem. She wants to rent it to you and you will have to sign a letter that if it is damaged, the motion picture company will be responsible. And, of course, the keyboard is different. It's an Italian typewriter and the letters are in different places. But that won't make too much difference, will it?"

"I don't need the typewriter anymore, thank you." God, what she would like to have said to him!

"I'm sorry, Signora . . . we tried our best." Now his feelings were hurt. "Oh, yes . . . Signora, you have an overseas call that's holding. I just thought I'd give you the good news about the typewriter first . . . but it seems . . ."

Stevie interrupted him. "Please put through the call. And what time is it?"

"Of course, Signora . . . and it's six-thirty."

"Morning or night?"

He left the line without answering.

Sy Rosen was on the line. What was happening? Why couldn't Stevie solve the problem? Where was Jerry Fentris? What did she mean about his wife attempting suicide? Stevie must be joking. This was no time for jokes. Jerry's wife is in Palm Springs at a tennis tournament.

Stevie ended the conversation. "Bad joke, Sy . . . Jerry is laid up with a bad case of the trots. Can't even answer a phone, he's so weak. I'll call you tomorrow. By the way, what time is it?"

"What the hell kind of question is that? It's ten o'clock."

Stevie still wasn't sure whether it was day or night until she got up and pulled the drapes open. It was night and Rome was dotted with lights. The view of the Spanish Steps, with St. Peter's in the background, was stunning. She had had all of three hours of sleep, but she felt refreshed, which she couldn't understand. She had no better idea of how to lick this problem than she had thirty-nine hours ago, but it was evening in Rome, and she felt good and she was hungry . . . There were superb restaurants in Rome, and she didn't know anybody at all except Ralph Berlin, who was a dope . . . or Dimity Edwards, who was a pain in the ass. But she didn't want to eat alone, so she phoned Dimity.

"Oh, how lovely. What a super idea. Just the two of us for dinner. Why don't we go to the Hosteria della Orso? You'll just love it, Stephanie."

"Wonderful, Dimity . . . will you make the reservation? Say in about an hour and a half?"

"Make it two, Stephanie. Night life in Rome doesn't start that early."

When Stevie Tree and Dimity Edwards walked into
the reception at the Hosteria della Orso, one of Rome's
most elegant restaurants, the maitre d' stopped dead.
He had been lavishing his commanding attitude on a
rich, middle-aged American couple who looked under-
dressed and scruffy by his standards, and who, although
the concierge at the Hilton had made the reservation
and reconfirmed it, now had had their reservations
"lost." The maitre d' had looked at his list for their
names. He failed to find it once again, and suggested
that they come back another night, perhaps next year.

In the middle of this annoyance he caught sight of
two ravishingly beautiful women. One was Stevie Tree,
who wore a gown she had bought a month ago at Holly
Harp's, California's most elegant designer. It was pale
yellow chiffon, loosely flowing over a gauze-thin under-
slip of the same color. It was soft, romantic and sexy.
Stevie's ash blonde hair had been put into fighting trim
by a youthful hairdresser at the Hassler, who came to
her room and for a tip of ten thousand lire stayed after
work. He was a genius who should have been imported
to Beverly Hills. He was also so extravagantly hetero-
sexual that he tried thirteen different times and ways of
getting Stevie into bed. Federico was only nineteen and
stunning. His only fault was his technique, not in his
styling, but with his come-on.

"Signora . . . I am at last in love, but for the first
time."

"Yes, that's the way I like it."

"If we could only fuck for a little while, I wouldn't
keep you from your appointment, and it would make
me so happy."

"That's fine . . . not so much curl, Federico."

"You have such a magnificent body. I have such a
magnificent body, too. Would you like to see my
prick?" he said simply. "There is always time for a
fuck, Signora. Maybe you would like to suck my cock. I
like that too."

"I'm sure you do, Federico . . . and that's as it
should be . . . but I have a dinner appointment." And

suddenly Stevie hit on an idea that would solve the
problem. "I have a dinner appointment with a
woman."

Federico suddenly turned all business. "It is against
my religion. Catholics have no respect for a woman
with a woman. I am American in my thinking . . . but
no matter, Signora . . . I too have no respect for that."

"It is good of you to be so understanding."

"Always a pleasure to serve you, Signora . . . That
will be fifteen thousand lire."

"But you said ten thousand when we made the
arrangement."

"But that was before I learned you were . . . like
that, Signora."

Dimity Edwards looked beautiful too. Yes, Dimity
Edwards!

It was as if *Lady for a Day* had been remade in
Technicolor. In the Bette Davis film the charlady is
befriended by loving gangsters, who change the charlady into a beauty, for a day.

First, Dimity Edwards, that long, gaunt drink of
icewater, with hair pulled back tight into a bun, flat,
sensible shoes, a dark-blue wool skirt and brown
cardigan sweater, so shapeless that it looked like
chocolate syrup.

Fade in on Dimity Edwards, tall, regal, ravishingly
beautiful in a Norman Norell lavender sheath. Her red
hair hung below her shoulders. Her gray eyes appeared
like gem stones. The eyeglasses that hid them had been
consigned to the dressing table and the persona that
was Miss Dimity Edwards, schoolmarm, stuffed prig
and pain in the ass, was left there, too.

Stevie was astonished when she saw Dimity in the
lobby of the Hassler. With a flick of the eye Dimity
coolly acknowledged how stunning Stevie looked.

Two of the most beautiful women in Rome were
dining alone in a town where Italian men would kill for
a moment with either of them. The evening started
alone, but the gravitational pull of their beauty had
such a dazzling effect that as soon as they were seated

at the best table in the restaurant men began to appear as if by magic.

"Signore . . . permit me to introduce myself. I'm sure we met at . . . perhaps you remember the trip we took on the Principessa's yacht . . ."

Another one said to Stevie, "Miss Lauren Hutton . . . I'd recognize you from your photographs. We have a friend in common. Burt Reynolds. He is a very good friend of mine."

And someone addressed them both. "I am at another table in the restaurant with some friends. However, if you like, we can leave right now. My villa is only a few miles away and I have some very pure cocaine."

That was only part of the proceedings. Amidst all the goings and comings of half the most attractive men in Rome, circulating around the table, sending bottles of wine, notes, business cards, flowers and even waiting outside the ladies' room, the two of them got to know one another.

"Stevie . . . how the hell could you stand that pile of *merde* that I was giving out in your suite?"

Stevie broke into laughter and leaned over and kissed Dimity on the cheek. "I love you. Let's have fun."

The rest of the evening taxed the resources of Dimity Edwards, who had the stamina of a soccer player. It taxed the resources of Stevie Tree, who was hanging on by her thumbs. It was now forty-two hours and she had still had only three hours of sleep. God knew when she would be struck down. But God knew how much she adored Rome. The Italian men were awful. More accurately, they were so full of shit that they were awful, but they were so much fun they were wonderful. Never in the history of the Italian republic, with the possible exception of Mussolini's campaign in Ethiopia, had so much manpower been lavished in search of the ultimate treasure. For Mussolini it was simply the lure of empire. For what seemed like half of Rome, it was getting one of the two very beautiful, very particular ladies into bed.

Stevie was in awe of Dimity. She handled the entire evening with wit and charm and a kind of understated sexiness that indicated a finely tuned point of view and an appreciation of herself that could only have come from a lifetime of being courted and adored by men around the world.

Stevie caught an occasional appraising glance from Dimity. Reading her mind, Stevie knew that for this evening, and for the rest of their lives, they would be sisters. They shared a moment that women who learn to respect and adore each other find only occasionally. They were beautiful, both of them, each in a different way that left them free to shine without competing with each other. Moreover they were skilled professionals. They were not only good at their jobs, they were superb. Each had the assurance of knowing that she was at least half again better than the male competition she had to face, and possibly twice as good as the man who employed her. They had to be that good. Their time would come, but for the moment, Dimity Edwards had to present the face of a schoolmarm with the manners of a headmistress and the humor of the Tower of London for a chance to be with a director who would be helpful to her career. As what? As anything that the world of men would allow her to be. For Stevie, further advanced along that road, it would forever be a battle. No man would treat her as an equal, ever. And Stevie had decided just a while ago to scrap her attempt at the middle-sized mountain and aim for Everest. If no man would treat her as an equal, so be it. Let it be said that he would learn to treat her as a superior.

Neither of them spoke a minute's worth of business that night. They were having too much fun. There was too much laughter. There were too many men. There was too much dancing at Rome's discos. There wasn't a moment's thought that Stevie gave to the outcome of her trip. It was unsaid between them. The two of them would solve it. Two women working together were unbeatable.

At three in the morning, Stevie and Dimity were

deposited at the Hassler. The elevator operator unlocked the door and sleepily took them upstairs. They had given their floor numbers, and in the slow-moving elevator, Dimity leaned against the wall and smiled.

"Walker has been fucking the property man, a beautiful Italian, and Diedre has also been fucking that same beauty, without Walker's knowing it until the property man told him."

Stevie murmured, "Mmmmm."

"And Diedre attempted suicide after Walker told her that her acting stinks."

"Mmmmm."

"Walker loved your letter. You know a lot about film, don't you, Stevie? He respects that. He's really a talented man, but a kid."

"Mmmmm. Would he write a letter to Diedre to apologize?"

"Sure . . . whatever you want him to say. I'll compose it myself."

Dimity continued in the slow-moving elevator. The operator was nearly asleep. "If you see Diedre, I think it would be nice to get her to write and say she'll stop fucking the property man."

"Good idea . . . I'll write that before I see her tomorrow."

"Right, but you'll have Walker's letter first thing in the morning." Dimity was nearly asleep on her feet. "I'll have it for you right after breakfast. Then after it's all settled, why don't you give a reconciliation party and we can all get back to work."

"Dimity, it's your floor."

"Good night, Stevie. We're going to be good friends. I mean really good friends."

"Good night, Dimity. We really are."

Dimity Edwards walked out of the elevator a little unsteadily, and the operator closed the door. Stevie got out on the next floor and walked slowly to the door of her suite. She looked at the clock. Fifty-five hours with only three hours' sleep. She lay down on the bed after depositing her Holly Harp on the chair and fell asleep.

To be sure that the switchboard would not disturb her this time with a phone call, she cut the telephone cord with the scissors that Federico had accidently left behind.

Stevie woke absolutely refreshed. She had slept as if dead from three in the morning till eight, when she was wakened by the ring of the phone. The ringing was insistent and in the light of the bedside table, Stevie could see that it couldn't be her phone, since some idiot had cut the wire. The ringing continued and she went into the sitting room of the suite. There it was, ringing its little heart out.

"Signora, you had an overseas call on the line."

"Put it on."

"No, they hung up five minutes ago."

"Why did you keep ringing?"

"Signora, to tell you that your other phone wasn't working. Don't worry, the overseas call will ring back, but maybe not today. There is a work stoppage on the phone people."

"When does this start?"

"I'm not sure, but I think it started already. Maybe your party didn't hang up. Maybe the operators—*comunisti*, Signora—maybe they cut them off. If you like, I can phone them and find out if that was the reason that your phone call did not come through."

"Fuck it."

"What did you say, Signora?"

"I said that I want you to connect me with room service."

"I'm sorry, Signora . . . they're on a work stoppage, in sympathy with other unions."

"Thank you very much. I'm hanging up now."

"You're welcome, Signora . . . glad I could be of help."

At eleven o'clock that morning, Stevie walked into Diedre Magee's suite at the Hassler. Diedre was a radiant picture of happiness. At twenty-three, the

former photographer's model had the unspoiled look of
the typical American girl—tall, blonde and statuesque.
Her smile made Stevie aware that a million guys loved
that look, the girl next door but prettier. Diedre came
over to Stevie and hugged her.

"Stevie, we haven't met, but Dimity told me all
about you—about how you fixed up everything. Here's
the letter that Walker wrote me, in his own handwriting. It's very personal . . . otherwise I'd read it to you.
Of course I'll go back to work. God, I admire Walker
so much. He's a genius. I'm learning so much just being
with him—but you know that already. He wrote in this
letter how wonderful your note to him was—explaining
the things in his films that he thought nobody but
nobody—even John Simon—ever picked up on. Stevie,
I just know you and I are going to be good friends."

Stevie smiled. She liked Diedre. She saw how simple
and sweet she was, how outgoing and how vulnerable.
If Walker Perkins was anything at all like Diedre,
Stevie wondered how movie companies could entrust
millions of dollars to kids, talented kids, who had a
tough time looking at themselves in the mirror and
getting their personal acts together.

"Diedre, I couldn't have picked a more wonderful
thing to hear—first that we're going to be friends and
second that you're going to go back to work. Now that
only leaves Walker . . ."

Diedre laughed. "Oh, that's already solved. I spoke
to him on the phone, just a few minutes ago. We both
cried. I explained that I did something wrong . . . and I
apologized. It's too personal, otherwise I'd tell you.
Maybe someday. Yes, absolutely someday."

"Diedre . . . thank you so much."

"Dimity called Ralph Berlin. We're going to be back
on the set at two this afternoon. Walker thinks that we
can make up some of the time we lost. But we wanted
to thank you, Stevie, for all you did in straightening
things out. Dimity says that you are giving us a dinner
party tonight at the Hostería della Orso. It'll give you a

chance to know Walker . . . and for him to get to know you. I'm so happy and the picture is going to be a *success!*"

Stevie went over to Diedre and hugged that very darling, very innocent young lady who wanted so much to have it so, and who was so unsure of herself and what she was doing on the planet that she attempted to kill herself because the man in her life abandoned her for a moment with a few jealous words. As she held on to Diedre, she heard the sounds of tears, but they were tears of relief.

Stevie retreated from the suite. It was all over except for the dinner that night. She would send a cable to Sy Rosen that the picture was back on track.

As Stevie walked down the stairs at the Hassler to her own suite, she smiled to herself at the remarkable Dimity Edwards. What an extraordinary person she was! What a wonderful thing it was to know that a person like Dimity existed.

What a pain in the ass it was to climb stairs at the Hassler after sixty-eight hours with only eight hours of sleep.

Among other tragedies, the elevator operators were on strike, too.

20

A week had gone by since Stevie's triumphant return from Rome. She had thought hard about how to treat the Jerry Fentris desertion, and although he really didn't deserve her loyalty, she decided he would get it because it was practical. She said nothing about it to Sy Rosen or the rest. She figured that she would clue Jerry to his supposed illness and he could invent any other cover story that was necessary.

It was an academic exercise. When Stevie got to New York after the flight from Rome, she called the office and spoke to Brenda. Brenda informed her that Jerry Fentris was at home and transferred the call there. The person at the end of the line was a woman.

"Hello . . ."

"This is Stevie Tree . . . Is Jerry Fentris there?"

"Hi, Stevie . . . this is Mildred Fentris. Jerry has told me so much about you. I hope we can meet soon. Just a minute, I assume you want to talk to Jerry."

"Thank you, Mildred." Stevie wondered what was going on.

"Stevie . . . hi, kiddo. Well, I'm a new man. That jet lag thing worked."

"Jerry, what are you talking about?"

"Hard as a rock. Like a piece of castiron pipe. Came late, came often. Like a fifteen-year-old kid. Fuck 'em all."

Stevie laughed out loud. "I suppose you don't want to hear about what happened in Rome?"

"Yeah, what happened? It's hard right now. Can you

imagine at this time of the morning, and while I'm on the phone? Can't wait to get off the goddam phone."

"I won't keep you from your work, Jerry. Everyone's back on the job and everyone's happy, and I'll let you go. How do you want me to cover for you at the office?"

"Don't bother, Stevie . . . They know that I'm back . . . I never knew before that Sy Rosen reads copies of all outgoing cables. Should have known better than to send that phony from the office."

"Are you in hot water?"

"Nah—he thinks I got something going on the side . . . There are things more important than a picture in trouble. Got to hang up. See you in a couple of days. Welcome back."

In the next few weeks at the agency, Stevie really didn't have time to comprehend fully the change in her situation. But it began to mount up with small incidents, only to work itself into a *cause célèbre* about the simple matter of a secretary. Brenda was at the center of the controversy that had the agency as divided as if it had been the classic confrontation between U.S.C. and U.C.L.A., except that it involved an even bigger battle, the war of the sexes.

Stevie had reported that Rome affair in very sketchy detail, leaving out the particulars concerning the love-life of Walker and Diedre. There was no need to explain or dwell upon the causes of the delay. In her opinion, it was enough to bring the matter to a successful conclusion. The rest of the staff at the meeting didn't fully agree, and resentment seemed to flow because of her unwillingness to share the bedroom details among her associates. That was item number one.

Next, a client of Stevie's, a writer for a situation-comedy series, had developed a musical play and was interested in having Stevie represent the material for production on Broadway. The project had special interest for Stevie because she liked the writer and it had potential as a starring vehicle for Zelma Hurwitz.

The agency, Sy Rosen told her at the meeting, had an entire department devoted to the legitimate theater. It was a New York operation and Stevie should keep her nose out of it.

And then something else happened.

Principal photography had been completed on *Camille*. Walker Perkins and Diedre Magee were back in L.A. to edit the picture and to complete the post production. A day following their arrival, Stevie received a phone call from Walker. He thanked her for the kindness and thoughtfulness she had shown him and Diedre and the wonderful evening that they had spent together at the Hosteria della Orso. Following the restarting of production, Walker had made up most of the lost time, and the studio had been so excited by the dailies that Walker himself was truly exultant. He admitted, he told Stevie, that he might have made originally a mistake in casting Diedre. As it turned out, though, the end product seemed to be terrific. Walker added that he and Diedre had considered their representation by IA, and that even though it was three months before the contract terminated, the only way they would continue would be if Stevie handled the two of them herself. Throw another log on the fire! In other words, as Stevie went, so went Walker Perkins and Diedre Magee.

But the real trouble revolved around Brenda.

With the continuing growth of the agency, IA took another 5,000 feet of space in the adjacent building it owned and had previously leased to a computer corporation. The closely packed agents welcomed the expansion and for months, while the plans were being formulated, Fred Wine sent around tentative plans for the reallocation of agency space. Each third or fourth day would find new floor plans in circulation, with penciled names of agents and secretaries in ever-changing locations. Stevie now occupied a small office next to Jerry Fentris. They shared Brenda as mutual secretary. As the volume of Stevie's activity increased, a second secretary was added. Her name was Margie

Quinn and she was new, both to secretarial work and
the agency business. Margie took the longest lunches,
the longest coffee breaks, forgot the most messages and
would win any contest for the greatest number of typing
errors in a single letter. She complained about the lack
of air conditioning when it got too hot, the absence of
heat when it got cold, and the general lack of consider-
ation for her leisure when she was asked to work.

Stevie had repeatedly asked Jerry Fentris to fire her.
Some perverse streak in Jerry had reinforced Margie in
her job, or it may just have been that it was the only
way in which Jerry could enforce his authority over
Stevie. Whatever the reason for perpetuating this
walking tragedy in secretary's clothing, Margie Quinn
continued to thrive and prosper as part of the joint
secretarial team serving Jerry Fentris and Stevie Tree.

With the proposed change in the physical setup in the
offices, Stevie would be located farther away from
Jerry, and when the agents compared the size of the
office each would get and the number of windows each
would have, they noted that Stevie Tree not only had
the same-size office as all of them, but also had one
more window than most. From the standpoint of office
geography, Stevie was an important person. She was
equal, and that made it very important, because after
all, she was still a woman.

The relocation of offices also called for separation of
the umbilical cord that tied Jerry and Stevie to both
secretaries. How they would be broken apart was a
matter of concern to both Jerry, Stevie, Brenda and
Margie. Since Jerry was senior, he had the choice.
Despite the aberrant behavior that made him protect
Margie's job, he was not insane. He chose to take
Brenda as his own. The problem was that Brenda said
she would quit unless she stayed with Stevie.

Stevie was flattered but tried to persuade Brenda to
accept the roll of the dice. She was sincere, but so was
Brenda.

"Damn it, Stevie . . . I dig you. I like you. If I don't

work for you, I'll quit. I didn't go through college and secretarial school to work for some jerk, and you can quote me."

The agents discussed the matter as seriously and importantly as they might discuss the fate of Israel. And in the sexist privacy of the men's room, the comments really flew.

"That black cunt . . . I know we've got to have spades for appearance sake, but shit . . . it's too much. Now she's telling the whole fucking agency to stuff it."

And . . . "If we didn't have so many black acts, we wouldn't have to have so many black office people."

And . . . "Do you suppose Stevie put her up to it? After all, women will try to protect each other."

And . . . "Hey, while you're talking so much, you're pissing on my trousers. Forget it . . . I was only kidding."

The resolution of the secretary rebellion took place in Sy Rosen's office with Stevie and Fred Wine.

"Stevie, Fred is here because he's in charge of these things, and frankly I don't know what to do."

Fred Wine interjected, "You know the situation with Brenda . . . and if we give in to her, it'll mean disaster in the agency."

"How so, Fred? I'm afraid I don't understand," Stevie inquired.

Sy spoke before Fred could answer. "Stevie . . . if we run a business, we run it. No secretary is within her rights to tell us how to assign her. If we allow her to tell us, then the entire business of seniority goes out the window and we'll have the goddam secretaries running the place."

Fred Wine added. "I don't foresee that as a possibility, Sy, but there are some serious problems, Stevie. Jerry Fentris has been with the agency for fifteen years. He started in the mailroom. You've been with us less than three years, and we have a responsibility to the men—rather, the people who have been here a long while and who have given their all for years."

Stevie stood up. "OK, fellows, I'll quit."

Sy stood up quickly. "Stevie, I know you're joking, but it's not funny . . . and what we're looking for is your help."

"No, Sy, I wasn't joking. I believe that this is the straw that dumped the camel—but it's not my camel, and if we have to come to blows on this, I'd rather fight it out on this insane territory rather than the real issues you fellows don't want to deal with."

There was panic in Fred Wine's voice. "Stevie . . . our relationship is rock solid. You're IA, and IA is you, just as it is with every senior member of our family."

Sy Rosen quickly added, "Stevie, maybe we've been a little overdramatic. It's a tendency us older fellows have, but it's nothing that experienced people, people who truly admire and respect each other, can't work out. Brenda is only a secretary, after all. Let's put these things in their true context."

Stevie sat there a moment quietly. They were awaiting a quieter word, a thoughtful reconsideration, and each felt that perhaps they had been too strong, but Stevie was overreacting. They were both wrong. She was just beginning to react.

"Fred . . . Sy . . . let's put it on the table. I've been here almost three years and I've accomplished a good deal. You've recognized that in a practical way, and I'm pleased that you've included me in the profit plan. This year instead of my junior participation, I'm sure you plan on the same participation that all of my senior colleagues have. I'll expect it, and I'm sure I won't be disappointed."

Fred Wine looked at Sy Rosen meaningfully.

"But I think there's a hint of something else in the air. It started when I spent two thousand dollars of the agency's money on a commitment to fund computer training for Zelma Hurwitz. I had overreached myself in your eyes. I spend more than that on lunches in a month. Jerry Fentris and the other boys spend more than that on greens fees. Then it continued with some of the deals I made. I took some chances, but I never double-dealt. I never lied to a client. I never lied to a customer. I won't do that. I never will."

Sy Rosen looked at Fred Wine. You couldn't be an agent and tell the truth, the look said.

"Then, fellows, there was the matter of Walker Perkins and Diedre Magee, not to mention Zelma Hurwitz . . . all of whom stipulated that they would remain with the agency only as long as I was part of it. It was their request, not mine. Now, I'll do this kind of deal with you. I won't resign from the agency, which will protect your position with the clients I've mentioned, not to mention others who may have some respect and affection for me. I'll stay on . . . draw my salary . . . and you can give me any secretary you want to, or none at all, 'cause I'll just occupy my space. Even if I do nothing, you'll be getting your money's worth, just by keeping those clients . . . or . . . you can act as if I am really equal. Whether I'm a woman, or a three-year-veteran, both Brenda and I are entitled to free choice. Nobody but you fellows is going to run this agency till you drop dead, don't worry. In the meantime, make it a fruitful place to work, and let's go on to more important things."

Sy Rosen sat there quietly. Fred Wine blew on his fingernails. Stevie got up from her chair and looked out the window.

"Stevie . . . please understand . . . we're one family. We love you like our own. Brenda isn't important. You are, and if that would make you happy, of course she goes with you," Sy Rosen said.

"Stevie . . . we all say things in haste . . . whatever Sy says goes double for me," added Fred Wine.

"Sy . . . Fred . . . thanks a lot, and Brenda will be pleased, too. I've got to get back to work." Stevie left without turning back.

When Stevie had left, Sy Rosen said to Fred, "Baby, we've got a problem with that little lady. It's her or me. I know what I'm talking about."

"Sy, you're wrong."

Sy Rosen stood up and roared. "Don't tell me I'm wrong. I know people, goddammit. I know that lady, and I can tell you she's on one big power trip, and I'm telling you one other thing . . . fuck this agency . . . only one person's gonna run it, not Brenda or whatever her name is . . . or Stevie Tree . . . or *anybody*. I'm gonna turn off that little lady's water, even if it costs us a couple of clients, Fred—even if it costs us a lot of clients. I spent too many years at this desk to move aside for Miss Blow Job."

Fred Wine winced. "You told me to fire her the first day. I shouldn't have convinced you to change your mind . . . I shouldn't have convinced you."

"You're damn right you shouldn't, and nobody is going to make me change my mind now."

Over a period of months, Ginny Tree had become a permanent fixture in the life of Morgan Oliver. It was an addiction, and the seventeen-year-old girl knew it and used it. From that first afternoon meeting in his bungalow, Ginny had built the relationship she intended to have, step by step, like a methodical stone mason would build a wall. It wasn't only that Ginny was a tiger in bed. It wasn't only the fact that she would do anything, the kinkier the better. The thing that turned Morgan on was the fact that she didn't want him exclusively, she didn't need him exclusively, but most of all, that she was unabashedly and unashamedly wild and uncontrollable.

In the afternoons, or evening, or mornings, whenever Ginny felt it, she stopped at his bungalow at the Beverly Hills Hotel. Morgan could be busy at anything, or even not there at all, and Ginny felt absolutely free to enter his life. The first few times it happened found Morgan in several unusual situations. Ginny walked into the suite when Morgan was in a meeting with his agent, a producer, a director and a writer. Ginny didn't say a word to anyone. She just walked purposefully through the living room into the bedroom. Another writer was on the phone in the bedroom. She removed her clothes and slipped into the huge bed.

A second time, Morgan was making it with a showgirl he had known from a weekend in Las Vegas. Ginny walked through the bedroom and into the bathroom. She left the door open while she peed. She waited there in the dark. Very soon the front door slammed. The showgirl had left.

On another occasion Ginny was in the suite for an entire night and Morgan hadn't arrived. When he did show up the next day he found Ginny asleep in bed with a black man. A nude couple were sleeping on the couch.

Morgan reveled in every detail of every trick Ginny turned, every john she had. He made her describe in full detail the size of their cocks, what she did while fucking or sucking, how much she got, what they said, how much she stole. The more outrageous her actions, the more fascinated he became with her stories.

Morgan loved to hit her. It started with spankings and became more abusive. Soon it happened with sufficient frequency and force that Ginny was more than occasionally bruised. Each time it occurred, it curiously deepened the hold that she had over him, and each time it happened Ginny became more elusive. She wouldn't show up for days when in fact she had promised to see him. There would never be an explanation or an excuse. Their fights were frequent and violent. And they almost always ended with Morgan beating her.

Morgan had changed drastically. He was strange with his friends, as if his reach into Ginny's black soul had given him a taste of darkness that he had looked for and searched for, but had never been able to find before.

At the same time, Morgan's career was in a no-man's land. His most recent pictures were unsuccessful. The last was yet to be released, but gossip labeled it the worst yet. He was on a continual merry-go-round of meetings with producers and writers to discuss new projects, all of them unformed and in process. Morgan didn't really know what was good or bad anymore. There were no blacks or whites in his career—everything seemed gray.

In addition, Morgan was under severe money pressure as a result of some bad investments by his business manager. The important people in his life went unpaid: the Internal Revenue Service and his lawyer. The others could wait for their money, although not too long.

One night when Ginny walked in, Morgan was on the phone talking with his accountant. Ginny had repeatedly heard conversations about his problems, but now they appeared to be more acute.

"You're a fucking bore, Oliver."

"You're a stupid cunt."

"At least I'm not going bankrupt, Oliver. If you had a pussy, I could teach you a few things."

Morgan sat down on the bed. "Lovely talk."

"What you need is a new agent."

"What I need is a new life."

"Same thing. I'm smarter than I look, Oliver. Yep, what you need is a new agent. I happen to know one."

"Who, your pimp?"

"No, my sister . . . same thing."

Stevie had occupied the house on Laurel Canyon for six months, at which time the back-to-back deal for ownership had been completed. The subterfuge avoided the roadblock created by David's sister. During free moments away from her work, she concentrated on furnishing it. In a testament to the memories of the place that Stevie held dear, she unconsciously copied the style of the house when she and David had occupied it, four years previously. Everything the decorator showed her was wrong, until he went in the direction of what had been, and so, although no piece of furniture remained from that earlier time, it still had the brown and chrome look that made it appear very masculine. Rich oranges and earth tones topped the terra cotta base. Deep and lustrous leathers covered the chairs. Huge Brazilian couches, soft and luxurious, covered with the thinnest of skins, took their place in the living room as before.

Her first night back in the house on Laurel Canyon, Stevie smoked some grass as she sat in the huge armchair in the living room. All but one of the lights were out, dimly illuminating the tasteful warmth of the large room, without obscuring the full view out the picture window, while she stared and reflected. The matter of the secretary campaign, or "Operation Brenda," as it was known in the ladies' room at the agency, had not in itself been trying, but Stevie knew that she had finally pressed the wrong buttons with Sy Rosen and Fred Wine. She was not concerned about Fred. Since the first run-in she had had with him, when he had threatened to fire her, he had been her staunchest supporter in the agency. It was as if, by defanging him that one time, he had been released from a moral purgatory, a false position of an avenging angel, which he had unconsciously abhorred, and that release had allowed him to act as a human being.

But Sy Rosen was different. She had marveled, time after time, at the two sides of the man. He was the pillar of the community, the dean of the industry, the man who was regarded as the oracle with vision and as the conscience of entertainment. But he was also the Sy Rosen she had seen at staff meetings and indirectly through others' eyes—hard as nails, cold as ice.

Like a superb commander, he maintained an attitude of complete deniability. No game, no trick that he had instructed an employee to perform, no fast shuffle, no underhanded thrust could ever be traced to his door, and on the few occasions when an agent was caught off base Sy never seemed responsible. It was the way he worked, quietly, effectively. Sy was the resident guru at IA, and he treasured that reputation. Beware those who crossed him—the guru had claws of steel.

And Stevie knew that she *had* crossed him. She knew

that each client who felt a loyalty to Stevie Tree, and not to the grand old dame International Artists, was a threat to Sy's corpus and a thrust at his heart.

The hi-fi was playing Joni Mitchell, and the grass was settling into her brain, bringing with it flashes of inspiration. She felt that if only she were able to instantaneously record each and every insight she had while she was high, it would have been a document as important as the Magna Carta. She smiled, she had tried that a few times, but the meandering notes were both incomprehensible and idiotic. Stevie had asked her Mexican maid to make her some sandwiches and leave them in the fridge before she left. Stevie wanted to be alone, and when she got home, she opened a bottle of white wine and sat in the living room drinking slowly, sipping deeply, in the haze of the grass.

Earlier that day she had received a phone call from Diedre Magee, who had behaved very mysteriously. When Stevie inquired if there was a problem, Diedre said, "No!" Would Stevie be home tonight? Stevie said she would. Diedre would call her again, privately, away from the office. Was it trouble with Walker? "No," said Diedre, and, hung up, leaving Stevie wondering.

By nine o'clock the grass had brought Stevie to a strange high. Each high was different for her, and this one made her full of anxieties. Disasters in her life were parading before her in kaleidoscopic fashion. She saw her mother. She saw Ginny as a baby again, and then that image changed to people in her present life. Huge, cavernous jaws were opening, and in their depths was Laurie, wordlessly crying out. The visions vanished, and she realized that she was indeed fixating her worries on the little girl, even though she shouldn't. It was late, and stupid, but she reached for the telephone and dialed Laurie's mother.

The telephone rang repeatedly. Where was Laurie? Was she sick or dead? Was the phone in the bedroom? Was Sam screwing his wife? What kind of lay was she? She was about to hang up when a woman's voice answered.

"Yes?"

"Excuse me for calling so late . . . I wondered if Laurie was all right?"

"Who is this?" the voice inquired.

"I'm sorry . . . I guess I didn't say. This is Stevie Tree. You're Laurie's mother."

"Why are you calling, Miss Tree." Her voice sounded cold and bitter.

"I don't want to talk to Laurie, Mrs. Di Benedetto . . . I just want to find out how she is. I was worried."

"Miss Tree, I suppose you're a decent person. Laurie thinks so, but don't you think that you're assuming a little bit too much. This kind of thing is a mother's job. Laurie is my child. I'll take care of her. Thank you for calling. Goodbye."

Stevie looked at the phone in her hand. What had she done? She'd loused it up completely. My God, how *was* Laurie? Now, Laurie would be completely off limits. She cried quietly. She dialed another number. A recorded message spoke to her.

"Hello, you star-fuckers. This is your favorite star-fuckee, Jon. As you can see, I'm not home. Bet you can't guess where I am. Leave your guess and your name when you hear the beep. Maybe I'll call you, and then maybe I won't. If your guess wins, you get to split a bottle of champagne with me, but a French brand, p-u-l-e-e-s-e. Here's the beep."

Stevie hung up again. The grass still hung high, and she walked over to the window and placed her hands on the pane. It was blessedly cool, and she pressed her forehead against it. Wonderful. Pray the glass would never get warm. Pray that her forehead would always be cool. As she looked down a strange car pulled into the driveway. The light inside went on as the door opened, and she recognized Diedre Magee. Stevie weaved a bit, went to the door and opened it. Diedre climbed the stairs and walked in.

"Hi, Diedre . . . This is a surprise."

"Do you mind, Stevie? I had to talk to you."

"No, not at all. It's wonderful to see you. Have a glass of wine, and I'll show you around."

Diedre moved into the living room and sat in a deep chair facing the coffee table. "I'll take some wine, Stevie . . . but I'll take a raincheck on the tour of the house. I've passed by this place a hundred times . . . and I wondered what it was like since you wanted it so, but I'm too nervous to get up and walk around."

Stevie found a glass in the kitchen and returned. She poured wine for Diedre and sat opposite on the couch. 'Jesus, what cooks?' Stevie thought. 'Here is this extraordinary young girl, beautiful, talented and tied up with a strange but enormously talented and complex man, Walker Perkins . . . Together they seem at home in work but totally out of step in the rest of their lives. Stevie laughed to herself. The story of my life!'

"Stevie," Diedre started haltingly, "this is the most difficult thing I've ever experienced. I never thought it would be this way, ever . . . and I dreaded this moment, and at the same time I so longed for it."

Diedre stood for a moment, trying to decide something. She seemed uncertain, then she sat down again slowly.

"Stevie . . . you mean more to me than anyone else I've ever met. You know what I mean, not in a professional way, but in a human way. I think of you all the time. It's crazy. I even dream about you. I admire you—your courage, your honesty—your complete sincerity."

Stevie refilled her glass. The marijuana haze was fast disappearing.

"Please don't interrupt me, Stevie . . . otherwise I won't have the courage to say it. I love you. I know what kind of life you've been through. You don't have to tell me. I know that scar on your face is from something very deep and very sad. You know that I know, and even if I didn't, I would still feel every hurt in your life."

"Do you really know, Diedre?"

"You tried to kill yourself over somebody. I don't know who. I hope it was a man . . . because I want to be the only woman in your life."

The single lamp in the living room silhouetted the back of Diedre's head, and behind her was the sparkling panorama of Los Angeles. The music on the hi-fi had suddenly stopped, as if the director of this scene were about to give a cue for action. Diedre got up from her chair and sat alongside Stevie. She left space between them as if not daring to bridge that gap without further permission.

Diedre sat on the edge of the couch, breathing heavily. Stevie was quiet, unwilling to say a word, unsure what she herself might say or do.

"Stevie . . . please don't interrupt, and don't look at me . . . I don't take love for granted. It is the most important thing in my life—something I've been looking for. I thought I found it once, but I was wrong. Not with Walker—with another girl, years ago."

Stevie reached forward and lifted the glass of wine to her lips. She didn't look at the figure sitting next to her in the dark.

"You don't know how good I can be for you, Stevie. I could be your face in the mirror . . . that loves you . . . without a doubt, without hesitation, without excuses."

Diedre put her hand on Stevie's. Stevie didn't move. The soft, hot touch of the hand on hers was charged with electricity.

Stevie sighed deeply. "Diedre . . . you know how fond I am of you . . . and of Walker, too. I don't know if I'm ready for any relationship—with a man or a woman. I've never been with a woman . . . and I can't seem to find one with a man . . . any man. You're right about a lot of things. About a half mile farther up the canyon, I tried to kill myself. But before that I lived with someone I loved in this house. Coming back here after all these years, I've been trying to relive a part of my life that was happy."

Diedre just sat there, breathing deeply.

"I keep wanting to find someone who will let me care for him . . . and let me feel I'm a good person. Someone wise said the person I tried to kill that night four years ago was a bad person, and that I did kill that part of me. But Diedre . . . if that's true, what's left of me? Where is the part I didn't kill?"

Stevie hadn't meant to let down so many barriers, but Diedre seemed to force her to. Diedre moved to her slowly and held her. Beautiful, alluring, desirable, adoring Diedre took Stevie's face in her hands and kissed her on the lips. Diedre didn't dare let herself or Stevie move for minutes. She was desperate that the next step taken by both of them should not break the spell.

In a tidal wave of emotion, Stevie dissolved in tears. She couldn't stop crying. Diedre pressed Stevie close and felt the pulses run through to her own body.

Then Stevie broke away and took Diedre's hands. "Oh, Diedre . . . darling Diedre . . . I'm not alive inside . . . Diedre, forgive me . . . please. I don't feel a thing. It's not a man thing. It's not a woman thing. It's me."

Diedre kissed her softly on the forehead and after a moment she turned and left.

Stevie sat in the dark for several hours, until she fell asleep in the chair overlooking Laurel Canyon.

Saturday—5 P.M.

District Attorney John Daniels started the chain with a phone call to Ralph Stanton, president of Magna Pictures. His assistant, Henry Borris had had the good sense to check with Daniels before he went off like a rocket. Borris had seen too many promising careers destroyed by the wrong move, made at the wrong time.

Ralph Stanton's delight at having pulled off the coup that gave him two more Morgan Oliver pictures, despite the Randy Davis piece of trash that might make its money back on TV, was short-lived.

"Mr. Stanton, this is John Daniels, and I'm sorry to disturb you on a weekend, but something quite nasty has just come up that may involve you and your studio."

"Mr. Daniels, in what way could the district attorney be interested in me? And why today?"

John Daniels proceeded to give Ralph Stanton the information that Stevie had given his assistant.

"Look, Mr. Daniels, I appreciate, more than I can say, the fact that you telephoned me first. Can I ask you for a small favor?"

"Mr. Stanton, I'm up for re-election this year. There might be room for a favor—provided I can do it in good conscience."

"I wouldn't expect it any other way, Mr. Daniels. Can you give me the telephone number where you can be reached for the next half hour, and can I ask you just to hold off doing *anything* until I phone you back?"

"Certainly, Mr. Stanton. Please call me John."

"John . . . thanks . . . let's stick to a first-name basis."

"Good, Ralph. Then I'll hear from you in a half hour."

"Absolutely. My word is my bond."

"Good, Ralph. We understand each other."

Ralph Stanton hung up and phoned Sy Rosen in Palm Springs. He told Sy what had transpired.

"It's a very sad situation, Ralph. You know that Stevie Tree was the one who shopped Morgan around with that pirated print of *Young Dillinger*. Somehow I let it slip when we spoke earlier. You see, the truth of the matter is that she used to be Morgan's girl—years ago. I guess she never got over him."

"Really, Sy?"

"It's a part of youth, Ralph. You and I are about the same age, and when you've seen as much of life as we both have, then you're not surprised at *anything*. It's not telling too big a secret, Ralph, to let you know that the poor girl attempted suicide because of Morgan."

"Then this whole business with the D.A. is just to get even?" Ralph Stanton whistled under his breath. "'Hell hath no fury . . .'"

Sy continued. "'. . . like a woman scorned.' Shakespeare was right. Never could touch him for ideas—that stuff is solid gold. What we both couldn't do with a writer half as good. What motion pictures we could make."

"Sy, what should I do? I have to phone Daniels back."

"Don't you bother, Ralph. Just give me his number. I know some people who are very close to him. I can solve the whole thing with a phone call."

"You'll do *that*? I gave him my word I'd call him back within the half hour."

"Rest easy, Ralph . . . within fifteen minutes. Just give me the information."

"What about Stevie Tree? She sounds very unstable."

"Ralph, I feel like a father to that girl . . . like a father. Wait, I'll get a pencil and you'll give me Mr. Daniel's phone number. I'm getting old and I can't trust my memory the way I used to."

Three minutes later, Sy Rosen was on the telephone with Jerry Fentris.

"Jerry, we have a small additional problem, but I think it can be handled. Do you know John Daniels?"

"Who the hell is he? And what's the problem?"

"Jerry, you should take more of an interest in civic matters. He happens to be our district attorney." Sy told Jerry the story of Stevie's escapade with justice. Jerry whistled.

"Holy shit. That's the end of it. We're cooked now."

"No, Jerry, you don't understand the nuances. I must ask you to think these things through. Mr. Daniels would not have phoned Ralph Stanton first unless he wanted something. So I would like you to phone Mr. Daniels and tell him that through the kind intercession of Ralph Stanton, International Artists will devote the services and talent of its *top* artists to entertain at money-raising rallies for Mr. Daniels' campaign. Tell him also that Ted Caramia and his friends will be grateful."

"What?"

"Don't forget to add that. I think that it will help."

"Ted Caramia and his friends . . . you know who his friends are?"

"Yes," said Sy, "and so does John Daniels."

"What about the charges?"

"Stevie is a vengeful girl, Jerry. Invite Mr. Daniels to phone Nicholas Long if he cares to. It might also help if you alerted our doctor friend to expect a call. Mr. Daniels might wish to follow up, although I don't really think so."

"I hope you know what you're talking about, Sy."

"Jerry, Jerry, Jerry . . . listen to an old man. It's not that I'm clever or smart. It's just that I've lived longer. Get a pencil and take down the number."

"OK, Sy. What about Stevie?"

"One thing at a time, Jerry. First this item, and then we will proceed to dispose of that person you mentioned, like they say in the CIA, 'with extreme prejudice' . . . Do you have a pencil, Jerry?"

"Yeah, Sy. Go ahead."

21

Morgan Oliver had just completed a potboiler of a movie called *Dealer's Choice*, which was filmed in three different European countries to qualify for tax advantages in all three. The countries were France, Italy and Germany, and because the innovative producers had structured the contractual aspects in a creatively lucrative way, it really didn't make any difference to them if the picture was ever released. They had made their money in front.

From France there were subsidies in a refund on admission prices. Because the production qualified as Italian, under a liberal interpretation of corporate hopscotching, it also qualified for those subsidies as well. Additionally, a new gimmick that made a German production a tax shelter for rich German doctors allowed for additional funds to be handed back to the producers.

The unfortunate aspect of the deal was that the contracts binding all the parties were more entertaining than the script. For the deal to go through, there had to be a star and an acceptable director. In an atmosphere in which Morgan Oliver pictures were not in great demand on the home front, Morgan's agent was offered a contract departing from his usual picture price, but providing gainful employment for him at a time when he desperately needed the money.

The agent presented the offer to Morgan. It was a no-quote offer, which meant that the producer was solemnly sworn not to reveal to any other party how much Morgan actually was paid. In the industry, the information about previous fees paid to actors, writers, producers and directors is a fact that most studios and many independents share with each other. A fact that drives some agents to distraction because they are powerless to lie to a customer who can and will check up on the price previously paid to the talent in question.

The other ingredient that made the deal agreeable to Morgan was the possibility of a share of the profits from the picture. This his agent negotiated for him and told him would make up for the difference in the salary he was asked to accept. It was fool's gold. No one would see a nickel's worth of profits except the imaginative producers who remained in Paris during the shoot, so as not to confuse profit with art.

Lastly, Morgan was being beset by the Hollywood game of "Who's on top?" and it would have been bad politics to stay in a town where people looked the other way when he came into a room. His last three pictures had been disastrous. He had developed a reputation for serious coke addiction and had had a number of ugly fights, which had led to two separate lawsuits against him. One involved his having beaten a stagehand. The union closed down the set for three days, during which the picture people had to make redress for his behavior. Even that didn't stop the man from filing a civil suit against him. The second lawsuit was for destroying plate-glass windows on Rodeo Drive during a drunken spree. No one was particularly fond of doing business with Morgan even when he was on top, and even his dearest friends began to avoid him now that he was down.

His isolation intensified his relationship with Ginny Tree. At night Morgan wouldn't leave the bungalow at the Beverly Hills Hotel, and even though Ginny continued to keep her clothes with Frank and Betty, more and more she stayed with Morgan. The bungalow took on the appearance of a town under siege. The mess was extraordinary. Scripts, old newspapers, magazines and articles of clothing were all over. Try as they could, the cleaning people at the hotel were unable to keep it tidy. They didn't dare disturb the personal articles, and they hardly were able to get to the beds, the bathroom, and have room service retrieve the endless pile of dirty dishes.

Ginny continued to turn tricks during the day and, in addition, began to steal to supplement her income. Ginny's cocaine habit had reached a hundred dollars a day. During all this time, she never asked Morgan for any money. Little by little, Ginny was beginning to dominate his life. The two of them hardly had sex together. What sex Morgan enjoyed was either an occasional call girl or a bit actress or extra on the set.

Ginny and Morgan fought constantly. Their arguments continued to be loud and violent. Frequently, security at the hotel was forced to phone and request that they quiet down. When they acceded, they would return to the unmade bed and eat huge quantities of junk food, watching TV into the late hours, dozing and waking again to stare zombielike at the set.

Stevie had learned almost immediately after it began about her sister Ginny's relationship with Morgan Oliver. She took the news grimly. Each time she heard more about Ginny and Morgan, she wondered where it was going. Too much of the news reflected the relationship she herself had had with him years earlier. Stevie knew that Ginny was a prostitute, and although it deeply troubled her, she was forced to realize that she had been little more than that in the past. Perhaps she hadn't turned tricks off the street, but nights and weekends for her pimp Morgan Oliver were the same thing. Who was she kidding? Fifty-dollar and hundred-dollar "taxi fares." A whore was a whore. Sometimes Stevie thought of calling Ginny. On one occasion she did, and clicked down on the phone when her sister answered. What could she say to her? What right did she have to say anything? Had she been somehow to blame? Had there ever been a time when she could have been a real sister? Was Ginny right in her anger?

Her thoughts darkened. It wasn't so. Stevie had been barely staying alive herself.

The last three weeks of Morgan's European picture were being shot in Germany, at Studio Hamburg, a modern and complete studio complex well within that city. Morgan had urged Ginny to stay with him during the filming. It seemed like a very natural thing to do. Their circle was being drawn tighter and tighter. The last weeks of the shoot were spent together in a suite at the Hotel Atlantic, a giant of an old-world hotel, with huge rooms and fireplaces.

The shoot would finish several days before Christmas, and they would fly back to California. Hamburg was gray and cold in late December. It became more and more difficult to get Morgan out of bed and to the studio for his morning calls. When he did go, Ginny would sleep through the day. To help in completing photography, one of the assistants on the picture was detailed to obtain cocaine for Morgan. It was easy to get.

On the last day of the shoot, the rest of the cast held a "wrap party," which Morgan didn't attend. Alone, he and Ginny got riotously drunk and ran up and down the halls of the hotel at three in the morning. Morgan set fire to draperies in the lobby and the fire and police departments were summoned. The hotel management insisted on prosecuting, but the heads of the film studio finally talked them out of it.

Morgan and Ginny made a sullen pair, as they cut their last ties with civilized behavior. In the living room of the suite, waiting for the limousine to take them to the airport and then to Frankfurt, New York and L.A., Morgan surveyed the mountain of luggage that awaited the bellboys. He looked over at the couch on which Ginny was dozing, bundled up in a coat and muffler. Morgan came over to Ginny and tapped her on the shoulder.

"Hey you, wake up . . . wake up, goddammit, and get me another agent . . . That's what I need, another agent. Your sister is Miss Hotshot. Put in a phone call right now—don't wait. It'll be Christmas soon and I want to have a new agent by Christmas."

Ginny barely stirred, and with difficulty the two of them made their way to the limousine that took them to the airport.

It wasn't until Morgan got to New York that he was able to contact International Artists. The more he thought about it, the more convinced he was that the answer to all problems lay in finding a new agent. In some curious twist of his mind, he became obsessed with the notion that the right person was Stevie Tree. Whether this conviction came out of a real understanding of Stevie's importance in the industry, or whether it was his unconscious wish to get the other Tree into the grimy playpen with him, was not important. The more frustrated he was in his attempt to get overseas phone calls to the States from Hamburg, then Frankfurt, then London, finally reaching IA from New York, the more convinced he was that the devil himself was attempting to exercise one last bit of control over his life.

Finally, at ten o'clock California time, he reached Fred Wine at home through the IA switchboard. It was Christmas Eve. Agents are used to intrusion in their personal lives from troubled clients, but Morgan's voice on the phone suggested near frenzy and hysteria.

"Fred . . . Morgan Oliver. Jesus Christ, you people are impossible to get hold of. Do you know how long I've been trying? Forget it . . . Look, I want to change representation. I'm prepared to sign with IA. Yeah, you motherfuckers finally got me. One thing, Fred— there's only one person I want handling me. I want to meet with Stevie Tree tomorrow when I get back. Have her at the Beverly Hills Hotel at five."

Despite the hour, Fred Wine phoned Sy Rosen at home. "Sy, Morgan Oliver phoned me just now from New York. He's been making a picture in Europe."

"What does *he* want?"

"He wants us to represent him, and wait till you hear this—he wants Stevie."

"Jesus, his career is nowhere—and Christ knows she's the last person to want to represent him. She tried to kill herself over that bastard."

"Yeah, I know, Sy."

"Fred, I bet she'd do it . . . Not that I think that there's a nickel in Morgan Oliver. He's destroying himself, but something tells me that the chemistry between him and our girl could help us. Christ knows I'm not looking for her to try suicide again, though frankly, Fred, that *would* solve a lot of problems . . . Something good will come out of it, I feel it in my bones."

"Do you really think so, Sy?"

"Yeah, the more I think of it, the better I like it. You call her. It'll stink if I call her."

"It'll still stink, Sy."

"Yeah, but so what? Do it tomorrow. It's Christmas."

Early Christmas morning, Stevie received a phone call from Fred Wine.

"Stevie, Merry Christmas."

"Thanks, Fred . . . and to you too."

"Stevie, I got a phone call last night from someone you know very well, and this party wanted to know if IA would handle him. His representation terminated some time ago at another agency."

"Who is it?"

"Morgan."

"Yes, Fred? Is there something else you have to say?"

"Well, now you don't have to do it, but maybe it would be useful, kind of get him out of your system." There was a silence on the phone.

"Fred, if Morgan Oliver wants me to handle him . . . I'd be more than pleased."

"You're sure, Stevie?"

Stevie paused a moment. "Yes, Fred . . . I'm absolutely sure."

"OK then, Stevie . . . five o'clock today at the Beverly Hills Hotel, his bungalow. I know it's Christmas day, but he seems in a panic."

"Merry Christmas, Fred."

Stevie hung up the phone slowly and walked to her closet, which bulged with the valises of Morgan Oliver clippings. Then she walked over to her wardrobe racks and looked at the array of beautiful things: silk shirts and slacks, Adolfo suits, Galanos and Holly Harp gowns, Gucci loafers, Charles Jourdan shoes. 'What do you wear to an execution?' she wondered. 'And whose execution will it be?'

At four-thirty that afternoon, Stevie left the house. On an impulse, she drove up Laurel Canyon and found the house off Mulholland where Morgan had lived five years ago. She parked the car in the driveway at the foot of the stairs and walked the two flights up to the terrace. Midway, she was assaulted by the sounds of kids running in and out of doors and down steps. Two young boys were racing ahead, and a young girl, not more than six, was navigating the stairs slowly in an attempt to keep up with the boys. The little girl stopped to say "hello."

"My mommy and daddy aren't home. Did you come to see them?"

"No darling . . . a friend a mine used to live here. Do you think that your mommy and daddy would let me take a look out from your terrace?"

"Oh, sure . . . come on. I'll show you the way. Who was your friend? Do I know him?"

Stevie walked up the stairs to the terrace, holding the little girl's hand. She remembered it very well, and at the edge she looked around and saw the vast panorama of the San Fernando Valley. The bright December sun painted a golden haze above the valley and cast deep shadows into the ravines. Then she looked down below and saw the dark recesses of the canyon, the rocks and boulders and the sharp edge of the scrub trees that lined the bottom of the steep drop.

"Does your mommy let you play on the terrace?"

"Oh, sure . . . I'm very careful. Are you scared of heights?"

"No, darling."

"My mommy says some people are . . . Excuse me, I got to go catch my brothers. Come back again . . . I like you."

After several minutes alone, Stevie retreated to her Porsche. She drove slowly to the Beverly Hills Hotel, depositing the car with the doorman, then announced herself on the house phone, and walked the seventy-five feet to Morgan's bungalow.

The door to the bungalow was open and as Stevie entered, Morgan Oliver walked out of the bedroom in a blue terrycloth robe and bare feet. His hair was uncombed and at five o'clock he was unshaven. He sat down in an easy chair opposite the coffee table, reached for a cigarette in his pocket and lit it. Stevie sat down in a chair opposite him. She looked at Morgan carefully. 'My God, he is still beautiful,' she thought incredulously. His deep blue eyes captivated her, locked her in. His coal-black hair hung down on his forehead, nearly in his eyes, giving him the appearance of a rumpled, sleepy, beautiful boy. Morgan was still a magnificent-looking man. She wondered where Ginny was.

"Stevie, it's been a long time. How have you been? You look like a million bucks."

"Thanks, Morgan . . . I'm doing fine."

"Your sister tells me you're the best in the business."

Stevie pulled a cigarette from the open pack and lit it. Except for grass, it was the first cigarette she had smoked in years. She looked at her fingers as she lit it, surprised that they were steady.

"Sisters are notoriously bad witnesses, Morgan . . ."

"What I need is a good picture."

"Morgan, what you need is a whole new act."

"What the hell are you talking about?" He slammed his feet on the floor.

"Morgan . . . I might resurrect you. It would be like turning loaves into fishes, and parting the waters of the Red Sea, no doubt . . . but you've got to behave."

"Come off it, lady . . . I don't need some smartass telling me what to do."

"So long, Morgan . . . You don't need an agent, you need a miracle."

Stevie started to get up and turned to go. Out of the bedroom came the figure of Ginny Tree. She was in a stained shorty nightgown, her hair askew, her left eye bruised and one side of her face black and blue. Bruises marked her upper arm and her other shoulder.

"Morgan." It was a word. It was a command. "Listen to the lady." Ginny had aged. Stevie recognized the signs of drugs in her reddened eyes and in the cold, measured manner of her movements. Stevie wondered whether Ginny was on heroin. She looked at her sister. Their eyes didn't meet. Ginny sat down on the couch and lit a roach that was in the ashtray.

Stevie sat down and continued. "There isn't a place in this town that doesn't know you, Morgan, and doesn't hate your guts. Your problem is that you're trouble. Now I don't care what you do in your private life, but I'll say this . . . the first meeting you take with me, you behave . . . and when you get a picture—and I'll get you one—you behave on the picture too. I don't care whether someone has to give you the catechism every day to make you shape up, but find that someone."

He stared up at her with his incredible blue eyes. "Otherwise?"

"There's no otherwise, Morgan. Feel the floor. You've hit bottom. Man, this is it. You've got no place to go."

Stevie turned her attention to Ginny, who sat there sucking on the joint. Their eyes had still not met. She realized they would never connect, and turned away.

"Get me a picture," he commanded.

"Stevie got up to leave. "You'll be hearing from me—and return my calls when I call, or I'll stop calling. Once is enough, Morgan." He had no clue to her full meaning.

Stevie walked out of the bungalow and onto the green manicured hotel lawn. Back inside the main part of the hotel, she walked into the powder room beyond the Polo Lounge and stared at the mirror. She cried until someone came in. She wasn't crying for herself. She was crying for an early image of her baby sister years ago, tiny and forlorn, and for the Ginny she saw today—as lost as on that day sixteen years ago.

Stevie drove slowly back along Sunset. The Christmas lights illuminated all the shop windows she passed, but the streets were quiet and empty. Hollywood was at home in the bosom of family.

Stevie wanted desperately to find her own home. There had been days at the agency when it seemed as if the world were tumbling down, days when clients were rebellious and unwilling to behave, days when customers would make the most outrageous demands and then ask for more. Bad days were never easy, but none of them had the quality of this day. There was Ginny, whose hatred had led to a path of destruction, whose jealousy of Stevie had brought her to the brink of disaster. And Morgan Oliver, a devil incarnate and a beautiful devil. A man whose utter contempt for the women in his life led him to brutalize and degrade them. Stevie remembered her sister's bruises and knew that Morgan had caused them and a hundred more that had disappeared. With all her heart, Stevie wanted to free her sister. And yet she knew she didn't have the power or the right. Ginny had found her own path of self-destruction. Stevie's dream was to destroy Morgan Oliver, and now she was, it seemed, to be the means of his resurrection.

Stevie parked the car in the garage and walked slowly upstairs to the front door. The telephone was ringing as she put the key in the lock and Stevie quickly walked over to a hall table and picked it up. It was Sam.

"I'm glad I got you, Stevie."

"Sam . . . I know that this is a tough day for you to call—Christmas at home. Did Laurie get my present?"

"Wait, Stevie—I'll put her on the phone. She wants to thank you herself."

"Hi, Stevie. Merry Christmas."

"Merry Christmas to you too, Laurie. I send you a big kiss."

"And me too, Stevie. I love the present. The *Oz* books are my very favorites. I thought that they were second-hand books, until Daddy explained them to me. They're first editions. They must have cost a lot of money."

"Not a lot, Laurie . . . a very little for a very special young lady."

"I didn't send you a present . . . but I made you one . . . I didn't send it because I want to give it to you myself when I see you. And Stevie, something wonderful happened."

"Tell me, honey."

"Well, it's the thing that I've been hoping for . . . Remember I wanted to be the girl on the poster . . . with Jerry Lewis?"

"Yes . . . are you going to be it?"

"Maybe . . . maybe . . . I'm in the finals . . . Do you know why I couldn't qualify before? It was because I didn't look as if I was really sick. But now I can . . . You haven't seen me in a while, Stevie. Why haven't you come to visit me? I'm wearing heavy braces now, so I look OK for the poster."

"Yes, baby . . . yes, Laurie."

"And I've got an autographed picture of Jerry Lewis for Christmas. Bet you never had one of them."

"No, never, Laurie."

"Hold on, Stevie. Daddy wants to say hello."

Sam spoke. "Stevie . . . you understand, don't you?"

"Yes, Sam . . . I understand. God help me, I understand."

The phone call marked the end of Christmas day.

22

Through the nonprofessional spy systems that agents use to obtain information in Hollywood, Stevie became aware of a highly regarded script owned by Magna Films. The script, by a new young writer, was titled *Young Dillinger*.

An occasional note of thanks, a pair of tickets to a screening, a friendly conversation on the phone with the secretary to an important producer or a production executive had paid off many times for Stevie, in the ability to get the man on the phone, and occasionally, as it did now, in a tip on a hot property in need of casting.

Stevie phoned the producer and asked to see a script in order to submit casting ideas. The producer, Nicholas Long, was unwilling to send her a script, saying there was no one she represented who would fit. And that was that, and goodbye to you.

A wholly unsatisfactory phone call to a producer she had never liked, and vice versa. The problem now was how to get a script. It was too much to ask of the secretary who gave Stevie the tip. It was out of proportion to the risk if someone ever discovered that the secretary had done something that disloyal. Leaks are permitted in Washington, but never in Hollywood, where the worry is that someone will beat you to the market with a quick version of the picture you're in the process of making.

Stevie considered phoning the head of the studio. He

would send her a script, but she would lose points with him. Why, he would ask, had the producer not sent her one? A good question. 'Because the producer is a prick,' she said to herself, 'and thinks that I don't have any clients he wants—or even worse, he hates my guts and doesn't want to do business with me even if I had a client he wanted, which I don't even know, because I have no idea who to suggest since I haven't read the script in the first place.' Everything got more complicated as you went along.

At the end of the day, Brenda came into Stevie's office and closed the door. Brenda took out a cigarette case and passed a joint over to Stevie. Stevie lit up, as the senior member, and then after a deep drag passed it back to Brenda.

"Another day, another dollar."

"You ought to join a union, Stevie."

"It won't pay any better."

"Yeah . . . but you get longer lunches, free Kotex in the ladies' room, and a feel-up at the Christmas party."

Brenda reached over and took the joint expertly between her thumb and forefinger. She drew deeply and finally coughed. "Damn! You white folks are always able to do that without coughing."

Stevie retrieved the joint and drew in on the smoke. "There, you have it, Brenda . . . the natural superiority of the honky."

"Stevie . . . what do you want out of life?"

"Well, I would like to take a pee . . . and second in importance I would like to get a copy of a script called *Young . . . Young . . .* I forget the man's name. It was on the tip of my tongue."

"What kind of tongue?"

"Sliced tongue with mustard on rye. *Dillinger.*"

"My name is Brenda . . . you can remember that, even if you're stoned."

"That's the name of the movie. *Young Dillinger.*"

"And you can't get a script?" Brenda was deep in thought.

"The producer won't hand it over . . . and it is not

behooving for a behoover in my position to ask around him."

"Which producer?"

"Nicholas Long."

Brenda inhaled. "Oh, that motherfucker."

"The same one." Stevie nodded to Brenda.

Brenda tapped her finger on her teeth. "Go pee. Where there's a *schwarze*, there's a way."

Exactly five minutes later, Stevie came back to her office. The smell of grass would have given Beverly Hills a contact high had the window been left open. Only some cleaning women and the two of them were still in the building. Brenda was on the telephone saying her ritual, "Uh-huhs," and then a final "goodbye."

"Stevie . . . you got it. If you can spare the bread and send a cab to this address, you got a script of *Young Dillinger*." Brenda handed Stevie a slip of paper with an East Los Angeles address.

Stevie grabbed her and hugged her. "No shit?"

Brenda smiled. "No shit. Wanna know how, white lady?"

"Yeah . . . yeah . . . do it." Stevie's eyes sparkled.

"Well, the idea came to me when I saw our cleaning ladies. Cleaning ladies see the insides of more offices and more stuff that people don't want them to see than their psychiatrists."

"Roll on, oh little mother of all the Russias."

"And so all those cleaning ladies are unionized and friendly. I called in our cleaning lady, a *black* lady, mind you, and I said to her, 'There's a wastebasket at Magna Studios, in the office of producer Nicholas Long, in which I would like to find a script. And the script I would like to find in it is a script titled *Young Dillinger*.'"

"Then what happened? Oh my God, I missed the whole thing because of a weak bladder."

"Black folks don't *have* weak bladders. We're too *poor*."

"Fuck you, Brenda . . . go on."

"So the cleaning lady over here phoned the head cleaning lady over at Magna, on our phone, and told her what to look for in the wastebasket."

"Christ, Brenda . . . it's one chance in a million that there'll be a script of *Young Dillinger* in his wastebasket."

"No risk at all, honey . . . If it ain't there now, the cleaning lady will *put* it there."

"Where will she get it, Brenda?"

"From the files, Stevie! Where else?"

The script was as good as the secretary had indicated. Stevie read it that night and sent it by messenger to Morgan Oliver first thing the next morning with a note that read: Read this at once, and phone me."

Later that afternoon Morgan was on the phone. "OK, what's the joke?"

Stevie steeled herself at the sound of his voice. "Do you like it? Will you do it?"

"Are you kidding? Of course I'll do it. Was it offered to me?"

"Of course not . . . but we'll see."

"Yeah . . . big deal . . . very funny." Morgan hung up.

Twenty-four hours later Stevie met Ralph Stanton, the head of Magna, for lunch in his private dining room.

Early that morning, Ralph Stanton's secretary, one of his three, who was charged with many personal matters for her boss, conducted one of her most important functions, that of making luncheon arrangements for Ralph Stanton's guests who lunched daily with him in his private dining room. The conversation about arrangements was entertaining for Brenda.

"This is Mr. Ralph Stanton's secretary. Am I speaking to the secretary of Miss Stevie Tree?"

Brenda began to swing with the punch. "Right on."

"I'd like to confirm the fact that Miss Tree will be lunching today with Mr. Stanton in Mr. Stanton's private dining room. I've arranged a drive-on pass for

Miss Tree at the main gate on Dunbar. That's the main gate on Dunbar, D-U-N-B-A-R. When Miss Tree drives through the gate the guard will wave her on. Miss Tree drives a red Porsche, I believe, license plate 768 MJ?"

"My God, how do you know that? I don't even know her license plate."

"I make a record of the license plates of people who visit Mr. Stanton, so when they come a second time they don't have the inconvenience of stopping at the guard gate."

"That's thoughtful," Brenda marveled.

"When Miss Tree drives on, she is to park in the executive parking lot, which is just alongside the fountains that we used in the musical version of *Tom Sawyer*."

"Oh, *them* fountains. Loved the fountains, but didn't care for the flick."

Stanton's secretary was not tuned into Brenda's comments, so she continued. She appeared to be reading from something like the checklist a pilot uses to prepare a 747 takeoff.

"The parking space reserved for Miss Tree is number 205, which is next to Mr. Stanton's tan Corniche. In the event that Miss Tree forgets the number, all she has to do is remember the color of Mr. Stanton's Corniche."

Brenda offered, "brown . . . light . . . sort of tannish."

"Yes . . . and Miss Tree should take the elevator to the third floor of the administration building. Miss Tree has been here before so she will know the way."

"Oh, *yeah*."

"What would Miss Tree care for in the way of lunch?"

"You suggest," Brenda was testing.

"Well, it's all prepared by Mr. Stanton's cook. He could make anything that Miss Tree had a preference for."

"Whale."

"Sorry, did you say kale? That's a vegetable, isn't it?"

"Look, Miss Tree will take a salad, or a hot dog or anything else you're serving. My other phone is ringing. Thanks for the nice chat." Brenda broke up laughing first, and then Stevie, who had been listening on the standard agency earpiece.

At lunch, Ralph Stanton sat at the opposite of a ten-foot-long table until Stevie picked up her placemat and moved down the to his side. He seemed startled at the break in tradition, but pleased at sitting next to a very pretty lady who didn't wear a brassiere.

"Ralph, I love this room."

"This is your first time here for lunch, Stevie . . . We should do it more often. My chef is an absolute master. He made you a seafood salad, as you ordered, but there are a few extra treats.

"He likes to surprise people . . . There's a superb quiche to start with, and a wonderful white wine from the Mount St. Helena vineyard that they send me only six cases of every year . . . and then there's a wonderful soufflé, Grand Marnier, I think, or maybe chocolate . . . and of course some very pleasant claret with the dessert. Then we can have coffee or espresso if you wish, back in my office."

"Ralph . . . you will be a legend in your own time."

"In the industry?"

"No, Ralph, with Weight Watchers. You're a killer, but I'm game."

After lunch, Ralph Stanton led Stevie back to his office, which had a small corner set with comfortable chairs, a coffee table and a pot of espresso kept warm over a flame. Ralph poured, sighed and lit a cigar.

"Can I offer you a cigar, Stevie?"

"Ralph, thank you, but no . . . Now that I've put on thirty pounds, can we talk about *The Last Command?*"

"Of course, Stevie, always ready to talk business. I like the book. My people like the book, but we're not interested."

"Can I ask why, Ralph?"

"Let me tell you what I think about *The Last Command*. It is one of the most brilliantly written books in the last decade. There are two extravagantly important parts, eminently castable with major stars, and such a package would attract a major director, but nevertheless we're not interested. That's all there is to it. When I took over the studio, I promised the board of directors that I would dispense with the extravagances my predecessor engaged in, the ridiculous bidding for hot properties. Stevie, as much as I would like to own *The Last Command*, I will not get into a bidding game with the other studios in town. What they do is their business. I run my studio the way it should be run—efficiently *and* economically."

"Ralph . . . you can have *The Last Command* at your price."

"Of course . . . would you like some more espresso?" he paid no attention.

"Ralph . . . I'm serious. Just write a number down on a sheet of paper . . . Here's one on the coffee table . . . the amount you'd like to pay up front, and what percentage of the gross, from the first dollar, that you think is fair for the property."

Ralph Stanton looked up from his cigar, into Stevie's eyes. "I believe you mean it."

He reached for the pad and took a pen from his pocket. He paused a moment and wrote down a figure then paused another moment and crossed that out. He wrote down several other numbers, and without looking at the slip he handed her, Stevie folded it and said, "OK, you own *The Last Command*."

Ralph Stanton smiled. "I really don't believe you."

Stevie stared at him. "Ralph, if it's a bad joke, you'll never let me back on the lot. Trust me, it's yours . . . Now I would like to talk about *Young Dillinger*. I have the perfect casting for it—Morgan Oliver."

Ralph Stanton put his pen down. "I might have known it. A tie-in deal. No deal, Miss Tree."

"Excuse me, Ralph . . . no tie-in deal. *The Last Command* deal stands . . . on its own. What I'm talking about now is a superb actor, a former box-office winner who could be again . . . and who is absolutely right for the part. He'll work for very small front money against a piece of the profit."

Ralph Stanton picked up his pen. "He's no good."

Stevie drank some espresso. "Granted."

"He's trouble on the set."

"No . . . no more, Ralph. He has an interested agent who won't let him be."

"How cheap?"

"This cheap." Stevie took his pen and pad and wrote down a half-dozen numbers. Ralph Stanton smiled.

"OK, you've got a deal. I like doing business with you, young lady."

"Your producer hates him, Ralph."

"Fuck Nicholas Long. He does what I tell him."

"My point exactly," Stevie replied, smiling.

Before Stevie phoned Morgan Oliver, she recounted the entire story for Brenda.

"And you folded it up without looking at it?"

"It's useful to read upside-down, Brenda. Try it, and you'll never want to read right-side-up again."

"And this whole story that you're telling me . . . that's not just for the greater glory of Stevie Tree. I know it, Stevie . . . I heard from the office grapevine that you went to bat for me to become an agent."

Stevie smiled. "Mighty white of me, Brenda . . . Get me what's-his-name on the phone, while you're still my secretary."

Brenda picked up the phone and started dialing the Beverly Hills Hotel. "You mean *what's his name*?"

"Yeah, what's-his-name, dammit."

The next weeks were a blur of activity as far as Morgan Oliver was concerned. When Stevie told him the news, he asked to review the deal. He complained bitterly that there wasn't enough front money to make it worthwhile. Stevie pointed out to him from her complete knowledge of every deal he had done, every business venture that Morgan Oliver had engaged in these past five years, that it was equal to the price he got on his last picture. Nevertheless, he said, the percentage of profits was below his customary amount. Stevie pointed out that this was the first occasion when he would be getting a percentage of the gross income rather than an unpredictable amount of a larger percentage of the elusive net profits. These had a tendency to disappear when the studio's mysterious salves and unguents were applied to reports to profit participants.

Lastly, Morgan complained that there was no guarantee of his own Winnebago, his own car and limousine. Stevie acknowledged that was true and muttered, "Morgan . . . you were unemployable yesterday. You've got a job today," ending the conversation. Preparation for the film was already under way. The production called for an eight-week schedule, and principal photography would take place in Churubusco Studios in Mexico.

Later that same day, Stevie was at home when the phone rang. The maid came out of the kitchen and announced to Stevie that it was her sister. Stevie moved toward the telephone on the coffee table and sat down before she picked up the receiver. Maria hung up the phone in the kitchen.

"Ginny . . ."

"Look, Stevie . . . I'm not very good at these things, but I want to thank you for what you did for Morgan . . . things have been very bad for us . . . I guess you know it, and this comes at an important time . . ."

"Ginny, could I see you? Could we talk? There's so much we need to say to each other."

"I don't know, Stevie. I'm so full of anger. I don't really know what to do about myself. I love Morgan . . . I really do. He doesn't care anything about me." It sounded all too familiar to Stevie.

"Ginny, he beat you."

"That's nothing. It's been a lot worse, but maybe with this picture it will be different."

"Ginny, anything I say will sound like jealousy, but this is your chance to get out."

"I can't, sister . . . I'm hooked."

"Morgan or heroin?"

"Both . . . but I've been clean for a while. I promised myself that I'll stay clean through the picture and then we'll see. Well, goodbye, Stevie . . . I'm glad I called you . . . I really am. Maybe when we get back from Mexico. Who knows?"

The phone clicked off. There was only the dull buzz in her ear.

That night Stevie ate dinner alone at home. Her Mexican maid had set a small table next to the picture window in the living room, on which she placed a vase of wildflowers. Eating alone had become a habit with Stevie, except for the occasions that she had a business appointment. Maria went out of her way to make new dishes to tempt her. With the lights dimmed in the living room behind her and the lights of the flickering candle on the table reflected in the window, the dinner setting was romantic enough to be shared.

Stevie had finished her second cup of coffee when she heard a loud sound coming from the kitchen, then voices—Maria's familiar Spanish cadences and a male voice. The voices got louder and Stevie was frightened. Laurel Canyon, and most particularly houses like hers away from the main road, had known violence. Stevie started for the phone to call the police. At that moment, Maria raced into the living room.

"Señora . . . I think you should come into the kitchen."

Stevie had the phone in her hand. "Maria, should I call the police?"

"Señora, I don't know. But you come, please."

Stevie followed Maria. "Who is in there, Maria?"

Maria turned just before she pushed open the kitchen door. "A strange man. He come to the kitchen door. He say he is your father. Is possible, your father, Señora?"

Stevie had been eleven years old when she last saw Ray Tree, a gun in his hand, sitting alongside the dead bodies of her mother and her mother's lover. Sixteen years had gone by. My god, she thought, could it be? And the answer lay behind the kitchen door.

Ray Tree, now forty-eight, had spent the last sixteen years in a Federal prison in Kansas. Stevie opened the door and saw an old man standing before her. Quickly, he tried to hide behind the door. Dressed in a plaid mackintosh, tan workpants and boots, his hair completely gray and closely cropped, his face was gaunt and unshaven. His eyes darted around the kitchen, looking first at Stevie, then Maria, then behind him, as if he expected someone to snatch him away.

He looked at Stevie with the eyes of a frightened rabbit, wanting to run, but with no place to run to. Stevie, stunned by the sight, turned to Maria. "Maria, get this man out of my house, and if he won't go, telephone the police."

Maria put her hand on Stevie's arm. "Señora . . . whatever you say, but the man is sick."

Stevie looked at Maria and then at her father.

"Señora, I can let him rest on that cot in the garage downstairs. Señora, is the man your father? ¿Verdad?"

Stevie looked slowly. "Yes, Maria . . . verdad. Take him downstairs." Stevie left the two of them in the kitchen and went back into the living room to piece together her jumbled thoughts.

With each passing day, and without any further words between Stevie and Maria, Stevie acknowledged Ray Tree's presence. She had in effect given sanction to it. Stevie could catch hints of his presence. Maria would prepare a sandwich or some fruit while Stevie was out and bring it down to him. A week went by, and as if in response to an unasked question, Maria remarked, "Señora . . . he is getting better."

Stevie didn't know what to do. Her feelings for her father were now confused. She had always wanted him dead, and for that matter, had never even considered that he might be alive. She had never put it together that since he *had* been alive when last she saw him, he might still be.

Some perverse streak in Stevie made her want Ray Tree near her, now that he had found her. It was, in its own way, not unlike the need for control that made her collect scraps of information about Morgan Oliver—as if she could magically contain both their souls. Tacitly, Stevie was giving permission for him to be there. Maria would occasionally whisper asides about him, as if there were a secret conspiracy among the three of them. Maria confided to her that he was much improved, and that while Stevie was away, he was helping her, not in the house, never, but outside, clearing trees and removing trash. As far as Maria was concerned, Ray Tree was another resident of the house.

23

The musical play *Hello Sucker* with Zelma Hurwitz
opened on Broadway, and for Zelma it was a personal
triumph. The critics and public alike regarded it as
fresh, charming, funny, delightful—a huge hit. Stevie,
in New York for the opening, had set up a deal for the
movie version, which would be filmed at the conclusion
of the first year's run. At that point, by contract, Zelma
would be free of the play. Back in L.A., Stevie
imagined Zelma luxuriating in New York with adoring
friends and family. But it wasn't quite that way, as
Stevie learned in a phone call from her New York
counterpart at IA. There was trouble. Stevie flew east
the next day and drove from the airport directly to the
Pierre Hotel on Fifth Avenue. She had arranged to
meet with Zelma first and then go to the IA apartment
at the Sherry Netherland.

It was four in the afternoon. When Zelma opened
the door to the suite at the Pierre, she was drunk.
Stevie kissed her on the cheek. Her hair was uncombed
and wild. She was still in a bathrobe. Dishes littered
with food and silver serving pieces from room service
covered two carts in the corner of the living room.
Zelma hadn't eaten anything.

"Welcome to sin city, Stevie."

"Should I comment on how terrific you look,
Zelma?"

"Sure, lie a little. That's what agents do."

"What are you drinking?"

"Southern Comfort . . . I love it. It's just like Fox's U-Bet chocolate syrup, but you wouldn't know anything about those Jew drinks. You're a *shiksa* . . . a beautiful *shiksa*."

"Is there any coffee? Never mind, I see a pot on the table." Stevie poured out a cup of cold coffee, took some ice cubes from the bucket and made a rudimentary iced coffee, figuring that action might help carry the conversation.

"It's about time you came, Stevie . . . My God, how they treat me on the show. It's worse than that bar and grill I used to sing at in Brooklyn."

Stevie took one sip of the bitter concoction. "Tell me about it."

"I'm supposed to have a limo pick me up every night . . . Well, he does. He was late once or twice, not serious . . . but the driver is some Arab. Now, I'm not about to say something to him about Israel or about me being Jewish . . . 'cause after all, he may be with Al Fatah or Black September or one of those things . . . and I'm petrified every time I get in. He could abduct me . . . or turn around when we're stuck in traffic and shoot me."

"Did you try to get a different driver?"

"Who can I talk to? What can I say, my driver is Arafat. Get rid of him. I'd sound like a loony."

Stevie changed the attack. "How's the cast . . . and the director?"

"Let me tell you about that director. He's a faggot, of that I'm sure. The first night I went on stage, he reaches into my dress and rearranges my boobs for their opening night entrance. That's what the son of a bitch said. Can you imagine the nerve of that man?"

Stevie smiled. "Did he goose you too?"

"That's not funny . . . I don't make an entrance with my ass."

"OK, what else, Zelma . . ."

"Well, there's the dressing room. The air conditioning doesn't work, and I've been asking for a refrigerator for three weeks now. The one I have doesn't make any ice . . . and you'd think that for a star they'd do that one simple thing."

"Zelma . . . I'm sure that there's more, and I have a couple of suggestions to make. First, I'd lighten up on the booze—that *isn't* chocolate syrup—and take a short nap before you go to the theater. I'm going over to my hotel and take a shower, and I'll pick you up here. We'll check out Mr. Arafat. I'll go to the theater with you and grab the director's *cojones* to get even, provided he has them. Then after the show, we can go to the Stage Delicatessen, get something to eat, and we'll talk and work things out."

Zelma pouted. "You think I'm behaving like a spoiled brat."

"No, but close . . . and you're lonely . . . It's all very strange, Zelma. You're a star, and all you really want is an egg cream with chocolate syrup at the neighborhood candy store."

Zelma glared at Stevie. "How the hell did you know about egg creams? They're Jewish, dammit."

Stevie smiled and got up to leave. "My real name is Esther and I'm queen of the Jews . . . I was stolen by gypsies. See you in an hour and a half."

At the apartment at the Sherry Netherland, Stevie found a pile of messages waiting for her. She put them aside, called for ice and a bottle of dry vermouth from room service and proceeded to take a shower. Fifteen minutes later, damp and holding a drink in her hand, she felt in a fit condition to tune into the last half of her day—the California half.

She tucked a huge towel around her, pulled her feet under her and called the Coast. Brenda answered.

"OK, Stevie . . . which is it first, the good news or the bad news?"

"Well, your father is in jail."

"That's nice."

"That's the bad news, but the good news is that he's out. The cops picked him up on the complaint of some tourists who were wandering around near your house.

He thought they were trespassers and threatened them with a shotgun."

Stevie took another sip. "So far, so good. And then what happened?"

"Well, they weren't exactly tourists . . . they were the FBI. He threatened to shoot them if they didn't get off the property."

"Nothing wrong with that."

"They were looking for Timothy Leary . . . he lives somewhere in Laurel Canyon . . . and they got lost."

"Terrific. Who got him out?"

"Maria called me and I got one of our lawyers. Everything's OK. As for the rest, there are three messages for you from Diedre Magee. Please call when you get back. NBC wants to talk to you. Oh, there's a new man there, I have his name."

"He may not be there when I get back."

"Uh-huh . . . and a call from Mexico—*Young Dillinger* is on budget and on schedule."

"Who phoned?"

"Your sister." Stevie felt a pang of fear, and she didn't know why.

"Jesus, it's wonderful to have a family that keeps in touch."

"Sy Rosen wants you to see him first thing Monday . . . it's about the Filmgroup thing. Sounds like trouble. And then there are calls from clients and customers. I'll handle the ones I can. The rest you can get into on Monday."

Stevie took another mouthful of vermouth. "He threatened the FBI with a shotgun. Do you suppose he would have shot them?"

"Why not? I think they stepped on some of his flowers."

Standing backstage at *Hello Sucker*, Stevie realized what a great performer Zelma was. It was an extraordinary experience to see someone take an audience from the first minute, play with them, thrill, enchant, and then leave them just as they were panting for more. The curtain calls were thunderous and never-ending. Zelma rushed back to her dressing room and started to remove her makeup.

"Feel the air conditioning, Stevie . . . Look, I ask you to feel it. Is it actually cooling? And then look at the refrigerator. It's absolutely a disaster. Even my cousin on the Grand Concourse has a better refrigerator than that. When are we going to eat? Jesus, I'm famished."

"Zelma, I have a surprise for you . . . As soon as we leave the dressing room, an army of carpenters, paperhangers and interior decorators are going to turn this place into a fairyland."

"You mean for faggots?" Zelma paused in mid-cold-cream.

"No, for you. Either that or a disaster. I got the producer to spring for redecorating the entire place, putting in a kitchen, a new refrigerator and a soda bar, with six cases of seltzer and a gallon of Fox's U-Bet chocolate syrup. The wallpaper is going to be floral, a whole outdoor feeling. Either that, or the decorator will be looking for a new tushy."

Zelma rushed over to Stevie and hugged her. "Oh, Stevie, I knew you could make it all right."

Stevie extricated herself from the embrace. "Let's get out of here and get something to eat. Your hunger is catching."

At the Stage Delicatessen, the two were shown immediately to a table in the rear. A parade of waiters, customers, management and people off the street accidentally-on-purpose wandered back to gawk at Zelma, who signed autographs whenever they were asked. Finally as the crowd subsided, the two of them were able to talk between bites of pastrami.

"Do you think you could call my mother, Stevie?"

"Well, why not, but what do you want me to say?"

"Please, we're not talking . . . She's angry at me

because I'm not getting enough sleep and I'm eating the wrong things."

"How does she know that?"

"Well, she asks me . . . and I tell her. A girl shouldn't lie to her own mother. But tell her that I'm OK, and that she doesn't have to worry about me."

"OK, Zelma . . . and by the way I checked on your driver."

"You mean the one in the limo outside," Zelma asked.

"Yes."

"Oh, that's OK, too, Stevie. I spoke to him . . . and he turns out to be Israeli. I swear, though, he looks like an Arab."

"Yes, indeed, Zelma . . . and one more thing."

"What's that?"

"Go out and buy a dog, preferably one that's pregnant and needs orthodontia."

"I don't get it." Zelma paused with a mouthful of food.

"Baby . . . life is too good. You need something to worry about, and when that dog has puppies in your suite at the Pierre, you'll have lots to worry about."

Before Stevie checked out of the Sherry Netherland the next day, she phoned Zelma's mother and reassured her that her daughter would not get rickets, tuberculosis, pneumonia or dysentery from the life she was leading. Mrs. Hurwitz listened intently, but Stevie guessed that she remained unconvinced.

The second call was to Mrs. Harriet Daniel. Since Stevie took over the house on Laurel Canyon, it bothered her that she had obtained it in an underhanded way. There was no reason why she should feel guilty, but she did. After dialing, she waited. Finally someone answered.

"Mrs. Daniel . . . this is Stevie Tree. I expect you remember me."

The flat voice was damning. "Yes, I do . . ."

"Mrs. Daniel, I want you to know I own the house on Laurel Canyon now. I purchased it from a friend and I just wanted to set the record straight. I don't like doing things that way."

"Then why did you do it, Miss Tree?"

"Because I had to have the house, Mrs. Daniel. Maybe now you'll understand how much David meant to me."

"Why are you telling me this now? To hurt me?"

"Mrs. Daniel . . . I don't think it's that, honestly. I just don't want to live a lie."

There was silence for a long time and then Mrs. Daniel's voice. "I don't think we have anything further to talk about, Miss Tree. Goodbye."

24

The rest of the shoot on *Young Dillinger* didn't match the early reports. Despite Morgan's promises to behave, he caused the usual endless problems on the set. He was frequently late in the morning and after lunch. He argued with the director and threatened to punch him. He was out of contact with the other members of the cast, and he wouldn't talk to the crew, which was made up of a combination of Mexican and American technicians.

Still, the dailies sent to the studio at the end of each production day were extraordinarily good. Nicholas Long, the producer, wouldn't permit Stevie to see them. The two of them didn't talk at all. If there was any communication necessary, his secretary spoke with Brenda.

Stevie did see a rough twenty-minute section of the film, when the producer was in Mexico City. Ralph Stanton, head of Magna, telephoned her to see it with him. At the conclusion of the run, he slapped her back and said, "Congratulations, Stevie . . . We've done it together . . . It's got the smell of hit."

"He's got fire, Ralph, and the rest of the cast is working too."

"How would you like to talk a multiple-picture deal for your man?"

"Ralph . . . I don't think so . . . I'd like the smoke to settle."

"You mean, you want this picture to get out first."

"Exactly. By the way, what's happening to *The Last Command*?"

"Nothing . . . absolutely nothing. We can't lick the script problem. I frankly don't know why we bought it, Stevie."

"Ralph, we'll buy it back from you, dollar for dollar. I'm serious."

Ralph Stanton looked across at her in his private screening room. "You'd do that?"

"Absolutely."

"Forget it. It's too valuable to let go of. We'll try another draft." Casually he added, "Can you think of a writer?"

"How about the guy who wrote the book?" Stevie replied, just as casually.

Ralph looked at her incredulously. "That's a great idea."

If there was trouble on the set in Mexico, and there was lots of it, it never entered the conversation with Ralph Stanton. When you were delivering and Morgan Oliver was, too, they would accept all kinds of shit from him.

Five weeks later, when Stevie arrived in her office, there was a message from Nicholas Long.

"You're sure it's for me," Stevie inquired of Brenda.

"Honest, it's for you. Maybe your horse won . . . or maybe he needs some Kaopectate. He's still in Mexico."

"Please get him for me."

In several minutes, Brenda buzzed and Stevie picked up.

"Hello, Nicholas." She was curious.

"I shouldn't even be talking to you . . . after what you've done."

"Nicholas, all I did was give you a star for a hit picture. What's so bad about that?"

"Never mind. Your sister is coming back in a Lear Jet and should be landing at Van Nuys Airport in a couple of hours. As a favor to you, Ralph Stanton told me to put her in a plane and send her back to L.A."

"What's the matter? Is she sick?"

"Well, I guess you could say so . . . We told the

authorities that she broke her leg, to avoid complications, but the truth of the matter is she attempted suicide with a bottle of pills."

"Is she all right?" It surprised Stevie to be so calm in the face of this news—almost as if it was to be expected.

"Yeah, I guess so . . . the air ambulance says she'll be OK. But we just caught her in time. In any event, she's all yours, thanks to Magna Pictures."

"Thank you. I really can't thank you enough." And then the pain of the moment hit her—as though she were looking into a mirror at a painful reflection of herself.

Nicholas Long continued. "I don't suppose you'd like to know why she did it."

Stevie waited. "Tell me."

"Your client . . . the charming and lovable star of *Young Dillinger*. Goodbye, Stevie."

Stevie telephoned Sam Di Benedetto. He advised her that Ginny should be hospitalized. Sam sounded very curt, and Stevie hung up dissatisfied. She had Brenda telephone a private ambulance service and with their assistance found out the time the plane was to arrive. They couldn't make arrangements for a private hospital; she would have to do that. Asking Brenda to find a hospital, Stevie strode out to the parking lot and her Porsche for the drive to the airport.

At the airport, she located the waiting ambulance. The driver, a tall, dark, muscular young man in his late twenties did a double-take when Stevie got out of her car, then gave her a broad smile. Stevie recognized the look. His companion, a slight, bookish type, stared in a more subdued fashion.

Muscles called out, "Hi, lady . . . Are you the one we're supposed to meet? You don't look sick at all."

"Thanks . . . What time is the plane due?"

"In fifteen minutes. We could grab a brew if you like, kind of get to know each other. My partner will watch for the plane."

Stevie ignored him and searched out a phone. She reached Brenda who had a room waiting for Ginny at

Cedars. Sam Di Benedetto had called back with the name of a doctor who could treat Ginny.

Stevie returned to the landing strip. The ambulance driver refused to let up. "My name is Dwight . . . and I'm all right. That's what the girls say about me. They also say I'm 'all-night Dwight.' Get what I mean?"

Stevie asked the other driver, "Can I ride in the ambulance with her? I'll send someone to pick up my car."

Dwight interrupted. "You can do more than that, honey. We'll get it on in the back while my partner drives. Bet you never tried that before."

Stevie stared straight ahead. At the end of the runway she saw the sleek shape of the Lear sliding down for a landing. It roared to the end of the runway, reversed thrust and slowly made its way to the ramp. A ground mechanic motioned to the pilot to bring it into the dock and at last the engines were shut down.

The door of the Lear opened, and the stairs folded down out of the side. Stevie watched as the two ambulance attendants started up the stairs with a portable stretcher, but they returned in a few moments and Stevie wondered why. Slowly, with the aid of the stewardess, Ginny made her way down the stairs and Stevie ran over to her.

"Ginny . . . baby."

"Stevie . . . I just want to go home."

"Baby . . . I've got an ambulance here to take you to the hospital."

"Stevie . . . I'll live. Please don't send me to the hospital . . . please don't . . . I couldn't stand it. Please don't send me away. Take me with you."

Ginny looked frail and weak. Her exquisite, sensuous beauty had disappeared and been replaced with grayish skin and deep, sunken eyes. She was in tears. Stevie took her elbow, supporting her weight, and led her over to the Porsche.

Ambulance driver Dwight called out. "Hey, she's OK, cutie, maybe we can double-date with my buddy."

Stevie looked up and motioned, "In a minute." She

opened the door of the Porsche and gently lowered
Ginny inside. Closing the door slowly, she walked over
to the ambulance driver.

"I've been listening to you for a while. I didn't say a
word because I thought I needed you to drive my sister
to the hospital."

Dwight fidgeted. "I hope you didn't take offense,
lady. After all, you're a good-looking chick and I'm a
hundred percent man . . . and that's what it's all
about."

Stevie looked into his eyes. "Yes, that's what it's all
about." Stevie reached down suddenly, grabbed his
balls and squeezed them as hard as she could. He
screamed wildly and fell to his knees in pain.

As Stevie walked off, she called over her shoulder,
"Phone me when you feel better." She got into the
Porsche, gingerly revved it up and started the drive
back to the house on Laurel Canyon.

Maria fell desperately in love with Ginny, and that
was all to the good since Stevie's schedule didn't allow
her to spend the time she wanted to with her. Once
Ginny moved into the guest room next to Stevie's, she
lived in the room. She appeared fearful of *ever* leaving
it. It was a nest into which Ginny could finally crawl,
and Maria was the loving mother whose patient attention was tender and limitless.

Stevie came home from the office early during the
first weeks, taking her meals in Ginny's room. The
doctor recommended by Sam Di Benedetto came
occasionally and told Stevie that she was making a
mistake. Ginny was an addict and couldn't be treated at
home. He warned Stevie that she would find drugs, and
possibly even had them with her. She should be
institutionalized, he advised. It was the only way.
Stevie listened, but refused, unwilling to reject her
sister, no matter what.

Stevie wondered how long she could keep the
presence of Ray Tree secret from her sister. But she
needn't have bothered worrying. Maria had told Ginny

the first day. Neither of the sisters mentioned any more about it.

And neither of them spoke of Morgan Oliver. Despite these strange circumstances the two sisters grew very close. They laughed and chatted as if they were young girls, trying to make up for the years apart. They were never serious. The dark patches in each of their lives they pushed aside to find pleasure in the present. During this time, Stevie had made a decision, and she awaited Sy Rosen's return from vacation nervously.

The day of Sy's return, he conducted the regular staff meeting. Afterward, Stevie stopped him on the way out of the conference room. She had a matter of importance to talk to him about.

Stevie followed him into his office and asked his secretary to hold his calls. Then she shut the door.

"Sy, I've come to a hard realization that despite my trying to be Wonder Woman, I'm only human."

"Stevie, I never thought you were anything but human. What's the problem? You know that you can tell me."

"Sy, for personal reasons which I won't bore you with, I want to forgo my handling of Morgan Oliver."

"Sy whistled. "My God, why? Everything seems to be going fine."

"Not so, Sy . . . at least not for me."

"Stevie, I'll accede to your wishes . . . and I'll try and convince Morgan that it's for the best . . . but surely I have the right to know why, as head of the agency, and as your friend."

"Sy—I'm sorry. It's nothing that I can talk about. It's personal."

"Well, Stevie, at least you ought to break the news to Morgan, and pass him on to someone else in an orderly fashion. We've got to do these things, painful as they sometimes are."

"Sorry, Sy, I won't do that either."

"Stevie, you're behaving badly. Just because you and he had a relationship years ago . . . and you were all

around town . . . then finally attempted to . . ." Sy
trailed off. He had committed the one unforgivable sin
for an agent—he had said too damn much.

Stevie noted every word. He *had* known all about
her. He had always known it, and still he had pushed
her together with Morgan Oliver.

The silence was broken when Sy rose from his seat.
"Look, forget it, Stevie. We'll work it out. I'll take over
handling Morgan myself. He can't object to that."

"I'm sure, Sy."

"Look, Stevie, I wanted to add something to what I
said at the staff meeting, about that directors' group
you're forming. What do you call it?"

"THE Filmgroup, Sy—that's the working name. I
believe it can be a force in the industry. We have
Walker Perkins, who is ready to fly with it, and Roger
Curtin. He's another good name, and in our stable."

"Yes, Stevie . . . But why reach outside for Kubrick
and Ingmar Bergman? We don't represent them, we
don't commission them."

"Sy, as I said . . . we have good directors, but only
two very good directors. With Kubrick and Bergman, it
would be a powerhouse. *And* be salable. Without
them, it might go nowhere. We owe it to our clients—
Perkins and Curtin."

"I'm afraid not, Stevie. They come and go—that's
clients for you. The agency will live forever. Forget it.
That's the last word on the Filmgroup."

Stevie stared straight ahead at the door. She hadn't
looked at Sy Rosen since he had made the slip about
her and Morgan Oliver.

"Then you'll take care of the Morgan Oliver thing as
of now, Sy?"

"Of course, Stevie. You just leave it to me." She left
the office without looking back.

Zelma developed a wide range of imaginary diseases
during the run of *Hello Sucker*, and she requested a
vacation. The grind of rehearsals, the punishment of
the out-of-town tryouts, the strain of opening night,

and the nightly pressure were legitimately too much for an inexperienced performer. Stevie phoned the producer and after a conversation on the merits of complying with Zelma's wishes, as opposed to having an "unhappy" star, he agreed. Zelma's understudy would take over for two weeks.

Zelma flew out to L.A. and borrowed a beach house where she planned to relax. It was Stevie who arranged with one of her clients to lend Zelma the luxurious house facing the ocean at Malibu.

On the second day after Zelma arrived, she telephoned Stevie, who was out. Zelma left a message with Brenda.

"Her majesty would like to see you tomorrow." Brenda sighed.

"Which one, British or Yiddish?"

"Not Queen Elizabeth, Queen Zelma."

It was three months since Stevie had seen Zelma in New York, she thought, driving out the beautiful winding road that is Sunset Boulevard, west to the Pacific. It was a bright, clear day, and at eleven in the morning the sun was slanting behind her as she drove. Once at the ocean, Stevie headed north on Pacific Coast Highway and soon arrived at the house. On the highway side, the beach houses looked simple and nondescript, with clapboard fronts of no particular style. Inside, however, they were highly individual and magnificently furnished. It was almost as if the properties were purposely camouflaged.

During the heyday of movie madness, the torrid '40's and '50's, the beach-front houses were hideaways for the stars, producers and studio moguls. More liaisons were conducted on the west side of the Pacific Coast Highway than in the court of Louis XIV. On the shore side, huge mountain bluffs led to a startling highland above the ocean.

Stevie parked her red Porsche off the main road, next to a redwood wall that hid the house from prying eyes, pressed a buzzer and explained her presence on the intercom. When it buzzed back, Stevie passed through the gate and strode out on a beautifully terraced landscape, cascading with flowers, topped by a breathtakingly modern home of "graying" redwood and glass.

Stevie was admitted into the extravagant interior by a Chinese butler. The home belonged to a client, a hugely successful choreographer. The Chinese butler was an obvious legacy. Stevie walked into the huge living room, which stretched for thirty feet along the beach, with a clear and unrestricted view of the sparkling Pacific through a picture window the length of the room. The furnishings consisted of large comfortable stuffed sofas and chairs, and on the walls were hung exquisite modern paintings. Stevie sat in one of the chairs and waited. Ten minutes later she located the butler. "Did you tell Miss Hurwitz that I was here?" He looked at her respectfully and replied, "Yes, Miss . . . as soon as you came in." Stevie waited another ten minutes, becoming visibly disturbed.

Finally she heard the sound of voices and Zelma appeared with a handsome, young black man. She kissed Stevie on the cheek and the two of them seated themselves on the couch holding hands. Zelma was wearing bright red toreador pants and a lace top with nothing beneath it. The full globes of her breasts, which Stevie had noticed at their first lunch at the Bistro, when Zelma was an ingenue in show business, were center stage and happy to be there. Stevie turned to Zelma's friend. He was coal black and stunning. For a moment, Stevie thought he might be gay, but reconsidered quickly. He was tall and graceful in fawn-colored slacks and a thin, white cashmere sweater with rolled-up sleeves.

"Stevie, this is Mark."

"Hello, Mark." Mark's hand moved out of Zelma's, and began to massage her back.

"Hi." Mark didn't even look up.

"I like this place," Stevie remarked, at a loss for

what to say. The situation, Stevie thought to herself, was about to explode, with the shrapnel headed her way.

"I don't think I'm going back to Broadway, Stevie."

"Oh, when was that decision made?"

"Just recently . . . It's too much work, and it's too boring. I'm sure that I can get out of the contract."

Mark was still massaging. "No sweat, baby."

Stevie looked at Mark. "What does Mark have to do with it?"

"Mark and I are partners, Stevie. We formed a production company to make movies . . . it's going right to the top. I'm tired of working for others. I want to work for myself."

Mark stopped his hand routine on various parts of Zelma's body. "I don't see any reason why Zelma here has to kiss-ass to no one. She's a superstar and ought to be treated like one. They's millions of dollars out there that she can capitalize on, without her having to bust her ass every night. When I saw what this little lady had to do to earn a living, with *her* talent, why, I got real angry. Do you get where I'm coming from?"

Stevie rose from her chair and reached for a cigarette from a box on the table. The box was empty.

Mark commented, "We don't have no cigarettes."

"Never mind. Shouldn't smoke anyway. Well, if you aren't going to continue with the play—and, of course, there's going to be one hell of a lawsuit—what are you going to do?"

Mark broke in. "Lady, they can sue our asses till the end of time. Ain't no way they gonna get this lady back in that ghet-to. I seen the way she was living in New York."

"Jesus, Zelma . . . I never thought it was that bad. They gave you a new refrigerator and paid you twenty-five thousand dollars a week." The humor was lost on the pair.

Mark broke in again. "We got some scripts. Some of my friends are very good script writers . . . and one of them is a natural for Clint Eastwood. Do you know Clint Eastwood, lady?"

"Doesn't everybody? What about the motion picture version of *Hello Sucker*, Zelma? What are your plans in that regard?"

"Well, I'm willing to do the movie, so I can get out of the play . . . because the producer of the play has a piece of the movie and he'll be willing to forget the whole thing."

"Who told you that?" Stevie said slowly.

"Sy Rosen. Mark and I had a long talk with Sy yesterday."

"Yeah, lady, your boss came all the way out here to see Zelma. Tells you what *he* thinks of her."

The bottom was falling out of Stevie's life. Sy Rosen hadn't said a word. And when she next saw Sy, he would just say that he was handling it, the same way that he was handling Morgan Oliver. He really wasn't going behind her back. It was just to assist. That's what the head of an organization is for—to serve as a backup for his people.

The truth of the matter was simple. Sy Rosen wanted Stevie out. He was closing in on her clients, denuding her of her power, and when she was no longer a threat she would be asked to resign. Stevie saw it all, but she had no idea what she would do about it. Sy was the fiercest adversary she had ever known. How do you win against twenty-five years of cunning?

Stevie rose to leave. "I don't think there's much more to say, Zelma. You're in good hands with Sy, and I'm sure all your wishes will come to pass—all the movies you two want to produce, being your own boss and being worthwhile members of our wonderful community."

Zelma started to ring for the butler and then decided to walk Stevie to the door as one last gesture of *noblesse oblige*. As the two of them stood at the door, Stevie turned to Zelma.

"How long have you been doing coke, honey?" There was no response, but the look in the eyes scored.

"Coke will do it every time, baby. And the guy who brings it to you all the time, he's king."

And Stevie walked out without another word. She got into her Porsche, heading north on the Pacific Coast Highway away from town. She needed some time to think.

25

Stevie discovered nothing on the drive up the Pacific Coast Highway to Ventura that she couldn't have discovered eating a hamburger at McDonalds, which might also have saved her a fifty-dollar ticket. She was clocked at 85 mph by a very polite, attractive, business-like California highway patrol officer on a Honda. For the sake of gallantry, he lowered the speed he marked on the ticket to 80, thereby ensuring his place in the firmament of well-meaning good guys who only hit you when you're down.

In fact, Stevie couldn't have cared less about the ticket or the formalities of being penitent. The highway patrol officer had rather liked her style as he chased her down, particularly her looks when she got out of the car. Had Stevie been the least bit sorry, she might have gotten off with a warning.

As it was, after pocketing the ticket, she floored the Porsche, made a 180-degree turn at 30 mph, accelerating to 50 and then to 85 again, as she roared back to town. The motorcycle officer watched her, shaking his head. As far as he was concerned, Stevie was now in someone else's territory.

On her way back to the office, Stevie wondered to herself what strategy would work. She was being forced to take a position in the agency, and go against Sy Rosen. She knew what the outcome would be. Sy would get out of his chair and come over to her. He would put his hand on her shoulder and say, "Stevie, the most important thing in the world, outside of health, is to be happy at your work. If you think for a minute . . . one tiny minute . . . that I've done anything against you, then you're wrong. My only love is the agency, and what will make it prosper. If it works, Stevie, we all work. On the other hand, it's easy to see that you're not happy here. That's the last thing that I want for the agency, or for you as a person. You've got a contract, but don't let that interfere with your thinking, we'll work that out. We want you to be happy. I, Sy Rosen, want you to be happy."

There was, Stevie knew, nothing you could say to a carefully orchestrated campaign to exterminate you, not even, "Bullshit, Sy." Any apparent loss of cool would be very demeaning, even as you were getting your throat cut.

On the last portion of the drive back, Stevie remembered something that Morrie Amster had said to her, which she hadn't understood at first. It was one of those apocryphal stories that was mysterious when heard but the utmost of wisdom when she finally absorbed its lesson. Morrie told Stevie about one of the greatest salesmen the world of entertainment had ever seen. Matty Fox had been a legend in the business. In his early thirties, Matty was the head of a major motion picture company, but his insatiable appetite for danger and new challenge took him to other pastures. In the later years of his life, Matty had a half interest in French Indochina—literally. The story of Matty's legendary fortunes and misfortunes filled many hours of conversation. One of the observations eventually became a watchword for Stevie—a cryptic comment that Matty had once made to Morrie Amster that day. It was simply, "The first guy that talks is dead."

Deciphered, it meant that the first trader to name a price or even to signify that a negotiation was in progress was at a disadvantage. That's all it meant, and today a blonde and very resolute female named Stevie Tree was going to follow that advice. 'Fuck it,' she advised herself. 'We're in a negotiation. There's no need for me to open the discussion. Someone else will.'

Then she smiled to herself grimly, as she put the speeding ticket in her pocketbook. 'I'll take five new cards, Mr. Dealer.'

As Stevie walked past Brenda's desk on her return to the office, Brenda caught her eye. The look was unmistakable. Brenda knew, and if Brenda knew about the Zelma Hurwitz incident, then everyone in the agency knew. Furthermore, if the proper signals were in effect, there would be a few words dropped at every restaurant in town during the next few days about the impending departure of Stevie Tree. That was the way the business worked. Stevie had seen it happen before and now it was happening to her.

Brenda brought in Stevie's messages.

"So you want to be an agent, Brenda?"

"I'm not so sure, Stevie."

"The messages, please, Doctor . . ."

"Well, the usual claptrap from three writers who are doing a screenplay for Paramount—all of them clients of IA and all of them sent out for the same assignment, at the same time, by three different agents."

"Which one is ours?"

"Stan James . . . and he got the job."

"That will make the rest of the boys happy." Her tone was more than cynical. "What else?"

"A call from Morgan Oliver's tailor, wanting money. I gave that call to our illustrious president . . . another from Walker Perkins: 'What's happening with Kubrick and the Filmgroup project?' A dozen or so other things—contracts, prices and stuff. I handled most of it. There's a list of what's left." Then Brenda paused. "Diedre called. She asked me to tell you it was important. I said I would. Who do you want first?"

The conversation with Diedre was very short. All Stevie said, "I'm sorry to have been so difficult to reach . . . Can you forgive me?" And all Diedre said was, "Can you meet me at the Beverly Wilshire . . . El Padrino . . . at five?" Stevie said, "Yes," and that was that.

Everything in Stevie's life was conspiring to force decisions. But she didn't want to make them. She was happier in limbo. Up till that moment she had been able to push everything aside, like a grocery list that didn't have to be made, as long as you ate out. But Stevie was running out of days. She felt more than ever that she was playing in a sporting event, hoping it would never end. The action, the challenge, the thrill of the game were very heady. Phone calls in the middle of the night, early in the morning, on the weekends, from New York and all over the world. The worry and delight of playing mother, big sister and confessor to a family of insecure children. All of these obscured the need to come to grips with her own decisions. If the noise and the confusion ever stopped, where would she be? What would she do? And it *was* stopping slowly, surely, just as if someone had put a heavy hand on the wheel of her tricycle. Sy Rosen was seeing to that.

Stevie felt a panic she had known before so often in her life. Panic that had caused her to run breathlessly home to her uncle in Urbana. Panic that she had once felt in her quest for Morgan's love. Here with Diedre was another chance, the possibility of a commitment to someone to replace a void. Here, she thought, might be an answer to the panic she felt in her life. The reason why Stevie resisted a relationship with Diedre had nothing to do with disdain for the word *lesbian*, or the life it implied either. But it wasn't the life that interested her. It was the possibility that Diedre could fill that empty place, still that fear and prevent her from being alone.

The Beverly Wilshire Hotel stood at the foot of Rodeo Drive in Beverly Hills, a grand, luxurious way station for international travelers. Inside the old wing, in quiet, red-carpeted splendor, were restaurants, shops and discreet dispensers of luxury goods to a world of strangers. The El Padrino room, a bar and restaurant, had, as its premium quality, darkness. Not so dark that you couldn't find your way, but dark enough, lit only by a soft glow of electricity and the flickering candles on the red-checked tablecloths. Dark enough so that words and faces were obscure.

She waited in a black-leather-covered booth for Diedre to appear. Piercing through the darkness, the lovely figure of movie star Diedre Magee, tall and regal, slid in beside her.

"Hi, Diedre."

"Hi, Stevie."

"I ordered you a glass of white wine . . . Was that what you wanted?"

"Yes, thanks . . . Stevie. I know that there's trouble at the agency . . . and the last thing I want to do is add to it, Stevie."

Stevie looked at Diedre. Her beautiful face had adorned dozens of magazine covers in the years before she got into the movies. It was now adored by millions of motion picture fans . . . but even more it held such sweetness and such love. She was so touched when Diedre touched her hand that Stevie did not withdraw hers.

The waiter appeared and deposited the glass of white wine and the vermouth on the rocks for Stevie, then he disappeared. The hubbub of the Beverly Hills cocktail hour filled the room, and Stevie was almost mesmerized by the sounds around her.

Diedre broke the quiet. "Walker wants me to go to England with him. I'm not sure I want to, Stevie."

"Why England? And why don't you want to?"

"I'm not supposed to tell you . . . but you'll find it out anyway. Walker is very unhappy about what's been happening at IA. He doesn't blame you, but the whole notion of the Filmgroup is something very near and dear to his heart. He really believes that three or four dedicated film directors could be a huge force for good in the industry."

"I agree . . . and I tried to make it work, Diedre, but the agency won't let me—won't let it include clients outside the agency."

"I know . . . but Walker says that he's going to do it

himself. The contract he has with the agency is coming
to an end . . . and after this next picture, he wants to
sit it out the rest of the time in London. He'll
write . . . and see."

"And what will you do, Diedre?"

"Stevie . . . I really don't want to act anymore. It's
something that I can do a little . . . like I can play
tennis a little . . . or sail a little, and always with
perfect form. I can take any pose in the world . . . and
it'll photograph up a storm. I make beautiful pictures,
Stevie, but there's nothing inside, absolutely nothing."

The conversation was taking a tack that Stevie hadn't
counted on. She had hoped and feared the need to say
something to Diedre as a commitment to her or a final
rejection. Stevie was bewildered by what seemed to be
the lack of having to do either. The matter might just
be taken out of her hands completely.

"Diedre . . . please don't say that. My God, nothing
inside? How can you say that? I have never known
anyone more tender, more loving than you. How could
there be nothing inside when you came to me in a
moment when I desperately needed someone to love
me . . . and . . ."

But there it stopped, because Diedre filled in the
missing piece. "And Stevie . . . would you live with
me? Would we become lovers?"

Stevie withdrew her hand. "My God, Diedre, I don't
know. Can't it take its own time? Can't it find its own
way?"

"Stevie, it could . . . but it won't and I can't wait for
you to love me. I need someone just as much as you do.
If it can't be you, it *can* be Walker. He needs me and, I
think in his own way, loves me. I need that. It gives me
the missing part of my life, Stevie."

Silently, Diedre slipped out of the booth. She leaned
across the table toward Stevie's face. The sweet, gentle
touch of her fingers traced the line of Stevie's scar. In
the near dark, it was hard to pick out, but Diedre had
traced it from memory. And then she was gone.

The drive back to the house on Laurel Canyon was a

thoughtful, sad one for Stevie. She drove slowly up the winding hill as the darkness began to fill the canyon. A few lights were beginning to appear in windows alongside the drive. She passed the Country Store, and the windows were lit. Stevie turned on her headlights and headed further into the canyon. At the crossing, she made a turn and headed up the side road to her house. Her bright beams picked up a figure scurrying past the garage. It was Ray Tree, in the performance of his self-appointed vigil. Light glinted off the barrel of his shotgun. She was frightened for an instant, then she shook her head at the vision of the silent sentinel patrolling the house for imagined enemies. Ray Tree wasn't real. He was a ghost guardian of a ghost castle.

Stevie parked her Porsche and slowly walked up the stairs. When she opened the door, the house was ablaze with light. Maria raced to her, Brenda walking behind her.

"Stevie . . . Maria called the office after you left . . . your sister Ginny has disappeared."

Stevie addressed herself to Maria, who was in a state of near collapse. "What happened, Maria?"

"Your sister . . . she fine person, Señora . . . and I have no bad to say about her . . . but this afternoon when I come home from shopping, I find her leaving."

"Did you try to stop her, Maria? You know she's not well."

Maria was in tears. "I try like she my own, Señora . . . but even after I grab her, she not stop. She take my pocketbook with all the money left from the grocery and she hit me when I try to stop her. Señora . . . I love that girl. Why she hit me? I give her anything I got. I make up the grocery money to you, Señora . . . You not lose the money."

"Brenda, thank you for coming."

"When I heard Maria's story, I had to come right over."

Stevie took Maria by the arm and caressed her cheek. "Oh, Maria, you are so good . . . so very good.

How can I thank you for what you do for me and what you've done for my sister, too. I'm sure we'll find her, and it will be all right."

Maria spoke in between sobs. "Thank you, Señora. I try my best."

When the telephone rang, Stevie looked at Brenda, who walked to the hall phone and answered it. In the distance, she heard Brenda talking, and then it was quiet.

"Stevie! It was the City Hospital . . . an ambulance just brought Ginny to the emergency ward. She's unconscious. It was a hit and run accident. Someone found her on the street and phoned for an ambulance."

Stevie was too chilled to react, except to ask, "Where was she found? Did they say?"

"Near the Beverly Hills Hotel. Let's go to the hospital. I know where it is."

It was too late.

In the months that followed Ginny's death, Stevie immersed herself in the work at IA. The agency staff meetings found her quiet and reserved. Stevie's only comments consisted of answers to questions.

Brenda now attended the staff meetings herself, watching Stevie with a keen eye. Even the affectionate relationship that Stevie felt for Brenda, now an assistant agent, couldn't stir Stevie to a reaction toward anyone in the agency.

During those months, Nick Long the producer, Walker Perkins the director and two editors cut, shaped and polished *Young Dillinger*. The picture began to be talked about. Even at that early point, a picture that smells of success has its trumpeters. Finally the completed cut of the film was scored, sound effects were added, and picture and sound were brought together in a mixing session.

The first print came out of the laboratory, ready for screening by the studio. Nick Long was holding a

screening for the first people outside the studio to see
it.

It would take place Friday night at his Bel Air home.

Saturday—9 P.M.

Stevie made dinner reservations at Jimmy's in Beverly
Hills for Sam and herself. Sam was always reluctant to
call. Stevie was a star, and her name worked wonders,
so there was always a table, one of the best. Stevie
needed to talk to someone. The twenty-four hours
following the screening of *Young Dillinger* had been so
undeniably grim that she needed advice.

Stevie pulled her Porsche into the empty spot in front
of the entrance and one of the valet parkers rushed to
open her door. "Nice to see you again, Miss Tree. No
need for a ticket."

Jimmy's, the chic new restaurant for the rich and
elegant, belonged to a group of investors, local millionaires who adored having their own restaurant. Jimmy,
the guiding force behind the Bistro for many years, was
co-owner and blessedly in charge. The double doors led
to a spacious entrance with pale blue carpet and
gray-blue walls. Huge bouquets of fresh flowers, wherever one looked, lent the quietly glamorous restaurant
a springlike appearance.

Jimmy took Stevie's hand at the door and led her to a
banquette. As she sat, he smiled and murmured, "We
don't see enough of you, Miss Tree." From the corner
of her eye she saw Greg Peck with a party of six, and
across the room Linda Ronstadt and Jerry Brown, who
nodded to her as she was seated.

What Stevie needed was a drink. True to form,
Jimmy sent the waiter over promptly.

Stevie sat in the blue-plush banquette for almost ten
minutes before Sam came. It was unusual for him to be
late, but he had rearranged his previous plans to be
with her, recognizing the trouble in her voice.

Sam kissed her politely. Stevie had already finished
two scotches. When Sam motioned to the waiter and

gave his drink order, Stevie asked for a third. She wanted to get drunk.

Sam leaned over. "OK, what it's all about?"

Stevie polished off the third drink in two gulps. "Nothing, just wanted to see you."

"Uh-huh."

"No, really . . . It's been a while. How's Laurie?"

"About as well as can be expected, Stevie. Spill it."

"Sam, except for Morrie, you're the best friend I've ever had, and I've come to a crossroads—I need advice."

"You've come to a crossroads. OK, next."

"Something happened last night at the screening at Nick Long's house. His daughter OD'ed on heroin. She's dead".

"Oh, my god. I had no idea . . ."

"Yep . . ." Stevie was beginning to slur her words. She felt it and she was glad. Maybe the awareness would go away. "But the rest of it is that Morgan Oliver was involved. Twelve people know about it—and are covering it up."

"For the family?"

"Christ, no. For the money. Well, there's one . . . that's Nick's wife, Valerie . . . she just wants to protect Melinda's reputation, and her family's, but the whole thing has been engineered by the wonder workers of IA."

"You?"

"Gee, Sam"—now Stevie was really slurring—"not me. You *are* dumb for a smart guy . . . No, the guys at the agency. It's all deals, Sam . . . and pictures . . . and commissions . . . and shit."

"OK, I get it."

"Not quite. There's a doctor, I don't even know his name, who forged the death certificate . . . They worked that out . . . worked out the payoffs for everyone."

"What's your payoff, Stevie?"

"That's the point, Sam . . . there isn't any payoff. If I blow the whistle, then I destroy the lives of a couple of innocent people, not to mention destroying the career of a guy I hate . . . Morgan . . . and a movie that could be a classic. As you can see, it's a little confusing." Her voice was bitter.

"And yourself."

"Sam—I'm destroyed *now*. You are an innocent as far as the world is concerned. They're going to *get* me. Do you know what that means? When my buddies at IA decide to do a number on me, they will do such a job that I won't be employable by anybody . . . including a janitorial service."

"Marry me."

It was said simply, but Stevie responded to it with fury.

"Dammit. You're all alike. Men think that's the answer to every woman's problems. Chuck it. Chuck independence . . . everything I worked and fought for . . . and become a 'little woman.' You're no damn consolation prize Doctor Di Benedetto."

The meal continued in silence. Stevie asked Sam to order for her and when the food came, she toyed with it. Sam occasionally stared at Stevie, who looked down at the tablecloth for what seemed like hours at a time. Stevie was drunk, and what seemed hours was only forty-five minutes. Sam paid the check and they started to leave. The captain was panic-stricken when he saw Stevie leave early, but she was too numb to respond to his inquiry.

"Miss Tree isn't feeling well . . . it has nothing to do with the food . . . I'm taking her home," Sam explained.

Sam called for his car, leaving Stevie's at the restaurant, and managed to get her in and settled. The next hour was spent getting her into her house, undressing her and putting her to bed. When he left she was sound asleep.

Later, the telephone rang and continued ringing. Somehow, out of the fog she was in, Stevie had the strength to pick it up and turn on the bedside light. She looked at the clock—midnight. She had been asleep for two hours. "Stevie . . . it's late, I know, but I took the chance of calling you now. I tried to return your call all evening."

It was Sy Rosen. How could she talk to him now?

"That's all right, Sy. Just wait a minute till I pull myself together . . . You'll hold on, won't you?"

"Of course . . . do whatever you have to."

Stevie half stumbled into the bathroom and splashed water on her face. She didn't feel much better. She pinched her arm and couldn't feel it. She bit on her thumb. It hurt. She was almost awake. She put on a robe, returned to the bed and picked up the phone.

"Sorry to have kept you, Sy."

"No problem, Stevie . . . I've been awake a long while myself. Had trouble sleeping."

"How do you feel?"

"Like an old man, Stevie."

Stevie thought to herself in the midst of the cobwebs, Here it comes.

"We're all getting old, Sy."

"Some of us more than others, Stevie. Some of us more than others."

She was annoyed by the lullaby in the man's voice, by the repetition of words and phrases collected over eons. Words and phrases that made you think kindly of dear old philosopher Sy Rosen, with one foot in the grave and the other in heaven. Stevie had always been able to deal with Sy through thinking ahead, slugging from a position of strength, but her present strength was very uncertain. Christ, no, her strength was predictable— zero.

"Sy . . . I'm sure you've spoken to Jerry about last night."

"Yes, he came down here this morning with Fred."

"Do you understand how I feel?"

"Of course, Stevie. That's what saddens me."

"What do you mean?"

"I feel the same way you do." Sy crooned it.

Stevie wasn't awake enough to anticipate the trap.

"What do you mean, you feel the same way I do, Sy?"

"Just what I said. I hold no brief for Morgan

Oliver—none at all. I find him a contemptible human being . . . but Stevie, we have responsibilities . . . all of us . . . and me, most of all.''

"Sy, don't we have a responsibility to the law? We're party to a criminal act."

"I don't think of it that way, Stevie."

"How do you think of it?"

"It's a humanitarian act . . . an act of charity . . . and love. Love for a grieving family who could be destroyed by the publicity mills. You know how this would destroy Nick and Valerie Long . . . and the memory of a young girl." Man, was he righteous!

"What about the commissions?"

"What do you mean?"

"Sy, fuck the humanitarian crap. If you put this deal together and cover up the scandal, IA will earn four or five million dollars in commissions."

There was a long pause. "Stevie. I think you're overwrought because of an emotional involvement. I'm too old a man to be incensed by a momentary flash of youth . . . a remark, I might add, that was ungracious and inappropriate. I think that when you sleep on it, and wake up fresh and restored in the morning, you'll feel differently. In the meantime, I feel sleepy . . . and I hope that you can get to sleep, too. I'm sorry that I woke you, Stevie. Forgive me."

He hung up. Stevie Tree was dead at IA, and after they were finished she'd be dead in the industry. She had clinched it at dinner when she drank too damn much scotch, and she hated scotch.

Sunday—10 A.M.

Stevie felt better after a fifteen-minute shower, as cold as she could stand. Then breakfast and two cups of coffee. Maria had the day off, which was fine as far as Stevie was concerned. She desperately wanted to be alone.

Descending the stairs, Stevie walked to the road to retrieve the huge bundles of the LA *Sunday Times* and the *New York Times*. Hefting them under her arms, she felt restored in the morning air and happily anticipated several hours of working her way through the newspapers. As she started for the house, she saw the back of the fleeting, shadowy figure of Ray Tree. My God, she thought, doesn't he ever sleep? In a moment, the zombielike creature, still carrying his gun, disappeared magically into the deep, dark woods around the house.

The early morning fog had burned away and the day was brilliant. As Stevie began with the L.A. paper and was savoring a third cup of coffee, the phone rang.

"Stevie . . . Jerry Fentris."

"Yes, Jerry."

"Thought you might want to know that I've just returned from the funeral . . . It was a simple and lovely service."

"That's nice, Jerry . . ."

"A nondenominational ceremony."

"Really, Jerry?"

"Yeah, it was over in a couple of minutes . . . Nick and Valerie and a few friends. They're scattering the ashes at sea."

"Really, Jerry?"

"Yeah. Nick decided it was more in the spirit of youth to have her return to nature . . . as it were."

"Also solves the problem of an autopsy."

No answer, and then, "By the way, Stevie . . . Sy is feeling a little better. He's coming into the office tomorrow at noon . . . and specifically asked if you'd be sure to be there . . . I mean cancel any previous appointments. It's a general meeting to see where we're going."

"Really, Jerry?"

"Yeah . . . Why do you keep saying that?"

"Saying what?" she inquired innocently.

He replied with some annoyance, "*Really Jerry* . . . that's what."

"I didn't realize that's what I was saying . . . Really, Jerry."

Stevie hung up.

She didn't think it would be possible to get back to the newspapers, but she did. In that moment, she made her decision. From that time on, she felt incredibly free. The solution to her problems was available. The time wasn't right. She needed a bit of patience. There was a lot of repair work to do, a lot of ground she would have to do over again. It wasn't impossible. She'd done tougher things in a lifetime in Hollywood.

Her mind raced. She literally devoured every word in the papers. She could have scored high on a quiz of the day's newspapers. Everything about the living room began to take on a surreal quality. The texture of the very chair she sat on, she seemed to feel for the first time.

Charged with energy, Stevie walked out the door and down the stairs to take an unheard-of walk the length of Laurel Canyon. Every so often she had to step into the scrub alongside the road, as the progression of screeching cars threaded their way up the serpentine. Stevie's face was flushed from the exercise. Her blue eyes sparkled as she made her way down the canyon road. Dressed in white jeans, a blue and white French sailor's shirt and tennis shoes, Stevie looked like a blonde goddess, as she cheerfully ducked in and out to avoid cars and waved to the appreciative shouts of girl-watchers driving by.

She walked down to the center of life, the square next to the Country Store. Cars were parked, with Sunday shoppers piling out to buy groceries. Stevie sat on a packing case as she watched the parade, the people so young, so innocent, so free of care.

Smiling to herself, she started the climb back. It was a tough road to climb. Stevie was exhausted, perspiring but exhilarated.

When she got back to the house, it was five in the afternoon. Stevie had taken the phone off the hook and she kept it that way while she rolled herself a joint and sat near the window watching the setting sun.

At eight o'clock Stevie went into the kitchen to make a sandwich. The refrigerator was virtually empty.

Maria would have to go shopping tomorrow. Stevie would make a list and leave money.

She made a thick sandwich—bologna and cheese with a lot of mustard—and it tasted terrific. When she rummaged in the refrigerator for something to drink there was only a Shasta cola. Maria was intent on saving money. But it wasn't bad. How much cheaper was it than Coke? She would have to ask. Thousands of details raced through her mind.

With the rest of the sandwich and the cola, Stevie moved back to her position at the window. The night had fallen and the clear blue-black velvet sky full of lights made her happy once again that she had acquired the house. Stevie was hypnotized by the sight. When she turned on the lamp in the darkened room, the clock read ten-fifteen.

It was time, Stevie thought.

In the near dark, she brought the telephone by its long cord to her seat by the window and dialed a familiar number—it wasn't easy to forget Morgan Oliver or anything associated with him. She thought he would be at home, and she was right.

"Morgan? Stevie."

"Hi."

Stevie took a deep breath. "Well, we did it, baby. It took heaven and earth, but we did it . . . It's all over, Morgan. The incident is dead and buried."

"Yeah, I heard." He was matter-of-fact.

"Morgan, I don't have to blow my own horn, but the fellas were going to let you drown. I want you to know that I couldn't let it happen. We meant too much to each other years ago . . . I couldn't let them get you, Morgan."

The line was silent.

"Morgan . . . Friday night, I cried at the screening. I really did. Not only did I see Morgan the actor . . . and you've got to be a nomination . . . but I saw you, Morgan the man . . . it came through. We've been through an awful lot together and apart, Morgan. We really have, and in the last two days I've come to realize that you mean more to me than I ever thought. I was really jealous of Ginny, but that's over. And that's why I was glad when I had the chance to help you. Morgan, I did it for you."

Morgan listened and said nothing. Stevie went on.

"Morgan . . . can we ever get together again? I pray for it . . . Can we ever have what we used to have? We were the greatest. There's never been another one like you in bed . . . for me . . . the feel of your stiff cock in my hand. The heavenly first lick on the tip. The thrill of taking huge gulps of that incredible rod. Morgan, my pussy wants you . . . It's wet, soaking wet, Morgan, just thinking of you. Are you getting hard, Morgan? You used to with me instantly, when I started playing with myself. I'm doing it now . . . Oh, Morgan . . . Can't we do it one more time? Tonight is a night to celebrate . . . with someone who drives you crazy in bed. Morgan, you know I'm the best . . . Baby, come on over . . . now, baby . . . come now and fuck me . . . baby. I want you so bad . . . please, baby. I miss you so much."

There was a pause. "I'll be over . . ." The phone clicked off.

Stevie stripped down to her bra and panties. She brushed her smooth blonde hair in the mirror and stood in front of it examining herself. Then she took off her underwear and lit candles alongside the bed table and across the room. The red wax candles, combined with the incense she lit, made it seem like a bridal chamber.

From her dresser, Stevie took out a tape recorder, unwrapped a brand-new cassette and set it carefully in the deep shadow of the bedside table. She had used the Sony many times before to record meetings at home. It picked up everything within a range of twenty feet. For hours during the day Stevie had resolved that whatever cost she would destroy Morgan. Lying in bed, smoking a joint after sex, she would get him to admit his participation in the death of Melinda Long. She might even be able to get him to admit involvement in the destruction of Ginny Tree. She was sure it had been Morgan who lured her to her death.

The plan needed only one thing apart from luck—the most convincing performance in bed that a woman had ever given. Stevie needed to show that no matter what Morgan had done, she was still enslaved by him.

More than just a performance in bed, she must give evidence of the total surrender of a woman obsessed with a man, wanting him beyond any reason, beyond any sense of right or wrong, to the lowest form of self-degradation. The spirit of the Whore of Babylon. Stevie remembered back to an earlier time with Morgan. How far from that had she been?

In the afterglow of lovemaking, it would all be on tape. Even if that were not admissible in a court of law, and Stevie had no idea whether it would be, it would be enough to destroy him. In the proper hands that admission would be his destruction. It would end his career.

She heard the sound of a car. It pulled into the driveway and stopped. A car door opened. There were footsteps on the gravel and then up the stairs.

Stevie called out from the bedroom. "Morgan . . . it's open."

The front door banged shut and there were footsteps up the carpeted stairs. It took a few seconds for him to reach the open bedroom.

Morgan stood there in the soft light of the flickering candles.

"Baby . . ." Stevie murmured, lying on the bed under the light sheet that covered her nakedness.

Morgan stood as if frozen. He was not smiling.

"Listen, bitch."

Stevie recoiled.

"Listen to me, you cunt. I called Jerry Fentris after you phoned me. *You* saved my ass. Sure, you saved my ass. Over this last fucking weekend you tried to have me crucified. Well, if there's one body that's gonna be strung up on the cross, it's not mine. From what they tell me, it's all under wraps, for good." He pulled the cover off her. Stevie lay naked in terror. His eyes burned like blue coals.

"I don't know what you had in mind . . . you

planning some little number to turn me over to the
D.A. . . . for that hot-pants daughter of Nick Long
. . . and your goddam hot-pants chippy sister. You've
got one family resemblance, you and your sister . . .
pussy to the world."

He was shouting, he saw the tape recorder running
silently under the night table. He turned the table over
with a single move, sending the lamp crashing to the
floor. His thin lips twisted in a grimace, he pulled the
tape recorder out of its socket and smashed it on the
side of the bed, drunk on his own violence and
strength. Stevie was shaking with sobs, petrified from
fear. The noise of Morgan's yelling and the sound of
objects shattering, furniture being thrown over, consumed the house.

Then, just as he had walked in, Morgan turned and
left Stevie there. The footsteps retreated down the carpeted stairs. There was a sound of a door opening and
closing, the sound of footsteps down the outside stairs.

Then the sudden, cavernous sound of two gunshots.
The emptying of two barrels of a shotgun, a smoking
shotgun held by Ray Tree as he stood over the dead,
bloody body of Morgan Oliver. Ray Tree had heard
every word shouted in the bedroom above. He stood
their impassively, grimly smiling, a strange and mania-
cal victor over evil.

The echoes of the gunshots could still be heard
faintly down the recesses of the canyon.

Monday Morning

It was exactly ten-thirty when Stevie stepped into her
red Porsche. By this time, she was usually at work, but
today was different and Sy Rosen wouldn't be returning
from Palm Springs till noon. There was more than
enough time to have breakfast at Schwab's.

Stevie wore fawn-colored wool slacks, a light tan and
brown sweater over a tattersall shirt, open at the neck,
and a trim, brown suit coat. She carried a leather

portfolio, very worn and very expensive. Her blonde
hair was lustrous in the California sun, as she drove
down Laurel Canyon on the bright October day in less
than the usual time.

Stevie negotiated a space in Schwab's parking lot,
walked past the attendant, Cliff, and waved. Inside, the
noise level was less than usual. Only the regulars
remained, those who weren't even pretending that they
had anything to do. Stevie asked for *Daily Variety* and
the *Hollywood Reporter* at the counter. They wouldn't
have the story, but the L.A. *Times* would, and she
paused to pick up a copy. With all her reading material,
she walked to the restaurant area and sat down in a
booth. Only a few booths were occupied, and the
people in them were intent on their own conversations.
They neither knew nor recognized her—she could be
anonymous for a little while.

The headline in the L.A. *Times* said it all: MOVIE STAR
KILLED IN LAUREL CANYON. The story ran to over three
columns—in later editions Stevie was sure it would be a
banner head. There had been only a little time for the
paper to get the details, but they did get most of them.
Ray Tree, mentally unstable, had mistaken film star
Morgan Oliver for a prowler . . . shot twice with a
twelve-gauge shotgun . . . huge gaping holes . . .
killed instantly. Stevie Tree, well-known Hollywood
agent, hadn't expected Morgan Oliver's visit . . . They
had seen each other two days ago at a Bel Air screening
of his upcoming picture *Young Dillinger*, reported to be
highly promising . . . There was a brief bio of Morgan
Oliver . . . later editions would have more.

Stevie put the Monday *Times* on the seat. Obviously
she knew the story better than they did, having spent
most of the early hours of the morning with the police,
who arrived soon after she called.

Stevie had held the figure of Ray Tree, frightened
and bewildered, close to her. Photographers got the
pictures for later editions. Stevie was sure that her
father would be found guiltless of any crime and that

this would be the proper occasion to have him sent to a Veteran's Hospital, where he could be in the company of other ex-GI's. Stevie was sure she could arrange it.

The huge German waitress Gertrude came to take her order. She, too, had no idea of any connection between Stevie and the story in the papers.

"Terrible story in the papers," Gertrude remarked.

"Yes, terrible . . . I'll have a large orange juice . . . soft scrambled eggs, potatoes, toast and coffee . . . and the coffee now, please."

"How do you expect to keep your figure, you eat so much?"

"The same way you keep yours, Gertrude, a pleasant disposition."

The waitress didn't appreciate the joke and left.

Stevie read the trades while she drank her coffee and ate her breakfast. There was nothing much she hadn't already known. That was her business, to know things before others. She finished breakfast, left a dollar tip on the table and the trades for someone else who might not be able to spare the change. She hadn't known Ray Tree would kill again, until it happened. Was it a strange repetition of her mother's death? If he had come to her room, would he have killed her too? Or was this payment in kind for a daughter he had done nothing for all her life? Stevie could only wonder.

Stevie paid her check, tipped the attendant in the parking lot and unlocked her Porsche. She pulled the car out of the lot and proceeded west on Sunset in the direction of the agency. It was going to be a bitch of a day. She could see it coming, though the sky was cloudless and almost clear.

Stevie continued along Sunset and exited Hollywood, moving west into Beverly Hills. The huge, baroque homes of a bygone era stood out, brilliantly decorative in the sun. Stevie paused for a red light at the corner of Sunset and Doheny. Last night there had been no choices. There had been the certainty of terminating her relationship with IA. Before Morgan's death, she had thought that she would get money in the settlement of her contract, but what would there be after that? Another agency? Perhaps, but a smaller one with less choice and less power. IA *was* the best.

The car behind her was honking. The light had changed.

At International Artists, she could be one of the truly important agents and she still had a lot to learn. She might as well learn it at IA and from Sy Rosen. He was the best, but today Sy Rosen didn't want her . . . or maybe that was only what he *thought*. And Morrie Amster had told her she could be one of the stars. She had to try for him.

Last night's incident was playing right into her plans. With Morgan dead, all bets were off. Negotiations had to begin again in a game that Stevie understood very well. She had neutralized Sy Rosen's best chess moves. It was a new board.

And she had some other ammunition she could use. Zelma Hurwitz could be brought into line. Flack and Flaherty owed her a lot and she could control them. The writer of *Hello Sucker* would write something new for her to represent. She could sell *THE LIFE STORY OF MORGAN OLIVER* to Magna. Why not? A great idea! Who would be right to play Stevie Tree? She was planning again. The past was set, the future was something she could create.

Sy Rosen could be made to recognize that he needed her.

Maybe, just maybe, she should tune down her style. There were a million possibilities. She caught herself. 'Stevie, don't be so damn positive about things. Somebody else has a point of view.'

But if it didn't work . . . and sometimes it just wasn't your day . . . then she would come back to the table another time, and it wouldn't be too bad either. She once thought that it would be the end of the world not to have the power, not to have the set of electric trains to play with, the IA electric trains.

That's what she had said to Sam when she phoned

him at eight that morning. She and Sam had a date for tonight, who knew, she thought, perhaps there in bed, in his arms, she would tell him just how much she wanted him. How much she had wanted him all along and hadn't known it. She might be ready to feel, might be ready to love, maybe even ready to consider marriage.

The honking hadn't stopped. Thinking of tonight, Stevie brushed her ash blonde hair back with her hand and smiled at herself shyly in the mirror. Then she put the Porsche in gear and headed for work.

At the IA complex, she gave the obligatory greetings on the way to her office and walked smoothly into the conference room, head high, face composed, suit businesslike but not agency drab. The lady who engineered million-dollar contracts with the grace of a ballet choreographer acknowledged the men around the table.

"Good morning, gentlemen," Stevie Tree said, looking directly at Sy Rosen as she sat down. Her smile was commanding, her voice cool. She was going to win this one.